SE_
NO
EVIL

D.S. BUTLER

THOMAS & MERCER

Text copyright © 2025 by D. S. Butler
All rights reserved.

Published by Thomas & Mercer, Seattle

www.apub.com

Amazon, the Amazon logo, and Thomas & Mercer are trademarks of Amazon.com, Inc., or its affiliates.

EU Product Safety contact:
Amazon Publishing, Amazon Media EU S.à r.l.
38, avenue John F. Kennedy, L-1855 Luxembourg
amazonpublishing-gpsr@amazon.com

ISBN-13: 9781662512315
eISBN: 9781662512322

Cover design by @blacksheep-uk.com
Cover image: © Marie Carr / ArcAngel; © Tadeas-P / Shutterstock

Printed in the United States of America

SEE
NO
EVIL

ALSO BY
D. S. BUTLER

Deadly Justice
Deadly Ritual
Deadly Payback
Deadly Game
Deadly Intent

East End Series:

East End Trouble
East End Diamond
East End Retribution

Harper Grant Mystery Series:

A Witchy Bake Off
A Witchy Business
A Witchy Mystery
A Witchy Christmas
A Witchy Valentine
Harper Grant and the Poisoned Pumpkin Pie

For Sam – who finds strength in adversity and always finds a way.

Prologue

Ava Claywood strolled through Willingham Woods. Her dog, Max, bounded ahead, sniffing every tree and fern.

Humming along to Shakin' Stevens's 'Green Door' – the song that had been playing on every radio station lately – she breathed in the earthy, warm scent of the woods and felt the tension in her shoulders ease.

It was a perfect late-summer day. She smiled as the dog chased a butterfly, his tail wagging furiously. It was easy to forget about work out here. To forget the meetings behind closed doors and the money changing hands.

The bad things.

What would her boss do if she spoke out about what she'd seen? She didn't even want to consider it, but could she live with herself if she kept quiet?

She forced the thoughts away, concentrating on Max as he scampered ahead.

'No, Max! Not that way,' she called, ordering the excitable golden retriever away from the pond.

She wasn't going anywhere near that muddy water, not after the last episode with the biting insects. A whole week later and the bites were still itching like mad.

She glanced at her watch and sighed. As much as she loved these walks, she couldn't let them go on for too long.

'Come on, Max. Time to go home.'

The dog had no intention of giving up his freedom. Max leaped in and out of the ferns, edging closer to the pond.

'Don't you dare,' she warned, eyeing the cloud of midges hovering in the shade. 'I mean it,' she said sternly, and held up his lead. 'We're going home. Now.'

The dog's head dropped as he slunk towards her, tail between his legs. She couldn't help grinning at Max's woe-is-me act. 'Don't give me that hard-done-by look. Come here.'

Max reluctantly trotted over. She couldn't blame him for his overenthusiasm. The woods gave him a lot more freedom to run around than their little two-bed terrace in Market Rasen.

'Don't worry,' she said as she clipped the lead on to Max's collar. 'We'll come back tomorrow.'

A blackbird chirped an alarm call. Then the woods fell eerily quiet as the normal birdsong faded away to nothing.

A volley of alarm calls rang out.

She frowned, glancing around nervously and scanning the surrounding trees, but there was no one in sight. It was probably nothing. Most likely just the birds reacting to Max. Although they'd been singing happily up until now.

Max had gone still too. Body tensed, the dog stared into the undergrowth.

A twig snapped behind her and Ava turned, her heart pounding. Nothing. Just the dense greenery and lengthening shadows.

Uneasy now, she tugged at the dog's lead and hurried back to the path. It was definitely time to go home. She'd only taken a few steps when she heard a low growl from Max that made her freeze.

Was someone watching them? She stared in the direction of Max's gaze but couldn't see anything except green bushes and tree trunks.

Ava patted Max's head as her eyes focused on the treeline again. 'It's all right, boy. Time to go.'

They walked briskly. It would be okay. They'd be home soon.

As she quickened her pace, a rustling caught her attention. Her stomach lurched as a man emerged from behind a tree. Her eyes locked on to his.

Oh, no. *Not him. Not here. Not now.*

They were alone out here. No one would hear her cry for help.

Her dog's soft whine only fuelled her growing panic.

She had to get away.

Clutching Max's lead, she bolted deeper into the woods, flying over roots and dodging low-hanging branches. The trees closed in as Max frantically kept pace beside her.

Keep going. Don't look back.

But she did look back, glancing over her shoulder. He was fast, sprinting through the brambles. Just ten paces behind, his hate-filled eyes fixed on her.

The trees blurred as she ran faster, her breath coming in short gasps. He was gaining on her, and she couldn't outrun him.

Her lungs burned and her calves ached, but the instinct to survive drove her forward. She darted around the trees, the dog's lead still clutched tightly in her hand.

A branch slapped against her face, cutting her lip. It spurred her on, the metallic taste of blood reminding her of what would happen if he caught up.

How long could she keep going? Already her legs were rubbery and her lungs were on fire.

Finally she saw a clearing, a break in the trees. Was that the road? She sprinted towards it, her legs screaming in protest. She emerged into the open, gasping for air, her chest heaving. She looked around and realised with horror that she was nowhere near the road.

She was trapped.

The pond was on one side, the dense woods on the other.

She could hear him getting closer, but she couldn't see him.

He wouldn't stop until . . . until what? The reality of the situation hit her then. He wouldn't stop. Not ever.

She backed up until her feet were at the water's edge.

A figure burst through the trees.

'No use trying to get away,' he said, advancing towards her.

There was nowhere to run.

He straightened to his full height, hands on his hips as he caught his breath. 'That's quite the runaround you've given me.'

'Please . . .' The word rasped from her dry mouth. 'You don't have to do this. Let me go. I won't tell anyone. I promise.'

He shook his head. 'Too late.'

He lunged at her. As she tried to dodge him, she tripped on a rock and fell with a splash into the cold water. Then she struggled to her feet, but he was on her in an instant. Strong hands locked around her throat.

Max barked furiously. She tried to fight back, tried to scratch the man and kick out, but he was too strong.

His thick fingers crushed any chance she had of calling for help. She felt her airway closing and her vision blurring.

She kicked again, her foot connecting with his shin, but he didn't even flinch. He kept squeezing, his face inches from hers.

This was it. She was going to die.

4

Her husband would be at home by now, probably putting the kettle on, wondering where she was. And her daughter . . . her precious little girl.

Max was jumping up, barking and growling. But it had no effect.

People say your life flashes before your eyes when you're dying. But it wasn't her own life Ava saw; it was her daughter's.

She squeezed her eyes shut and let the memories wash over her.

Chubby cheeks and gummy smiles. First unsteady steps across their tiny living room. Sticky fingers and birthday cake. First day at school, with socks that wouldn't stay up. Learning to ride a bike, all wobbles and giggles. Summer holidays at the seaside, building sandcastles with little plastic spades. Homework battles and practising times tables.

Then all the milestones she'd miss. First crush, then first heartbreak. Exam nerves. First job. The woman she'd become, strong and kind and beautiful.

It wasn't fair. It wasn't nearly enough. But as the darkness crept in, Ava clung to those glimpses of the future that she'd never see, but desperately wanted for her little girl.

Present day

Lorraine Harrington's fingers trembled as she typed out the message. The words blurred on the screen.

She read the final sentence one last time, and her throat tightened.

> *I've kept things secret long enough and it's time for the truth to come out.*

Her cursor hovered over the send button as a prickle of sweat broke out across her forehead. Part of her wanted nothing more than to erase the whole message, to leave the past buried where it couldn't hurt anyone. But the guilt was a constant, gnawing ache. One she could no longer ignore.

Lorraine thought of her son, Mike, and the way he frowned when he was troubled. He projected an image of strength and toughness to the world. Grumpy on the surface, but sensitive underneath. A loyal, kind man. She'd certainly made mistakes, but her son was one thing she was proud of.

She imagined the hurt and betrayal she would see in his eyes when she told him everything.

And then there was Karen – the woman who'd managed to thaw Mike's heart after he'd been left devastated by the death of his little boy. The loss had destroyed his marriage, and he'd come close to following his child out of this world. But somehow Karen had found a way to get through Mike's prickly defences. And as much as she'd tried to resist, even Lorraine had grown fond of her.

Tears stung Lorraine's eyes as she thought of all the times she had put on a wounded act to stop Mike asking about his father. She'd let her voice shake and pretended to be upset, to trigger his protective side and end the conversation.

It was a cruel way of manipulating him, and it made her feel terrible every time. But putting up emotional barriers had seemed easier than dismantling the web of lies she had carefully built over the years.

But Karen wasn't so easy to control. She was too sharp, too observant. Lorraine had noticed the way her eyes narrowed, the wheels spinning in her mind, whenever Mike's biological father was mentioned.

Karen hadn't fallen for Lorraine's manipulation the way Mike had. She was tenacious – it wouldn't be long before she started digging into the past on her own. She wasn't put off by Lorraine's tears and trembling voice.

Lorraine had now accepted that Karen was in Mike's life for good, and she was glad. Mike was happier than she'd seen him in a long time. But Lorraine's ability to deflect and misdirect would only work for so long before Karen uncovered the truth. What if Mike heard the story from Karen, not her?

Lorraine's gaze drifted to the framed photographs on the wall. There was her wedding photo with James, Mike's stepfather, and one of Mike as a five-year-old, with messy hair and perpetually grubby knees, grinning at the camera.

Despite everything, her son had grown into a decent, kind man. She'd tried so hard to make up for the sins of the past – to build a stable home for Mike where he never wanted for anything.

But she'd kept secrets.

He'd asked so many times over the years, wanting to know more about his background and his father. When he was younger it had been easier to put him off. But in the last year, his questions had become more demanding, and she knew he wouldn't let it rest.

He deserved the truth. Even if he thought less of her for it.

Taking a deep breath, Lorraine hit send.

The whoosh of the email made her stomach churn with worry. There was no going back.

Now all she had to do was tell Mike.

She imagined his stunned expression changing to that hurt, brooding look that made her feel about two inches tall. And poor Karen would have to deal with the fallout.

Maybe it would work. Maybe she could explain, make them both understand how she'd only been trying to protect—

The shrill ring of Lorraine's mobile cut through her thoughts and made her jump. She snatched up her phone.

It was Mike.

Chapter One

Detective Sergeant Karen Hart shivered in the passenger seat of the unmarked police car. Beside her was DC Rick Cooper, a camera ready on his lap.

They had been sitting there for hours, staking out the location after receiving a tip-off that something was about to go down.

'Tea, and salt and vinegar crisps.' Rick popped open another packet from his stash in the glove compartment. 'Perfect combination.'

Karen shook her head when Rick offered her the packet.

'At least we've got proper snacks this time,' he said. 'I did the last one with Sophie and all she brought was celery sticks and hummus.'

Karen smiled despite the chill seeping into her bones. They were parked at the back of a supermarket car park, as the sheltered spot gave them a good view of the warehouse they were watching.

She scanned the area, willing something to happen. They knew that Quentin Chapman was dodgy – which was why they were here, waiting to catch him in the act – but the man was also careful. Too careful.

In recent weeks, they'd ramped up their investigations and surveillance based on intel from Ed Dawson, a local snitch whose past information had been spotty at best. But they couldn't risk dismissing any leads regarding Chapman. Even an unreliable source like Ed occasionally produced something worthwhile. He'd claimed a delivery of stripped parts from high-end vehicles was due at Chapman's warehouse today, but Karen wasn't convinced. Ed had been particularly keen to help lately, which usually meant he was trying to divert attention from whatever he was up to himself.

Today's operation was just another in a long line of frustrating days. They were watching for the white Transit van Ed had told them would be arriving with the stolen parts. But the only movement had been a DPD delivery to the premises next door.

Chapman couldn't be this squeaky clean. Something had to give eventually. Didn't it?

The car's heaters were on the blink. Karen rubbed her hands, but the friction did little to ward off the December cold. She sighed, her breath fogging the window. She had a horrible feeling they'd been played. Chapman always managed to outmanoeuvre them.

'Do you think he knows we're watching him?' Rick asked.

'It's possible. Chapman's got eyes and ears everywhere.'

She thought back to their last encounter, the way Chapman had smiled at her, all grandfatherly and polite. But Karen knew him better than that. Beneath the benign exterior was a ruthless man – one who wouldn't hesitate to eliminate his rivals.

Would he despatch a police officer just as easily? Maybe. Especially if that officer was constantly getting in his way. The thought made her shudder, and not just from the cold.

Karen had a complicated history with Chapman. It wasn't long ago that he had quite literally saved her life by pushing her out of the path of a bullet. She vividly recalled the force of his hands shoving her aside, the crack of the gunshot, and then Chapman crumpling to the ground.

He had survived, of course. Men like Quentin Chapman were hard to kill. And though he hadn't brought it up . . . yet . . . Karen had the uncomfortable sense that she owed him a debt for saving her life that day.

'I think this operation is another dud,' Rick said.

Karen thought he was probably right. She studied the warehouse through the windscreen. The building was old and run-down, its windows boarded up. Hours had passed, but there was still no sign of the white Transit. Maybe they were barking up the wrong tree entirely. Or perhaps Chapman had somehow cottoned on to their increased surveillance and decided to lie low.

'We should call it a day,' Rick said, scrunching his empty crisp packet into a ball.

Karen glanced at the clock on the dashboard. 'Just a little while longer.'

Rick let out a long-suffering sigh and checked his watch for the tenth time in as many minutes. 'Do you really think a few more minutes will make any difference? He's not here. No one is.'

'Chapman has had things go his way for too long. He'll get sloppy. We just need to be patient.'

Rick's leg bounced up and down with pent-up energy. 'It's so cold tonight.'

Karen nodded, her eyes still fixed on the warehouse as Rick reached for another bag of crisps.

'So,' he said, 'have you and Mike set a date for the wedding yet?'

'We're in no rush. We're both so busy with work, and we haven't even told Mike's parents yet.'

'Why not?'

She paused. 'I'm not sure how Lorraine's going to take the news. Mike wants to tell her tonight. We're having dinner with her and James.'

'They'll be happy for you both, won't they? I thought you were getting along better these days?'

Karen grimaced. 'We are. But Lorraine's still not my biggest fan.'

'Why?'

'I'm not sure. Maybe she thinks I'm too wrapped up in my job to make Mike happy.'

She thought of the last time she'd seen Lorraine. It had been James's birthday dinner last month. Karen had barely made it through the main course before getting called out to a suspected arson. Lorraine's eyes had narrowed in disapproval as Karen rushed off – and she'd said, *Well, I suppose that's something we'll have to get used to.*

Now Karen wondered if maybe Lorraine was right – Mike spent more evenings alone than any fiancé should have to.

But Mike said he understood. Having worked his way through the police ranks, then spent years as a police dog handler before his leg injury, he understood what the job demanded better than most.

She loved Mike, and he loved her. They were grown-ups and would figure out how to handle Lorraine together.

His relationship with his mum had been strained ever since Mike had asked again about the identity of his biological father. He'd always known James was his stepfather, since he was old enough when his mum and James first got together to remember. The question of his real father had always been avoided when he was younger, though. But he'd started asking again in recent years. When he'd kept on at Lorraine about it, she'd eventually handed over some old photographs. In every single one, his father's face had been scratched out.

Mike had backed off when his mum broke down in tears after he'd pressed her even further. He'd even burned the photos to prove to himself he was done with it all. But Karen knew him better than that – his need to understand where he came from wouldn't stay buried forever.

It was still a touchy subject, but Karen worried she'd made things worse when she tried to suggest to Lorraine that Mike had a right to know his own history. Lorraine had made it clear she didn't appreciate Karen's input.

Karen wished she could help him more, but wasn't sure how.

Rick shifted in his seat. 'Sorry, Sarge, too much tea.' He put his hand on the door. 'I'm going to have to use the supermarket toilets.'

So much for lying low. 'All right. Be quick.'

Rick flashed her a grateful smile, handing her the camera before slipping out of the car. Karen watched him jog to the supermarket, then she turned back towards the warehouse.

A flicker of light caught her eye. Two big security lights, either side of the main door to the warehouse, cut through the gloom of the December afternoon.

Karen sat up straighter and lifted the camera, zooming in.

She peered through the viewfinder, finger ready on the shutter button. But as the image came into focus, she groaned as a tough-looking tabby cat sauntered on the LCD screen.

Karen slumped back in her seat, lowering the camera. A false alarm.

Rick was right. Today had been another waste of time.

A few minutes later, Rick reappeared, jogging back towards the car. He slid into the passenger seat and closed the door with a thud. 'Anything?'

'Nothing.'

'Chapman is a crafty one,' Rick said with a scowl.

Karen agreed. He'd been involved in all sorts of criminal activities over the years, but he had an uncanny ability to remain just out of reach of the law.

If they were going to bring him down, they needed to be clever. Chapman was too careful to incriminate himself in an obvious way. Their best chance of getting him locked up was if they could persuade one of Chapman's soldiers to turn on him, giving them the evidence they needed.

But that wouldn't be easy. Chapman's people were fiercely loyal. Getting one of them to talk would be like squeezing blood from a stone.

Rick looked thoroughly fed up. 'I know we need to catch him in the act, but I don't think anything is going to happen here today.'

'You really want to head back to the station, don't you?'

'Well, I would like to feel my toes again at some point.'

And Karen needed to get home at a reasonable time. She couldn't miss dinner with Mike, Lorraine and James if she and Mike were announcing their engagement.

'All right. Let's pack it in for the day. We're not getting anywhere sitting here freezing our backsides off.'

'Music to my frostbitten ears,' Rick said, and he started gathering up the empty crisp packets.

Chapter Two

At six thirty that evening Karen stood in front of the full-length mirror in her bedroom. She'd already changed her outfit twice and was now on the verge of changing it for a third time. She'd never been the type to get flustered about what to wear, but tonight was different. Tonight, they were going to tell Mike's mother and stepfather about their engagement.

Karen tugged at the neckline of her blouse, feeling a knot of anxiety in her chest. She glared at her reflection, irritated with herself for being so on edge. Why did announcing their engagement feel like heading into battle?

She pulled off the blouse and traded it for a cosy cream cable-knit jumper. Better? No, now she looked like a fisherman. She put the jumper back on its hanger and selected a dress instead. Why was she so nervous?

Her gaze drifted to the delicate diamond ring on her finger, and her stomach fluttered with butterflies. This wasn't cold feet, was it?

No, she adored Mike. She wanted to spend the rest of her life with him. She'd never thought she'd find happiness again after losing Josh and Tilly, but Mike had surprised her and now she couldn't imagine life without him.

No, Mike wasn't the problem. It was Lorraine who had her on edge.

She smoothed her hands down the front of the dress. It was a simple navy shift – elegant, but tonight it felt wrong. Too plain and boring. She needed something special. But everything else in her wardrobe seemed either too casual or too fancy.

Mike came up behind her and slipped his arms around her waist. 'You look great,' he said, resting his chin on her shoulder.

Karen met his eyes in the mirror. 'I look like I'm dressed for a day at the office, not an engagement announcement.'

Mike kissed her cheek. 'You look perfect. And Mum and James will be too busy celebrating to notice what you're wearing anyway.'

Karen sighed. 'I want everything to go well tonight.'

'It will.'

She'd actually meant that she didn't want to give Lorraine the opportunity to find fault with anything.

'It's easy for you to say. Your mother adores you.'

'And I adore *you*.' He nuzzled into the crook of her neck, his stubble rough against her skin.

Karen relaxed into him, her nerves temporarily forgotten. 'You old softie,' she murmured, leaning into his solid frame.

'You love me for it. Seriously though, you have nothing to worry about. Tonight is going to be perfect.'

Karen looked at him doubtfully. 'I hope you're right.'

'Come on. How can *you* be afraid of my mum?'

Extricating herself from his arms, Karen turned to face him. 'I'm not afraid. It's just Lorraine can be . . . challenging.'

He grinned. 'Really? I hadn't noticed.'

Karen playfully swatted his arm. 'You know what I mean.'

'Unfortunately, I do.' Mike's expression softened. 'She can be prickly, but she does like you.'

'It doesn't always feel like it.'

'I know, and I appreciate the effort you put in.'

'I'm being ridiculous, aren't I?'

'I wouldn't go as far as ridiculous.'

'Oh? How far would you go?'

'I know better than to answer that.' He grinned. 'It's just an evening with my parents. You've faced down armed criminals without batting an eye.'

'Yes, but your mum is . . .' Karen hesitated. *Manipulative? Controlling?* No, that was unkind. 'She has a way of getting under my skin.'

'Believe me, I know how she can be. James is on his way back from a golf day with some old friends. He won't be home until seven thirty. So it will just be us and Mum for drinks before dinner. We can tell her before James gets home if you'd prefer?'

Karen wasn't sure. James was good at calming Lorraine when she got worked up. He'd been nothing but kind to Karen since they'd first met, always asking about her work and actually listening to her answers. She felt James's presence would be a welcome buffer. 'No, let's wait and tell them both at dinner.'

They went downstairs and made sure Sandy, Mike's dog, was settled for the evening.

Then, as Mike opened the front door, he turned and asked, 'Ready?'

'As I'll ever be.' She managed a smile. 'Let's go and tell your mum and James the good news.'

Mike pulled on to the driveway of his mother's house at seven p.m. Lorraine's car was parked in its usual spot in front of the garage.

Karen felt jittery, despite Mike's reassuring smile.

She frowned as they got out of the car, noticing the front door of the house was ajar. 'That's odd. The door's open.'

Mike shrugged. 'Maybe James just got back.'

Karen relaxed a little, thinking that might be a good thing. If James was already there, they could share the news of their engagement straightaway and there would be no need for making small talk with Lorraine while they waited for James to come home.

But something was wrong. Her police instincts were almost screaming at her. There was no sign of James's car.

And why were there no lights on? Karen followed Mike towards the house.

'It's quiet,' he said.

Karen was getting a bad feeling about this. She tried to push the growing unease aside, but it kept creeping back.

'Mike . . .' she began.

He was already striding ahead.

'Mum?' He pushed the front door open.

Silence.

They moved inside, and Mike switched on the hall light. 'Maybe she went for a nap and overslept.'

'Or she forgot we were coming over and went out?' Karen suggested. 'Her car is in the drive, so she can't have gone far.'

'She didn't forget,' Mike said. 'I spoke to her at lunchtime. She said she was going to cook roast chicken tonight.'

There was no smell of cooking in the house. Only a faint floral scent coming from a diffuser in the hall.

Karen put her bag on the floor beside the coat rack. Lorraine's red wool coat hung on its usual hook. Everything seemed in its place, but something about the stillness of the house made her skin prickle.

'Mum!' Mike called again, louder this time.

Still no response. Mike moved ahead of her, heading for the living room. Karen followed.

The room was tidy, the TV remote control still on the coffee table. The colourful cushions on the sofa neatly plumped as always.

They moved on to the kitchen. It was spotless. The oven was off. Maybe Lorraine had changed her mind about the roast chicken and was planning to get a takeaway tonight?

Karen touched the kettle. It was stone cold. Lorraine nearly always had a cup of tea on the go, so that wasn't normal. The detail nagged at her, adding to the dread pooling in her stomach.

There were no obvious signs of a break-in, and yet every instinct was screaming that something wasn't right. She stole a glance at Mike. His shoulders were tense as he called out again.

They checked the study next. The computer was on, and an address book lay on the floor.

Mike picked it up and put it on the desk. 'That's weird.'

Then they moved on to the dining room.

Mike pushed open the door and then stopped in his tracks, his broad shoulders blocking the doorway. Karen pulled up short, almost bumping into him.

'Mike, what . . . ?' The words faded on her lips as she looked past him and caught sight of what had made him stop.

A chair had been overturned. Lorraine's legs were just visible behind the table.

She was lying on the floor, her body crumpled and still.

Karen's first thought was that Lorraine had fainted or suffered a heart attack.

Mike made a strangled sound, his hand flying to cover his mouth. He was in shock. But they needed to move quickly. They might be able to resuscitate Lorraine.

'Call 999,' Karen ordered, gently nudging him, trying to get past.

Mike stood rooted to the spot.

'Mike! 999 now!'

As she manoeuvred around his rigid body to get to Lorraine, she suddenly stopped.

A shocked gasp escaped Karen's lips before she could prevent it.

Her faint hope that they could resuscitate Lorraine was viciously extinguished.

Now she realised why Mike had frozen like that.

Karen's stomach churned violently. Lorraine's eyes. Crude black stitches had been used to sew the lids shut.

Bile burned in her throat. This was no accident, no passing from natural causes. Who would have done something so vile?

She couldn't tear her gaze away from those mutilated eyelids. The stitches were harsh and uneven, coarse black thread puckering Lorraine's pale skin.

Mike still hadn't moved to call 999. Karen patted her pockets for her mobile.

Then a guttural sound, somewhere between a retch and a sob, tore from his throat. He stumbled forward, his expression contorted in horror and disbelief.

Karen watched as he crumpled to his knees beside his mother's body. She crouched beside him and pressed her fingers to Lorraine's neck, searching for a pulse she already knew wouldn't be there.

Lorraine's skin was cold.

A section of carpet below Lorraine's head was darker than usual, where blood had seeped into the fibres. A blow to the head, Karen guessed. Likely the initial attack to incapacitate her.

She sat back. 'I'm so sorry, Mike. She's gone.'

For a moment, he seemed not to hear her, rocking back on his haunches with his face buried in his hands. Karen reached out, touching his shoulder.

'Mike, I need to call this in.'

'No, we have to try CPR first.'

He moved forward, his face frantic, but Karen held up a hand.

It was pointless. Karen judged Lorraine had been dead for a few hours already. But she understood Mike's desperation.

'We have to try.'

'Mike, I'm so sorry, but she's been dead a while. We can't bring her back, and this is now a crime scene.'

The look of devastation he gave Karen lanced straight through her heart.

'I don't understand . . . why would anyone do this . . . who could do something so evil?'

Karen took Mike's hand, squeezing it as her gaze drifted back to those hideous stitches. 'I don't know, but we'll catch them, I promise.'

Chapter Three

Karen was still crouched next to Lorraine's body, her hand on Mike's shoulder.

She heard the uniformed officers before she saw them, their heavy footsteps accompanied by shouts of 'Police!'

'In here,' she called, her voice sounding far calmer than she felt.

Two officers appeared in the doorway, a man and a woman, both looking tense and alert. The male officer, tall with close-cropped hair, took a step into the room, his eyes darting from Karen to Mike and then to Lorraine's body on the floor.

'Did you call this in?' he asked, his hand resting on his radio.

'Yes. I'm Detective Sergeant Karen Hart, and this is Mike Harrington.' Karen gestured to Mike, who was still kneeling beside his mother's body, his face white. 'The deceased is Lorraine Harrington, Mike's mother.'

Karen moved to fetch her ID from her bag in the hall, but the female officer held up a hand to stop her. 'Please stay where you are for now,' she said, her tone not unkind, but firm.

Karen understood their caution. To them, she and Mike were just two people at a crime scene, their roles not yet established. She would have done the same in their position.

The officers seemed overwhelmed, their eyes wide as they took in the scene. Karen couldn't blame them. It was one thing to respond to a reported death; quite another to walk into a room and find a woman with her eyes sewn shut.

'Is she . . . ?' the male officer prompted.

'She's dead,' Karen confirmed. 'And her eyelids . . .' She swallowed hard, fighting back a wave of nausea. 'They've been sewn shut.'

The female officer's mouth set in a grim line. The other officer moved past her, his jaw clenched as he approached Lorraine's body. He looked down at her for a long moment, then swore under his breath.

He turned back to Karen and Mike. 'We need to secure the scene. Can you talk me through how you found her?'

Karen nodded. 'We came in through the front door, which was unlocked and ajar. We called out for Lorraine but got no response. We went from room to room and found her here.' She looked down at Lorraine's body. 'I checked for a pulse, but there wasn't one.'

'Thank you. We'll need to take statements from both of you, but that can wait for now. Can you please follow me?' He turned to his partner. 'SOCOs?'

'On their way,' the female officer said. 'I'll check on their progress.'

As Karen and Mike followed the officers out of the house, she asked, 'Do you know who'll be assigned the senior investigating officer role?'

'Not yet.'

The biting December chill hit them as they stepped outside. It felt much colder now than when they'd arrived. Mike was shivering, which was unusual. Mike, who'd sleep with the window open in winter and wear a T-shirt when everyone else had coats on, was shaking like a leaf. Karen knew it wasn't the cold. It was the shock.

The officer must have noticed too. He gestured to the marked police car. 'Let's get you warm. Sit in the back, and I'll put the heaters on.'

They got in the car and settled into the back seat. As the car's heaters worked overtime against the chill, Mike's shivering decreased.

Karen took a deep breath. This was her job – what she did every day. She looked at Mike, taking in his grief and shock, and felt a fierce surge of protectiveness. What could she say that would help?

There were no words that could make what he was going through any easier. She was used to talking to victims' families, but this was Mike – *her* Mike. All her experience suddenly felt useless. She wanted so badly to make things better for him, but she knew nothing she said could fix this.

A few minutes later, she saw DI Scott Morgan arrive on the scene. He spoke briefly with the officers outside before approaching the police car. He opened the door, letting in a gust of cold air.

Morgan's eyes met Karen's, a silent question in them. She gave Mike's shoulder a gentle squeeze before stepping out of the car to speak with Morgan.

He led her a few paces away, out of earshot of Mike. 'What happened?'

Karen took a deep breath. 'We found her like that. Mike and I were coming for dinner. To tell Lorraine and James about our engagement.'

Morgan's expression softened. 'I'm sorry, Karen. I know this is tough. But if you can run through exactly what happened for me, that would be a great help.'

Karen gave him the key details. Then, when she was done, Morgan asked her if Mike was holding up okay.

She glanced back at the car. 'He's in shock. I don't know what to say to him. Everything just feels useless.'

'There's not much you can say in a situation like this.' Morgan paused, seeming to weigh his next words. 'Where is James?'

She cursed under her breath. How could she have forgotten about James? 'He met up with friends for a day of golf. But he's on his way back.'

Morgan winced. 'That's not going to be a pleasant homecoming.'

'No, it's not.' Karen glanced again at the police car where Mike sat, looking utterly lost.

'We can break the news,' Morgan said. 'He's next of kin, so we'll need to talk to him anyway.'

Karen nodded slowly. But she hated the thought of James receiving such terrible news from strangers. 'Maybe I should call him first? If that's okay?'

'It might be better coming from you,' Morgan agreed.

As much as she dreaded making the call, James deserved to hear the news from someone who could deliver it as gently as possible.

'I'll do it,' she said. 'Can you stay with Mike while I make the call?'

'Of course. Take all the time you need.'

With a grateful nod, Karen moved a few steps away, pulling out her mobile. The cold evening air bit at her skin as she scrolled through her contacts until she found James's number.

Her finger hovered over the screen. How did you soften the blow when telling someone that their wife had been brutally murdered? She'd delivered bad news like this before, of course. But this was different. This time it was personal.

Karen hit the call button. The phone rang three times, then James's cheerful voice came on the line. 'Karen! So sorry, I'm running late. Traffic on the A46 is dire.'

Karen closed her eyes. 'James, I'm sorry. Something's happened . . .'

◆ ◆ ◆

Morgan stood outside the house, eyes fixed on the police car where Mike sat in the back, staring blankly ahead. His mind flashed to the gruesome scene inside – Lorraine with her eyelids cruelly sewn shut. A wave of revulsion made him shudder, and he was glad Mike couldn't see his reaction from here.

What a horrible way to go, Morgan thought, his stomach churning. And what an awful thing for Mike and Karen to find.

He approached the car, tapping gently on the window before opening the door. 'Mike, I'm so sorry for your loss.'

Mike didn't respond. He didn't even seem to hear him. His gaze remained fixed on some distant point.

Morgan tried again. 'Karen's just stepped away to call your stepdad and let him know what's happened.'

Still no response. Mike seemed lost in his own world of grief and horror.

Morgan crouched down beside the open door. 'Mike, I know this is a terrible shock, but I have to ask. Do you have any idea who could have done this?'

Slowly, Mike shook his head. 'No. I don't. I can't think.'

Of course he can't, Morgan thought. *Poor bloke's just found his mother murdered in her own home.*

He remembered the look on Karen's face when he'd arrived. The shock, the disbelief, the helplessness. It was a look he'd seen too many times in his career, and it never got easier.

Especially not when it was someone you knew. Someone you cared about.

His thoughts turned to the crime itself. The sewing of the eyes, the purposeful disfigurement. It wasn't a common type of MO, not in his experience. Most domestic murders were crimes of passion, of sudden, explosive anger. This felt like something else. More calculated, maybe ritualistic.

Could it be the son? The thought crept into his mind. It wouldn't be the first time he'd seen it. Twice in his career, he'd had cases where sons had turned on their mothers with brutal violence. But those had been very different. Frenzied stabbings and beatings. Not this cold, methodical mutilation.

This wasn't a son's rage. Probably not a husband's either, though they'd certainly need to check alibis. This was something else. Something sinister.

He straightened up and turned back towards the house. The gruesome handiwork on the victim's eyes pointed to a killer who wanted to send a message.

But what message? Morgan wondered. *And who is it intended for?*

It wasn't long before the driveway was full of vehicles. SOCOs filed into the house in their white suits, carrying their kits. They moved with brisk efficiency, disappearing inside to set up lights and label evidence.

After a scenes of crime officer took prints and DNA samples from Karen and Mike for elimination purposes, Morgan came over to them again. 'Why don't you two head home now? There's nothing more you can do here.'

Karen hesitated, her gaze drawn back to the house. Part of her wanted to stay, to oversee every detail of the investigation. But this was too personal. Her judgement would be clouded.

Tim Farthing, head SOCO, trudged along the drive.

'Well, this sounds like a nasty one,' he said, coming to a stop beside them. 'What have we got? Domestic?'

A flash of cold anger shot through Karen. He didn't know, she had to remind herself. It wasn't his fault, but right now his casual tone hit a raw nerve.

Before she had a chance to respond, Morgan stepped forward. 'Tim, a word?' He gestured for Tim to follow him a few paces away.

She watched as Morgan leaned in close to the SOCO, his expression grim. Though she couldn't hear the words, she could guess what was being said from the way Tim's expression changed.

Tim came back looking chastened. 'Sorry for your loss,' he muttered, avoiding Karen's gaze as he moved towards the house.

Morgan returned to Karen's side. 'You know the drill,' he said. 'SOCOs will go over everything and gather evidence. We'll need to talk to you and Mike again, but that can wait.'

Karen nodded, feeling grateful for Morgan's presence. He was steady, reliable – exactly what she needed right now. 'I'm glad you're handling this. I don't think I could . . .' Her voice faded to nothing as she glanced at Mike. His face was still pale, though the trembling had stopped.

Morgan followed her gaze. 'You should take him home.'

She nodded. 'I will. I suggested to James that he come straight to our house rather than here. I thought it might be easier.'

'That's a good idea. He doesn't need to see this.'

Karen turned to Mike and gently touched his shoulder. 'Mike? Let's go home.'

As Karen led him away, she felt like she was moving through a fog, her body operating on autopilot while her mind struggled to process what had happened.

Lorraine was dead. *Murdered.* Her eyes . . . She shuddered, pushing the horrible image from her mind. She couldn't think about that now. She had to focus on getting Mike through this nightmare.

They were almost to their car when a voice called out from behind them. 'Wait up!'

Karen and Mike both stopped and turned around to see Tim Farthing standing in the doorway of the house, holding something up.

The address book.

'I forgot to mention we found that on the floor when we were looking for Lorraine,' Karen said.

Tim frowned as he walked over to them. 'Why did you disturb it? It's evidence.'

Karen suppressed a surge of anger. 'I didn't know Lorraine was dead at that point. We were just trying to find her.'

Tim held up a hand in a placating gesture. 'Right. Sorry. It's just that a page has been ripped out. One of the letter "M" pages is missing. Any idea what that could mean?'

Morgan stepped between them. 'Let's save it until after Mike and Karen have left.'

Was Morgan edging her out?

Karen quickly pushed the thought aside. Of course not. It was just that she shouldn't be involved in the investigation. She was too close to it, too emotionally invested.

But a small voice whispered in the back of her mind: *You're a detective. You could help.*

Karen shook her head, trying to clear it. No. She needed to focus on Mike, on being there for him.

Morgan was gesturing at Tim to get back in the house, a look of exasperation on his face.

'Well, I wouldn't talk about it in front of normal witnesses, of course,' Tim said. 'But this is *Karen.*'

Morgan's jaw tightened. 'I'm perfectly aware of who it is, Tim.'

The unspoken message was clear. *Drop it.* But Tim, being Tim, couldn't seem to help himself.

'I'm just saying,' he continued, 'it's all a bit odd. The missing page, the eyes sewn shut. It's not your typical domestic murder.'

Beside her, Karen felt Mike tense. She'd been so caught up in the normal actions of a crime scene, she'd almost forgotten how each casual mention of the details must be hitting him. This was his *mother*. His childhood home was now a crime scene being dissected by strangers.

'Do you have to discuss it like this? Right here in front of me?' Mike snapped.

'Tim,' Morgan said, his voice taking on a hard edge, 'why don't you go back inside.'

It was a clear dismissal, and even Tim couldn't miss it. With a curt nod and a mumbled apology to Mike, he turned and headed back into the house.

When Morgan looked at Karen and Mike, his face showed both sympathy and frustration. 'I'm sorry about that,' he said. 'You know what Tim's like. No filter.'

Karen nodded, too drained to muster much of a response. She glanced at Mike, who had gone very still beside her. His face was pale; Tim's words about the eyes had clearly hit home. She knew Tim hadn't meant any harm, but his behaviour could be grating at the best of times. And this was far from the best of times.

She touched Mike's arm gently. 'Come on,' she said softly. 'Let's get out of here.'

Get Mike home, she told herself. *Be there for him. Let Morgan and the team handle the rest.*

But even as she thought it, she knew things wouldn't be that simple. Her mind was already speculating – wondering if that missing page in the address book had anything to do with Lorraine's murder. Had the address book fallen to the floor during Lorraine's struggle with her attacker? Or had her killer been searching through it?

Had the killer torn out the page for a name or an address?

Or maybe it was a coincidence. Maybe it wasn't related to the murder at all. Lorraine might have ripped the page out ages ago, needing a scrap of paper or to remove old contacts.

If the killer *had* handled the book, that meant she and Mike might have contaminated evidence.

She glanced at Mike, putting the idea aside. Speculation wouldn't help now. He needed her full attention.

Morgan followed them to the car. 'Do you want a lift home? I can have someone drive your car back later.'

'No, it's okay. I'll drive.' Karen needed something to focus on – something to keep her mind from spiralling.

'Call me if you need anything, okay?' Morgan said. 'Anything at all.'

Karen managed a small smile. 'Thanks, Morgan. I will.'

As they got into the car, Karen felt a wave of exhaustion wash over her. The initial adrenaline was fading, leaving her feeling drained and empty.

Focus, she told herself firmly. *Mike needs you. James needs you. You can fall apart later.*

As she pulled away from the kerb, she glanced in the rear-view mirror. Morgan was standing in the driveway, watching them go, his expression unreadable.

Karen was already imagining the difficult conversations that lay ahead. How would she answer the questions James was bound to have? What could she say to comfort Mike?

One thing at a time, she told herself. *Just take it one thing at a time.*

But that was easier said than done. Because no matter how hard she tried to narrow her focus and concentrate on the practicalities, the image of Lorraine's pale face, her eyes sewn shut with black thread, kept running through her mind.

The gruesome sight would haunt her dreams for a long time to come.

Chapter Four

Morgan watched Raj, the pathologist, crouch beside the body, his gloved hands gently examining the stitches.

The sound of footsteps made Morgan turn. DS Arnie Hodgson stood in the doorway.

'What on earth . . .' Arnie's craggy face screwed up in disgust as he looked at the stitches over Lorraine's eyelids.

He attempted to zip the white protective suit over his ample stomach, then gave up, dropping his hands to his sides. His broad shoulders seemed to sag under the weight of what he saw.

'It's Lorraine Harrington,' Morgan said. 'Mike's mother.'

Arnie's gaze snapped to Morgan's face. 'Karen's Mike? Does she know?'

'It was Karen and Mike who found her.'

Arnie shook his head. 'Poor Karen. How's she holding up?'

'As well as can be expected.' Morgan glanced back at the body. 'We need to look at all angles here, Arnie. Family, friends, enemies. Anyone who might have had a grudge. What do you think about Mike or James?'

'You don't think either of them could have . . . ?'

'We can't rule anything out. You've spent more time with Mike than I have. What do you think?'

'Last month Sylvie and I went up to the Highlands with Karen and Mike. He seems like a good bloke to me. Never met James, though.'

'We'll keep an open mind. It's often a male relative who—'

'Well, yes, but not like this . . .' Arnie said, cutting him off. 'What kind of son or husband would sew her eyes shut? No – if you ask me, this is symbolic. Maybe Lorraine saw something she shouldn't have . . . Or perhaps her husband did, and this was intended as a warning to him.'

'We'll look into Lorraine and James's recent movements.'

'Alibis?' Arnie asked, his gaze dropping back down to where Raj was working.

'James was out all day at a golf event with friends, and Mike was with Karen for at least an hour before they found the body. We'll need to verify of course.'

Arnie nodded, his expression thoughtful. 'Any idea on time of death, Raj?'

Morgan and Arnie both turned to Raj, who was examining Lorraine's hands. He looked up, his usually cheerful face sombre. 'I'd estimate she died sometime between two and four p.m.'

Morgan glanced at his watch. It was now just past eight p.m.

'Cause of death?' Arnie asked.

'Blunt force trauma to the occipital region of the skull. Considerable blood loss. I'd guess she was hit from behind.'

Arnie was already making notes in his battered notebook. 'I'll organise talking to the neighbours, see if anyone saw or heard anything unusual around that time.'

'Good. There's another thing that might be relevant,' Morgan said. 'An address book was on the floor in the study. Karen and Mike found it when they were looking for Lorraine. There's a page missing from the "M" section.'

Morgan could practically see Arnie's mind working. Just like Morgan, he'd be wondering if the killer had taken it, or if it had been ripped out long ago.

'You don't think Chapman could've done this, do you?' Arnie's gruff voice cut through Morgan's thoughts. 'Some kind of threat? Maybe a warning for Karen. You know she and Rick were watching one of his warehouses today?'

Leave it to Arnie to voice the possibility they both feared. Morgan exhaled slowly. Chapman throwing his weight around wouldn't be out of character. But having Karen's future mother-in-law killed? That seemed a step too far, even for him.

Unless she had crossed him in some way. Or had some information she hadn't yet shared with the team. But that wouldn't be like Karen. She knew how important it was for the team to function as one. Especially after what had happened to Sophie. She'd been out investigating alone when someone cracked her skull with an iron bar. They'd almost lost her. Even now, she lived with the consequences, though she did her best to hide the effects of the assault, both physical and otherwise.

Arnie was still silently mulling the idea over. His bushy brows knitted together. Arnie would be a terrible poker player. 'Karen needs to know it's a possibility. If you won't tell her, I will.'

'I'll handle it, DS Hodgson.'

Arnie gave a curt nod, though his frown remained.

Morgan knew the older detective didn't always agree with his methodical approach. But at the end of the day, they both wanted the same thing. And Morgan would never leave Karen at risk.

But there could be another explanation. They couldn't leap to conclusions without evidence. Morgan couldn't remember what sort of work Lorraine did. She was retired, wasn't she?

Getting a full picture of her life would be a top priority.

Morgan noticed Arnie was still looking at him. 'Why don't you make a start with the neighbours?' he said.

'Brilliant idea. Never would have thought of that myself.'

Morgan watched him stomp off. Arnie's worry for Karen was making him even more abrasive than usual. Morgan could understand, even if he was handling it differently. Karen's situation had them both on edge, but Arnie wore his concern like a prickly armour.

Morgan sighed. Different methods, same goal. But at the end of the day, having the same goal was what mattered.

As he exited the house, Arnie took one last glance back. Above the porch, nailed in place, was a horseshoe. A superstitious gesture meant to ward off evil spirits.

Well, that definitely hadn't worked today.

Arnie stripped off the too-tight white coveralls and tucked his notebook into the pocket of his rumpled suit jacket. It was a nice neighbourhood. He took in the tidy row of semi-detached houses and neat front gardens.

Word had clearly spread about Lorraine's murder. He could see curtains twitching as he walked to the next house. A concerned face peered out from behind net curtains before disappearing again.

He couldn't blame the residents for being jittery. A violent crime in a sleepy little community shook people's sense of safety.

Surely someone in this street would have noticed something out of the ordinary today. Something to help them work out what had happened to Lorraine. They needed to start building a timeline, establishing who had seen or spoken to Lorraine in those final critical hours.

One thing was certain: Arnie wouldn't be resting until the responsible party was caught and brought to justice. He owed Karen and Mike that much.

A male face appeared at an upstairs window in the house opposite. It was an older man watching him warily before closing the curtains. The insidious nature of violent crime didn't just steal lives and tear families apart. It robbed entire communities of their sense of security.

The man's nervous glance reminded Arnie that everyone was touched by this kind of violence, but no one would be worse affected than James. Losing the woman he loved like that would tear his world apart.

Thinking of how James would feel made Arnie's thoughts drift to Sylvie. The TV producer had crashed into his life during that nasty business with the murder on her TV set a couple of months ago, and somehow he still hadn't scared her off. Was she starting to mean something to him? He wished he was with her tonight instead of knee-deep in this grisly murder investigation. Things were going remarkably well between them, and Arnie could scarcely believe his luck.

He'd expected Sylvie's interest to cool once she got to know him better. His gruff demeanour and cynical outlook weren't exactly ideal for charming the ladies. But if anything, the opposite had happened. It had only been a matter of weeks since they'd met, but they'd already grown close.

A smile tugged at the corner of Arnie's mouth. Sylvie made him happy. Really happy. A feeling he hadn't experienced in longer than he cared to admit.

He didn't want to get ahead of himself, but he could imagine a real future with her. Maybe even finally giving up his old bachelor pad for something a bit more domestic.

Arnie shook his head, dispersing the uncharacteristically rosy thoughts. His gaze drifted back to the Harrington house.

Poor Karen and Mike. Finding Lorraine like that would haunt them both. Arnie had spent enough time around the pair to find it nearly impossible to believe Mike would be involved in such a horrific crime against his own mother. Sure, you never really knew what went on behind closed doors, but Mike seemed a solid bloke. Down-to-earth and devoted to Karen. Something like this just didn't fit.

Arnie frowned, pondering the other potential suspect: James Harrington. Now there was a possibility that couldn't be dismissed out of hand. His apparent absence from the home at the time of the murder was certainly convenient; almost too convenient. Could it have been a prearranged alibi?

But then, what possible motive could the man have? Arnie had encountered more than his fair share of domestic disputes, but this seemed to surpass that level of violence.

Those stitched eyelids were unsettling. It didn't seem like the kind of thing a nasty, hot-headed husband would do after losing his temper in the midst of a heated row. That sort of calculated mutilation hinted at the workings of a truly deranged mind. An absolute sicko.

Arnie's hands curled into fists at his sides as a surge of anger flooded him. Whoever had done this, whatever their reasons, they wouldn't be enjoying their freedom for much longer. Not if he had any say in it.

He heard squealing brakes and stopped walking.

Someone jumped out of a blue Peugeot and began ranting and gesturing wildly outside the Harrington house.

Arnie squinted. Who *was* that?

Chapter Five

Arnie headed towards the commotion as fast as his stocky frame would allow. The Peugeot sat in the quiet residential street with the driver's-side door thrown open and its hazard lights flashing.

A grey-haired man wearing beige trousers and a blue jacket paced the pavement, waving his arms and shouting at the police officers who stood at the perimeter of the Harrington house.

'This is ridiculous!' the man shouted, his face beet red. 'You can't stop me entering my own home.'

One of the uniformed officers stepped forward. 'Sir, you need to calm down and step back from the premises.'

'Calm down?' He let out a hysterical bark of laughter. 'My wife has been murdered! How can I possibly be calm?'

Arnie had never met the man before, but he knew that this had to be James Harrington, the husband of the recently deceased Lorraine – Mike's stepfather.

Wheezing, Arnie slowed his pace to a jog. By the time he reached them, James had grabbed the officer by the lapels.

'You listen to me,' James said. 'That woman in there is my wife. And someone has . . .' He choked, the words seeming to catch in his throat. His face crumpled.

Arnie intervened. 'Mr Harrington. I'm DS Hodgson. Why don't you let go of the officer and we can talk about this?'

James turned to him, eyes wild. 'Can you tell me what happened? It doesn't make sense.'

DI Morgan's familiar voice came from behind Arnie. 'Mr Harrington, I'm very sorry for your loss. You've spoken to Karen? I thought you were going straight to her house to be with Mike?'

James's anger seemed to subside when he heard Morgan's voice. His arms fell to his sides. 'We were supposed to have dinner tonight, all four of us.' He swallowed hard and raised a shaking hand to his forehead. 'Karen called me on the way home, but I couldn't believe it. I had to come here to see for myself and make sure there hadn't been some terrible mistake.'

Sympathy formed a lump in Arnie's throat. No matter how many years he'd been a copper, he could never become numb to scenes like this.

'Let's go somewhere quieter and discuss what information we have. I can assure you that we are doing everything in our power to find out what happened here tonight.' Morgan looked at Arnie and gave him a subtle nod.

Arnie understood the unspoken request. 'Come along, Mr Harrington. Let's have a chat.'

He placed a gentle hand on the man's elbow and steered him towards the police car parked at the kerb. James let himself be led into the back seat. Arnie closed the door.

'Poor bloke's in a state of shock,' he said quietly to Morgan. 'And who can blame him?'

'He seems upset. But keep an open mind. We have to consider all possible suspects.' Morgan's eyes narrowed. 'Especially those closest to the victim.'

The implication hung heavily between them. James himself couldn't be definitively ruled out until the evidence said so. Arnie felt his mouth turn down at the corners as he studied his colleague.

Morgan had the ability to detach on the job. To a mind like his, all parties were suspects until proven otherwise. He didn't let feelings or emotions get in the way. It was an approach that Arnie both respected and sometimes found disturbing.

'Talk to him. Find out what you can, then take him back to Karen and Mike,' Morgan said. 'They'll start to worry if he doesn't turn up soon.'

'Will do,' Arnie said, walking around to the other side of the car.

There were some cases that really knocked the stuffing out of you. And Arnie was pretty sure this would be one of them.

Karen stared at the tabletop as she struggled to find the right words. Mike sat motionless across from her.

Curled up beside him, Sandy let out a soft whine, sensing the tension. Without a word, Mike reached down and stroked the spaniel's head. The dog nuzzled into his hand.

Karen watched the simple interaction, her chest tightening. Sandy was doing a better job than her. How could she console Mike when his world had been shattered? She knew the devastation of grief all too well – that hollow ache that never truly went away. Yet despite going through loss herself, she didn't even know how to begin helping him through this. He'd already lost his son in a tragic drowning years before she met him, and she knew how close he'd come to giving up then. How would he get through another cruel loss?

'Mike.' Her voice cracked. 'I'm so sorry.'

His gaze remained fixed ahead, his face blank. For a long moment, Karen thought he wouldn't respond at all. Then finally, he spoke, his tone flat. 'Why would someone do that to her?'

Karen fought back the lump forming in her throat. 'I don't know. Whoever did this, they're . . .' She trailed off. The obvious word like *evil* seemed inadequate.

Sick. Twisted. A monster.

'We will find them,' she said. 'And we'll find out why they did it.'

Mike said nothing, and his face remained expressionless. Part of Karen wanted him to rage against what had happened – to vent all the emotions she knew he was experiencing.

She reached across the table, covering his hand with her own. She worried he would pull away, putting up walls she couldn't cross. But he turned his hand over, allowing their fingers to intertwine.

'I can't get my head around it. Help me understand,' he said. 'Why would someone sew her eyes shut?' He shuddered, repulsed by the memory. 'It's like something out of a nightmare.'

Karen agreed. She'd been trying to work it out and analyse what it meant. But so far she hadn't come up with any solid theories.

All she managed was 'I don't understand it either.'

'The stitches . . .' He swallowed before continuing. 'They would have done that after she was dead, don't you think? She wouldn't have felt it. She would have died quickly without suffering, right?'

Karen's instinct was to protect him. She wanted to tell him Lorraine had died quickly with no pain. But she didn't know if that was true and didn't want to lie.

As if sensing her hesitation, Mike squeezed her hand. 'Please, Karen. I need to know what you think.'

He looked at her then, properly, for the first time since they'd got home, and Karen saw everything in his expression – his pain, his confusion, his desperate need for answers. No matter how horrific it was, he wanted the truth.

But she couldn't give it to him, because she didn't have the full story yet.

'We'll have to wait for the post-mortem results to know for sure. But I think the stitches were probably done after she died, because there was minimal blood around her eyes.'

The clinical words left her mouth before she could stop them. She heard herself speaking like a detective instead of Mike's partner, and her stomach twisted. Was this how she was going to comfort him – with forensic observations?

But he nodded slowly, seeming satisfied with her answer. Maybe that was what he needed right now – straightforward facts, something concrete to hold on to in all this.

She thought again about the ripped page from the address book.

She wanted to ask Mike if he knew why the address book might be important, or if he knew what names and addresses would have been on the missing "M" page. But should she really burden him with speculation and theories now?

Her instinct told her to wait and let the dust settle before trying to get answers.

Karen glanced at the clock above the oven. 'I wonder where James has got to. When I spoke to him, he told me he was about thirty minutes away.'

He should have been here by now. Finding Lorraine had left Karen on edge, and her mind immediately leaped to the worst possibility. He'd sounded so shocked on the phone. Maybe she shouldn't have told him while he was driving. What if he'd had an accident?

Mike didn't reply, but he kept his hand linked with hers.

Karen's phone lit up. Three new messages. Then four. Five. Six. A stream of messages from her family WhatsApp group.

Dad: *Why did the scarecrow win an award? Because he was outstanding in his field!* 😄

Emma: *Dad, that's terrible even for you.*

Dad: *I've got loads more!*

Emma: *One a day is more than enough!*

Emma: *Has anyone heard from Karen? She's been quiet today.*

Mum: *She's having dinner at Mike's parents' tonight and telling them about the engagement! Bet they're having a lovely time.*

42

Karen stared at the messages. They had no idea. She'd have to call them.

Her own family had been so easy to tell about the engagement. She and Mike had told them over Sunday lunch a couple of weeks ago, and they'd reacted exactly as she'd known they would: her dad pretending to be stern – *Just make sure you treat her right* – and Emma gushing and demanding to see the ring. Her mother dabbing at happy tears. And her niece, Mallory, asking if she could be a bridesmaid.

No drama, no loaded comments about whether they were rushing things, no subtle digs about Karen's career choices.

That's why they'd put off telling Lorraine. They'd known it would be . . . well, an ordeal was the only way she could describe it, if she were being honest.

Lorraine would probably have found some way to put a damper on things. She would have questioned their decision, maybe thrown in a few passive-aggressive comments about Karen's job for good measure.

But now she'd never know about the engagement, would she?

Poor Lorraine. She'd never get her chance to pick apart their decision, or arch an eyebrow and say *Oh, I see* in that cutting way she had.

The realisation struck Karen as she stared at her phone: she was actually feeling bad that Lorraine wouldn't get a chance to purse her lips and make those little judgemental remarks. She would put up with hundreds of those barbed comments if it would bring Mike's mum back. They shouldn't have put off telling her. It wasn't fair they'd told Karen's family and held back before telling Mike's.

The doorbell rang. Karen went to the door.

Arnie stood on the doorstep with James next to him.

When Karen had spoken to James earlier, he'd said he was on his way directly to her house. Yet here he was with Arnie, as if he'd needed an escort. Had he gone to his home first despite what she'd told him?

She pushed her questions aside for now, not wanting to add to James's obvious distress. There would be time for questions later.

'I'm so sorry, James.'

He met her gaze and said nothing, but the sadness in his eyes spoke volumes.

'Mike's in the kitchen,' she said. 'Come on in, both of you.'

James went through to the kitchen, but Arnie shook his head. 'Can't stay, I'm afraid. Got to head back to the scene.' His face softened as he looked at Karen. 'I just wanted to make sure James got here all right. I've asked him some preliminary questions, but we'll need to talk to him and Mike again tomorrow, when things are less . . . fresh.' After James was out of earshot, Arnie leaned in closer and added, 'Have you got a minute? I need a quick word in private.'

Part of her wanted to get back to Mike. She was worried about him, but she knew anything case-related from Arnie could be important. She glanced over her shoulder to where James had joined Mike at the kitchen table.

She stepped out on to the front porch, pulling the door almost closed behind her to give them some privacy. 'What is it?'

Arnie's face was grave, his craggy features somehow more lined than usual. 'I'm sorry about all this, Karen.' He paused, almost as if searching for the right words – which was unusual behaviour for the typically blunt detective, who could talk nineteen to the dozen under normal circumstances. 'But I need to ask. I've talked it over with Morgan and . . . we think there's a chance this could be related to the Chapman case.'

Karen felt her chest tighten. 'Chapman? Why would he be involved?'

'It seems . . . convenient timing? With you looking into Chapman's dealings recently.'

Karen's mouth went dry. The implication was clear. If Chapman had killed Lorraine, then it was to get at Karen, which meant Karen was responsible for Lorraine's murder.

But surely even Chapman wouldn't . . .

'It's a stretch.' Karen kept her voice hushed, not wanting Mike to overhear.

Arnie's expression was grim.

She couldn't imagine how Mike would react to the news. If he found out this had happened because of Karen's work . . . Despite the freezing temperatures, a prickle of sweat broke out on her forehead.

She shuddered to think what Mike would do if he thought Chapman had murdered his mother. Perhaps it was better to keep him in the dark for now. At least until they had concrete proof.

'Maybe I shouldn't have brought it up.'

'You did the right thing telling me,' Karen said. 'But I won't mention it to Mike until we have more to go on.'

'We could organise a panic button, maybe a unit to sit outside tonight?' Arnie offered.

Karen thought it through, then shook her head. 'We'll be okay. We've got our security cameras, and Sandy's our early alarm system.'

Arnie nodded. 'All right then. Focus on taking care of yourself and those two in there.' His voice softened so it was almost fatherly. 'Let me and Morgan handle things.'

For all his gruffness, Arnie had a big heart. 'Thanks, Arnie.'

He cleared his throat, the tender moment ending as quickly as it had begun. 'Well, you know where I am if you need anything.' With a nod, he turned and headed for his car.

Karen hesitated before joining Mike and James in the kitchen. A chill ran through her as the horrifying implications sank in. If Chapman had gone after Lorraine because of Karen . . . then this was all Karen's fault.

Had she placed a target on the back of Mike's mother? How could Mike ever forgive Karen for that?

In the kitchen, Mike sat silently. James sat opposite, his face clearly showing his pain.

'I can't believe this is happening,' he muttered. 'Why would someone do this to Lorraine?' His voice broke as he said her name.

Karen's gaze flicked briefly to Mike. But he didn't respond.

'We don't have answers right now,' she said. 'But we will. We're going to figure out who did this, and why.'

'Will they let you work on the investigation?' James asked.

'No, I'm too close to it, but I'm sure they'll keep us informed.'

'Mike.' James turned his gaze on his stepson. 'I'm sorry you had to find her like that.'

Mike remained still for so long that Karen wondered if he'd even heard what James had said. But finally, he nodded.

Karen decided to make some tea and toast as Mike and James sat in silence. She switched on the kettle, wondering if Arnie's suspicions about Chapman could be wrong.

The man was ruthless, yes, but would he really stoop to killing an innocent woman? Why not target Karen directly if she was the thorn in his side?

Lorraine's eyes being sewn shut had to be significant. Was it a warning for Karen to keep her eyes closed to Chapman's exploits?

She felt ill just considering the possibilities.

But this didn't fit Chapman's pattern. The man was methodical and careful. He eliminated threats with precision – usually making them look like accidents or suicides. That's why it was so hard to pin things on him. He'd never gone after family members, viewing it as messy and crude. *I'm not some common thug, Detective Hart,* he'd told her once. *Everything I do is simply business.*

And whatever this was, it definitely wasn't business.

Chapter Six

The following morning, Karen was stifling yawns as she drove to Nettleham police station.

She'd called her parents late last night and broken the bad news. They'd both been stunned into silence at first, and then came the questions she couldn't really answer. She'd stuck to the basics and said nothing about Lorraine's eyelids being sewn shut.

That was partly her being professional – no discussing case details – but if she was honest, she didn't want that image taking up residence in her parents' heads the way it had in hers.

She'd slept badly, her mind full of unanswered questions about Lorraine's murder. Every time she'd started to drift off, another question would form. She knew she should be focused on supporting Mike, not lying there picking apart crime scene details in her head. But the detective part of her wouldn't shut up, even when she wanted it to.

Mike had risen before dawn, after a restless night of his own. He'd muttered something about needing the distraction of work before heading off for a shower. She couldn't blame him. Being around animals was calming in a way human company could never be right now.

She'd tried to persuade him to take some time off, but Mike was stubborn. *I need to work*, he'd insisted, his voice flat. *Don't worry about me.*

It was impossible to stop worrying just because someone told you to. But Karen knew better than to push him. Maybe some time at work would help.

After Mike left, James had decided to visit his brother in person to break the devastating news. With them both gone, the house had felt oppressively quiet. So she'd decided to go to work.

She parked, and as she got out of her car, she noticed a huge bloke running towards her from the other side of the car park.

It took Karen a moment to recognise the bulky man behind the camera, but when she did, her temper flared. It was the photographer who often worked with Cindy Connor, the irritating reporter who always seemed to show up at the worst possible moments.

'What do you think you're doing?' Karen demanded.

Cindy sauntered into view, her helmet-like blonde bob perfectly rigid as always. 'Sorry for your loss, DS Hart,' she said.

'Who told you?' Karen asked.

'We just need a photograph for the new story,' Cindy said, completely ignoring Karen's question.

A photograph of her? Why? Were they writing about Lorraine?

'What new story?' she asked, dreading the answer.

Cindy's lips curved into a smug smile. 'It publishes on the *Lincolnshire Post* website at noon. You can see for yourself.'

If they wanted a picture of her, the story must be about Lorraine's murder. How could Cindy stoop so low, exploiting this for clickbait?

Karen held back, fighting the urge to give the pair a mouthful. That would only give Cindy more ammunition.

'Things must be pretty bad career-wise if you can't even make it into print,' Karen said, grabbing her bag from the back seat.

Cindy didn't miss a beat. 'Online is where all the important stories get published these days. Paper publishing is old news. Too slow.'

Before Karen could respond, the photographer stepped forward, his camera raised again. The lens was inches from her face. Instinctively, she pushed it away, causing him to stumble.

'Hey, watch it!' he protested, cradling the camera protectively. 'This equipment is expensive. I'm going to file a complaint!'

Karen shook her head. They had such nerve, ambushing her like this and then acting like the victim. She wanted nothing more than to rip into them both, but she knew her emotions were too raw. In her current state, she couldn't trust herself not to say something she'd regret.

Clenching her fists, she pushed past them and made her way towards the station entrance. She couldn't let them get under her skin. She had work to do, and Cindy Connor's sensationalism wasn't going to distract her.

As she entered the reception area, a cluster of uniformed officers murmured condolences. Karen acknowledged them with a tight nod and a forced half-smile. Word of Lorraine's brutal death had clearly spread.

'I'm so sorry.'

'Dreadful business, just dreadful.'

'Let us know if you need anything.'

She murmured her thanks as their well-intentioned words washed over her, and walked quickly towards the stairs.

On the second floor, she was greeted by a mercifully empty hallway.

Karen stepped into the open-plan office, and immediately all heads swivelled in her direction. A hush fell over the room as conversations stopped abruptly.

Before she could even make it to her desk, DC Sophie Jones rushed over, her face tight with worry. 'Oh, Karen, I'm so sorry. I didn't come around last night because I knew you and Mike would need some space.'

Accepting Sophie's hug, Karen smiled. 'I got your text, Sophie. Thanks for thinking of us.'

Sophie awkwardly tried to find the right words. 'If there's anything, *anything,* I can do.'

'Thanks,' Karen said gently. 'I appreciate it. I'll be okay.'

From the corner of her eye, she caught sight of Morgan emerging from his office.

He strode towards them, his gaze fixed on Karen. 'What are you doing here?'

Her defences immediately bristled. 'I'm here to work. The same as you.'

Seeming to realise how harsh his words had sounded, Morgan said, 'Sorry, that came out wrong. I just meant are you sure you should be back so soon? Doesn't Mike need you at home?'

'Being at home wouldn't help because Mike isn't there. He's gone to work.'

Karen's jaw clenched at Morgan's look of pity. Of course she *should* be with Mike right now. But the truth was, she had no clue how to help him through this. Every attempt to comfort him felt clumsy and inadequate. She didn't need Morgan to remind her how useless she felt right now.

She was trying to be there for him, but Mike had retreated into himself. His grief was like a wall, and she couldn't get past it. When he'd announced he was going to work this morning, Karen had felt both guilt and relief. Relief that she wouldn't have to face a day of awkward silences and stilted conversations. And guilt that she was failing him when he needed her most.

What was she supposed to do? Sit at home, twiddling her thumbs, while Mike went to work? No, she needed to keep busy.

Karen forced a smile that felt more like a grimace. 'Mike and I both thought work would be a good distraction.'

They were both the same – her diving into case files while Mike took refuge with his four-legged friends. Different jobs, same escape plan. She was running to the station to bury herself in work, while Mike wanted to spend time with his dogs. At least the dogs didn't judge his coping mechanism.

Sophie exchanged a sceptical look with Morgan. 'I'm not sure that's a good idea. Maybe you should both take some time—'

Karen waved off her concern. 'I'm fine, Sophie. Really. I need to be here.'

Morgan studied her. After a moment, he said, 'Karen, can I have a word in my office?'

Great. Now she was going to get a lecture from Morgan about taking care of herself or some other well-meaning tripe.

But she couldn't exactly refuse. With a nod, she followed him into his office, acutely aware of the curious glances from the rest of the team.

As soon as the door closed behind them, Morgan gestured for her to take a seat. Karen perched on the edge of the chair.

Morgan settled behind his desk, his hands clasped in front of him. 'Karen, I know you want to be here, but are you sure you're ready for this? It's not even been a day since . . .' He left the sentence unfinished.

Since my future mother-in-law was brutally murdered, Karen thought, mentally completing his sentence.

And since Mike's world was shattered.

Out loud, she said, 'I appreciate your concern, Morgan, but I need to work. I can't just sit at home and dwell on what happened.'

'I understand that. But you've been through a trauma. It would be wise to take some time to process it.'

Karen shook her head. 'I can't. Not when there's a killer out there who needs to be caught.'

And not when the alternative to being at the station was facing the fact that she had no idea how to be there for Mike, and that she was failing him.

She couldn't say that to Morgan, though. She didn't want to admit that she was floundering. So instead, she met his gaze head-on. 'I'm not going to sit on the sidelines while someone else investigates Lorraine's murder. I need to be a part of this, Morgan. I need to find out who did this to her.'

'You know that's impossible. Completely against procedure. You can't work the case.'

Of course she knew that. Technically, it was an iron-clad rule. But she was still going to try. She'd spent most of the night trying to find a loophole that would allow her to be part of the investigation. 'I can help. I—'

'No.'

'But I could just—'

'No.'

Karen narrowed her eyes. 'Most people would be a little gentler in their approach considering what I've just been through.'

'I'm not trying to hurt you. I'm trying to keep you safe.'

'Then why didn't you tell me about the possible Chapman connection?' The words left her mouth as she realised that this was why she was angry with Morgan. Unfairly, perhaps. But she was hurt he was pushing her out.

Morgan went quiet. Then, after a moment, he said, 'I take it Arnie shared that information with you?'

'I should have realised it was a possibility myself. I was in shock.'

Morgan sighed. 'I thought about telling you, then decided you didn't need the extra stress. We've had a unit on Chapman since last night.'

'What good is having a unit on Chapman when we know he doesn't do his own dirty work?'

'There was also a unit on your road last night.'

'I told Arnie I didn't want that.'

'And I overruled him.'

Karen glared at Morgan.

And then she realised what she was doing. Why was she pushing back? He was trying to help. It made sense to have a police presence outside to keep them safe, just in case whoever had killed and mutilated Lorraine decided they weren't done.

'Karen, I only want what's best for you.'

'I'll decide what's best for me, thanks.'

'No, you won't. I know this is hard for you, because you're not in control. That's scary. I'd feel the same. So you're trying to control other things, trying to get in on the case.'

Karen felt a flash of anger at Morgan's words, even though she knew he was right. She hated feeling powerless. It terrified her.

'I just want to be involved.'

Morgan's expression remained infuriatingly calm. 'I know you do. But you're too close to this. You need to step back and let the team handle it.'

'So you're just going to shut me out completely?' The words came out sharper than she'd intended.

'Of course not.' Morgan leaned back in his chair. 'You'll be kept in the loop. But you can't actively work the case, Karen. It's a clear conflict of interest.'

She opened her mouth to argue, but Morgan held up a hand, stopping her. 'I'm not saying this to be cruel. I'm looking out for you. For your well-being *and* your career.'

She had all her arguments ready – that her judgment wouldn't be compromised, that she could keep her feelings in check and stay objective, and that she had a strong track record of handling difficult cases. But the words stuck in her throat. She *was* too emotionally invested.

Karen let out a slow breath. As a professional, she had to recognise when her involvement could do more harm than good. 'Okay. You're right.'

Morgan gave her a sympathetic look. 'I know how hard this is for you. I wish I could let you work the case. But it's for the best that you take a step back. Besides, DCI Churchill is bringing in people from outside to oversee the investigation.'

Karen's fingers dug into the arms of the chair. *Outsiders.* She didn't like the sound of that. Morgan's clinical, by-the-book methods might drive her up the wall at times, but she knew he was good. She could trust he'd do his best to find Lorraine's killer. 'Who is Churchill bringing in?'

'DI Falkner and DS Cunnings from Sleaford. Churchill says they're good. I haven't worked with them before, but Arnie has. Arnie's not Falkner's biggest fan, but he admits the man's a sharp detective. Cunnings is a hard worker, fair and compassionate. The case is in good hands. Our team will still be involved, and you have my word I will put my all into this investigation. But you have to step back.'

Part of her was relieved to have this taken out of her hands. But another part – the stubborn, headstrong part – hated being sidelined.

'I feel so useless,' she admitted.

'You're not useless. You're taking care of Mike. That's the most important thing right now.'

Karen gave a humourless laugh. 'I'm doing a pretty poor job of *that* so far.'

The words were out before she could stop them. She immediately wished she could take them back. The guilt and inadequacy that had been eating away at her since Lorraine's murder was something she wanted to keep private.

But Morgan didn't look shocked or judgemental. He simply nodded.

'Mike's grieving,' he said gently. 'There's no right way to handle that. Just be there for him. However you can. That's all anyone can ask.'

Be there for him. She was trying, really trying. But it felt like it wasn't enough. She was failing Mike when he needed her most.

'All right,' she said. 'I'll step back. Let you and the new detectives handle it.'

Morgan looked relieved. 'Thank you. I know this isn't easy, but it's for the best.'

'What's your initial hunch? Do you think Chapman could be behind Lorraine's murder?' Karen studied Morgan carefully, searching his face for any hint he might be holding something back.

'I don't think so. It doesn't fit his usual pattern.'

Her fingers tapped on the armrest. 'But the fact I've been tracking him . . .'

'Likely a coincidence,' Morgan said. 'We have no evidence Chapman has ever directly targeted an officer's family before.'

Karen felt a wave of relief. 'So you don't think it's my fault? You don't think that Lorraine was killed because of my history with Chapman?'

The words tasted bitter as she voiced the fear that had been lurking in the back of her mind since Arnie's visit last night.

Morgan's expression softened. 'No, I don't. Even with his rivals or those who've crossed him, Chapman has never stooped to attacking their loved ones. It's not his style.'

Karen exhaled slowly, thinking. Morgan's calm logic had helped ease some of the guilt that had been weighing her down.

Morgan met her gaze steadily, his expression open and sincere.

She believed him. 'If it wasn't Chapman, where does that leave us? Any leads on who could have done this to Lorraine?'

'Karen . . .' He paused, then seemed to decide something. 'Look, I know what you're doing.'

'Imagining what might be happening will drive me mad. At least if I know what's going on, I can . . .' She shrugged. 'I don't know . . . process it better.'

'You don't want to be kept in the dark, and I understand. But I need you to be clear on this: I can give you some information, but you can't investigate.'

'All right.'

'We're looking into Lorraine's life, her contacts and associates. We'll need to speak to Mike and James again. All routine stuff.' He held her gaze. 'And you need to let us handle it.'

'I know. I will. But what about the missing page from her address book?' Karen asked.

Morgan frowned, and Karen knew she was pushing her luck.

'It could be relevant,' he finally said. 'We're trying to determine the names that might have been on that page. James and Mike could be able to help us with that.'

'So, if we don't think this is related to Chapman, then Rick and I can resume our investigation?'

'You can continue working the Chapman case *if* Churchill gives the go-ahead. But promise me you'll stay away from anything to do with Lorraine's murder.'

Karen couldn't promise any such thing. Instead, she simply said, 'I'll speak to Churchill.'

Morgan sighed, but there was understanding in his eyes. 'Okay. But if work gets to be too much, if you need compassionate leave or counselling, you tell me. Understood?'

Karen nodded. 'Understood. There's one more thing. Mike wanted to know if the killer stitched up Lorraine's eyes after . . . that she wouldn't have felt it.'

For the first time, Morgan's raw emotion broke through. His jaw clenched. He leaned forward, elbows on his desk. When he spoke, his voice was low. 'I'm sorry, Karen. Whoever did that is depraved. Raj's initial assessment was that the stitches were carried out after she died.'

She stood up. 'At least that's one small mercy. She didn't suffer *that* while still alive.'

As she reached for the door handle, Morgan's voice stopped her. 'Karen?'

She turned back to face him, bracing herself for more well-meaning advice.

But all he said was: 'I'm here if you need anything. We all are. Even if all you need is to talk. You can call me anytime.'

'Thanks, Morgan. I appreciate it.'

And she did. Even if she couldn't bring herself to take him up on the offer. Because talking wouldn't help her. The only thing that would make her feel better was seeing the evil person who'd murdered and mutilated Lorraine behind bars.

Chapter Seven

Arnie slurped his tea, hunched over his desk, staring at the computer screen. His eyes felt dry and gritty. It had been a long night, and the email Churchill had sent earlier hadn't improved his mood. DI Falkner and DS Cunnings had been temporarily assigned to Lorraine Harrington's murder case. He'd already moaned about it to Morgan.

Cunnings wasn't so bad, Arnie supposed. She seemed pretty laid-back, but worked hard and always got the job done. Falkner, though . . . That man was the most pedantic know-all Arnie had ever worked with, and he'd never once seen him crack a smile.

Of course, the brass thought the sun shone out of his backside because he always seemed to get results. The pair of them were a rescue team of sorts, regularly parachuted in when a case was going south.

At least Falkner was tenacious, Arnie had to give him that. He would dig deep to get answers, which was exactly what they needed right now. Just a shame Arnie would have to put up with the man's annoying superiority complex until they got those answers.

Arnie closed the email and pulled up the background check he'd been running on a delivery driver seen hanging around and 'looking suspicious', according to one of Lorraine's neighbours.

Arnie had identified him as Jason Wilkes. Wilkes had been working for the delivery company for just four months. A short stint, but not unheard of in that line of work. High turnover was pretty standard.

Wilkes had a rap sheet longer than Arnie's arm. Petty theft, affray, even a charge of possession back in his youth. But murder? That was a whole different kettle of fish. Arnie scrolled through the file again, tapping his pen on the desk as he read the details.

It was a lead, sure, but Wilkes didn't really fit the profile of a killer who'd sew up a victim's eyelids. That kind of act spoke to a deeply disturbed individual who wanted to send a message.

Wilkes, on the other hand, seemed like your run-of-the-mill petty criminal. A bit of a waster, maybe, but not the type to suddenly escalate to something so gruesome. Still, Arnie knew he couldn't afford to overlook any potential suspects. He had to dot all the i's and cross all the t's, no matter how unlikely the lead might seem.

He sighed, leaned back in his chair and rubbed his eyes. His mind wandered to Karen. He'd just seen her heading into Morgan's office.

Karen would be champing at the bit to be involved in the investigation, but it was for the best that she'd been shut out. She was too close to the victim.

He took another swig of tea. He'd talk to Karen later and see how she was holding up. For now, though, he had work to do.

Arnie picked up the phone and called the delivery company. He needed to arrange a chat with Wilkes, see if he could shake loose any new information.

The line clicked, and a cheerful-sounding receptionist answered. Arnie identified himself and asked when Jason Wilkes's next shift would be. The receptionist put him on hold, and Arnie drummed his fingers on the desk impatiently.

Karen emerged from Morgan's office, her face pale and drawn. Arnie could only imagine how she must be feeling, forced to sit on the sidelines while Lorraine's murder was investigated.

Knowing Karen, she'd probably tried to persuade Morgan to let her in on the case. But Morgan was a stickler for the rules, and he'd never allow her to work an investigation with such a personal connection. Just as well Arnie wasn't the one in charge – he'd fold like a beach chair if he thought it would make Karen feel better.

The receptionist's voice came back on the line. 'Mr Wilkes should be arriving for his shift at the depot in about an hour.'

'Thanks for your help. I'll be there.' He hung up.

If he left soon, he'd arrive at the depot in plenty of time to greet Wilkes. Even if Wilkes wasn't likely to be Lorraine's killer, he might have seen something useful. Arnie could only hope.

Karen was making her way over, and Arnie subtly angled his monitor away so she couldn't see the screen.

'Hiding something?' She raised an eyebrow.

Apparently, he wasn't as subtle as he thought. Either that or Karen had eyes like a flipping hawk.

Arnie shrugged. 'You know how it is.' He nodded in the direction of Morgan's office. 'How did it go in there?'

'Banned from Lorraine's investigation, but Morgan thinks it's probably okay to carry on with Chapman.'

'Seriously?' Arnie slapped his pen down on the desk. 'Do you think that's a good idea?'

'I need to get Churchill's go-ahead, but Morgan doesn't think Chapman is behind Lorraine's murder, and I agree with him. I need to do something. I want to carry on with the Chapman investigation.'

Arnie stared at her. Was she out of her mind? That was a very bad idea. What was Morgan thinking? He was normally such a sensible bloke. Annoyingly pedantic at times, yes, but always sensible.

Chapman wasn't stupid. He'd be aware of this investigation. And Karen had been stalked by his goons before, hadn't she? Chapman had confided in Karen in the past, but that was only because it had suited him when he thought his life was in danger. Now he had no need of Karen's help, and there were only so many times you could poke a bear before it came for you, teeth bared.

'Oh, and apparently they're bringing in some new officers to help with the investigation,' Karen said. 'DI Falkner and DS Cunnings.'

Arnie grimaced. 'Can't wait.' Falkner wouldn't just *help* with the investigation; he'd swoop in like some self-appointed genius, explaining basic police work to them like they were all thick as planks. The man had a special talent for making experienced officers feel like they were back in training college.

'You know them?'

'Unfortunately.' Arnie suddenly became very interested in straightening the files on his desk.

'What are they like?'

'They're . . . decent officers.' He paused. 'Hard workers.'

'But?'

'Falkner and I don't exactly see eye to eye.'

'Why not?'

'He's the sort who thinks having a posh accent and a master's degree makes him better than the rest of us common folk. Last time we worked together, he actually corrected my grammar in the middle of interviewing a suspect.'

Arnie was sure it wouldn't be long after Falkner arrived that he would be giving his condescending lectures about how their simple minds had missed all the obvious clues that his brilliant brain had spotted.

Karen frowned. 'Well, as long as they're good at what they do, I can put up with a few grammar pointers. We need to move quickly on this. You know how cases can lose momentum if we don't get off to a strong start.' She glanced at her watch. 'Speaking of which, I should go and talk to Churchill.'

After she headed off, an uneasy feeling settled over Arnie.

Karen was one of the best officers he knew, determined and sharp and she didn't give up easily. For once, he wished she would.

Arnie just hoped that if Karen tried to bring down Chapman, she wouldn't get hurt in the process.

Karen made her way up to Churchill's office. Outside the door, she took a moment to compose herself. He trusted her instincts. Or, at least, he used to.

Things had been strained between them ever since Cindy Connor had published photographs of a crime scene that should have been sealed from the press. Churchill had been furious with Karen for letting the journalist and her photographer get close enough for photos. And while Karen understood his frustration with the media, there wasn't much she could do about reporters lingering around crime scenes.

She took a deep breath and knocked.

'Come in,' Churchill called from inside.

Karen pushed open the door and stepped into the office. Churchill sat behind his desk, a stack of paperwork in front of him.

He looked up as she entered. 'Karen. I thought you'd want to take some time off. A few days, at least.'

'I need to keep busy. I want to keep trailing Chapman. Morgan told me to ask your permission.'

Churchill leaned back in his chair, studying her. 'And you think that's a good idea?'

Karen nodded. 'I won't go near the investigation into Lorraine's murder. But I don't want to waste all the work we've done trying to build a case against Chapman.'

'My instinct is to keep you away from both investigations.'

Karen said nothing.

'I'd be happier if you took some time off.'

Karen still said nothing. Churchill hadn't actually asked any questions.

'You've just experienced a horrendous shock. Don't you think your current circumstances might cloud your judgement?'

She met his gaze. 'I won't let my personal feelings compromise the investigation.'

Churchill was silent for a long moment, considering her words. Finally he sighed, shaking his head. 'I'm sorry, Karen, but the answer's no.'

Karen's jaw clenched. Once again Chapman would slip through their fingers. She needed to be out there, on active cases. Not stuck inside with her thoughts. 'All right, I could look into those agricultural machinery thefts in Potterhanworth—'

'That will be handled by other officers.'

'The burglaries in the villages, then?'

His tone softened. 'If you don't want to take compassionate leave, I understand. But I don't want you out there until we know what we're dealing with. If you want to work at the station, there's plenty of paperwork needs sorting.'

Paperwork wouldn't stop her mind from wandering to . . . to places she didn't want it to go. 'Sir—'

'This isn't a negotiation, Karen. I want you where I know you're safe.'

A sharp rap on the office door made them both turn.

'Come in,' Churchill said.

Karen turned as the door swung open, and two unfamiliar figures stepped inside – a tall, lean man in an ill-fitting suit and a petite blonde woman with dimpled cheeks.

'Let me introduce you,' Churchill said, rising from his chair. 'DS Hart, this is DI Simon Falkner and DS Bridget Cunnings. They'll be taking the lead on Lorraine's case. Morgan and the rest of the team will still be working on the investigation, but they'll be following Falkner's direction.'

Falkner's gaze settled on Karen, his pale eyes studying her intently. She resisted the urge to squirm under his scrutiny, and met his stare head-on. She could sense him sizing her up. It was hard to tell what he was thinking. His expression was impassive.

Falkner had the sort of nondescript features that would allow him to blend seamlessly into a crowd. The lack of animation in his expression was unnerving.

DS Cunnings, on the other hand, had a friendly, open face. She offered a warm smile, the dimples in her cheek deepening. 'It's a pleasure to meet you, DS Hart, though I wish it were under better circumstances.'

Karen forced a tight smile in return. These were the people tasked with tracking down the evil person who'd killed Mike's mother. Would they be able to? Could she trust them?

'If you don't mind, sir, we'd like to have an informal chat with DS Hart after we've finished up here,' Falkner said, his voice clipped in a distinctly upper-crust way, devoid of any emotion.

Churchill glanced towards Karen.

'Yes, that's fine.' The words felt thick on her tongue.

'Very well,' Churchill said. 'We won't be long. Just a few things to discuss. DI Falkner and DS Cunnings will come down to the open-plan office in ten minutes or so.'

Karen hesitated, her gaze flickering between Churchill and the two new detectives. This was Churchill's way of dismissing her. They would soon be discussing her behind her back – analysing, judging, and talking about her private life.

It wasn't their fault. Their job involved digging into Lorraine's background, and like it or not, Karen was part of that background.

She stood and exited the office, pulling the door closed behind her.

Two officers she knew hardly anything about were now leading the investigation into Lorraine's death. Their skills and tenacity would determine whether her killer was brought to justice.

They needed to be good, Karen thought, her jaw clenching. Really, really good.

Karen checked her phone as she headed back downstairs. She had messaged Mike earlier to see if he wanted to meet for lunch, but there was still no response. A knot of worry twisted in her stomach. She knew he had every right to deal with the loss of his mother in his own way, but the silence was unsettling.

She tapped out another quick message.

Thinking of you. Let me know if you'd like me to pick up dinner on my way home tonight. xx

Her thumb hovered over the send button. Was it insensitive to ask about something as mundane as dinner when all this was going on?

Karen sighed and hit send anyway. She needed to at least make the offer, even if he didn't feel up to eating.

As she entered the open-plan office, she noticed Rick, Sophie and Morgan gathered around Sophie's workstation. They seemed to be deep in discussion, their heads bent over something on the desk.

As Karen drew closer, they looked up. Rick quickly shuffled some papers, turning them over, trying to cover whatever they'd been looking at. Sophie flipped the folder shut, while Morgan straightened, his expression unreadable.

They were treating her like an outsider. She knew it was protocol, and that she couldn't be involved in Lorraine's case, but it still stung. These were her colleagues, her friends.

Had they found something? Had they identified Lorraine's killer? She wanted to demand that they tell her what they knew.

Her hands balled into fists at her sides as she forced herself to hold back from demanding information. It wasn't fair on them.

She had to be professional. She couldn't just barrel up to them and order them to tell her what they had all been looking at.

But it was hard to hold back.

She stopped by the desk. 'What's going on?'

Rick and Sophie exchanged a glance, then looked to Morgan.

He cleared his throat. 'Karen, you might want to sit down for this.'

Chapter Eight

Karen sat down, as she'd been asked. Morgan, Sophie and Rick's eyes were all fixed on her. She felt like a slide under a microscope. Morgan passed over the thick file, and she tensed.

'What am I looking at?' she asked, flipping through the pages.

'Lorraine's bank statements, going back years,' Morgan said.

Physical paper statements. Lorraine had liked keeping meticulous records, it seemed. Lots of different payments were listed.

'Anything stand out?' Morgan asked.

Karen didn't like the way they were watching her reactions, like hawks. She took a closer look at one of the statements. Lorraine's name was printed at the top along with an address Karen didn't recognise. The statement was dated September 1981. She scanned the incomings and outgoings.

Then she hesitated on one, a payment from 'Regency Holdings' for three hundred pounds.

That name rang a bell.

One of Quentin Chapman's companies.

Karen lifted her head. 'Regency Holdings?'

'The same amount every month. Did Lorraine ever mention these payments to you?' Rick asked carefully.

'Of course not!' Karen snapped, annoyed at being on the other side of the questioning. She didn't like it at all.

She considered what it could mean. Had Lorraine been some kind of informant for Chapman? But these payments had started long before Karen had ever known her. In fact, this was only a couple of years after Mike was born. A sickening realisation washed over her.

Sophie, Rick and Morgan were all watching her with thinly veiled pity in their eyes. She hated it. And she hated being kept in the dark even more. What weren't they telling her?

Did they suspect, as she suddenly did, that these payments indicated that the career criminal could be Mike's biological father? Why else would Chapman be sending Lorraine regular payments?

All this time, she'd thought Chapman's interest in her was because he thought her investigation was getting too close for comfort. She closed her eyes, remembering finding one of Chapman's men lurking outside Mike's apartment all those months ago, and Mike being followed back home by Chapman's Range Rover . . . She had thought it was all because of her connection to the crime boss. But what if it had been about keeping tabs on Mike . . . his *son*?

And what about when Chapman had pushed her out of the way of a bullet? She'd thought that was an odd act of heroism for a man like him . . . but had he been doing it for Mike?

She met Morgan's knowing gaze and saw the same thoughts reflected there. Of course he would have come to the same conclusion.

'I'm sorry to ask such a personal question,' Morgan said. 'I know Mike talked about wanting to know who his biological father was. Did he ever find out?'

Karen winced, the question hitting a nerve. 'No. Lorraine was very reluctant to discuss it.'

Did Mike's father have something to do with Lorraine's murder? Was Chapman trying to stop the truth from coming out? So much so that he'd killed Lorraine to stop her talking? But that didn't add up. Surely Chapman wouldn't have done something so vile.

'Had Lorraine kept in contact with Mike's father?' Morgan asked.

'As far as I know, she hadn't spoken to him since he left her and Mike,' Karen replied, rubbing her temples.

Morgan looked thoughtful. 'So she never received any financial support from Mike's biological father?'

Karen stared down at the payments from Regency Holdings. 'I don't know.'

'Do you think Mike could be the reason Chapman was making the payments to Lorraine?' Rick asked. 'Mike could be Chapman's son.'

Karen shook her head slowly, feeling ill. 'Mike's nothing like Chapman.'

'It would explain why he was transferring money to Lorraine though,' Sophie said gently. 'Unless you have another explanation?'

She didn't. Karen stared down at the evidence, her mind reeling. Could the kind, down-to-earth man she loved really be the son of Lincolnshire's most notorious criminal? The possibility made her head spin.

How would she break the news to Mike? Karen slumped back in her chair, wishing she could wake up from this nightmare.

'DS Hart?'

Karen jumped at the sound of DI Falkner's voice from behind them.

She turned to face him. DS Cunnings hovered beside him, her expression halfway between sympathy and discomfort.

Falkner's pale eyes narrowed as they took in the documents on the desk in front of Karen. His thin lips pressed into a firm line.

'I'll have to ask you to move these files, DI Morgan,' he said. 'It's not appropriate for DS Hart to be privy to this evidence.'

'We're just going through some old payments,' Morgan said. 'Karen is giving us her insights.'

'Not here. Let's discuss this in your office.'

As the others reluctantly gathered up the files, Karen felt a gentle hand on her arm. 'I know this all must be terribly difficult for you, Karen,' Cunnings said. 'But DI Falkner does have a point. It's no reflection on you, of course. But this isn't just a normal case for you.'

Karen swallowed hard, her throat tight. She knew Cunnings was right, but Lorraine's murder had taken on a whole new dimension with the revelations about Mike's potential connection to Chapman. She felt sick at the thought of having to tell him that the father he'd always longed to know could be the criminal Karen had been trying to bring down.

'I want you to know we're on your side,' Cunnings assured her.

Karen managed a nod, caught between gratitude for Cunnings's kindness, frustration at Falkner's coldness, and dread at the potential bombshell that could be awaiting Mike. Should she even tell him, when the evidence was so shaky? But if he found out later that she'd kept this from him, he'd be upset.

'Are you free to have that quick chat now?' Cunnings asked. 'Just a few questions. I'm sure you have some for me, too.'

Through the closed door, Karen could hear Morgan's raised voice. Morgan didn't usually get angry. It wasn't like him at all.

She realised he cared, too. It was hard for all of them, not just her. Maybe Churchill had been right to bring in outsiders.

'Sure,' Karen said, 'but don't you want to wait for DI Falkner?'

'He'll be along shortly. But we can make a start. I've booked interview room three.'

◆ ◆ ◆

Arnie slouched in one of the plastic chairs in the depot's break room, his eyes fixed on the door. The vending machine hummed behind him, a steady drone that threatened to lull him to sleep. He'd been up half the night, and the lack of sleep was catching up with him.

Through the thin walls, he could hear the beeping of reversing forklifts and the shouts of workers calling to each other.

He'd bumped into Cunnings and Falkner just before leaving the station. Falkner hadn't changed, unless you counted him getting even more pompous and patronising. Still the same old self-important bore who thought having a master's degree made him God's gift to policing.

Cunnings was all right though. They'd had a quick flutter on how long it would take Falkner to mention his precious degree. Arnie had won a fiver when Falkner dropped it into conversation within the first five minutes.

He checked his watch. Jason Wilkes was due to start his shift any minute now. Arnie hoped the bloke would actually show up. It would be just his luck if Wilkes had decided to pull a sickie today. Though, if he did, that would make him look even more suspicious.

The door swung open, and a wiry man with unkempt hair stepped in. His eyes widened when he saw Arnie, and for a moment, it looked like he might bolt.

Arnie stood up, his knees creaking in protest. 'Jason Wilkes?'

The man nodded, his Adam's apple bobbing as he swallowed hard.

'DS Hodgson.' Arnie flashed his warrant card. 'I'd like to have a quick chat, if you don't mind.'

Wilkes glanced at the door, then back at Arnie. His fingers twitched at his sides.

Arnie sighed. 'Look, mate. I'm too old and too tired to be chasing you around this depot. If you make me run, I'll be in a foul mood, and trust me, neither of us wants that. So why don't we sit down and have a civilised conversation?'

Wilkes hesitated for a moment, then nodded. He perched on the edge of a chair, looking like he might take flight at any moment.

Arnie lowered himself back into his seat. 'I want to ask you about a delivery you made yesterday. Three p.m. To a Mrs Lorraine Harrington.'

Wilkes shrugged. 'I make a lot of deliveries. Can't remember them all.'

'This one might stand out. Because Mrs Harrington was murdered around the time you were seen near her house.'

Wilkes paled. 'I didn't have anything to do with that.'

'I didn't say you did. I just want to know what you saw when you made your delivery.'

'Nothing,' Wilkes said quickly. Too quickly. 'I rang the bell, no one answered. I took the parcel back to the depot.'

Arnie leaned forward, his elbows on his knees. 'See, that's interesting. Because a neighbour saw you hanging around, peering in the windows. Care to explain that?'

Wilkes shifted in his seat, his eyes darting around the room. 'I was just checking to see if anyone was home.'

'By looking in the windows?' Arnie raised an eyebrow. 'Bit invasive, don't you think?'

'I needed a signature,' Wilkes mumbled.

'What did you see?'

Wilkes was silent for a long moment, nervously bouncing his leg up and down. When he spoke, his voice was just a quiet mumble. 'I thought I heard something.'

Arnie's ears pricked up. 'What kind of something?'

'A noise. Inside the house. And I saw a shadow moving.'

If Wilkes had seen someone inside, it wouldn't have been Lorraine as she would have answered the door. Which meant . . .

'This shadow,' Arnie said carefully. 'Could you tell if it was a man or a woman?'

Wilkes shook his head. 'It was just a shadow. Could've been anyone.'

Arnie leaned back in his chair, processing this new information. It wasn't much, but it was something. Wilkes had been at the scene around the time Lorraine was murdered. He might have seen the killer. Arnie sensed the man was holding something back.

'Come on, Jason,' Arnie pressed gently. 'I reckon there's more to it than that. What else did you see?'

Wilkes shrugged, his eyes fixed on the floor. 'It's probably not important. And, well, with my record, I don't want to get involved.'

Arnie could understand that. Wilkes's charges could fill a book. He probably broke out in a cold sweat every time he saw a copper.

'Don't be daft, Jason. A woman was murdered. Of course it's important.'

Wilkes shifted uncomfortably, then sighed. 'All right. At first, it was just a shadow. I thought the person inside might be hard of hearing, so I waved at the window, trying to get their attention.' He paused, a visible shudder running through his body. 'Then, as they came closer, I saw a face. A man with evil eyes.'

'Evil eyes, eh?' Arnie raised an eyebrow, feeling like he might be on to something but sceptical of Wilkes's dramatic description. Was he just making this up to direct attention away from himself?

Wilkes bristled, folding his arms over his chest. 'You asked. I'm telling you what I saw, all right? Those eyes . . . they weren't right.'

'Fair enough,' Arnie said. 'I believe you saw something that spooked you. Can you give me any more details? Height? Build? Was he white, black, young, old?'

'White bloke, maybe mid-twenties? Clean shaven. Couldn't tell his height since I only saw his face, and even then, only for a second or two. I couldn't see much else.'

It wasn't a perfect description, but it was more than they'd had before. 'Would you mind working with us to generate a photofit image? Might help us to identify this bloke.'

Wilkes hesitated for a moment before nodding. 'Yeah, all right.'

Arnie stood up, his knees protesting again. 'Good man, Jason. Thanks for your time. I'll contact you later today about the photofit. If you remember anything else, give me a call.'

He handed Wilkes his card. The man took it gingerly, as if it might burn him.

As Arnie headed for the door, he turned back. 'Oh, and Jason? Next time you see something suspicious, call it in. It's the right thing to do, even with your record. Might even help you stay on the straight and narrow.'

Wilkes nodded, but Arnie wasn't entirely sure what to make of him. The story seemed genuine enough, and Wilkes didn't strike Arnie as the type to go around sewing up victims' eyes. But years on the job had taught him that people with a record often tried to point the finger elsewhere, even when they were innocent. Could Wilkes have invented this mysterious man with the evil eyes just to get the police off his back? After all, people who didn't trust the system often thought they'd get blamed anyway. Some habits were hard to break.

Outside, Arnie squinted in the bright sunlight. He pulled out his phone and dialled Morgan's number.

Morgan answered on the first ring. 'Got something?'

times, but Mike had the patience of a saint. There's no way he would ever be violent towards her.'

Cunnings nodded, making a note. 'And what about James? How did he get on with Lorraine?'

'As far as I could tell, they had a good marriage. James adored her, really. He was a bit blind to her faults, but that's love, I suppose.'

'I see.' Cunnings paused. 'Can you think of anyone who might have wanted to harm Lorraine? Anyone she may have had a run-in with recently?'

'No, I can't. Lorraine could be abrasive occasionally, but she was a good person. I can't imagine anyone wanting to do something so gruesome as . . .' She trailed off as the image of Lorraine's mutilated eyelids flashed through her mind.

Before she could compose herself and continue, the door opened, and Detective Inspector Falkner strode in, a file in his hand. His pale eyes swept over Karen, assessing, before turning to Cunnings.

'I'm sorry to keep you waiting.'

Cunnings offered him a polite smile, but Falkner's expression remained blank. Karen found herself wondering if his face would crack if he ever attempted a smile.

Falkner placed the file on the table between them. 'SOCOs found something at Lorraine Harrington's house.'

'The bank statements?' Karen said. 'I just told DS Cunnings—'

'No. Not the statements.' He sat down and nudged the folder towards her. 'Take a look. It was in the filing cabinet in the study.'

Karen frowned as she opened it. Inside were a stack of yellowed newspaper clippings. The headlines were faded but still legible.

She read the words emblazoned across the articles:

Woman Strangled in Woods!

Karen bit her lip as she scanned the articles. A young woman, Ava Claywood, had been found dead in Willingham Woods in 1981. She'd been strangled, and her body had been left by the pond.

Karen looked up in confusion. 'I don't understand. What does this have to do with Lorraine?'

Neither Falkner nor Cunnings replied.

'Ava Claywood,' Karen murmured, looking back down at the articles and focusing on the date. '1981.'

Falkner's eyes narrowed. 'That was a couple of years after Mike was born, wasn't it?'

Karen nodded slowly, her mind racing. 'Yes, it was. But I've never heard of Ava Claywood. Lorraine never mentioned her.'

Cunnings leaned forward. 'We think there has to be a connection between Lorraine and Ava Claywood. Is there anything you can tell us that might shed light on why Lorraine kept these articles?'

Karen shook her head helplessly. 'I don't know. Lorraine never said anything about it.'

Why would Lorraine have old newspaper clippings about a murder that happened nearly forty-five years ago? What possible connection could there be between Ava and Lorraine? Or had *James* stashed them in the back of the filing cabinet? Perhaps Lorraine hadn't even known they were there . . .

'Do you really think this case could be related to Lorraine's murder?' Karen asked.

'We don't know. We'll obviously need to talk to Mike about this,' Falkner said. 'And his stepfather as well.'

That sparked Karen's protective instinct. 'Of course, but I don't think they'll know anything. This has never come up before. It's odd. And we can't assume it was Lorraine who kept these articles. For all we know, they could have belonged to James.'

Falkner's gaze hardened. 'We are not *assuming* anything, DS Hart.'

Karen nodded slowly, her mouth dry. She really wasn't enjoying being on the other side of things. And she couldn't imagine becoming friendly with Falkner anytime soon.

'The team needs to speak to Mike and James again, anyway,' Cunnings said with a reassuring smile. 'See if there's anything else they can tell us. I imagine everyone was in shock yesterday, so there might be something they can recall by now.'

'Yes,' Karen said quietly.

'Do you think this afternoon would be suitable for them? We can come to your house, so the whole thing isn't so . . . overwhelming.'

'James went to break the news to his brother this morning, but he should be back this afternoon. It should be okay for Mike, too.'

At least, she hoped it would be. Mike hadn't replied to the messages she'd sent earlier, so she really didn't know how he was, let alone whether he'd be up to an interview this afternoon.

Karen looked at the newspaper clippings again, focusing on the grainy black-and-white photo of Ava Claywood.

She was a young woman who should have had her whole life ahead of her. 'Did they catch Ava's killer?'

Falkner gathered up the newspaper clippings. 'No, Ava Claywood's murder has been unsolved for more than forty years.'

The interview room was stuffy and Karen felt like she'd been answering questions from DI Falkner and DS Cunnings for hours.

She had just finished going through what had happened when she and Mike arrived at Lorraine's house the night before.

Falkner's gaze lingered on her. He was waiting for her to say more, but she'd told them everything.

The door creaked open, and the new press officer, Callum Turner, poked his head inside, looking apologetic. 'I'm really sorry to interrupt,' he said, his eyes darting between Karen and Falkner. 'But I desperately need to speak to DS Hart. Things are hitting the fan big-time.'

'Who are you?' Falkner snapped.

'Oh, sorry. I'm Callum Turner, press officer and media liaison.' He walked forward, holding out his hand for Falkner and then Cunnings to shake in turn.

'We're in the middle of something here, Callum. Can't it wait?' Falkner asked.

Callum hesitated, then shook his head. 'I don't think so. It's quite urgent.'

With a sigh, Falkner waved a hand. 'Fine. But make it quick.'

Callum stood in front of Karen, twisting his hands. 'Um, Karen. I'm sorry. I know this is the last thing you need right now, but we've received a complaint from a photographer. He's accusing you of assaulting him in the station car park.'

Cindy Connor's photographer.

What a little worm. Karen hadn't honestly believed he would file a complaint, despite his threats. She'd barely touched his camera. She had better grounds for harassment against him than he did for assault.

'That's ridiculous, Callum. I never assaulted him.'

'I believe you,' Callum said, nodding. 'But he's claiming that you did. His name is Martin Green, and he's been working with Cindy Connor.'

'I know. Is she still here? I'd like a word with her.'

'No, she's already left, and so has the photographer.'

Karen stood up, her chair scraping against the floor. 'The car park has security cameras. Let's go and check them.'

She led the way as Cunnings, Falkner and Callum followed her along the corridor and downstairs towards the front desk. As she walked, she tried to recall every detail of her encounter with the photographer. She knew she hadn't assaulted him, but there had been physical contact.

At the front desk, Callum muttered something to the desk sergeant, before they went into the little side room behind reception.

After Karen gave him the time of her arrival, Callum tapped a few keys, pulling up the security feed on the computer. The footage appeared on the screen. 'Here we go,' he said. 'From the car park this morning.'

Karen, Cunnings and Falkner huddled around Callum and the monitor. The video showed Karen getting out of her car and then Martin Green, holding up his camera and rushing across the car park towards her. The security footage was crystal clear thanks to the new HD cameras installed just last month.

The picture was so sharp she could even see her own expression change. On screen, Karen's face twisted into a scowl when she saw Cindy and Martin. She looked furious as the photographer began snapping pictures.

Karen watched herself confront him, her finger jabbing the air as she spoke. Martin took a step back, a hand raised in a defensive gesture. Then, Karen saw her own hand reach out, brushing against the camera lens as she pushed it away.

'Well,' Callum said, pointing at the screen. 'I think that's the moment he's claiming you assaulted him.'

Karen shook her head in disbelief. 'My hand hardly touched the camera. It's not an assault.'

Falkner leaned in closer, his eyes narrowing as he studied the footage. 'I agree there was no assault here. The photographer is exaggerating, at best.'

The accusation might have been baseless, but it still left a bitter taste in Karen's mouth.

Callum chuckled. 'What a relief! It's a nothing burger.'

Falkner looked at Callum as though he was speaking double Dutch. 'A what? Please use proper English, Callum. That sort of juvenile language has no place in a professional environment.'

Karen had to bite her tongue. She hadn't known Falkner long, but she could already tell he was the type who thought he was above everyone else. As if using a bit of slang was going to bring down the reputation of the entire police force. No wonder Arnie wasn't keen on him.

Cunnings placed a hand on Karen's shoulder. 'Let us handle this, Karen. It's clearly not assault. We'll sort it out. You don't need anything else on your plate at the moment.'

Karen nodded, grateful for the support. 'The woman who's with him is a journalist called Cindy Connor. She has an article publishing online at midday for the *Lincolnshire Post*. I presume it's about Lorraine's murder, but I have no idea where she got her information. You haven't briefed the press yet, have you, Callum?'

'No official information has been released beyond the standard statement. If I recall correctly, the statement was: "Police were called to an address in Lincoln where the body of a woman was discovered. The cause of death is currently undetermined, and we are treating this as an ongoing investigation." I've no idea how Cindy got more information than that. I didn't reveal your relationship to the deceased, Karen.'

Cunnings gave Karen a sympathetic smile. 'It's practically impossible to keep this sort of crime quiet. One of the neighbours could have spoken to the press.'

'Quite possibly,' Falkner said, and glanced at his watch. 'Why don't we take a break for lunch. We'll be at your house at two p.m. to talk to Mike and James if that's convenient?'

Karen nodded, her mind still reeling from the accusation and the impending article. At least the security footage had proven her innocence. It was a small victory, but she'd take it.

After she left Falkner, Cunnings and the press officer, Karen pulled out her phone and sent texts to Mike and James, letting them know about the meeting.

Then she got a cup of coffee from the machine and carried it to her desk. She needed the caffeine to help her focus. Her phone buzzed with replies from both Mike and James. They agreed to be back at the house by two p.m. to talk to DI Falkner and DS Cunnings.

She sat down and logged on to her computer.

Feeling sick, she typed *Lincolnshire Post* into the search bar. The home page was filled with sensational headlines, but Karen ignored the majority of them to concentrate on finding Cindy's article.

It didn't take long. The article was accompanied by a large, unflattering photo of Karen taken by the photographer Martin Green. The scumbag.

Karen took a deep breath and began to read.

Tragedy Strikes Curtois Close: New Evidence Links Death to 43-Year-Old Murder.

Lorraine Harrington, a resident of Curtois Close, was found dead in her home yesterday, sending shockwaves through a quiet neighbourhood. She leaves behind a husband, James, and son, Mike. The family has chosen not to comment at this time.

In a dramatic turn of events, the Lincolnshire Post has learned investigators have discovered a link between Lorraine Harrington's untimely death and the unsolved murder of Ava Claywood, which has haunted the community for over forty years. This connection has yet to be officially confirmed by Lincolnshire Police, who have not responded to a request for comment.

Lorraine Harrington's son, Mike, is in a relationship with Detective Sergeant Karen Hart of Lincolnshire Police, putting the detective in the eye of the storm as the investigation continues.

Police are appealing for witnesses who may have seen or heard anything out of the ordinary at Curtois Close.

Ava Claywood's family have expressed their disappointment that her murder remains unsolved after so many years. They hope that the investigation into Lorraine Harrington's death will lead to a renewed effort to uncover the truth behind Ava's murder.

As this story unfolds, the Lincolnshire Post is committed to keeping the public informed of the latest developments in this intriguing case.

Karen pressed a hand against her churning stomach.

She'd known the article would be bad, but this was worse than she'd expected. It was clear that Cindy had been digging deep, uncovering information that hadn't been released yet.

How had she found out about the Ava Claywood connection? Karen had only just been told about the newspaper articles found in the filing cabinet at the Harrington house herself. How long had they kept that from her? Was there more evidence that Karen wasn't privy to?

She looked around the room at her colleagues. Morgan was in his office, on the phone. Rick and Sophie were at their desks, heads bent over their work. Would they keep things from her?

Of course they would.

They were good detectives, and it was their job to follow leads and gather evidence. She was a witness, and connected to the victim. She wasn't – couldn't be – part of the investigation team.

She knew all that. But it was unsettling to think that they might uncover important information without keeping her in the loop.

Karen looked back at the website and focused on the pictures.

A grainy, unflattering shot of herself dominated the article. She looked wild and angry. Below that was a small portrait of Ava smiling, oblivious to her fate. Then, inset into the main article was an old photograph of Ava's husband, John, and daughter, Ruth.

John looked haunted, his face gaunt and unshaven. Ruth, probably around eleven or twelve, clutched her father's arm as though afraid he might disappear too. How cruel to take the young girl's picture for the papers after her mother had just died.

Karen closed the website window and took a sip of her coffee. She needed to get on top of this. The actions of a pushy journalist and that worm of a photographer wouldn't throw her off balance. She was a police officer. She had to act like one.

Looking into Ava Claywood's murder would be a logical first step. Her fingers itched to search the police database. But she was supposed to keep her distance from the investigation, and she needed to make a move if she was going to be home when Mike and James were questioned by Cunnings and Falkner.

Karen was about to shut down her computer when she thought to check her emails one last time. A new message had just arrived.

Subject line: A Friendly Warning

Her finger hesitated over the mouse before clicking it open.

I know you want answers about Lorraine's death. But it's safer not to ask questions. Some doors are better left closed. For everyone's sake, step back. You've been warned.

The sender was NoMoreQuestions@protonmail.com.

Karen's stomach dropped.

She glanced around the room, but everything was carrying on as normal. Officers typing at their computers, phones ringing, the usual hum of police work.

She stood up and headed straight for Sophie's desk, opening the email app on her phone. 'Have a look at this.'

Sophie looked up from her paperwork. Her eyes widened as she read the message. 'That's awful! Who would send something like that?'

'I know a man who can help us find out.' Karen nodded towards the door. 'Fancy a trip to the tech lab?'

The basement lab was Harinder's domain. Huge monitors and humming servers took up half the large lab. The team fondly called him Harry, their very own lab wizard.

He looked up from his three screens, his face brightening when he spotted Sophie.

'What brings my favourite detective down here?' he asked, spinning his chair to face them.

When he saw Karen, his smile faltered. 'I'm so sorry, Karen. I meant to come and give my condolences, but I thought you could use some space.'

'Thank you.'

'If there is anything I can do . . .'

'As a matter of fact, there is,' Sophie said. 'Karen just received a threatening email, which essentially warned her to back off. We were hoping you might be able to trace the sender?'

Karen showed him the email. His usually cheerful expression turned serious as he read the text.

'I'll have a go, but it won't be easy,' he said, adjusting his glasses. 'They've used Proton Mail. It's an encrypted server, based in Switzerland. And if they've used a VPN as well . . .' He spread his hands. 'I can try to trace the IP address, but these anonymous email services are designed to protect user privacy. That's why criminals love them.'

'So you're saying it's impossible?' Sophie asked.

'Nothing's impossible.' Harinder grinned. 'Just really, really difficult. I'll see what I can do, but you'd better tell Morgan about this.'

'I will,' Karen said. 'Thanks, Harry.'

Sophie touched Karen's arm as they walked out of the lab. 'This is the last thing you need right now. It must be terrifying for you.'

Karen shook her head. 'Actually, I'm not scared. I'm furious. If they think they can intimidate me into backing off, they're wrong.'

Chapter Ten

As Sophie entered the police station canteen, she spotted Arnie and Cunnings sitting at a table in the corner. As she joined the queue for food, she glanced at the menu board. Something was different.

Where were the usual fried offerings? The sausage sandwiches and bacon that were staples of the canteen diet had vanished, replaced by plant-based alternatives.

'What'll it be, love?' Diane asked as Sophie reached the counter.

'I'll try the vegetable cannelloni, please,' Sophie said, eyeing the steaming dish. It actually looked quite appetising. 'What's with all the changes?'

Diane sighed. 'Chief Constable's new initiative. Apparently, we're spending too much on meat, it's not good for health, and the carbon footprint is through the roof. So now we've got to cut meat options down to once a week.' She began scooping cannelloni on to Sophie's plate. 'Mind you, I don't disagree. Half this lot could do with eating more veg. But try telling them that.' She nodded towards a group of officers grumbling over their plates. 'I've had more earache today than a GP on Monday morning.'

Sophie grinned. 'I bet. How's Arnie taking it?'

Diane rolled her eyes. 'Like a toddler who's had his favourite toy taken away. He was in here twice before lunch to check it wasn't all some cruel joke.'

Sophie thanked Diane and made her way to Arnie and Cunnings's table.

As she approached, she could hear Arnie mid-rant. '. . . next thing you know, they'll be banning coffee and biscuits. It's a slippery slope.'

Sophie slid into an empty chair, setting her tray down. 'I see you're taking the menu changes well, Arnie.'

He glowered at her, gesturing dramatically at the sad-looking sandwich on his plate. 'This,' he declared, 'is not food. It's an abomination.'

Sophie peered at the sandwich. It didn't look too bad. 'Plant-based sausages? They're probably a good thing, health-wise. Did you know the WHO classified processed meat as a carcinogen?'

Arnie scoffed. 'Flipping food police, ruining everything. Anything can be bad for you in excess.'

Sophie thought a *daily* sausage sandwich probably counted as excess, but decided Arnie wasn't in the mood for that particular nugget of wisdom. Instead, she tried for a sympathetic tone. 'It must have been quite a shock to see the new menu.'

'Shock?' Arnie's voice rose, attracting amused glances from nearby tables. 'Of course it was a shock. We're in Lincolnshire – a county known for its delicious sausages. I've a good mind to start a petition.' He turned in his chair, addressing the room. 'You'll all sign it, won't you?'

A chorus of agreement rose from the surrounding tables.

Cunnings grinned. 'Good for you, Arnie. I'll bet you a fiver they'll have real sausages back on the menu by the end of the week.'

Arnie extended his hand across the table. 'You're on. For once, I really hope I lose a bet.'

As they shook on it, a new face appeared at their table. It was Callum Turner, the press officer, balancing a tray with a cheese sandwich and a bottle of orange juice. 'Mind if I join you?'

They nodded, and he took a seat. Sophie studied him as he pulled his sandwich out of the wrapper. He was slim, almost waifish, with an expression that seemed like he was always on the verge of apologising for something.

A ringtone burst through the canteen's background noise. It was a smooth, jazzy melody that Sophie vaguely recognised. The noise caught everyone's attention.

At the counter, a member of the admin staff fumbled for his phone, struggling to extract it from his pocket while balancing a tray of food.

Detective Inspector Harris, sitting at the table next to theirs, leaned back in his chair, eyes closed, air-conducting with his fork.

Arnie grumbled as he squeezed an alarming amount of brown sauce on to his sandwich. 'What's with all the fancy ringtones these days? What's wrong with an old-fashioned ring?'

Cunnings said, 'I like it. It's definitely better than my cousin's ringtone – a car backfiring. Makes me jump every time it goes off.'

'Reminds me of where I grew up,' Callum said, his face lighting up. 'That's "The Girl from Ipanema". It's a classic.'

Sophie looked at him with interest. 'Oh? You grew up in Brazil?'

'Florianópolis,' Callum replied.

'How are you finding things here?' she asked him. 'Settling in okay?'

Callum smiled. 'Everyone's been really welcoming. Still getting used to everything, but it's been good.'

Arnie grunted. 'Well, if you can handle our miserable weather, you're tougher than most.'

'And the questionable canteen food,' Cunnings added with a wink.

They all laughed. Sophie was pleased to see Callum joining in. He seemed nice. Maybe too nice. He'd probably get eaten alive, working with the press.

'I've faced worse,' Callum said, still smiling. 'I've been back in the UK a few years now. Besides, the people here seem nice, and that makes up for it.'

Callum's phone rang. His cheeks flushed. 'Sorry.' He glanced at it before rejecting the call and laying the phone face down on the table.

Sophie smiled. 'You are allowed to use phones in here, you know. It's not a library.'

He shrugged. 'Oh, it wasn't important. I'll return the call later.'

Sophie watched Arnie eye his plant-based-sausage sandwich with the kind of suspicion usually reserved for unattended packages in train stations. Finally, he took a bite.

His face contorted in exaggerated disgust. 'This,' he declared, swallowing with visible effort, 'tastes like seasoned rubber!'

Sophie laughed. 'Oh, come on, it can't be that bad. And it *is* healthier. It could lower your cholesterol.'

Arnie fixed her with a baleful stare. 'I don't care. Even if it does that *and* finishes all my paperwork *and* miraculously fixes the station's dodgy plumbing, I'd still rather take my chances with the real deal.' Arnie pushed his sandwich away. 'I'm off to find real food. Luckily, I'm prepared for emergencies. I have a stash of chocolate hobnobs in my desk.'

As he walked away, Sophie smiled. Despite his grumbling, there was something comforting about Arnie. In a job that could chuck all sorts of nasty surprises their way, his reliable moodiness over daft things like menu changes and cheerful ringtones was reassuring.

Arnie was grouchy and obstinate. But she wouldn't want him any other way.

Sophie realised she was smiling and immediately felt guilty. All this ordinary lunchtime chat and friendly teasing suddenly felt jarring. Here she was, laughing about Arnie's reaction to plant-based sausages while Karen was throwing herself into work, trying to keep her mind off Lorraine's murder. And that threatening email Karen had received . . . Sophie's appetite vanished.

The cheerful atmosphere felt almost disrespectful given what had happened. She should be working on tracking down whoever sent that message, not sitting here casually chatting over lunch like it was just another ordinary day.

Sophie pulled out her phone and sent a quick text to Harinder:

Any luck with Karen's email?

His reply came through almost immediately:

No joy. As I suspected, it's proving difficult. I've put in a formal request with Proton Mail, but there's another layer of IP-hopping on top of the encryption. Whoever sent it knows what they're doing. They've been very, very careful.

Sophie frowned at her phone. She'd been hoping for better news. Karen was putting on a brave face, but receiving a threatening email was no joke. Especially not with everything else going on.

She slipped her phone back in her pocket. Whoever had sent that email telling Karen to back off obviously didn't know her. Karen was even more stubborn than Arnie when she got her teeth into something.

◆　◆　◆

Morgan pushed the lab door open. The chill of the air-conditioned room did nothing to cool his simmering anger. He was still seething from his argument with Falkner. The man was infuriating.

Removing Karen from the case was an understandable and sensible decision. Morgan understood the need to follow protocol, but by freezing her out completely, Falkner was being unnecessarily cruel.

And now Karen had been sent an anonymous email. As if she didn't have enough on her plate already.

'Morgan.' Raj stood at the entrance to the laboratory's office area. The pathologist's lab coat strained slightly over his belly, and his thick moustache lifted up as he smiled.

'Raj.' Morgan inclined his head as he approached. He wasn't in the mood for small talk today. 'What can you give me on Lorraine Harrington?'

Raj's warm expression turned solemn. He sat in front of one of the computers and Morgan took the seat beside him. Raj clicked a button, and a black-and-white image of Lorraine Harrington's skull appeared on the monitor.

Raj moved the cursor over an area at the back of the skull, and clicked to zoom in closer until the fracture pattern became clear.

'The cause of death was a blunt force trauma to the occipital bone, here at the base of the skull. One powerful blow.' He paused, then added, 'This area contains the foramen magnum, the large opening where the spinal cord passes through to connect to the brain. A blow to this region can be instantly fatal, due to its proximity to crucial brain structures.'

Morgan's gaze sharpened, focusing on the pattern of cracks webbing out from the crushed section of skull.

Raj tapped on the screen, outlining the fracture lines that radiated out like a shattered windowpane. 'The shape and pattern of the break suggest a metal tool was used. Something heavy, with a small, flat head. You can see how the impact point is depressed inward.'

Morgan took in the detail, leaning closer. One swing, one brutal strike, had been enough. Lorraine wouldn't have had time to process anything before she lost consciousness.

'A hammer?' Morgan suggested.

'Yes, most likely. We've recovered some microscopic metal fragments from the wound site. We should have the full analysis soon.'

'And then her eyes,' Morgan prompted, turning back towards Raj. 'They were sewn shut.'

Raj sighed softly and moved to another desk, pulling a sleeve of autopsy photographs into view. He put them on a stainless-steel bench. Morgan looked down at the clinical images of Lorraine's eyelids crudely stitched together.

'Yes, the sewing,' Raj said, his tone reflecting the grimness of the act. 'Whoever did it wasn't skilled or medically trained, in my opinion. It's basic cotton thread, something you'd find in a household sewing kit. The needle was small – maybe one you'd use for embroidery.'

Morgan stared at the images. The stitching was rough, erratic.

Raj continued, 'There were some small flakes of dried blood on the face, but not enough to indicate any bleeding from the eye area while she was alive.'

'So, your initial assessment at the scene was correct. She was dead before the sewing happened?'

'Exactly,' Raj confirmed. 'Her eyelids were stitched post-mortem.'

'But what does it mean?' Morgan muttered. His hands pressed against the cool metal edge of the table as he tried to think.

Why the eyes? This wasn't a random act of violence.

It was deliberate. A message. And not just for Lorraine.

'See no evil?' Raj offered quietly, only half joking.

Morgan frowned. His instincts told him this wasn't Chapman's style, although he hadn't discounted him entirely. It wasn't unheard of for Chapman to send nasty messages or threats if rumours about him were to be believed, but. . . The stitching was something new.

If all that cash he'd been sending Lorraine was hush money, maybe he'd finally lost patience and resorted to something far more brutal. On the other hand, it could still be tied to their investigations into his operations.

'If Chapman did this, maybe it really is a "see no evil" message. He's telling us not to look too closely. To turn a blind eye to him and his dealings. It might not be a coincidence that this happened just as we've ramped up our investigations into his businesses.'

Lorraine might have been the victim, but the message could have been for them . . . for Karen. A vicious threat to keep their eyes shut to his affairs.

Raj went through the rest of his findings, then he paused. 'There's more.'

Morgan inclined his head. 'Go on.'

The pathologist opened another folder on the screen, bringing up a scanned copy of a medical report. It had been filled in with the messy handwriting doctors seemed to master in medical school. 'Lorraine Harrington was in the advanced stages of lymphoma. Stage four.'

Morgan stilled. He blinked, processing the words slower than he normally would. 'Lymphoma? She was . . .'

'Yes, she was dying.' Raj finished Morgan's sentence. 'The cancer was very aggressive.'

Morgan stared at the report. Lorraine Harrington had been dying when someone had taken her life. 'Did she know?'

'Yes,' Raj confirmed. 'According to her medical records, she was diagnosed just a couple of weeks ago.'

Morgan straightened. 'Karen didn't mention it.'

'Perhaps Mrs Harrington hadn't had the time to break it to her family yet. It's hard to know for sure.'

Morgan stayed where he was, staring at the monitor in silence. A terminal prognosis. Lorraine had been receiving money from

Chapman, in secret, for decades. Could that have made her do something drastic? Sell Chapman out, maybe? Expose old secrets, thinking she had nothing left to lose.

Maybe the cash had been enough to keep her silent. But had Lorraine finally decided enough was enough? Had she come to the conclusion that Chapman, Mike's potential father and the man funding her all these years, needed to face justice?

But if that were true, then Lorraine's fatal error was believing that her terminal diagnosis meant she had nothing to lose.

'How long?' Morgan asked softly. 'How long would she have had?'

Raj leaned back in his chair, thinking. 'Difficult to predict precisely. Based on her last scan and bloodwork, I'd guess she might have had a few months left. Six months . . . no more.'

'She knew time was running out,' Morgan muttered, more to himself than to Raj.

Had Lorraine decided the truth was worth more than whatever deal she had with Chapman? With death approaching, had she chosen to speak up?

'So you think Quentin Chapman is behind this?' Raj asked.

Morgan nodded. 'I think it's a possibility. Lorraine may have grown tired of hiding what she knew about him. Maybe, with death looming, she chose to stand up to him. Chapman's too careful to do his own dirty work, though. He's the type to keep his hands clean and get someone else to handle it. If he is involved, he'll have used one of his thugs to carry out the murder.'

Raj looked thoughtful.

The case wasn't a regular murder investigation – it had spilled out into Karen's personal life. If Chapman had wanted Lorraine, and whatever it was she knew, out of the picture, there was no telling who else could be collateral damage.

Chapman had a strange preoccupation with Karen, which bordered on a fixation. The old gangster was almost protective. He'd even saved her life once. Morgan had assumed it was because Karen had got under Chapman's skin, but was it because her fiancé, Mike, was his son?

Either way, security needed to be tightened. Karen needed protection.

Morgan stood. 'I'll need those results from the metal fragments as soon as they're ready.'

Raj nodded. 'Shouldn't take long.'

Morgan turned to leave the lab, already mentally drafting the request to DCI Churchill for more surveillance on Karen's home. If Churchill wouldn't sign off on it, he'd park outside her house himself tonight.

This gruesome murder might not be a simple warning – if Chapman was behind it, then it could be his opening move. And in Chapman's world, the next move was always more brutal than the last.

Chapter Eleven

Karen sat at the kitchen table, staring at the closed door. Mike had firmly shut it behind him when it was his turn to be questioned.

Mike and DI Falkner and DS Cunnings had gone into the living room, leaving Karen in the kitchen with James and Sandy.

She couldn't help feeling hurt that he was shutting her out.

Across the table, James sat hunched, his shoulders slumped under an invisible weight. His gaze was fixed on his hands as he twisted his gold wedding band. The deep creases in his face had become more pronounced overnight.

The muffled murmur of voices drifted through the closed door. It wasn't a formal interview. She could have been in there, supporting Mike, if he'd wanted her to. But she would respect his wishes, no matter how difficult. And he wanted to do this alone.

Pushing back her chair, Karen rose and moved to the counter, then picked up the kettle. 'Fancy another cup of tea, James? I thought I'd take another one through to Mike and the detectives.'

James lifted his head, a ghost of a smile flickering across his features. 'You really want to know what they're talking about, don't you?'

Karen paused, the kettle hovering above the sink. She considered denying it, but James was right.

'I do,' she admitted. 'I'm worried about Mike, and I don't know Falkner or Cunnings. It's hard not being in there.'

James nodded. 'They were nice enough to me, given the circumstances.' His gaze drifted back to his hands. 'They said they should be able to let me back in the house in a couple of days, but I don't know if I'll ever be ready to face it.'

Karen's grip tightened on the kettle's handle as she imagined James stepping back into the home where Lorraine had taken her last breath; the scene of such violence.

After putting the kettle down, she crossed the kitchen and sat opposite James again, reaching out to cover his hand with her own. 'You can stay with us for as long as you need,' she said. 'Mike and I are here for you, James. You're not alone in this.'

James managed a small smile. 'Thank you, love.'

Karen patted his hand. 'I know you've always been there for Mike.'

'He's my son,' James said simply. 'I know he's been looking for answers lately, wanting to connect with his . . . *real* father, but I've always considered him my boy.'

'I'm sure he sees *you* as his *real* dad. He just wants to know who his biological father is. That doesn't change how much he cares about you.'

Karen watched James's face tighten as he struggled to control his emotions. 'I know that I'm Mike's dad in all the ways that matter. But I have to admit . . .' He paused, swallowing hard. 'It stings a bit that he feels the need to look for someone else.'

'That's understandable.' James had been a father to Mike since he'd moved in with Lorraine in the late eighties. He didn't deserve the hurt this had all brought up.

'I would never deny Mike the opportunity to find his biological father,' James added quickly.

'Did Lorraine ever talk to you about him?'

'No. It wasn't something Lorraine and I talked about. She said it was a very bad time in her life, and she didn't want to discuss it. I respected that. She said the only good thing that came out of that period was Mike.' He managed a watery chuckle, dabbing his eyes with a handkerchief. 'I don't know if you'd noticed, but when Lorraine put her foot down, I listened!' Despite the gentle joke, fresh tears spilled down his cheeks. 'She could be a little headstrong, but I loved her. I loved her so much.'

Her chest ached as she watched him struggle. Then James broke down, his shoulders shaking with sobs as he gripped her hand.

After a moment, he steadied himself, swiping the back of his hand across his eyes. Karen waited patiently, not wanting to rush him.

'What sort of questions did the detectives ask you?' she asked carefully when he had regained control.

James took a deep breath. 'They asked where I was yesterday, and whether I'd seen anything unusual. Standard questions, really. They also wanted to know if Lorraine had fallen out with anyone, or if she'd been acting strangely. They wanted to know what my relationship with Lorraine was like. How well she got on with Mike . . . with you . . .'

Karen nodded slowly, digesting the information. It seemed like a straightforward line of questioning. Nothing unusual for a murder investigation. 'Did they ask you about Ava Claywood?'

The question seemed to hit James like a physical blow. His face drained of colour, and he abruptly pulled his hand away from Karen's grasp.

He cleared his throat. 'Actually, I think I would like another cup of tea. I'll make it.'

'James?'

He didn't reply, instead busying himself with making a fresh pot of tea, his movements stiff and jerky. His reaction to the mention of Ava Claywood's name had been dramatic, almost panicked.

He was hiding something.

She was good at reading between the lines and detecting things that people tried to conceal. But anyone would have picked up on that dramatic shift in James. No training needed.

A part of her understood his reluctance to talk about the past. Lorraine's murder had already devastated him. Dredging up painful memories might add to his suffering. But Karen knew she had to push forward, no matter how uncomfortable it was.

She watched as James poured the tea, his movements smoother now. When he turned back towards her, his expression was composed.

'I'm sorry,' he said, handing her a cup. 'It's just . . . It's difficult.'

Karen accepted the tea with a nod of thanks. 'I understand this is painful for you, James. But anything you can tell me about how Lorraine is connected to Ava Claywood could be vitally important.'

He sank back into a chair, cradling his cup. 'I don't see why. It happened over forty years ago. It's not related to Lorraine's murder.'

'You don't know that. It could be related. Did Lorraine know Ava?'

'Ava was a young woman who died tragically, a long time ago. Lorraine did know her, but she never told me how.'

Karen leaned forward. 'What did she tell you?'

James took a sip of tea, buying himself a few more seconds. 'Not much, I'm afraid. It happened before Lorraine and I met, back when I was living in London. She never liked to talk about that time in her life.'

Karen studied her future father-in-law's face. She felt torn between treating him as family and as someone who might be holding back vital information. Frustration simmered within her. Without Lorraine to provide context, they might never uncover the full truth – and James's evasive answers weren't helping. She could sense the truth hovering just out of reach.

'If there's even the slightest chance that Ava's death is connected to Lorraine's murder, I need to know,' Karen said. 'It could help us find her killer.'

He met her gaze, and she saw the conflicted look in his eyes. The desire to protect his late wife's privacy warred with the knowledge that withholding information could hinder the investigation.

'James, please,' Karen said, her tone softening.

Finally, he seemed to reach a decision, his shoulders sagging.

'All right. I'll tell you what I know, but it's not much. The first I knew of Ava Claywood was when I came home early from work one day in the late eighties and found Lorraine looking through newspaper cuttings. She'd been crying. She tried to hide it, but I could see how upset she was.

'When she saw me, she quickly gathered up the papers, trying to hide them from me. I saw the name "Ava Claywood" printed on one of the articles. Of course, I asked her what was wrong, but she brushed it off, saying it was nothing. Just a friend from a long time ago.' James shook his head slowly. 'But I could tell it was more than that. The way she reacted, so many tears. I'd never seen her so upset.'

'Why do you seem so desperate not to talk about this?'

'What do you mean?'

'As soon as I mentioned Ava Claywood, you couldn't change the subject fast enough.'

James sighed. 'I feel so guilty talking about Lorraine like this. She was a very private person. She hadn't even confided in me about Ava, and she'd hate all these people digging into her past.'

'So she never explained her connection to Ava?' Karen asked gently.

James sighed. 'Not really. All she said was that Ava had been a friend, but that part of her life was over now. She'd had to move on.' He paused with a sad smile. 'Except she never really did.'

'What do you mean?'

'Sometimes I'd come home and find her looking through that file again. Newspaper articles, old photos, anything she could get her hands on about Ava.' He looked up at Karen. 'She never told me what happened. I just assumed they'd been friends. I didn't push the issue because she became very upset when I asked her about it.'

Karen thought Lorraine's behaviour sounded familiar. She'd had a pattern. She'd shut down conversations she didn't want to have by getting upset and emotionally manipulating the situation until the other person backed off. It was a tactic Karen had seen her use, particularly when Mike had asked her about his biological father.

Lorraine had been a devoted wife and mother, a strong woman who had weathered life's storms. But something had happened to her. Whatever it was, it had left her with the need to protect herself, even from those closest to her. It was a survival mechanism.

Karen wondered what price Lorraine had paid for that self-preservation. How had her relationships suffered because of the secrets she kept locked away?

Karen felt a pang of empathy for Lorraine. She knew what it was like to face grief and loss so overwhelming that it threatened to consume her. When she'd lost Josh and Tilly it had felt like her heart had been ripped from her chest. Mike was no stranger to grief either. The loss of his son had nearly destroyed him.

But they had both learned that the only way to truly heal was to face those demons head-on, and to let others in.

Perhaps that was true strength – not hiding from pain, but having the courage to confront it.

The loss of their children had changed Karen and Mike. It had shaped them, but it no longer defined them.

Lorraine had chosen a different path – one of self-imposed emotional isolation.

And that path had led them here, to this.

Chapter Twelve

The doorbell rang. Karen exchanged a glance with James, who was still nursing his cup of tea.

'I'll get it,' she said, rising from her chair.

She made her way to the front door. Through the side glass panel, she could make out the silhouettes of two figures. The living room door was closed because Mike was still being questioned by Falkner and Cunnings. The last thing he needed was a disruption that might prolong the questioning.

Karen opened the door. A woman in her fifties with brown hair brushed back from her face stood alongside an elderly man with white hair. They both looked tense.

'Can I help you?' Karen asked.

The woman opened her mouth, but no words came out. The man cleared his throat. 'Are you Detective Sergeant Karen Hart?'

His question caught Karen off guard. At first glance, she had assumed they were door-to-door salespeople or maybe from a religious group. But the nervous energy they were giving off suggested something more serious.

The woman's fingers fidgeted with the strap of her large handbag, while the man simply stared at her.

'Yes, that's me,' Karen said cautiously.

The woman finally found her voice. 'I'm Ruth Claywood, and this is my father, John.' She gestured to the man beside her.

A jolt of shock went through Karen. The Claywoods.

Ava Claywood's family?

She hadn't recognised them from their photographs. But that wasn't really surprising since more than forty years had passed.

What were they doing here, at her home?

Karen had to tread carefully. Her personal link to Lorraine's murder meant she couldn't let herself get pulled in any deeper than she already was. One wrong step, and she could compromise not just the investigation but also her career.

John Claywood cleared his throat again. 'We were hoping we could have a moment of your time, Detective.'

'I'm afraid now really isn't a good time.'

The crestfallen looks on both their faces made Karen waver. She could see the desperation, that deep need for answers that she'd seen so often in the eyes of victims' loved ones. But she couldn't allow herself to get drawn in.

'How did you get my address?'

'A journalist, Cindy Connor, gave it to us,' Ruth said.

A rush of anger filled Karen. Of course it was Cindy Connor. Always going too far. So much for journalistic integrity. She tried to keep her expression neutral. The Claywoods weren't to blame for the reporter's unethical behaviour.

'I'm sorry, but I can't discuss any details of an ongoing investigation,' Karen said.

John reached over and put a hand on his daughter's shoulder. 'Let's go,' he said in a defeated tone. 'I said there was no point. The police didn't help us then. They're not going to help us now.'

But Ruth wasn't ready to give up. 'I saw your picture in the article, DS Hart. I thought you looked . . . kind.'

Kind? Karen thought she'd looked like a wild-eyed maniac.

Ruth continued, 'I know it's been a long time. I was twelve when my mother was killed. But I thought now maybe . . .' Her voice faded away. 'Never mind.'

Something inside Karen weakened at the raw pain in Ruth's expression.

Before she could think better of it, she said, 'Wait.' And she grabbed her bag that was hooked over the banister before taking out her small notepad and pen. She scrawled her mobile number on a sheet, ripped it out and handed it to Ruth. 'Give me your contact details too, and I'll make sure someone reaches out.'

John frowned. 'Why not you?'

'Because I'm too close to things. I can't work this particular case.'

He raised his bushy white eyebrows. 'So you *do* think there's a link between Ava's death and the new murder?'

'I don't know,' Karen admitted honestly.

As Ruth printed their contact details neatly in Karen's notebook, John said, 'I'm sorry you lost someone close to you, Detective. I hope you get more answers than we did.'

He gave a solemn nod and Ruth handed Karen back her notebook and pen.

Karen couldn't resist asking, 'Did Ava know Lorraine Harrington?'

John paused, thinking. 'I've been wracking my brain since the journalist approached us. I don't remember Lorraine. But it's been a long time. My memory isn't what it was.'

'DI Falkner is here. He's the senior investigating officer on the case. If you wait just a moment, I can get him to speak with you.'

John's expression hardened. 'Don't bother. We spoke to Falkner already. I don't have much faith in him.'

Karen knew she should defend Falkner, but she thought back to her experience with him earlier that day. The man was about as soothing as sandpaper on a sunburn. She didn't find it surprising to learn he hadn't won the Claywoods over.

Before she could ask what had happened with Falkner, John continued, his tone bitter with disappointment, 'I thought you'd be different, Detective. I thought you'd understand what we're going through.'

Ruth placed a hand on her father's arm. 'Dad, maybe we should speak to Falkner again. He might have made some progress.'

John shook his head emphatically. 'No. I've had enough of the police to last me a lifetime. I only let you persuade me to come here because this detective' – he nodded towards Karen – 'was close to that other woman who died. I thought her personal involvement might make one of them get a shift on.'

'Dad!' Ruth looked apologetically at Karen, clearly embarrassed.

As John made his frustration with the police clear, Karen could see his point. She'd only known Falkner since this morning, and already she could see why he might not inspire confidence in grieving families. John and Ruth had every right to be angry. The police service had let them down. More than forty years with no one brought to account for Ava's murder was unacceptable.

'The investigation team are trying their best,' Karen said, knowing her words sounded weak.

John muttered, 'Then I'd hate to see them at their worst.'

Karen watched them walk away.

Her gaze dropped to the notebook clutched in her hand, the Claywoods' phone number and address printed on the page. She should have insisted on interrupting Mike's interview and letting Cunnings or Falkner deal with them. But she hadn't.

Why? Because a big part of her wanted to look into it herself.

She knew she shouldn't. Both Morgan and Churchill had made it clear she was to take a back seat on this case. But she felt drawn to it, and it wasn't easy to step back.

A small, traitorous part of her mind whispered: *Why shouldn't I speak to the Claywoods again?* After all, they'd come to her.

But she would be playing a dangerous game if she started digging and asking questions when she had been explicitly told not to.

After the Claywoods had driven off, Karen stepped outside into the front garden, her breath puffing out in small clouds. The December afternoon was crisp and chilly. Across the street, a neighbour was struggling to untangle a string of Christmas lights, grumbling under his breath.

Karen took out her mobile. After a couple of rings, Cindy answered. 'Hello, DS Hart. To what do I owe the pleasure?'

'You gave my home address to the Claywoods,' Karen said, cutting straight to the point. 'Why would you put me at risk like that? Mike's mother has just been murdered, and you're giving out my address to just anyone.'

There was a pause before Cindy responded. 'I'm sorry, Karen. I didn't mean any harm. The Claywoods aren't just anyone, though. I really thought you could help them. They're good people, and they deserve answers.'

'That may be,' Karen replied, 'but the point still stands. You can't give out my address without my permission. If you do, you're putting me at risk.'

'You're right. I'm sorry, I should have asked first.' Cindy's tone softened. 'So, any new developments?'

'Nice try, but you're not getting any details out of me.'

'Can't blame me for taking the chance. Seriously, though, I was very sorry to hear about your loss.'

The comment caught Karen off guard. Her professional detachment cracked for a moment. This wasn't just any case. This was someone she knew. It was Mike's *mother*.

'Thank you,' she said after a pause.

Sensing an opportunity, Cindy pressed on. 'So how did you discover the link between Ava Claywood and Lorraine? I'm dying to know.'

'I could ask you the same thing,' Karen countered. 'How did you find out about the connection?'

'A reporter never reveals her sources.'

'So you have a source inside the police?'

Cindy let out a loud laugh. 'I didn't say that.'

'This isn't a game, Cindy,' Karen said, her voice hardening. 'After what's happened, I'm really not in the mood. Do us both a favour and back off from this one.'

'You know that can't happen, Karen,' Cindy said. 'It's not in my nature to back off. This isn't personal, you know.'

It felt personal. This whole thing felt like a punch to the gut. Lorraine's murder had knocked Karen's feet from under her, shattering the happiness she'd found with Mike after years of grieving her own family.

'Why did your photographer register a complaint against me?' Karen asked. 'You know I never touched him. You were there.'

Cindy scoffed. 'Don't blame me for that. I told him he was being stupid, but he's such a fusspot when it comes to his camera equipment.'

'The complaint was the last thing I needed,' she said.

'I did try to stop him,' Cindy said. 'But I'll talk to someone if you like. Your boss maybe? Whoever you want me to tell that it wasn't your fault, I will.'

Karen appreciated the offer, but it didn't erase the annoyance she felt. The security footage from the car park had already proved the photographer was making a mountain out of a molehill, but it could still cause her trouble if the complaint gained traction. 'Thanks,' she said, her tone cold. 'But it was all caught on camera, so it's clear that he was hugely exaggerating the incident.'

'I'll ask him to drop it. Look, why don't we meet up, have a chat?' Cindy suggested. 'Maybe we could help each other out with this.'

Karen pulled the phone away from her ear and stared at it. What planet was Cindy on? Did she really think Karen would reveal sensitive information about an ongoing investigation? To a journalist, of all people?

'I'm not working the case, Cindy,' Karen said bluntly. 'I'm too close to it.'

The words tasted bitter. She desperately wanted to be involved, to seek justice for Lorraine and answers for Mike, despite both Morgan and Churchill making it explicitly clear she was to remain on the sidelines.

A slight pause. 'Really? So you're not looking into the Ava Claywood case either?'

'No.'

'It was a pretty shocking murder. And the family never got any answers,' Cindy continued. 'Don't you feel like the police owe them another look?'

Gritting her teeth, Karen fought to keep her tone even. 'It doesn't matter what I feel about the Claywoods. What matters is that I'm here to support Mike after he has just lost his mother in the most brutal way I can imagine. This isn't just another story, another case. Lorraine was . . .' Karen stopped talking. What was the point of trying to make someone like Cindy understand? The journalist seemed to view the world solely through the lens of her next sensational article.

Regaining her composure, Karen added, 'Anyway, you need to back off and leave me alone. And do not give out my address to anyone else, understood?'

'Of course,' Cindy said.

Karen ended the call, still seething with anger. It was nearly half three, and the winter afternoon was fading into dusk.

The sound of car doors made Karen turn. Karen's sister, Emma, was helping Mallory out of the back seat; Karen's little niece was clutching something that looked like artwork.

Emma rushed over, wrapping Karen in a fierce hug. 'I'm so sorry. How're you doing?'

'Surviving,' Karen said. 'Just about.'

Mallory, usually first to chatter about her day, hung back shyly.

'Someone's been very busy doing art at school today,' Emma said. 'Show Auntie Karen what you made.'

Mallory stepped forward, carefully smoothing her drawing. 'It's everyone. There's Grandpa and Nanny, and you and Uncle Mike, and Mummy and Daddy and me . . .'

'That's amazing, Mallory. I can tell that's Grandpa. I like his hat.'

Mallory frowned. 'That's his hair.'

Karen smiled. 'Of course, I knew that. I was just teasing.'

'Mum and Dad said not to crowd you,' Emma said quietly. 'But I needed to see how you were holding up.'

'Can I go and show Uncle Mike?' Mallory asked hopefully.

'He's a bit busy at the moment, sweetheart. But I'll show him your lovely picture later, I promise,' Karen said, and then turned to Emma. 'He's talking to the police, but you should both come in. It's freezing out here.'

'No, we won't stay. Just . . . promise you'll call if you need anything?'

'I will.'

Karen waved as they drove away. When they disappeared around the corner, the warmth of their brief visit faded, leaving her feeling weighed down with the reality of everything. Her gaze drifted back to the house. Through the living room window, she caught sight of Falkner's silhouette, the stern detective staring out at her.

She shivered. She didn't know why, but she didn't trust Falkner – or Cunnings, for that matter – to handle this case properly.

Was it simply because they were outsiders? Unfamiliar faces brought in with no connection to the area or those involved? Or was it because this investigation cut so deeply, so personally, that no one would ever seem good enough in her eyes? Not when she wanted to be the one uncovering the truth.

Karen gave a nod towards Falkner's shadowy form, making it clear she knew he'd been watching her, before turning and making her way back inside.

Chapter Thirteen

Karen let DI Falkner and DS Cunnings leave her house without telling them about her visit from the Claywoods. She wasn't really sure why – perhaps it was her way of holding on to a small part of the case after they'd frozen her out of the rest of the investigation.

It wasn't as though the Claywoods had any information about Lorraine's murder, so she didn't feel obliged to tell Falkner and Cunnings anything. Plus, part of her thought if she mentioned the visit, they might try to ban her from speaking to the Claywoods again, and she didn't want that.

As for Mike and James, they were dealing with enough right now. Their grief was still raw, and she couldn't bring herself to add more complications, especially when Ava Claywood's murder might have nothing to do with Lorraine's death. It wouldn't hurt to keep the Claywoods' visit to herself, at least for now.

Karen returned to the kitchen, where Mike and James were waiting.

James sat hunched at the table, his fingers tracing invisible patterns on the wood, and Mike leaned against the counter, his gaze fixed on some distant point beyond the window.

Karen was used to dealing with grief-stricken families, but this was much harder. This was Mike looking lost and broken. And

James, the man who'd raised him, looking like he'd aged a decade in the span of a day.

What could she say to them now their family had been shattered? When she was supposed to be the one making things better, but she felt almost as lost as they did?

There was no manual for this kind of thing. No checklist she could follow.

But, in true British fashion, there was always tea.

Karen cleared her throat. 'Anyone fancy another cuppa?'

Mike attempted to smile. 'I think if I have any more tea, I'll start sloshing when I walk.'

'Fair point,' she said. 'We've probably single-handedly kept the tea industry afloat today.'

James let out a soft chuckle. 'Your mum would have approved, Mike. She always said a good cup of tea could solve most of life's problems.'

Mike's face clouded over again at the mention of Lorraine.

'I could pop out and grab something for dinner,' Karen offered. 'Or we could order a takeaway if you prefer?'

Mike shrugged. 'I'm not really hungry.'

'Me neither,' James added.

Karen understood. Grief had a way of hollowing you out, leaving no room for practical concerns like food. But they needed to eat. To keep their strength up.

'I'll just pick up something simple from the shop then,' she decided. 'Nothing fancy, but we should try to eat something.'

She'd moved towards the hallway to grab her bag when Sandy let out a warning bark, and then the doorbell rang. Who could that be? Falkner and Cunnings had only just left, and they weren't expecting anyone else.

Karen went to answer. Through the glass panel, she could make out the shape of a large figure. She opened the door.

The man on the doorstep was indeed large, with broad shoulders that seemed to fill the entire doorframe. He carried a partially open black holdall and wore a baseball cap pulled low.

There was something about him that seemed familiar, but Karen couldn't place him. He had a hard, chiselled face, and narrowed eyes that made him look unfriendly. The brim of his cap cast shadows across his face, turning his features into sinister sharp angles and dark hollows.

But when he spoke, his voice was surprisingly soft, almost gentle, and he didn't sound local.

'Sorry to bother you, love,' he said, plastering on a smile. 'I'm just calling at homes in the neighbourhood, hoping people might want to buy something. I've fallen on hard times and I'm trying to get back on my feet. It would be great if you could buy some of these. They're good prices – tea towels, dishcloths, rubber gloves, scrubbing things.' He nodded down at the bag but made no move to show her its contents. Instead, he seemed more interested in peering over her shoulder into the house.

Karen's suspicion ratcheted up a notch. Just last month, Cindy Connor had written an article about a gang of burglars using exactly this tactic – seemingly innocent door-to-door salesmen, casing the area for future break-ins. Cindy and the rest of the press had named them the Doorstep Devils.

The gang probably loved that, thinking it made them sound like criminal masterminds. Among the police officers though, they'd been dubbed the Ding Dong Crew. Karen imagined the burglars probably weren't too chuffed about that one.

Was this man a member of that gang?

Her years in the police had taught her to trust her instincts, and right now, every fibre of her being was telling her that this man was trouble.

'No, thanks,' she said firmly, her hand reaching to close the door. 'It's not a good time.'

The man's smile faltered for a moment before returning, a bit too wide, a bit too eager. 'Nothing at all? I've got some real bargains here, and it would really help me out.'

'I said no,' Karen repeated, her voice taking on the steely edge she usually reserved for uncooperative suspects. 'Have a good evening.'

She closed the door before he could respond. Through the glass, she watched as he lingered for a moment before trudging down the drive, his holdall swinging at his side.

Karen frowned. It was sad how suspicious she'd become of people. Maybe the chap really was down on his luck and just trying to make an honest living. But something about him had set off alarm bells. Karen had learned the hard way in her job that it was better to be safe than sorry.

She grabbed her mobile, quickly tapping out a text to Christine next door. Good old Christine, the Neighbourhood Watch Queen. If there was anything dodgy going on, she'd have the whole street on alert.

'Everything okay?' Mike's voice startled her. He was standing in the kitchen doorway.

Karen managed a smile. 'Yes, it was just some bloke trying to sell stuff door-to-door. Could be genuine, but I've let Christine know, just in case.'

Mike nodded, a flicker of his old self showing through as he peered out through the window. 'Good call. With all the elderly folks living alone on this street, it's best not to take any chances. Are you heading out now?'

'Yes, just to grab a few bits from the shop. Won't be long.'

Twenty minutes later, Karen was back home. The local co-op had been quiet, and the food shop hadn't taken long. She was surprised to see James's car missing from the driveway when she returned.

'Mike? I'm back!' she called out, but the house remained silent.

Even Sandy didn't come to greet her. That was *really* odd. Frowning, she flicked on the hallway light and made her way to the kitchen.

Putting the reusable shopping bag on the counter, Karen pulled her mobile from her pocket and called Mike. It rang a few times, then switched over to voicemail. '*You've reached Mike Harrington . . .*'

She ended the call with an irritated sigh.

Had he gone out somewhere with James? Maybe taking Sandy along? But why not even send a text to let her know? Karen pulled up the security camera app on her phone, scrolling back through the footage. About twenty minutes earlier, James had marched out of the house. He'd got into his car and slammed the door. Just a few minutes later, Mike had left with Sandy, heading off on foot. It looked like a normal evening walk for Mike and Sandy, but something had clearly upset James.

Karen yanked open the fridge and began unpacking the shopping. She'd been out for less than half an hour. They knew she was getting something for dinner. Would it have killed them to send her a quick message?

Then guilt crept in. Mike and James were understandably distracted after losing Lorraine.

She typed out a quick text. *Just got in. Where have you gone?* Lowering the phone, she gazed out the window at the darkness that had enveloped the garden.

She hated the short days of winter.

Karen knew better than most how loss could drive a person to the brink. Mike's mother's death would have dredged up all his memories of losing Nathan.

Surely, Mike wouldn't do anything rash, would he?

After he'd lost his son, Mike had been in a very dark place and had tried to take his own life by driving his car into a wall. The incident had left him with a metal plate in his leg and a limp that was more severe on some days than others.

What if . . . Her heart gave a painful twist at the thought. No, surely he wouldn't try anything like that? Not now, not when they'd finally found their way back to happiness. She was sure he wouldn't.

Still, that didn't stop the cold dread from creeping over her skin.

Abandoning the half-unpacked bags, Karen moved through to the living room and looked out at the driveway. She wanted to see Mike walking home with Sandy, or hear the crunch of tyres on the driveway as James drove them all back home.

She wished James was with him. Mike wouldn't do anything stupid with his stepfather around.

Karen's pulse spiked as a sleek black Range Rover turned into her driveway. She recognised the vehicle instantly. Her mouth went dry.

Quentin Chapman.

What was he doing here?

She peered through the curtains, wondering if there was still a police unit keeping watch nearby. On her way back from the shops, she'd been too preoccupied with thoughts of Mike and James to notice any unmarked cars stationed in the close opposite. Perhaps Morgan had listened when she'd stupidly insisted they didn't need anyone watching the house.

The idea of Chapman having Lorraine killed seemed far-fetched to Karen. He might be ruthless in business, but sewing someone's eyelids shut? That wasn't something he'd do himself, and she couldn't imagine him ordering one of his thugs to do it either. This felt personal, ritualistic even. Nothing like Chapman's usual style of intimidation.

Indecision gripped her. What should she do – stay inside with the door firmly closed, or go out and confront him? He obviously had something to say; Chapman didn't make social calls.

She could pretend to be out. But they needed answers. Maybe he'd explain why he'd been paying Lorraine all those years.

Squaring her shoulders, Karen opened the front door and came face to face with the imposing figure of Quentin Chapman.

One of his men stayed by the Range Rover, watching menacingly from a distance.

'Good evening, Karen.' His polite, grandfatherly demeanour didn't fool her. 'I hope I'm not interrupting.'

He craned his neck, trying to look over her shoulder into the house. But Karen moved to block his view.

'I have a few questions for you,' she said, keeping her tone even. 'About my partner's mother's murder.'

Chapman's expression remained impassive. 'I did hear about that. Please accept my condolences and pass them on to your partner. In fact, I hoped I might have a word with him. Mike, isn't it?'

The way he said Mike's name made Karen's instincts prickle. Could he really be Mike's biological father? He didn't resemble Mike, but that didn't prove anything. Was he here to see Mike now that Mike was at his most vulnerable, with Lorraine gone?

'You can't talk to him. He's not here. And even if he was, he's not up to having visitors right now.'

'No, I imagine it must be a very difficult time.' Chapman's gaze didn't waver. 'Even so, I think I have some information that might interest him.'

Karen held his stare. 'Well, why don't you give it to me, then? I'll be sure to pass it on.'

Chapman's eyes narrowed. 'No, I don't think so.'

Karen stared at him defiantly. The sound of footsteps caught her attention, and she turned to see two familiar figures hurrying down the driveway – Davis and Perrot, two young but capable officers she'd worked with before.

The heavy, still lingering by the Range Rover, called out in warning, 'Boss!'

Chapman pivoted smoothly to see who was approaching. 'It seems we have visitors, DS Hart.'

Karen stepped past him, moving towards the approaching officers. 'It's okay,' she said quickly, raising a hand to slow the men hurtling down the drive.

One of them, Davis, pulled her aside. 'He's on the list of people we have to watch out for,' he murmured in a low voice, his gaze flickering to Chapman.

'I know,' Karen replied evenly, 'but it's okay. I need to talk to him. He might be able to tell us something important.'

Davis looked uncertain. 'Are you sure? Do you want me to call DI Morgan?'

'Yes, update DI Morgan. But I'll be okay. Can you just give us a minute?'

Perrot frowned, but after exchanging a glance with Davis, he nodded reluctantly. 'All right, we'll just be over here.' The two men took up positions near the front of the drive, keeping a watchful eye on Chapman and his goon.

Karen went back to Chapman.

'You have officers watching your house?' he asked, one silver brow arched.

She nodded curtly. 'As a precaution. Lorraine's murder was pretty shocking.'

'And they think you're at risk? Or maybe it's Mike?' Chapman's expression grew pensive, and he actually looked concerned.

'It's just a precaution, like I said.'

Chapman frowned. 'I'll look into it. You don't have to worry.'

Unease rippled through her. What was he talking about? She didn't want him meddling. Was he messing with her? She wanted no part of his criminal dealings.

If he'd ordered the killing, he wouldn't be standing here offering to help – even if this was some twisted game to get her in his debt. But something in his concern seemed genuine, and that brutal murder and disfigurement of Lorraine's eyes didn't fit with Chapman's usual methods.

'No. Don't interfere. The police have it handled.'

Chapman's gaze sharpened. 'Do they? So they know who killed your partner's mother?'

'Not yet, but we're making progress.' She paused. 'But I do have some questions for you. You had a relationship with Lorraine, didn't you?'

She wasn't sure what she expected, but she certainly didn't anticipate Chapman's reaction – a slow smile spread across his face, followed by a chuckle.

'I knew Lorraine for a long time, yes,' he admitted easily.

'And are you . . .' She gathered her courage. 'Are you Mike's father?'

Chapman threw back his head and let out a hearty burst of laughter. 'Am I what?'

His amusement annoyed Karen. 'It's not funny. What am I supposed to think? You're keeping tabs on me, and apparently you've been making payments to Lorraine that go back years, to just after Mike was born. It makes sense.'

Wiping away a tear and stifling his laughter, Chapman shook his head. 'I think you're adding two plus two and coming up with five, Detective.'

Karen stared at Chapman. 'Then how do you know Lorraine?'

'She worked for me before Mike was born.'

Karen felt like she'd been slapped. The man who'd been giving Lincolnshire Police the runaround for decades had employed Mike's mother?

'In what capacity?'

'A secretary. She was very good, a hard worker. And she got on well with my late wife.'

Karen was struggling to get her head around the fact that a man whose name came up in connection with everything from protection rackets to high-end car theft rings, yet somehow always emerged untouchable, had been Lorraine's boss. Both Karen and Mike had worked for the police, yet neither of them had known about this.

'And what were your payments to Lorraine for?'

'Lorraine got into a spot of trouble after Mike was born. She couldn't work when he was tiny, so I helped her out. I repay loyalty, Karen.'

It was hardly a subtle hint. He expected something in return for his supposed generosity, but Karen wasn't going to become one of his loyal servants, his officer on the inside. She knew all too well what kind of man he really was.

Even if he had been helping Lorraine out of the goodness of his heart, one good deed didn't make a good man.

'So if you knew Lorraine back then, do you know who Mike's biological father is?'

A slow nod was Chapman's only response.

'Well?' Karen prompted, her patience wearing thin. 'Tell me.'

A twisted smile crept across Chapman's face. He loved having information someone else wanted – it gave him power over them.

'I think that's something I should discuss with Mike, don't you?' he said.

Karen bristled. 'I've already told you you're not talking to him. He's fragile at the moment.'

'Well, I'll be here when he's ready.'

'But I need to know.'

Chapman merely shrugged. 'Then let me talk to Mike.'

'No.' Karen held her ground, refusing to be bullied. 'Lorraine's been murdered. It could have something to do with Mike's biological father, for all you know. So you need to tell me who he is.'

'I'll talk to Mike about it. No one else.'

She shook her head, frustration building. Images of Lorraine's dead body flashed through her mind. Her eyes, brutally disfigured. The way Chapman treated this like some sort of power trip was really getting under her skin.

'I can give you something that might help though,' Chapman offered. 'Lorraine has a sister. Michelle Matthews. I assume that's still her name, although she might have married. Been a long time since I talked to her. She and Lorraine were very close at one time.'

Karen frowned. She hadn't known Lorraine had a sister – which meant Mike had an aunt he'd never mentioned. Did Mike know about Michelle? Did James?

Chapman continued, 'As far as I know, Michelle lives near Scunthorpe. She might be able to give you some answers. I think the sisters had a falling-out, but at one time they were as thick as thieves.'

If she couldn't get the identity of Mike's biological father from Chapman, maybe she could get it from Michelle. If the sisters had once been close, Michelle might be the key to finally unlocking the truth about Mike's father.

Karen knew what she had to do, though Falkner wouldn't like it one bit. Morgan wouldn't be best pleased either. They wouldn't want her to track down Michelle. But she had to do it. Michelle might be able to give Mike the closure he deserved.

Michelle probably didn't even know Lorraine was dead. Karen didn't look forward to being the one to break the devastating news, but she was glad to have some purpose. It was something she could do to actually help Mike.

A sudden realisation jolted Karen. The torn 'M' page from Lorraine's address book . . . *Michelle Matthews.*

Had the killer wanted Michelle's address?

Karen's instincts were on high alert now. Finding Michelle wasn't just about closure for Mike. There was a very real possibility that Michelle's life was in danger.

Chapter Fourteen

Arnie let out a weary sigh as he settled into his seat. An evening briefing was always a trying affair, and tonight's was no exception.

DI Falkner and DI Morgan stood at the front of the room. Arnie caught the two men exchanging terse glances, their jaws clenched tight. He could practically feel the unspoken friction. You didn't need to be a detective to recognise the signs of a brewing storm between the two lead investigators. Arnie couldn't blame Morgan – Falkner walked around the station as though he owned the place.

Arnie glanced around the room, nodding at Rick, Sophie, DC Farzana Shah and DS Bridget Cunnings, all of whom had gathered for the update on the Harrington case.

He wondered how Karen was holding up. Cases were so much harder when they involved someone you knew. It would be bad enough to find any victim with their eyes sewn shut, but Mike's mum? And then to be told you couldn't investigate? Being shut out of the case had to be eating Karen alive.

Falkner cleared his throat, drawing everyone's attention. 'Right, let's get started. Arnie, what have you got?'

'Neighbours spotted a bloke peering through the windows around the time Lorraine Harrington was killed yesterday. Turns out the chap was a delivery driver called Jason Wilkes. He has a record. Petty theft, affray, possession.'

'Minor crimes, compared to murder,' Falkner said.

'Yes, I don't think he's the person we're looking for. I went to the depot to have a word before he started his shift. He told me he'd been looking through the living room window because he'd knocked and no one had answered, but then he thought he saw a shadow moving inside.'

'Forensics will tell us if he's lying and he went inside the property,' Morgan said.

'He wasn't a star witness. Did say it was a man he saw inside Lorraine's house, though, and that he had "evil eyes".'

'Evil eyes?' Rick snorted. 'What next? A twirly moustache and a cape?'

Arnie chuckled. 'If Jason had been any more unobservant, I'd suspect he'd have trouble finding his own backside with both hands. I was lucky to get the evil eyes description.'

A ripple of laughter went through the room, but Falkner's gaze remained cold. 'So, no other information from the delivery driver then?'

'He's agreed to help us generate a photofit,' Arnie replied, shrugging. Though, given Jason's lack of observational skills, they were likely to end up with a sketch of an evil Mr Potato Head.

Sophie frowned. 'Given Wilkes's record, how reliable is he? Can we believe that he really saw someone in the house?'

'He might be making it up,' Arnie said. 'But if he isn't, then the evil eyes he saw might belong to our killer.'

He could practically see the cogs turning in Falkner's mind as the DI considered the new angle.

Rick spoke next. 'Farzana and I have been checking the neighbourhood security cameras and traffic cams, but no luck so far. Not a single useful lead.'

Falkner's lips thinned into a disapproving line, and Arnie braced himself for the inevitable lecture on the importance of thorough investigative work. That was Falkner's style.

But before the DI could speak, Cunnings jumped in, her sunny disposition cutting through the gloomy mood. 'Well, we'll just have to keep looking. We've made a strong start.'

Why was she always so cheerful?

Cunnings gave the group an encouraging smile.

Farzana was the only one who managed to return it. But Arnie had to admit, Cunnings's slightly grating optimism was nicer than Falkner's perpetual sourness.

Falkner turned back to Rick. 'What about Chapman? We need answers on those payments to Lorraine.'

Rick shifted uncomfortably. 'I've invited him in for a voluntary interview but haven't heard back yet.'

'Then chase it. Go and see him at home.'

'Right. I'll do my best.'

Falkner's gaze lingered on Rick, and Arnie could see the impatience in the DI's eyes. 'See that you do. We need results, and we need them quickly. If you can't manage Chapman, perhaps I should assign the task to someone else?'

Rick's cheeks flushed. His confidence was taking a hammering. Falkner was out of line. Rick was a good copper, and a good leader shouldn't speak down to his team like that.

Falkner didn't seem to grasp how slippery Quentin Chapman could be. 'With respect, you don't understand Chapman,' Arnie said. 'He'll drag this out. It's what he does. The bloke's a weasel. If you're lucky enough to get him to attend a voluntary interview, he'll evade every question. Trying to get a helpful response from Chapman is like trying to nail jelly to a tree.'

Falkner levelled his pale, assessing gaze at Arnie. 'Are you saying we shouldn't bother, DS Hodgson?'

'No, of course not.' Arnie held up his hands. 'I'm just saying Chapman's crafty. You've got to approach him the right way, that's all.'

Falkner's lips twitched slightly, the barest hint of a smirk. 'I have no intention of playing his games. We simply need the facts from Chapman, and we'll extract them by whatever means necessary. Think you can manage, DC Jones? Or should I assign a more competent officer? Perhaps you need me to show you how it's done.'

Rick swallowed hard, embarrassment mixing with annoyance. 'I can do it.'

Falkner's condescending behaviour really wasn't helping anyone right now. Dealing with characters like Chapman required finesse, not brute force. But trying to convince Falkner of that would be like arguing with an orange. Arnie slumped back in his seat. He wasn't going to win this one, and he'd been in the police long enough to know when to pick his battles.

Just then, Morgan's mobile rang. His face tensed as he glanced at the caller ID. 'Sorry, I need to take this. It's Davis, one of the officers I have watching Karen's place.'

A hush fell over the room. Farzana caught Arnie's eye. She looked scared.

Morgan pressed the speaker button. Davis's voice filled the tense silence. 'Sir, Chapman's just turned up at Karen's place.' Sophie looked concerned as Davis continued, 'She's all right. He asked to speak to her privately and she agreed. But given everything that's going on, I thought you should know.'

'Who else is with him?' Morgan asked sharply.

'One other man – his driver, I think. Big white bloke, long dark hair in a ponytail.'

'We know him. He's one of Chapman's heavies, Jamie Goode.' Morgan's knuckles were white where he gripped the phone. 'Are they trying to intimidate Karen?'

'No, I don't think so. She seems to have it handled.'

'Are they inside?'

'No. Talking on the doorstep.'

'Good. Keep eyes on them at all times.'

'Of course, sir. I'll keep you posted.'

Davis hung up.

Arnie stood. 'Talking to Chapman alone? Is she mad? I'm going round there.'

Falkner's icy gaze pinned him in place. 'That would be highly improper, DS Hodgson. Karen should not be involved in this case, let alone speaking to Chapman.' He shot a pointed look at Morgan, as if blaming him for the situation. 'DS Cunnings and I will go and speak to Karen.'

Arnie watched as Cunnings followed Falkner out the door.

He knew better than to argue, but he was worried. Karen had been through enough.

Mike paced the kitchen. Karen watched him, waiting for him to either speak or explode. He'd just returned from walking Sandy, but the walk hadn't done anything to reduce the tension radiating from him. She wanted to tell him about Michelle, but wasn't sure now was the best time.

He was furious. Something must have happened between him and James.

'So James has gone to stay at Washingborough Hall?' she asked carefully, studying his face.

Mike stopped pacing and gave a jerky nod, not meeting her eyes. 'Yes, it was his choice.'

'We have a perfectly good spare room here.'

'That's what I said.' Mike's jaw tightened. 'He wasn't interested.'

Karen waited, giving him space to elaborate, but he just stood there, shoulders rigid, staring out the window at nothing in particular. She'd seen that look before – she'd worn it herself often enough after losing Josh and Tilly.

'Want to talk about what happened between you two?'

'Nothing happened.' Mike's voice was flat. 'He wanted space, that's all.'

Karen took a deep breath. 'Talking to someone helped after you lost Nathan.'

Mike nodded.

'You know, not too long ago, someone very wise told me that talking to a professional might help me process my grief.' She gave him a pointed look. 'Ring any bells?'

Mike's laugh was harsh. 'That was different.'

'Was it?'

'Yes.' He finally turned to face her. 'You'd lost Josh and Tilly. You were trying to cope alone for *years*. Just like I was without Nathan. This . . .' He gestured vaguely, helplessly. 'This just happened. I need time to process it myself first. I can't even think straight right now, let alone talk to some stranger about my feelings.'

'I thought the same thing back then.' Karen kept her voice gentle. 'Convinced myself I could handle it alone.'

'Karen.' His voice held a warning note. 'I know you're trying to help, but I can't do this right now. My mum's only been . . .' He broke off, swallowing hard. 'I just need some time, okay?'

Before Karen could respond, Sandy started barking from the living room and the doorbell rang.

'I'll get it.' Mike seemed almost relieved by the interruption.

Karen heard voices in the hallway, then Mike returned with DI Falkner and DS Cunnings in tow. *Fantastic.* Just what she needed.

'DS Hart.' Falkner's voice was cold. 'We need to discuss your conversation with Chapman.'

Karen caught Mike's questioning look, but before she could explain about Michelle Matthews or anything else, Falkner and Cunnings asked to speak to Karen privately. Mike retreated to his study, and Falkner launched into what felt like an endless lecture about protocol and chain of command. She half listened, nodding in what she hoped were the right places, while fighting the urge to pour her coffee over his head. When she finally managed to get a word in edgewise, she told him about Michelle. He paused, his gaze turning razor-sharp. A barrage of pointed questions followed, but once he'd extracted the necessary facts his lecture continued.

Twenty minutes later, Falkner was still going strong. 'Do you understand, DS Hart?' he asked in his piercing cut-glass accent.

Oh, she understood all right. She understood that Falkner was an insufferable man who could do with being taken down a peg or two. But she managed to nod, swallowing her real thoughts along with the last of her now-cold coffee.

She had tried to explain that Chapman had approached her, not the other way around, but Falkner didn't seem interested in hearing her side of things.

'What about Michelle Matthews?' she asked, refusing to be completely silenced.

Falkner's eyes narrowed to slits. 'DS Hart, are you being deliberately obtuse? You're not on this case. I understand you've been through a lot, but that doesn't mean—'

'With all due respect, sir, me being off the case doesn't change the fact that a woman's life might be at risk. If the killer took that "M" page for her address, she's a sitting duck. We need to warn her.'

Falkner sighed, pinching the bridge of his nose. 'I wasn't going to ignore it. Believe it or not, I have been an SIO on a murder case before. I'll get Sophie to locate Michelle Matthews's address and ask a local unit to do a wellness check. They can break the news about Lorraine while they're at it.'

'Shouldn't we suggest Michelle stay somewhere else for a few days as well? Just to be safe?'

Falkner looked like he'd bitten into a lemon, but after a moment, he nodded grudgingly. 'That's not a bad idea. I'll recommend it.'

'Thank you, sir.'

'Good, then we'll leave it there for now.' Falkner's words were clipped, final. Then, his phone began to ring. 'Excuse me,' he said, stepping out into the hallway to take the call.

As soon as he was out of earshot, Cunnings leaned in, her voice laced with sympathy. 'I'm sorry about that. This must be really difficult for you.'

She knew Cunnings was trying to be kind, but she couldn't wait to see the back of her and Falkner. Because Mike had returned not long before Falkner and Cunnings had shown up, they hadn't had a chance to have a proper chat. She hadn't even had the opportunity to tell him about Michelle yet or ask him whether he'd known his mother used to work for Quentin Chapman.

Karen knew Mike well enough to know when he was holding back. Clearly, something had gone down between him and James, but before she'd been able to squeeze more out of him, the dynamic detective duo had arrived.

Now she was stuck in her kitchen, facing Falkner and Cunnings and defending her actions, when she should have been talking to Mike, asking him if he'd had any idea he had an aunt, and finding out what had really gone on between him and James.

She wished it was Arnie or Morgan sitting across from her; she'd feel much more at ease talking to them. But at least Cunnings was doing her best to tone down Falkner's brashness.

'I know this must feel very unfair,' Cunnings said in a low voice, glancing towards the hallway where Falkner had gone to take his call. 'You shouldn't be completely left out of this, especially when it comes to information about Mike's biological father.' She paused, then added, 'Falkner is the sort of DI you want working the investigation, though. You should see how he connects the dots. He's sharp as they come.'

He might be brilliant at connecting dots, but he was rubbish at connecting with actual human beings. 'Glad to hear it. I do understand why he wants to keep me away from the investigation.'

Her mind wandered back to Mike. Karen appreciated Cunnings's support, but she really just wanted both detectives to leave so she could have a proper heart-to-heart with her fiancé.

Cunnings smiled. 'We'll make sure you're kept in the loop, at least about that part. I'll do whatever I can to get you the info you need about Mike's father.'

'Thank you. I really appreciate that.'

The sound of footsteps in the hallway announced Falkner's return. Cunnings straightened in her seat.

'We're leaving now,' he said. 'Thank you for your time.'

Karen looked up at him, wondering what the phone call had been about. 'Have there been any new developments?'

Falkner shook his head. 'No, we're still chasing leads.' His expression softened slightly as he added, 'We're doing our best to get answers for you and Mike.'

Karen appreciated the words, but her frustration was still simmering away. 'Anything new from the Claywoods?'

'I've spoken to them personally,' Falkner replied with that air of self-importance that made Karen want to grind her teeth.

'My feeling is that the cuttings Lorraine kept are irrelevant to the current investigation. It's likely she knew Ava a long time ago, but I doubt Ava's strangulation has anything to do with Lorraine's murder. There are no similarities between the two murders, other than the victims were both female.' He gave Karen a patronising smile, like he was bestowing great wisdom. 'But of course, we'll keep an open mind.'

Karen nodded. A potential lead eliminated, but at least they were being thorough and hadn't dismissed it entirely.

As the two detectives made their way towards the door, Falkner turned back to Karen. 'I trust you won't be talking to anyone else involved with the case?'

Guilt swamped Karen as she remembered taking the Claywoods' contact details. She couldn't promise that. She was torn – part of her desperately wanted to reach out to them, to gather any information that might shed light on Lorraine's murder. But she also knew that going behind Falkner's back would only complicate matters.

Pushing down her conflicted emotions, Karen met his gaze. 'My priority right now is helping Mike through this.'

Chapter Fifteen

Karen watched from the window by the front door as Falkner's car pulled away. Finally, she could talk to Mike alone.

She made her way into the living room, where Mike sat hunched on the sofa. Sandy was next to him, her head on his thigh.

'They're gone,' Karen said, sitting beside him.

'Good,' Mike replied, but he didn't look up.

Should she tell him what Chapman had said about Lorraine having a sister now? The last thing she wanted was to add more to his plate. But this wasn't something she could keep to herself for long.

'I need to talk to you about something.'

Mike lifted his head, his eyes meeting hers. 'Can it wait until tomorrow? I'm shattered, and my head's still spinning from all of this.'

'I'm sorry, but I don't think it can wait,' she said. 'When Chapman turned up earlier, he told me two things. Your mum used to work for him, and your mum has a sister – a woman called Michelle Matthews.'

'What?' He paused, clearly shocked. 'Are you serious?'

'Yes, he seemed quite sure.'

Mike leaned back, overwhelmed. 'I had no idea she even knew Quentin Chapman, and I didn't know I had an aunt. Why would Mum hide that from me?'

'I don't know.'

'When did she work for Chapman? What did she do for him?'

'Before you were born. She was his secretary.'

He exhaled slowly, shaking his head.

'Maybe we could talk to Michelle,' Karen suggested gently. 'She might have some answers about your biological father.'

He looked uncertain, wrestling with the idea. 'Maybe,' he said slowly. 'I'm sure you're right, and that's the best thing to do. But I don't think I'm ready to get into all this with a stranger. She might be my aunt, but I've never met her. Mum must have had a reason for cutting off contact and never telling me about her. Maybe she's awful.'

'I could go and talk to her, if you prefer? Ask her some questions?' Falkner had said to stay away from anyone involved in the case, but talking to Mike's aunt didn't count as interfering with the investigation as far as Karen was concerned. This was family. Even Falkner would have to see that.

For a long moment, Mike was silent as he mulled it over. At last, he said, 'I suppose someone should tell her that Mum's died.'

'I'll go and talk to her. See what she's like and if she can tell me anything about your mum's past.'

'I'd appreciate that. Thanks.'

Karen smiled, relieved to have something useful to do. 'No problem. I just wish I could do more.'

'There's nothing you can do. It's hard to believe how happy we were just a couple of days ago. I don't feel like the same person. I don't even know if I want to find out why Mum was so intent on keeping my father's identity a secret,' he said. 'Part of me wants to know the truth. But another part . . .' He trailed off with a helpless shrug.

Karen bit her lip, wishing she could say something to make him feel better. But this went deeper than anything she could say.

Mike had always been the strong, silent type, preferring to process his emotions alone before opening up. When they'd first met, he'd been a reclusive groundskeeper who'd shut himself away from the world after his son's death. It had taken so long for those walls to come down. Now she could see him building them back up, brick by bitter brick.

After a few minutes, Karen asked, 'What happened with James?'

Mike frowned. 'Nothing.'

'Then why is he staying at a hotel?'

Mike shrugged.

She studied his face, seeing the muscle twitch in his jaw. 'Did something happen between you two?'

Mike shook his head slowly. 'He just said he needed space to work through things.'

She opened her mouth to ask more, but something in his expression told her to stop. He was closed off. Pressing further wouldn't help. Something must have happened. But Mike clearly didn't want to talk about it.

She nodded. 'Okay. Fair enough.' She leaned on him, resting her head on his shoulder. He wrapped an arm around her.

After a brief silence, he sighed. 'I suppose I should call him at some point and ask if he knew about Michelle.'

'Good idea. What were DI Falkner's questions like earlier?' Karen asked. 'Did he go easy on you?'

'He was a typical detective. All self-importance and bluster. You know what they're like.'

Karen raised an eyebrow and lifted her head to see him grinning. A glimmer of the old Mike.

'Seriously though. He wasn't too bad. It's just hard to keep going over it. Constantly going over what it was like to find her like that.'

'I know. Hopefully they'll give us some space now. Falkner is behaving like such a pain,' Karen said. 'He was scolding me like I was a schoolgirl. It's not like I asked Chapman to turn up.'

'I know.' Mike yawned. 'I'm going to head up to bed. I didn't sleep well last night.'

It was only eight p.m. She nodded and smiled. 'Okay. I'll be up in a bit.'

Mike rose from the sofa and made his way towards the stairs, his limp seeming more pronounced.

Karen usually had the ability to connect with people, to offer them comfort and support. But with Mike, she was failing. She wasn't quite sure of the right thing to say or do.

She caught the murmur of Mike's voice upstairs – he must have decided to phone James now. The conversation didn't last long. Presumably James was as surprised by Michelle's existence as they had been.

Reaching down, she gave Sandy a gentle scratch behind the ears. 'Looks like it's just you and me tonight for Netflix.'

She switched on the TV but just flicked through the options, unable to settle on anything. With a frustrated sigh, she sank back against the sofa cushions, staring at the dark windows.

Falkner's stern reprimand from earlier played through her mind. The way he'd looked at her, as if she were a disobedient child rather than a capable police officer, had stung more than she wanted to admit.

Part of her still wanted to reach out to the Claywoods, to dig deeper into Ava's murder and its potential connection to Lorraine's death. But that would only earn her another lecture from Falkner. It would annoy Morgan, too.

She didn't care about being in Falkner's bad books, but the thought of letting Morgan down . . . She imagined him looking at her, sad and frustrated. Karen huffed. She was already failing Mike. She didn't want to disappoint Morgan, too.

She would put her need to solve everything aside for now. For once, she needed to stop being DS Hart and just be Karen – the person Mike needed most.

Tomorrow she'd visit Michelle Matthews, and hopefully get some answers.

Karen picked up her phone, intending to check her emails. A new notification caught her eye. Her throat seemed to close up as she saw the subject line: *Tread Carefully.*

You're not listening. I thought you were cleverer than this. You keep pushing your nose places it shouldn't be. Remember what happened to Lorraine. Some secrets are buried deep for a reason.

Karen's hand shook as she lowered the phone. Another message from NoMoreQuestions@protonmail.com. The same encrypted email service Harinder was having such trouble with. He'd called earlier to explain that Proton Mail would only release details if the request came through the Swiss authorities. Fat chance of that happening quickly.

She read the message again. The words seemed to pulse on the screen. *Remember what happened to Lorraine.* The threat couldn't be clearer.

There was something familiar about the tone though. That *I thought you were cleverer than this* – it felt personal, condescending. Like someone who knew her. Who thought they were smarter than her.

Who could it be? Someone who knew details of the investigation. Someone who knew she was asking questions. The list of people who fit that description was worryingly long.

She glanced towards the stairs. Mike didn't need to know about this. He was dealing with enough already.

But the team needed to know about this new development. She found Morgan's number in her contacts. Karen would much prefer to hear his calm, reassuring voice than Falkner's right now.

She pressed dial.

The following morning, Karen and Mike both woke early. Mike was quiet, not quite his usual self, but definitely better than yesterday. Getting through his grief would be a slow process, but at least they'd both slept a little better last night.

Karen buttered a slice of toast and tried to work out the best way to broach the subject of Mike calling James last night. He hadn't brought it up himself yet. Clearing her throat, she said, 'I thought I heard you on the phone last night after you went to bed. Did you call James?'

Mike glanced up. 'Yes, I forgot to mention it. He said he'd known Mum had a sister, but had never actually met Michelle. He said it completely slipped his mind with everything going on.'

Karen supposed that was understandable. 'Did he know what happened between them? Why they didn't keep in contact?'

Mike shrugged. 'He said they'd had some sort of falling-out, but he wasn't sure what it was about. It happened before he met Mum. He had no idea that she'd worked for Quentin Chapman either.'

Karen wanted to ask more questions but reminded herself this wasn't her job and she wasn't interrogating a witness. 'Is James doing okay?'

Mike swallowed his mouthful of toast. 'As far as I know.'

Karen poured herself another coffee and stifled a yawn. She was surprised she'd managed any sleep at all after that email.

But Morgan's steady voice and practical approach had helped. He'd arranged for extra patrols past the house and promised to apply some pressure to try to fast-track the request to the Swiss authorities. His calm efficiency had made the threat seem more manageable somehow.

She still hadn't mentioned the emails to Mike. He was dealing with enough already. Losing his mum, whatever weirdness was going on between him and James, and now all this business with an aunt he hadn't known about until yesterday. No, he had enough on his plate right now. She'd tell him once Harinder managed to trace the sender. No point in them both worrying about who was behind the threats.

After breakfast, Mike went off to work and Karen got in her car, preparing to visit Michelle Matthews to find out what she could about Mike's mystery aunt.

She was glad Falkner had promised to send local officers to do a wellness check yesterday and to break the news. Informing the family after a loved one's death was a part of the job she hated, but then again, Michelle was Mike's aunt. Should she have been there, rather than let local officers deliver the news of Lorraine's death?

A selfish part of her was relieved. The initial shock would have passed, giving Michelle time to process. Hopefully, she'd be in a better state to answer questions now. Unless she'd inherited Lorraine's prickly, emotionally distant nature. If so, extracting the truth would be like pulling teeth.

Karen had got Michelle's address from Sophie, which was maybe a little underhand. Ever since she'd come back to work after her attack, Sophie had been taking more risks and pushing back against rules she'd once followed rigidly. It was like her brush with death had made her reassess everything.

Karen felt a twinge of conscience for taking advantage of that newfound rebellious streak. But she'd convinced Sophie this was just about helping Mike connect with his aunt, nothing to do with Lorraine's murder investigation.

Sophie, trusting Karen implicitly, had readily given her the address. Which made Karen feel a bit guilty. She didn't want Sophie getting into trouble with Falkner.

She felt irritated just thinking about Falkner. Who did he think he was, telling her what she could and couldn't do? Chastising her for speaking to Chapman last night had been ridiculous. The more she thought about it, the more annoyed she felt.

What was she supposed to have done? Bolt the doors and pretend she wasn't home?

Actually, come to think of it, that was probably exactly what Falkner would have said she should do.

Chapman hadn't told her much, anyway. Nothing that would change the case from an investigative standpoint, at least. But he'd told Karen about Michelle. It was a start.

If Michelle hadn't seen her sister in years, she likely wouldn't have much insight into Lorraine's murder. But Mike's biological father? If the sisters had been close when they were younger, Michelle might have something useful to share about the man's identity.

Karen also thought that maybe building a relationship with his aunt might help Mike deal with the loss of his mother, especially if Michelle could tell him more about his paternal roots.

He still had his stepfather, James, even if something seemed off between the two of them at the moment. But another family connection couldn't hurt. You could never have too many people in your corner. Especially when it came to family.

She'd tried phoning James twice since yesterday, but he hadn't picked up or returned the messages she'd sent. She'd call in on him this afternoon at the hotel, to make sure he was doing all right. It wasn't a good idea for him to be alone after what he'd gone through. No matter what had happened between him and Mike.

As Karen fastened her seatbelt, her phone buzzed. Ruth Claywood's name flashed up on the screen.

Karen's mind conjured up an image of Falkner, his pinched face tightening in disapproval.

She answered the call. 'DS Hart.'

'Hello, Detective, I'm sorry to trouble you. I just wondered if you had time for a chat.'

Karen paused, conflicted. 'The thing is, Ruth, I'm not actually working the case. I wish I could help get you some answers, but my hands are tied.'

'I know you can't do anything officially. It's just that you . . . seem to understand,' Ruth said, her voice trembling slightly. 'And Dad's . . . well, he's taken this new development really hard. I think it would help reassure him if he could ask you some questions.'

Karen closed her eyes, leaning back in her seat. Falkner would have a fit if he knew she was even thinking about this. But she remembered Mike's face when they'd found Lorraine. Sometimes the human connection had to trump following the rule book.

She wanted to unravel the mystery surrounding Ava's murder and its potential connection to Lorraine. Yes, Falkner would disapprove if she got involved, but Karen felt a responsibility to provide some support to Ruth and her father. A brief chat to reassure them couldn't be so bad, could it?

'Has no one from the investigation been to see you?' Karen asked.

'Yes, we spoke with DI Falkner and another officer yesterday . . . and we've had a visit from a family liaison. I think his name was Jim?'

'Oh yes, Jim Willson, he's good.'

'He was nice. But he doesn't understand. Not like you do.'

Karen weighed her options. She glanced at the dashboard clock, a plan forming in her mind. 'Are you home now?'

'Yes, Dad and I are both home. He lives with me now.'

'Okay,' Karen said, mentally calculating the time she would need. If she made a quick stop at the Claywoods' and then headed straight to Michelle's, she could manage both visits this morning.

Ten minutes to offer some reassurance and then be on her way. That seemed reasonable.

'I'll come over to you now,' Karen said, her decision made.

The relief in Ruth's voice was obvious. 'Thank you so much. It will mean a lot. I'll tell Dad you're coming.'

After the call ended, Karen started the car. She felt better being proactive, actually doing something useful.

Falkner might not like it, but Karen trusted her instincts.

Chapter Sixteen

Morning frost coated the trees along Willingham Road as Karen drove to the Claywoods' home in Market Rasen. She slowed as she saw the sign for the De Aston School car park and then turned on to Kingfisher Drive. Rows of new-build homes lined the street. She pulled up outside a well-kept house with a double garage and a sizeable driveway.

Grabbing her bag from the passenger seat, Karen stepped out and made her way up the drive. Before she could knock, the door swung open. Ruth Claywood greeted her with a warm smile.

'Detective Sergeant Hart, thank you so much for coming.' Ruth's hazel eyes crinkled at the corners as she gestured for Karen to enter. 'Please, come in, out of the cold.'

Karen followed Ruth into a bright, open-plan living space, taking in the homey decor and family photos lining the walls. The smell of freshly brewed coffee wafted from the kitchen area.

'Can I get you a tea or coffee?' Ruth asked, leading the way.

'Coffee would be lovely, thanks.'

Ruth pulled out a stool at the breakfast bar as Karen shrugged off her coat.

Ruth busied herself with mugs and the filter coffee machine, while Karen took the opportunity to study the other woman. Ruth appeared relaxed, her movements unhurried. But Karen sensed an undercurrent of nervous energy. Not surprising, given the circumstances.

A few minutes later, Ruth set a steaming mug in front of Karen, along with a small plate of biscuits. 'I know this must be difficult for you, after you've just lost your partner's mother. I appreciate you making time to talk to us.'

'I'm glad to help if I can.' Karen offered a reassuring smile, trying to put Ruth at ease. 'To be honest, it's been challenging. Losing a loved one in such a terrible way is devastating. You and your father must have needed incredible strength to get through it.'

Ruth's gaze drifted to the window, her eyes clouding with a haunted look. 'After Mum died, Dad was so determined to find her killer, to get justice. When that didn't happen . . .' She gave a defeated shrug.

The ache of Karen's own grief stirred within her, familiar and bitter. She understood that all too well – the need to find purpose and meaning in the wake of tragedy. 'Is your dad around?'

'He is. He's in the garden shed, tinkering, as usual. He always goes out there when he needs time to think. I did tell him you were on your way.' Ruth rolled her eyes good-naturedly. 'I'll give him a shout.'

As she headed outside to fetch her father, Karen checked her messages on her phone. She had an email from Callum Turner, the press officer, telling her the photographer had dropped his assault complaint.

'Good,' Karen muttered, shaking her head. The photographer had been making it up from the start. That had been clear from the security footage. It was a complete waste of everyone's time and resources. But she supposed an apology was too much to hope for. At least the ridiculous distraction was out of the way.

She looked around the brightly lit kitchen, taking in the photos of kids at different ages, the cheerful fridge magnets and the muddy trainers by the back door. It was a warm family home. Somehow Ruth and her father had found a way to carry on after Ava's death, but Ava's unsolved murder must have left dark shadows over the family.

The back door opened, and John Claywood stepped inside. Ruth followed.

He shrugged off his large winter coat, hung it on a hook by the door and made his way to the filter coffee maker, pouring himself a mugful.

He greeted Karen with a nod. 'Hello again.'

'Come and sit with us, Dad,' Ruth said, pulling out a stool.

John eyed the stool – a sleek, modern design with a very small seat – dubiously, as though he didn't trust it. 'Don't know what's wrong with a normal table and chairs.'

At seventy-nine, he had the wiry frame of someone who'd spent time working outdoors. The whites of his eyes held a slight yellow cast, and his hands were gnarled, the knuckles swollen from arthritis.

When John finally managed to get himself comfortable on the stool, Karen said, 'I was just telling Ruth that I'd really like to help you. But I'm not working on the investigation. Because Lorraine was someone I knew well, the rules stop me getting involved in any way that might affect the outcome.'

'How do you feel about that?' John asked.

Karen paused. It was a simple question, but the answer was anything but. She understood the reasoning. Yet, knowing why didn't stop the pain of being sidelined, especially when the case hit so close to home.

She wanted to help Mike, to give him answers about his mum, and make things right for the Claywoods. If there was even a chance these two cases were connected . . . But was she seeing links that weren't there, just because she needed to feel useful?

She couldn't bring Lorraine back, but she could do the next best thing and make sure the person who'd committed this evil act was caught, and maybe get the Claywoods some answers too.

Police work was the one thing she knew how to do, and without it she felt lost.

But to John, she simply said, 'It's difficult.'

'I wish I could have faith in the system,' he said, his tone betraying a hint of bitterness. 'But they let us down.'

'Well, they sent us a family liaison officer this time and he seems very good,' Ruth said.

Her father shook his head. 'All talk, no action.'

'Dad, that's not fair. They're trying.' Ruth cast an apologetic glance towards Karen.

He softened slightly. 'Sometimes trying's not enough. You need to have somebody involved who's got a burning need to get to the truth. And nobody has that more than people who've been directly affected, like me and you.' Then his gaze shifted from Ruth to Karen. 'And like you.'

He was right. It was the personal connection – the raw, emotional drive – that often made the difference. But Karen had boundaries she needed to respect.

'Can you tell me about the day Ava died?' she asked.

Ruth set her mug down. 'It was a lovely sunny day.' Her voice was steady, as if she were recounting a story that had happened to someone else.

Karen nodded, encouraging her to go on.

'Mum had taken the dog for a walk after work. Our old golden retriever, Max. When Max came back on his own, Dad tried to stay calm, but I could see he was worried.'

John stared at the table, jaw clenched tight.

'Dad reported her missing, of course. He didn't want to scare me, but there was an edge to his voice that I'd never heard before,'

Ruth continued, her hands gripping the coffee mug as if clinging to the present while being pulled back into the past. 'The following morning, they found her body near the water in Willingham Woods. She'd been strangled.'

'I can't imagine what that was like for you. Losing your mother at such a young age, and in such a horrific way.'

Ruth's eyes met Karen's. 'It changed me. Changed us both really. And I suppose I grew up faster than I should have. I had to.'

Karen imagined the young girl Ruth had been, her world turned upside down in an instant.

'When it came to my own kids, it made me vigilant. Perhaps overly so.'

'Those are your two boys?' Karen said, nodding at the collection of framed family photos on the wall.

Ruth smiled. 'Yes, both flown the nest now. I still check their location apps daily though. It drives them mad, but after what happened to their grandmother . . .'

'They're good lads,' John said, patting Ruth's hand. 'A credit to their mum.'

'I split from their father when the boys were young, and sadly they've had no contact with him since,' Ruth explained. 'He had an affair, and then started a new family. At first he'd see them at Christmas and birthdays, but after a few years he just stopped bothering.' She shrugged, but Karen caught the old hurt in her voice. 'It was hard on them, but we got through it.'

'She filled both roles,' John said, squeezing Ruth's shoulder. Karen could see how proud he was of his daughter.

'You played a big part, too, Dad.' Ruth smiled at Karen. 'I wouldn't have coped without him.'

'Nonsense. You would have. Don't let her fool you, Detective. This one's made of tough stuff. Practically one of your lot now, too.'

'Oh really?'

'Yes,' John said, beaming with pride. 'A PCSO. A crucial role. The police service could do with more people like her – ones who actually care.' There was an edge to his voice. 'After what happened with Ava's case . . . well, let's just say Ruth shows what proper dedication looks like.'

'I didn't want another family to endure what we went through,' Ruth said. 'It's why I became a PCSO, to make a difference, to help where I can.'

Karen understood that drive, the need to turn personal loss into something meaningful.

'I've tried to get Mum's case looked at again, and even got a few of the senior officers interested. But without new evidence . . .' She spread her hands helplessly. 'I just don't want to let Mum down. I think she'd want me to keep pushing for answers.'

'I'm sure your mother would be proud of the woman you've become.'

'She most definitely would,' John said firmly, his eyes watery.

Ruth nodded, unshed tears making her hazel eyes shine brighter. 'I hope so. I like to think she's watching over us. That she's proud of her grandchildren, and of the life Dad and I lived after she died.'

'And you both live here now?' Karen asked.

'Yes, though Dad took some persuading to move in. He said it was because he was too old to change, but I think it was because he couldn't bear to leave the memories behind.'

John nodded slowly. 'There's probably some truth to that.'

Karen understood. Memories were all they had left of the person they had loved and lost.

'What can you tell me about the original investigation into your wife's murder? Were there any major suspects?'

John Claywood's weathered features darkened, the lines on his face deepening as he let out a weary sigh. 'It was a disaster, if I'm honest. The police back then seemed to be chasing their tails most of the time.' He shook his head, and a hint of frustration entered his voice. 'No strong suspects. At least, none they told me about. Though, in their defence, they didn't exactly have it easy.'

'Why do you say that?'

'Ava worked for a man called Kenneth Prescott. Everyone local was terrified of him.' John scowled, and Karen sensed his anger simmering just beneath the surface. 'Cowards, the lot of them. They all turned a blind eye to what he did. They were too scared to say a word to help the police.'

Kenneth Prescott . . . the name wasn't familiar. 'Do you know why everyone was so afraid of him?'

'Some dodgy gangster type. Fancied himself as a wheeler-dealer. There were lots of rumours about his gambling rings, debt collection, violence. I begged Ava to quit working for him. But she wouldn't leave until she found another job. We were struggling with the mortgage payments back then, couldn't manage on my salary alone. If only I'd insisted . . .' John's voice cracked. 'Then afterwards, no one would talk about what happened,' he said, his voice bitter. 'No one came forward. Evil thrives when people don't speak out against it.'

Ruth looked down at her hands, and Karen felt a wave of sympathy – how many times had they been asked to dredge up these painful memories? Karen had sat with enough grieving families to know how overwhelming these conversations could be.

'I realised a long time ago that it's pointless to blame the person who killed my mother,' Ruth said. 'They're either mentally ill or just a monster. Hating them won't change what happened. It won't bring my mother back.'

John waved his hand dismissively and scowled. 'How can you say that? They deserve to suffer like Ava suffered. Even after all these years, I want them to pay for what they did. What upsets me most,' he continued, his voice rising with each word, 'is knowing people could have helped, but didn't. Her co-workers . . . they must have seen signs, or known something was wrong. But no one came forward.'

'I think they were scared,' Ruth said quietly. 'No one would talk to the police or Dad. I suppose it was easier for them to close their eyes to it and pretend everything was fine.'

'You always see the best in people,' John muttered, but his voice had lost its edge. He turned to look at Ruth properly, then smiled fondly. 'Your mother did that too. At one point I thought Ava might have got too close to something, something Prescott was involved in. I wondered if she'd been poking around, asking too many questions. And then . . .' He fell silent, leaving the implication clear.

Karen felt a chill. Could Chapman and Prescott have worked together back in the day?

She watched John struggling to contain his anger and grief. Years after losing Josh and Tilly, she still recognized that pain – the desperate need for answers, mixed with helpless rage at a world that just kept turning while yours had stopped. 'I'm so sorry you had to go through that,' she said softly. 'It must have been awful for you to see the investigation stall, with no one willing to come forward and help.'

John nodded, his gaze distant, lost in the painful memories. 'It's been a long time, but the pain never really goes away. I'm trying not to get my hopes up. But maybe this time the police will finally get some answers.'

'They'll do their best. I know most of the officers investigating Lorraine's death. They're first-class. If there is a link to Ava's murder, I'm sure they'll find it.'

John sniffed. 'I'd prefer it if it was you working the case.'

'Dad, Detective Hart has already explained why she can't get involved.' Ruth looked at Karen. 'I'm sorry.'

'It's okay,' Karen said. 'I understand. I promise you they'll do everything in their power to find out what happened to Ava. She deserves justice, no matter how long it's been.'

John offered her a small, grateful smile. 'I appreciate that, Detective. Ava would too.'

As Karen made her way back to her car, she mulled over what the Claywoods had said. This visit was supposed to have been just to reassure them, but she wondered how deeply the police had looked at Kenneth Prescott back then. If people in the surrounding area had been genuinely scared of him, that suggested there could be truth behind the rumours. Maybe there was something to John's theory of his wife having stumbled across something that would incriminate Prescott.

Karen pressed the fob to unlock her car and then paused as she sensed a presence behind her.

Turning around, she sighed.

Brilliant. Just brilliant.

There was no way her visit to the Claywoods would fly under Falkner's radar now.

Chapter Seventeen

Karen spotted the family liaison officer Jim Willson approaching. Across the street, Cindy Connor was leaning back against her car, a smug smile plastered across her face like the cat that got the cream. She gave Karen a little mocking wave. Karen ignored her, focusing her attention on Jim instead.

'Karen, I didn't realise you were working with the Claywoods,' he said, frowning.

'I'm not. At least not officially. I just popped in to reassure them.'

Jim scratched his head, his bewilderment growing. 'Right. It's just . . . does Falkner know about this?'

Karen's lips pressed into a tight smile. Of course Falkner didn't know. He'd have her hauled in for another lecture if he found out she was poking around unofficially.

'No, he doesn't. But I understand you'll need to tell him that you saw me here.'

'I don't want to get you into any trouble,' Jim said quickly, holding up his hands. 'You've been through a terrible time, and I don't want to add to it.'

Karen shrugged. 'It's fine. I didn't tell the Claywoods anything they didn't already know. I don't *know* anything, because nobody's *told* me anything. I'm completely frozen out, so it's not like I *could* tell them anything, is it?'

Jim blinked at her long-winded spiel, clearly at a loss. 'Well, I'm not really sure.'

A wave of guilt hit Karen. She was being unfair. 'Sorry to put you in a tricky position,' she said, sighing as she realised she was making Jim's life ten times harder. It wasn't Jim's fault. He was just here to do his job. 'But you can tell Falkner you saw me here, it's not a problem.'

'Really?' Jim looked sceptical.

'Yes, absolutely. The Claywoods just asked me for a chat because I understand. Because I've lost someone I knew too.'

Understanding flickered in Jim's eyes and he nodded slowly. 'Right. How are you holding up?'

'As well as can be expected.' Karen forced another tight smile. 'And Mike?'

'It's hit him hard. But I think he'll be all right in time.'

Jim's expression softened with sympathy. 'If there's anything you need, just let me know.'

'Will do.'

Karen watched him head towards the Claywoods' front door and ring the bell.

Then, as though she'd been waiting for her moment, Cindy Connor sashayed over, still wearing that infuriatingly smug look.

Karen braced herself for whatever game Cindy was playing now. The journalist never approached without an angle – was she fishing for information about Ava or Lorraine's case, or had she discovered some juicy detail of her own she wanted to dangle just out of reach?

'Hello, Karen,' Cindy said, her tone dripping with fake sweetness. 'I knew you wouldn't be able to leave it alone for long. You're looking into Ava Claywood's murder, aren't you?'

'Actually, Cindy, I was just here to offer my support.'

Cindy's perfectly arched eyebrows lifted higher. 'Sure.' The single word conveyed her disbelief. 'So, any new developments you want to pass my way?'

'No.' Karen opened the car door, tossing her bag on to the passenger seat with more force than necessary. She turned back to Cindy, eyes narrowing. 'What about you? Anything you feel like you should be sharing with the police? Since, you know, this is actually a murder enquiry?'

Cindy waved a manicured hand dismissively. 'I'd tell you if there was anything I thought you needed to know.'

Frustration bubbled up inside Karen. 'It isn't up to you to decide that, Cindy.' Her tone was clipped. She was tired of arguing with this infuriating woman who never listened.

Undeterred, Cindy looked over Karen's shoulder towards the Claywoods' house. 'I just saw Jim Willson go inside. He must have something to tell them. Development?'

Karen sighed. 'I don't know.'

'What do you mean you don't know?'

Gritting her teeth, Karen tried to keep her tone even. 'I told you before, I'm not working the case. I'm too close to it.'

'Yes, but surely they would have told you if there'd been a development. They're not really keeping you on the outside, are they?'

The question hung in the air, and Karen swallowed hard, saying nothing.

'They are.' Cindy tutted. 'That's really unfair. Don't they trust you to be logical? Do they think you're going to be too emotional about things?' She shook her head slowly. 'I bet they wouldn't do that if you were a man.'

'They would, Cindy,' Karen said. 'They'd do it to any officer. No one is allowed to work a case when they have a personal connection to it.'

Cindy's gaze was assessing. 'I know you. You're not just going to step back and let everybody else investigate this.' She shook her head again, and that maddening smirk returned. Karen had seen that expression enough times to know Cindy was already drafting headlines in her head: *Detective Goes Rogue* or some other sensational nonsense. 'You want to get involved. I can see it in your eyes.'

The words struck a nerve, and Karen clenched her fists at her sides. 'Of course I *want* to get involved. But I can't.'

'All right.' Raising her hands in mock surrender, Cindy took a step back. 'I'm just going to hang around here, wait till Jim's finished, and then see if the Claywoods would like to talk to me.'

'You should leave them alone, Cindy. They've been through enough. They don't need press intrusion on top of everything.'

Cindy scoffed. 'The press generate more interest in the case. The police were more than willing to wipe their hands of it all forty years ago. The Claywoods are pleased to get some publicity. They hope it might get them some answers, finally.'

As much as Karen wanted to physically drag Cindy away from the Claywoods' house, she knew it wasn't appropriate. Besides, she had somewhere to be.

She needed to speak to Mike's aunt, Michelle. Mike was struggling. He was trying so hard to cope with it all, but Karen could tell the grief was eating him up inside. She hoped meeting his mum's sister would help. It might give him something to hold on to – not just a new connection to his mum, but possibly answers about his father's identity. Anything that might shift his focus away from the horror of Lorraine's murder.

And even if she couldn't get any answers from Michelle, it had to be less frustrating than standing here talking to Cindy Connor.

Karen got into her car and glanced at her travel mug in the cupholder. It had a cartoon dog holding a coffee cup, with the slogan *Paws and Enjoy the Coffee*. A silly gift from Mike to make her smile. It usually did. But not today.

Across the street, a woman slammed the boot of her car. Karen watched her carrying shopping bags to her house, envying her the simple task. That woman had no murders, no interfering DI breathing over her shoulder and no infuriating journalist writing invasive stories to worry about.

Karen started to program the satnav. She probably had an hour or two before news of her visit to the Claywoods got back to Falkner. She needed to make the most of it.

Her mobile rang. It was Sophie. Karen answered on the car's speaker system.

'Hi, Karen.' Sophie sounded casual yet cautious. 'Just a heads-up – Falkner's been asking where you are this morning.'

Karen gripped the wheel. Surely he couldn't have found out about her visit to the Claywoods already? 'What did you tell him?'

'Not much. Said I hadn't seen you.' She paused. 'He wasn't best pleased.'

'I bet,' Karen muttered.

'Listen, Karen,' Sophie continued, 'no one would blame you for taking a few days off after everything that's happened. I wouldn't mind telling Falkner that, actually. He can be quite annoying.'

'I had noticed,' Karen said drily.

She wanted answers desperately. Going to see Michelle felt right. It could be the key to unlocking Lorraine's past and potentially the identity of Mike's biological father. But if Falkner was already on her case, pushing him further could backfire spectacularly.

She closed her eyes. If he hadn't already, Falkner would soon find out she'd visited the Claywoods. She should go to the station and let him know before anyone else did. Head off any trouble.

Winding up Falkner would only make things worse. But she was already frozen out of the investigation. Visiting Michelle might be her one chance to get some answers for Mike about his biological father. This wasn't about the investigation into Lorraine's murder. It was about helping Mike establish a connection with his mother's sister. Would Falkner see it that way, though?

She was already stuck on desk duty. But annoying Falkner could mean filling out paperwork until her pension kicked in. If he lodged a formal complaint about her behaviour, her career would effectively be over.

It was an impossible choice. Follow her instincts and risk Falkner's temper or play it safe. She felt torn in two, wanting to do both but knowing she couldn't.

Karen exhaled slowly. She couldn't risk losing her job or being suspended. Painful as it was, she had to play by Falkner's rules for now.

'It's all right,' she said. 'I'll head to the station now. Tell Falkner I'm on my way.'

'Great,' Sophie said, sounding relieved. 'Need me to tell Falkner to back off? I think I'd quite enjoy it.'

A small smile tugged Karen's mouth at the idea of Sophie, the most type-A officer she'd ever known, telling anyone in charge to back off. The old Sophie had been such a goody-goody. She would have been horrified at the thought of talking back to a senior officer. But surviving her attack seemed to have given her a quiet confidence – and apparently, a subtle rebellious streak. 'I appreciate the support, Sophie, but don't make an enemy of Falkner on my account. I can handle him.'

'I know you can. See you soon.'

The call ended. Karen sat in silence, glancing at the Claywoods' home. Her questions for Michelle would have to wait. For now, keeping Falkner sweet and letting him know about the visit to the Claywoods was a priority.

Whatever Michelle knew about Lorraine's past would have to wait.

Chapter Eighteen

The doorbell chimed a tinny rendition of 'Greensleeves', seemingly determined to play through all the verses. Arnie groaned, wondering if he'd be retired by the time it finished.

'Coming!' a muffled voice called from inside.

Arnie glanced at Morgan, who stood beside him on the porch, apparently unbothered by the cheesy doorbell. How did the man always manage to look like he'd just stepped out of a magazine? Even his raincoat seemed to repel water more efficiently than Arnie's, which had dark splodges dotted over its fabric. The way Morgan and DCI Churchill dressed always made Arnie feel like a scruff. He reckoned they did it on purpose.

The door creaked open, revealing a frail-looking man in a wheelchair. An oxygen tube snaked across his face from the tank attached to the back of the chair. The man's eyes, though clouded with age, held a sharp glint of intelligence.

'DCI Brian Whitmore?' Arnie asked, flashing his warrant card. 'I'm DS Hodgson, and this is DI Morgan. We were hoping to have a word about an old case of yours.'

'I got your message. I'm intrigued. Come on in, then. Mind the threshold. That thing's a menace with this chair.'

Arnie carefully manoeuvred around the wheelchair. The living room was cosy, if a bit cluttered. Family photos covered every surface, and a half-finished jigsaw puzzle sprawled across the coffee table.

'Make yourselves comfortable,' Whitmore said, gesturing to the sofa. 'The wife's upstairs working. She does some sort of computer job. Never could wrap my head around it.'

As they sat, Whitmore wheeled himself into position and took a couple of deep breaths. 'Sorry. Believe it or not, I used to be pretty fit. Now I'm tethered to this thing.' He wiggled the oxygen tube. 'Pulmonary fibrosis. Nasty business. Don't recommend it.'

Arnie nodded sympathetically, unsure what to say. He'd never been good at this part of the job. The small talk, the pleasantries . . .

He exchanged a glance with Morgan. The DI's face was as impassive as ever, but Arnie caught the slight tightening around his eyes. He was even worse than Arnie when it came to the human touch.

'Wife's still fit as a fiddle,' Whitmore said, his voice raspy. 'Works from home these days, keeping an eye on me.'

Arnie nodded, still unsure what to say. What did you say to a bloke who'd gone from chasing down murderers to being attached to an oxygen cylinder for the rest of his days? He settled for 'Thanks for seeing us, Brian.'

'Happy to help.'

Morgan, as usual, was straight down to business. 'We're here about the Ava Claywood case. From 1981.'

The change in Whitmore was immediate. His shoulders stiffened, and a haunted look crept into his eyes. 'Ava Claywood,' he muttered. 'Didn't think I'd hear that name again. Why now, after all these years? Are they reopening the case?'

Arnie leaned forward, elbows on his knees. 'We've had a new murder that might be connected. We were hoping you could walk us through the original case.'

Whitmore nodded, his gaze distant. '1981. I was a DI back then, thought I knew everything, but that case hit me for six.' He paused, taking a laboured breath. 'It felt personal, you know? Ava had a little girl, Ruth. Only twelve years old. The thought of that child growing up without her mum. It haunted me. Still does.'

Arnie felt a familiar tightness in his chest. Cases where kids were affected always hit harder, no matter how long you'd been on the job.

'Ava was strangled in Willingham Woods,' Whitmore continued. 'She'd been out walking the family dog. But the dog came home without her.' He shook his head. 'The community joined in a search. Found her the next day.'

Morgan nodded. 'Who found her?'

'A group of civilians who were involved in the search discovered her body by the water. We checked them all out, but none of them had any connection to Ava, and all had good alibis. Then everyone went quiet,' Whitmore continued, frustration evident in his voice. 'I was naive at the time. Still a little green as detectives go. Figured someone must know something and would speak up eventually. But people were too scared.'

Arnie frowned. 'Scared of what?'

'Who, more like,' Whitmore corrected. 'Ava worked for a nasty piece of work called Ken Prescott. Owned a few betting shops, but everyone knew he was running illegal betting on the side too. Proving it was a different story.'

'You thought Prescott was involved?' Morgan asked.

Whitmore nodded. 'I was sure it was him. Still am. We just couldn't get the evidence. My theory was that Ava had information that could damage Prescott, so he killed her. I sat outside his house in my car for days on end. I wanted to keep the pressure on, but he left for Brazil a few months after the murder. As far as I know, he's still there.'

Arnie exchanged a glance with Morgan. This was where things got tricky.

'Brian,' Morgan said carefully, 'the reason we're interested in this case after all this time is because a woman named Lorraine Harrington was murdered two days ago. She kept newspaper clippings about Ava's murder. Her husband said she was very upset over it and would often look at the newspaper stories.'

Whitmore frowned. 'Lorraine Harrington? Doesn't ring a bell.'

'That's her married name,' Morgan explained. 'Her maiden name was Matthews.'

A spark of recognition lit up Whitmore's face. 'I think I interviewed her at the time. She'd had a relationship with Prescott. Jittery whenever he was around. Timid little thing. She had a son with him. He was just a toddler at the time.'

A jolt of shock ran through Arnie. He met Morgan's gaze, seeing the same realisation dawn in the DI's eyes.

'Was the lad's name Mike?' Arnie asked.

Whitmore nodded. 'Yes, I think it was. Sweet little lad.' He frowned, his eyes sharpening. 'You're looking at the son as a suspect?'

Arnie was about to say no, but Morgan spoke first. 'We're exploring all possibilities. Standard procedure.'

Whitmore wheezed out a sigh. 'I suppose it makes sense. Statistically speaking, partners, sons or other male family members are usually responsible. Last I checked, it was something like eighty per cent.' He shook his head. 'Felt sorry for the little mite back then, having a father like Prescott. But sometimes I wonder if that kind of evil can be in the genes.'

'That's not a theory I subscribe to,' Morgan said, his tone clipped. 'Nurture over nature. From what we know, Mike's made a good life for himself.'

Arnie remained silent, torn between the grim statistics Whitmore had quoted and his own instincts about Mike. Morgan hadn't even mentioned the fact Mike was an ex-copper or that they knew Mike personally. But Morgan always played his cards close to his chest, never revealing more information than he had to, even though Brian Whitmore used to be a DCI.

Arnie didn't suspect Mike had any real involvement in what had happened. Apart from the fact the killer had sewn Lorraine's eyelids together – something that suggested a true hatred or a psychotic break – Karen had good judgement; she wouldn't have missed signs of a violent nature in her husband-to-be.

'I'm glad,' Whitmore said. 'It must have been hard for Lorraine, raising Prescott's son on her own. I thought she'd had a lucky escape when he left for Brazil.' He adjusted his oxygen tube. 'Why do you think Lorraine's murder might be related to Ava's case after all this time?'

'We don't. We only know that Lorraine was deeply affected by Ava's murder.' Arnie hesitated. Even after years on the job, some things never got easier to say. 'Her own murder was very different, at least in terms of methodology. Lorraine was found with her eyes sewn shut.'

Whitmore's face contorted in disgust. 'Awful,' he muttered. 'The evil that lurks in some people. I don't miss that part of the job.'

Arnie nodded, feeling the weight of it all pressing down on him. He described the murder scene, watching as both Morgan and Whitmore's expressions grew increasingly grim. It was tough to talk about, even for seasoned coppers like them.

When Arnie had finished, Morgan asked Whitmore, 'Was Ken Prescott ever known to do anything like that? The eye-sewing?'

Whitmore barked a harsh laugh that turned into a cough. He shook his head vehemently. 'Sew people's eyes shut? No. He was an evil so-and-so, but nothing like that. Ava was strangled, but her body wasn't mutilated.' He paused, considering. 'I was convinced it was Ken who strangled her, but we could never prove it. Might have better luck these days with DNA, if you can persuade the powers that be to reopen the case.'

Arnie nodded. 'Let's hope so. Good for Ava's family to get closure after all this time.'

Brian's expression softened. 'How is the family? John and little Ruth? I suppose John is long gone now.'

'John's still around,' Morgan said.

Brian's eyebrows shot up. 'Really? He hit the drink hard after Ava's murder. Ruth was like a little caretaker for a while. Poor kid. No child should have to deal with what she went through.'

'Ruth's done well for herself,' Morgan added. 'She's got kids of her own who are at university, and she's a PCSO now.'

A genuine smile spread across Whitmore's face. 'Is she really? That's wonderful. Good for her.'

'Thank you for your time,' Arnie said, shaking the old detective's hand. 'You've been a great help.'

Outside, the rain had finally stopped, leaving the world looking washed clean. If only it were that easy to wash away the stains of past crimes.

Morgan turned to Arnie as they headed towards their car. 'We need to get in contact with Prescott as a priority.'

'Agreed.' As they climbed into the vehicle, Arnie fastened his seatbelt and added, 'Though I've got a feeling this Prescott bloke is going to be about as cooperative as a bookmaker who's just seen a lame underdog win the Grand National.'

Chapter Nineteen

As Karen walked into the open-plan office and made her way to her desk, she noticed people avoiding her gaze. They quickly looked away or suddenly became engrossed in their paperwork.

Even Farzana, usually quick with a smile, kept her eyes glued to her computer screen as she passed.

Karen frowned. What was going on?

She reached her desk, which was even more cluttered than usual, case files and witness statements strewn haphazardly across the surface. Cunnings was sharing the desk until another space could be found.

Karen had just sat down and turned on her computer when Sophie appeared at her side, fidgeting with the sleeve of her suit jacket.

'Hi, Karen,' she said, her tone tentative. 'How are you?'

Karen eyed her warily. 'Just the same as I was when I spoke to you twenty minutes ago. Why?'

'Oh, no reason.' Sophie tried for a smile, but it didn't reach her eyes. She glanced over at Rick, who returned her worried look. 'It's just, well, you're taking this a lot better than I expected.'

'Taking *what* better than you expected?'

Sophie bit her lip. 'Have you checked your email?'

Karen didn't like the sound of that. 'No, not yet. Why?'

'You might want to have a look. But please, don't shoot the messenger.'

Karen turned to her computer and opened her inbox. There, at the top, sent half an hour ago, was an email from Falkner with the subject line *MANDATORY PRESS TRAINING*. She clicked it open.

Detective Hart,

As discussed, you are required to attend a media training workshop today to enhance your skills in dealing with press enquiries. This is a crucial aspect of modern policing. Please report to Meeting Room 2 at 10 a.m. where you will meet with Callum Turner from the press office for the training.

DI Falkner

Karen stared at the screen, her confusion rapidly turning into a simmering anger. *Discussed?* They had discussed no such thing. This was clearly Falkner's way of sidelining her, keeping her away from the investigation.

She looked up at Sophie, who was watching her cautiously.

'Press training? Today?' Karen tried to keep her tone even, but some of her frustration came through. She wanted to work to keep her mind occupied and off the horrible murder of Mike's mother. Not to be stuck in some training session, bored out of her mind.

Sophie nodded, looking miserable. 'I'm sorry, Karen. I know it's not ideal timing.'

That was an understatement. Mike's mother had been murdered. But instead of letting her help find out who did it, Falkner wanted her polishing her PR skills.

It was 10.12 a.m. She was late. But Falkner hadn't given much notice.

The door swung open and Falkner strode into the office with DS Cunnings trailing behind. Karen was on her feet in an instant, crossing the room to confront him.

'DI Falkner, what is this about mandatory press training? I never agreed to that.' She kept her voice low but her irritation was unmistakable.

Cunnings gave her a sympathetic glance, but it was clear Karen would have to fend for herself on this one.

'I'm sure we discussed it,' Falkner said, dismissively, attempting to walk around Karen.

She stepped to the side to block his path. 'And while I have you here, you should know that I visited the Claywoods this morning.'

Falkner's eyes narrowed, annoyance flickering across his features. 'You did what? Detective Hart, I specifically told you to stay away from this investigation.'

Karen stood her ground. 'I know. But I didn't tell them anything about the case. They reached out to me, and I wanted to offer my support, given the circumstances.'

Falkner rubbed his temples. 'While your compassion is admirable, Detective, your involvement in this case is not. Which brings us back to the press training. Media engagement is a critical skill for any modern detective. In light of recent events with that photographer in the car park, I think it's imperative you undertake this training.'

Karen gritted her teeth. 'I understand you need to keep me out of the investigation. But I want to help find who did this. For Mike's sake.'

Falkner's expression softened a fraction, but Karen wasn't fooled. That patronising head tilt made her want to scream. 'I know you do, Karen. But the best thing you can do right now is to step back and let the rest of us handle it. Focus on this training. It's not a punishment. It's a development opportunity.'

Karen wanted to argue, but she knew it would be pointless. Falkner had made up his mind. Resentment burned in her chest, but she had no choice but to give in, for now at least.

'Fine,' she said tightly. 'I'll do the training.'

'Excellent,' Falkner said. 'Callum will be waiting for you in meeting room two. Best not keep him waiting.'

As if on cue, the door swung open and in walked Callum, a friendly smile on his face. 'Detective Hart, I came to find you. I thought maybe you hadn't got the message about the training.'

It was his way of gently pointing out the fact she was extremely late. 'I've only just been told.'

'Shall we get started then?' Callum said. 'We've got a lot to cover: interview techniques, press release writing, social media dos and don'ts. It's going to be a jam-packed session!'

'Lead the way,' Karen said, trying and failing to inject enthusiasm into her voice.

As she followed Callum out of the main office, a thought struck her. In her irritation, she'd forgotten to ask Falkner if he'd got any new information from the officers who'd visited Michelle Matthews for a wellness check yesterday. It was highly unlikely Michelle knew anything about Lorraine's murder if she hadn't seen her sister for decades. But she still might have some insight into the Ava Claywood connection. Maybe she had known Ava.

Karen glanced back over her shoulder, but Falkner was already deep in conversation with DI Goodridge and Morgan. It would have to wait. For now, she had to play along with this press training charade.

But Falkner had another thing coming if he thought this would keep her out of the loop.

Karen followed Callum into meeting room two.

The room was empty except for her and the young press officer, who now stood awkwardly by the whiteboard. His highlighted quiff seemed to defy gravity, and his slim-fit shirt looked like it was trying to strangle him.

No one else was here for this media training. Just her. It was painfully obvious that Falkner intended to get her out of the way.

If she hadn't been sure this was a stitch-up before, she certainly was now.

'Detective Hart.' He cleared his throat. 'Thanks for attending today's course.'

Karen raised an eyebrow. 'It's not like I had much choice, Callum.'

'Oh, um. I suppose not. Shall we get started?' He laughed nervously, a high-pitched sound that made Karen wince.

She took a seat in one of the uncomfortable chairs, crossing her arms. 'By all means.'

He looked so anxious that Karen started to feel guilty. It wasn't his fault Falkner was so devious. Callum seemed like a good kid. Polite, enthusiastic . . . perhaps a little too enthusiastic.

Callum fumbled with the projector remote, eventually managing to bring up his first slide. 'So, um, today we'll be covering various aspects of media handling. Press conferences, impromptu interviews, social media etiquette—'

Callum droned on, and Karen found it hard to concentrate.

'Maintaining public confidence is crucial,' he said. His nervousness evaporated as he warmed to his topic. 'We're a service. That's why the terminology has changed. "Police force" implies power over people. "Police service" reminds us who we work for.'

Karen half listened, noting how his voice had grown stronger.

'Transparency. Accountability. These aren't just buzzwords,' he said. 'They're vital principles. The public needs to trust us, and trust has to be earned.'

He changed the slide to one with brightly coloured pie charts. 'Gone are the days of unquestioned authority,' he continued, cheeks flushed. 'And good riddance, if you ask me. We need oversight. Scrutiny. The press pick up on cover-ups. They keep us honest.'

Karen nodded absently, her thoughts still with the Claywoods. For four decades Ava's killer had walked free. How terrible must that have been for her family?

A young mother's life taken, leaving behind a grieving husband and a daughter who would grow up with only fading memories of her mother. Though somehow, despite the odds, John and Ruth Claywood seemed to have rebuilt their lives and remained close. They'd managed to keep going despite the pain.

She thought of Mike. Of the anguish in his eyes when they'd found Lorraine's body. So many lives had been shattered by senseless violence. So many families torn apart.

Usually she was the one asking questions, gathering evidence and trying to make sense of senseless deaths. But trying to help Mike through his grief was different – being both a detective and connected to the family of the victim had left her floundering. Even losing Josh and Tilly hadn't prepared her for this strange middle ground.

'Detective Hart?'

Karen blinked, realising Callum had stopped his presentation and was looking at her expectantly. 'Sorry, what was that?'

'I asked how you might handle things differently if approached by a press photographer in the future?'

Karen felt a flare of annoyance. 'Handle things differently? I don't think I did anything wrong in the first place.'

'Well, pushing the camera—'

'I hardly touched it,' Karen interrupted. 'That photographer was harassing me. He's lucky all I did was push his camera away.'

Callum swallowed nervously. 'I understand your frustration, but we have to maintain a professional image—'

'Professional? That vulture was anything but professional.'

'Yes, but as representatives of the police service, we need to—'

'We need to protect people,' Karen cut in. 'That's our job. Not pander to sensationalist hacks looking for their next story.'

Callum looked like he wanted to melt into the floor. 'I know it can be challenging, especially when emotions are running high, and you're going through a very difficult time. But there are protocols we need to follow. It might have been different back when you first joined the police, but—'

'When I *first* joined the police?' Karen repeated, her voice rising. 'Just how old do you think I am, Callum?'

She stared at him. She was only just in her forties. Still, she supposed to someone in their early twenties, like Callum, that probably seemed ancient.

The young man's face turned an even deeper shade of red. 'I didn't mean . . . That is to say . . . I just meant that policing has changed over the years, and—'

'And you think I'm some fossil who can't keep up with the times?' Karen asked, torn between amusement and exasperation.

'No! Not at all!' Callum looked like he was about to have a panic attack. 'I have the utmost respect for your experience. I just meant that media relations have become a more integral part of policing in recent years.'

Karen leaned back in her chair, a smile playing on her lips. 'Relax, Callum. I'm not going to bite your head off. Though I might be tempted to if you keep implying I'm past it.'

Callum let out a nervous laugh. 'Right. Sorry. I'll just continue with the presentation, shall I?'

As he turned back to his slides, Karen's thoughts drifted once again. This time, she thought about Michelle Matthews. The woman who might hold the key to understanding Lorraine's past. Karen had promised Mike she'd speak to his aunt. That suddenly felt far more important than this press training nonsense.

'So, as you can see from this graph,' Callum was saying, 'the number of social media interactions has increased dramatically over the past five years. This means we need to be extra vigilant about—'

'Callum,' Karen interrupted, standing up. 'I'm sorry, but I can't do this right now.'

The young man's face fell. 'I didn't mean to offend you earlier—'

'It's not you,' she assured him. 'This just isn't where I need to be right now.'

'But what about the training?' Callum asked, looking panicked. 'DI Falkner said it was mandatory.'

Karen gathered her things. 'Tell Falkner I had a family matter to attend to.'

'A family matter?' he repeated, his voice rising an octave.

She paused at the door, turning back to face him. 'That's right.'

Callum opened and closed his mouth a few times, looking like a fish out of water. 'But should I tell DI Falkner we didn't finish the training?'

Karen smiled, feeling sorry for the young press officer. She didn't blame him for not wanting to get on Falkner's bad side. 'Tell him whatever you want, Callum. Tell him I was an exemplary student. Tell him I had to leave unexpectedly. Or tell him the truth. That there are more important things than press releases and social media etiquette when there's a murderer on the loose.'

She strode out of the room, leaving a bewildered Callum gaping after her. As the door clicked shut behind her, Karen took a deep breath. There would be consequences for her walking out, but right now, she couldn't bring herself to care.

Chapter Twenty

Arnie tried his best to look attentive as Falkner blathered on about protocol and press statements. The briefing room felt stuffy, and Arnie's mind wandered to the half-eaten packet of biscuits on his desk. He always thought about snacking when he was bored. What he wouldn't give to be out there, doing real police work, instead of being stuck in here listening to Falkner's greatest hits.

'Hodgson.' Falkner's sharp voice cut through Arnie's thoughts. 'Care to update us on your chat with Brian Whitmore?'

Arnie cleared his throat and summed up what Whitmore had told him. Before Falkner could respond, the door opened and Harinder Singh strode into the room.

'Sorry to interrupt,' he said, holding up a piece of paper. 'You need to see this. We've been going through Lorraine's emails, and I found this.' He handed the sheet to Falkner. 'It's an email she sent just days before she died.'

Arnie leaned forward, suddenly interested.

Falkner's eyes scanned the document, his frown deepening. 'Sent to someone by the name of Ken at a company called Presallion Exports?'

'Yes,' Harinder said. 'They're based in Brazil. Been trading for about thirty years.'

Arnie's copper's senses were tingling. 'Let me guess, the company is owned by Kenneth Prescott?'

Harinder nodded. 'Got it in one.'

Falkner cleared his throat and began to read the email aloud:

Ken,

I hope this email reaches you. I've no other way of getting in contact. It's taken me decades, but I've finally found the courage to write this.

Secrets have shaped my life for too long. It's time to face the music whether I'm ready for it or not.

I know the risks of reaching out to you. The memories of your threats and violence have never left me. But I can't do this anymore. You deserve to know that I can't – and won't – keep silent any longer.

I've denied the truth for years out of fear – fear of you, fear of the past. But I won't let that fear control me any longer.

This isn't a threat. It's a plea for understanding. I want you to be prepared. Please, don't try to stop me. We both know what you're capable of, but this has to end.

I've kept things secret long enough.

Lorraine

The room fell silent as everyone tried to process this new information. It seemed to imply what Whitmore had told them:

that Prescott was Mike's natural father. And it sounded like Lorraine had been about to break the news to Mike before she died.

It fit with Morgan's theory about Lorraine's illness being a catalyst for her sudden desire to do the right thing.

But was this really just about Mike's parentage? It seemed a tad dramatic to Arnie if that was what the email was about. Why not just sit the lad down and tell him his father was a bit of a wrong'un, but that it was all in the past? No need for emails and all that fuss – and certainly no need for anyone to kill her. It made Arnie suspect there was something more to be found. Another secret Lorraine knew about Prescott perhaps?

'Well,' Arnie said, breaking the stunned silence. 'That's certainly interesting.'

'Thank you, Harinder,' Falkner said. 'Is there anything else?'

'Not yet. That particular email had been deleted from the computer, hence the delay. We found it on a backup. I'll let you know if we come across anything else.'

He left the room.

Sophie spoke up, her voice hesitant. 'But what did Lorraine mean by "the truth"? Was she talking about the identity of Mike's biological father, or something else?'

Rick nodded, frowning. 'It's a bit vague, isn't it? Could be interpreted a couple of ways.'

Arnie scratched his chin. 'I agree. On one hand, she could have been talking about her plans to tell Mike his biological father was Prescott. But on the other—'

'She could be threatening to expose some past crime that Prescott was involved in,' Cunnings finished for him.

Falkner paced the room, his earlier irritation replaced by intense focus. 'Either way, it gives Prescott a motive. If Lorraine was planning to reveal something he wanted kept quiet . . .'

'But he has a pretty good alibi,' Sophie pointed out. 'He's been in Brazil for the past forty years, hasn't he?'

'We need to make sure,' Falkner said. 'Double-check he hasn't been back. We need to be one hundred per cent certain.'

Arnie leaned back in his chair, thinking. 'Even if he hasn't been back, he could have arranged it from abroad. Man like Prescott, he's bound to have connections.'

Falkner nodded. 'Very true. We need to dig deep into Prescott's background, his associates, anyone who might have done this for him.'

'What about Mike?' Rick asked, his voice quiet. 'Should we tell him about this?'

The room fell silent again. Arnie felt a pang of sympathy for Mike. Finding out your dad was a notorious criminal, who might have murdered your mother, wasn't exactly a cheery bit of news.

Falkner shook his head. 'Not yet. We need more information before we drop this bombshell. For now, this development doesn't leave this room. Understood?'

Everyone nodded, the gravity of the situation hitting them hard.

'Besides,' Falkner continued, his eyes narrowing, 'we can't rule out Mike's involvement just yet. For all we know, Lorraine told him this secret she's referring to in the email, and he snapped.'

Sophie's head jerked up. 'Mike's not the type to do something like that. He wouldn't—'

'With respect, DC Jones,' Falkner cut in, 'the fact you know Mike is a problem. Your judgement could be clouded.'

'It's not,' Sophie said, her voice tight, 'Karen's been with Mike for ages now. We all know he's not capable of—'

'That's precisely my point,' Falkner interrupted, his tone sharpening. 'I can't have personal relationships interfering with this investigation. That's why Cunnings and I were brought in – to keep emotional distance from the case.' He paused, his gaze fixed on Sophie. 'Perhaps it would be better if we removed you from the investigation entirely.'

She stiffened. 'I can assure you, sir, my personal feelings won't interfere with the investigation.'

'Hang on,' Arnie interrupted. 'Now this is nothing to do with my knowing Mike, but this crime doesn't feel like a fit of temper to me. Sewing Lorraine's eyes shut? That's cold. Methodical. It's not something you'd usually see from a hot-tempered son who'd "snapped".'

Falkner considered this, then gave a curt nod. 'Fair point, Hodgson. Still, I don't want Mike informed. Not yet.' His gaze swept the room. 'And that goes double for Karen. Not a word to her, understood?'

Arnie noticed Sophie flinch slightly. She idolised Karen; keeping this quiet would be hard for her.

'Right,' Falkner said, seemingly satisfied with their silent agreement. 'Hodgson, I want you to track down Prescott. Find out if he's been back to the UK. Land, sea or air, I want to know if he's stepped foot in this country in the last few weeks. Cunnings, focus on Prescott, too. Dig into his past, his associates, anything that might connect him to this murder. Jones, Cooper, you're still on Lorraine's background. Go through her life with a fine-toothed comb. There might be more skeletons in her closet we don't know about yet.' He gathered up a few loose papers. 'One more thing: Hodgson, Cooper, don't forget to go and have a word with Chapman. Let him know we haven't forgotten about him. Keep up the pressure – he needs to know we're still watching.'

Arnie nodded, already dreading the mountain of phone calls and paperwork ahead. Still, at least it was better than sitting through more of Falkner's lectures.

He glanced at Sophie, who looked as troubled as he felt. 'Fancy getting a coffee before we make a start?' he asked.

She nodded. 'I have a feeling I'm going to need it.'

As they walked towards the coffee machine, Arnie's mind wandered to Karen. He was glad she wasn't here for this. He made a mental note to check in on her later.

'So,' Sophie said as Arnie wrestled with the coffee machine, 'what's your take on all this?'

Arnie grunted, giving the machine a gentle thump. It spluttered to life, dispensing what he hoped was coffee and not some form of toxic sludge. 'I think we've stumbled into a right mess.'

He handed Sophie a mug, then took a sip from his own, wincing at the bitter taste. This was why he usually went down to the canteen. But they were in his bad books at the moment – he wasn't giving them his custom until proper sausages were back on the menu.

'Prescott being Mike's dad, that's one thing,' Arnie said. 'But if Lorraine was mixed up in some of Prescott's dodgy dealings back in the day . . .'

Sophie's forehead creased in thought. 'It could explain why she kept Mike's paternity secret all these years. Maybe she was protecting herself as much as Mike.'

'What could Prescott have done that was so bad, Lorraine felt she had to hide it for decades?'

'Could he have been involved in Ava Claywood's murder?' Sophie suggested.

Arnie shrugged. 'Possibly. DCI Whitmore was convinced Prescott strangled Ava. But Prescott was suspected of illegal betting, money laundering, that sort of thing. Violent crime wasn't really his style.'

'We don't have a record of him being violent. That doesn't mean he wasn't.'

'True. I almost hope Prescott is back in the country. If he did kill Ava, we should be able to prove it with DNA now. It was different back in the eighties.'

They lapsed into silence, lost in thought as they sipped their bitter coffees. Arnie's mind kept circling back to Mike and Karen. How would they react when they found out about all this? It was bound to cause some tension, to say the least.

They didn't deserve this. Why did awful things happen to good people?

In all his years in the job, Arnie had never found a satisfying answer to that question.

Chapter Twenty-One

Karen pulled her car up to the kerb on Windsor Way in the small town of Broughton, which was nestled between the larger towns of Scunthorpe and Brigg. The drive had taken her half an hour.

The frosty chill of the morning had given way to a damp, overcast day. The gardens along the residential street were a patchwork of muted greens, browns, and soggy grass.

This was where Michelle Matthews – Lorraine's estranged sister – supposedly lived, according to the address Sophie had provided. Karen eyed the row of bungalows lining the gently curving road. The neighbourhood felt open and pleasant, if a bit dreary in the grey weather.

Michelle's place stood out – a sandy brick bungalow with a neatly tended garden. Even in the dead of winter, a few evergreen plants remained glossy and green. A gravel driveway led to a cheerful red garage door. There was no car in the driveway. Karen hoped Michelle's car was in the garage and that she hadn't gone out.

Perhaps she should have phoned first.

The white front door was framed by a simple trellis, which was bare of any climbing plants except for some well-pruned roses at the base.

Karen didn't notice the front door was ajar until she was about to ring the doorbell.

A jolt of shock ran through her. It was unsettlingly similar to how she and Mike had found Lorraine's front door open before they'd found her body.

It's probably nothing, Karen told herself. *Don't read too much into it.* Michelle had likely just not closed it properly. Karen rang the bell.

After waiting a few moments with no response, she rang again, frowning. She listened for any sounds from inside the house, but it was quiet. Cautiously, she pushed the door open a bit further, peering inside.

'Hello? Mrs Matthews? It's Detective Sergeant Hart from Lincolnshire Police.' Her voice was loud in the stillness. 'I'm here to speak with you about your sister, Lorraine. Are you home?'

Still no answer. Karen's heart began to race as she stepped across the threshold. Tense, she moved further into the bungalow, senses on high alert. This didn't feel right.

'Mrs Matthews?' she called out again, with growing concern. 'Michelle?'

She turned into the living room first. It was empty. The room was cosy, with a large flatscreen TV mounted on the wall and a cream sofa facing it. The wallpaper had a shiny pattern that caught the light.

Most of the photographs on the wall showed a smiling woman Karen didn't recognise. She scanned the frames quickly for Lorraine or Mike, but there were no photos of them.

Nothing seemed out of place or disturbed.

She paused, listening intently for any sound of movement or life.

'Police! Is anyone home?' Karen tried again, even louder this time. But the bungalow remained unnaturally quiet, the stillness broken only by the soft ticking of a clock on the mantelpiece.

Karen moved on to the bedroom next. It was neat and tidy, the bed made.

A tapping sound made Karen flinch. But it was just a branch from a magnolia tree brushing against the window.

Finally, Karen reached the dining area. A chair was overturned, as if there had been a struggle. Karen stepped over it, and into the long galley-style kitchen on the left. That's when she saw her.

A woman, lying motionless on the tiled floor.

Karen's breath caught in her throat as she took in the horrific sight, her mind struggling to process the gruesome scene.

The woman was deathly pale, her skin almost greyish. Vivid red blood had formed a small pool around her head. She wore a pink dressing gown, the fabric bunched and twisted around her body.

There was no mistaking the unnatural stillness.

But the most horrifying detail was her eyes.

Just like Lorraine, the woman's eyelids had been crudely sewn shut with black thread, the ragged stitches shocking against the pale skin.

'Not again,' Karen whispered.

She'd walked into countless crime scenes over the years. But this one stole the air from her lungs. For a moment she couldn't move, couldn't breathe.

Another victim with sewn eyes.

First Lorraine, now Michelle.

Mike's mother and aunt must have been murdered by the same person. Why was the killer fixated on Mike's family?

She approached cautiously, crouching down beside the body, forcing herself to breathe. A part of her brain knew there was no point, that it was too late, but training and instinct compelled her to check.

Gently, she reached out with trembling fingers and pressed them to the woman's neck. The skin was still warm but felt lifeless under her touch. No pulse.

Straightening up, Karen pulled her phone from her pocket. She couldn't disturb things any further. This was now a crime scene, just like Lorraine's house had been. Another victim of this deranged killer.

Why hadn't Michelle taken their advice and stayed somewhere else for a few days? Karen should have pushed the point harder. If she had, maybe Michelle would still be alive.

Windsor Way was rammed with investigators. Police and SOCO vehicles were parked along the kerb, and officers bustled in and out of the bungalow.

Karen stood on the pavement, arms wrapped tightly around herself in a futile attempt to stop shivering. The murder scene kept replaying in her mind, each detail digging itself deeper into her memory.

How was she going to break this news to Mike? Not only had he lost his mother in the most horrific way, he'd now lost an aunt too. One he'd only just learned he had. The murders had to be connected, but why Lorraine and her sister? Did it mean that other family members could be at risk? Mike? Karen's trembling intensified as the thought sent pure terror through her. She couldn't lose anyone else she loved. The idea of something happening to Mike made her feel physically sick.

Morgan had spent a few minutes with Karen, checking she was okay and asking questions. He'd told her Raj was examining the body in the kitchen. When Farthing and Raj had emerged from the bungalow a few minutes later, their expressions were grave.

Just then, Karen felt the weight of Falkner's piercing stare. He was furious.

'I hope you have a good explanation for coming here, DS Hart,' he said. 'After I instructed you to stay away from this investigation.'

'Michelle Matthews was Mike's aunt,' Karen explained, trying to stop her teeth chattering. 'Lorraine's sister. I wanted to reach out to her on Mike's behalf.'

The words were partly true, though not the whole story. She'd also hoped to find out the identity of Mike's biological father and unravel the secrets buried in Lorraine's past.

But her questions would remain unanswered, because the poor woman was now lying dead in her kitchen.

Falkner ran a hand through his hair, clearly exasperated. 'Did you not think to tell me about your plans to come here?' He shook his head, carrying on ranting before Karen had a chance to defend herself.

Karen wanted to explain, to make him see that she wasn't actually trying to interfere but just wanted to help Mike. But from the look on Falkner's face, she didn't think he'd be in the mood to listen to her explanation, even if she could get a word in edgewise.

'Well, do you have anything to say to justify your behaviour?' he demanded.

Before Karen could gather her thoughts into a coherent sentence, Morgan stepped forward, his hand resting on her shoulder. The simple gesture eased her shivering by a fraction. 'Karen has just had quite a shock. Perhaps we could talk about this later?'

'I agree,' Cunnings chimed in from behind them. Karen hadn't even known she was there. She gave Karen a sympathetic smile. 'And it's reasonable for Karen to want to visit Mike's aunt.'

'It's far from reasonable to go off on her own recklessly,' Falkner said. 'Your behaviour has been extremely irresponsible, Karen. First Chapman, then the Claywoods, and now this!'

She'd just discovered Michelle's body. Couldn't he give her a few minutes to recover before launching into a dressing-down?

Yes, she'd seen dead bodies before, but this case was shocking. Seeing Michelle like that had brought back all the memories of finding Lorraine the same way. She gritted her teeth and resisted the urge to tell Falkner to shove his condescending attitude up his backside.

But Falkner wouldn't stop. 'Well? What do you have to say for yourself? How do you justify rushing over here alone?'

'I didn't rush anywhere,' Karen snapped, her frustration boiling over. 'That's the problem. I should have rushed . . . We should've been here sooner. That torn "M" page from Lorraine's address book. The killer likely ripped it out to get Michelle Matthews's information. If we'd acted earlier, maybe we could have found her before this happened.' Karen's voice caught as the grim reality of Michelle's death hit her again. 'What happened to the officers you sent to inform Michelle of her sister's death?'

'They called round yesterday, but there was no answer.'

'And you didn't find that concerning?'

Falkner's gaze sharpened. 'They were told to try again later today. My team has been working this case non-stop. You're not privy to all the details.'

The accusation stung, making Karen's cheeks heat with anger. 'Because you shut me out!' she shot back. 'If I'd been properly involved, maybe Michelle would still be alive. You didn't do your job properly.'

As her words landed, Karen saw their impact on Falkner. He flinched like she'd hit him.

Maybe she had gone too far. But at that moment she was filled with guilt over Michelle's death and meant every word. It wasn't just Falkner who'd failed Michelle. It was her too. She should have come to speak to her yesterday, as soon as Chapman had told her about Michelle.

If Karen had been able to speak to Michelle, maybe she could have persuaded her to go somewhere safe for a few days.

Karen caught the pleading look Cunnings gave Morgan, urging him to intervene before things escalated.

Morgan stepped in, positioning himself between her and Falkner. 'Karen, I know you're upset, but having a go at DI Falkner like this won't solve anything.' He turned to Falkner. 'And you're aware of how deeply this case has affected Karen. We're on the same side. We're all trying to find answers.'

Cunnings nodded. 'We all want to catch the evil person responsible for this, but fighting amongst ourselves isn't the way.'

The fury had drained from Falkner's face, leaving him looking merely irritated. 'You're right, of course. This is an extremely challenging situation for you, Karen.'

Karen felt her anger dissipating under the calming influence of Morgan and Cunnings. Despite her urge to lash out, they were trying to help. It was easy to see things in hindsight.

Taking a deep breath, she steadied herself. 'I apologise, I crossed a line.'

An uneasy silence lingered before Falkner spoke again, his voice composed. 'Why don't we continue this conversation back at the station later . . . when things aren't quite so heated?'

There was an awkward silence until Tim Farthing approached and cleared his throat. 'Can we get back to the matter at hand now?' he asked, oblivious to Falkner's foul mood.

'What is it?' Falkner snapped.

Unfazed, Tim continued, 'Raj said the cause of death appears to be a blow to the back of the head, just like Lorraine Harrington's murder. There's also the crude stitching of the eyelids, which is a disturbing similarity. I'm not a detective, but even I can see these two murders are linked.'

'Thank you, Tim,' Morgan said, taking charge. 'How long do you think you'll need to work the scene?'

'A couple more hours, at least, I think,' Tim replied. 'We'll do a thorough search, to look for further evidence. If we're lucky we might find whatever the killer used to hit her with.'

Morgan nodded slowly and put an arm through Karen's, leading her away from Falkner and the rest. 'Do you want me to drive you home? I can get someone to bring your car back.'

'No, thanks. I'll be okay.'

She wanted to drive home alone to clear her head, and process things before she had to break the news to Mike.

'How am I going to tell Mike?' Karen asked. 'I don't think he can take much more.'

Morgan's expression softened. 'It's a horrible situation. I'm sorry.' After a pause, he added, 'What about James? Did he know Michelle?'

'I don't think so,' Karen said, shrugging. 'As far as I know, Lorraine hadn't had anything to do with her sister for years. Mike was shocked when I told him about her. They'd obviously been close once because Chapman knew about Michelle, but something must have caused them to fall out, I suppose.'

She shivered again. 'This is now two members of the same family. Do you think Mike's at risk? He's at work today because he wants to keep busy, so he doesn't keep thinking about what's happened, but is he safe?'

'I really don't know,' Morgan said honestly. 'But we'll make sure he is. We'll get a unit on him specifically. We've kept the officers watching your house, of course, but if he's at work, maybe we need to assign more officers there during the day. Churchill will be ecstatically happy to spend more of the budget, I'm sure.'

He was trying to make Karen smile with the dig about Churchill and his budget, but she couldn't, her face felt frozen.

'Look, I know I can't officially be part of this investigation, but it's killing me,' Karen said. 'I need to know what's going on. Please tell me. I'm not just an ordinary person who's connected to the victim.'

A flicker of tension crossed his face. 'Karen, you know that—'

She cut him off. 'All I know is that you're my friend, and you should tell me.'

Morgan glanced around at the curious neighbours peering out of their windows, and the small crowd gathered near the SOCO van. 'Let's not talk about it here,' he said. 'We'll discuss it later. Go home, I'll come and see you and Mike later, all right? Tell you what we've found.'

'Thanks,' Karen said, though she wasn't convinced Morgan would keep his promise.

She admired him, liked him, cared about him . . . but did she really trust him to go against the rules and tell her what was going on?

If she was honest, she didn't.

Morgan was a stickler for procedure.

Sophie, on the other hand . . . Karen was sure Sophie would tell her everything.

Chapter Twenty-Two

Karen slammed her car door shut and grabbed her mobile, her fingers trembling. She wasn't about to break news like this over the phone, but she desperately needed to hear Mike's voice, to know he was okay.

She planned to ask him to meet her at home for lunch so she could tell him face to face about his aunt.

But Mike wasn't answering.

A cold, unwelcome thought crept into her mind. What if he couldn't answer? What if he was hurt?

'Don't be silly,' she muttered, shaking her head. She was on edge. She'd just found a body; a woman brutally murdered and left with mutilated eyes. It was natural to feel scared. Mike probably just had his phone on silent, that was all.

'Hi, Mike, it's me,' she said, trying to sound upbeat as she recorded a message on his voicemail. 'Give me a call when you get this. Can you meet me for lunch at home? I need to talk to you.'

Forty minutes later, Karen pulled into the empty driveway. No sign of Mike's car.

She checked her phone. No calls, no texts.

She went indoors, flicked the kettle on, and dialled Mike's number again. A faint, tinny ringing drifted from upstairs.

'Oh, great,' she grumbled, taking the stairs two at a time. Mike's phone sat on his nightstand, the screen flashing.

He must've left for work without it. So unlike him, but then again, their lives were far from normal these days. After his mum's murder, it was no surprise he was distracted.

Karen's mind flashed to Lorraine and Michelle, their faces pale, those horrible black stitches over their eyes. A fresh wave of fear washed over her. This killer had already targeted them both. What if Mike was next?

He could handle himself, sure. He was ex-police, still strong as an ox despite his leg injury. But the idea of Mike caught off guard, vulnerable . . . Maybe turning his back on the killer and—

She had to push that thought away before it overwhelmed her.

She called Morgan, made sure he'd assigned officers to shadow Mike at work. After Morgan's reassurances, she relaxed a bit. Would going to Mike's work be overkill? He was training today, and by the time she got there his lunch break would be nearly over.

She decided to call his office instead. If he was outside, exercising the dogs, he wouldn't hear the phone, but it was worth a try.

The ringing seemed to stretch on forever. Just as she was about to give up, he answered. 'Mike Harrington.'

Relief flooded through her. 'Hi, you left your phone at home this morning.'

'Yes, I noticed as soon as I got to work,' he said. 'Did you need me for something?'

Karen hesitated. This wasn't phone-conversation material, but could she wait? The thought of something happening to Mike because she'd kept quiet was unbearable. He needed to be on guard.

'Morgan's assigned some officers to keep an eye on you at work,' she said, her voice catching slightly. 'They won't get in the way. They're just there to make sure you're safe.'

'Are you sure that's necessary?'

She rubbed at her temple, knowing she couldn't keep this from him any longer. If his safety was at risk, he had to know.

'Actually, I've got some bad news.'

A beat of silence, then he said, 'More bad news? Well, I doubt it can be as bad as what we've already had, so go on.'

'You know I went to speak to Michelle today? Well, she's dead, Mike. Same as your mum. Eyes sewn shut and everything. Looks like the same killer did it.'

Silence stretched between them. Why had she blurted it out like that? Why hadn't she phrased it more compassionately? She should have gone and told him in person. She'd completely misjudged this.

She was falling back on her police training like a safety blanket – clinical, detached. But Mike wasn't a member of the public to be notified, or part of the investigating team. He was her partner, and his mother had just been murdered. He needed comfort and understanding, not a police report.

'Mike?'

'Yes,' he said quietly. 'Yes, I heard you.'

'I'm so sorry,' Karen said, feeling helpless. 'I know this is a huge shock.'

Another pause. 'Must've been awful for you, finding her like that. Are you okay? Need me to come home?'

'I'm all right,' Karen lied. 'If you want to finish the training sessions today, I understand.'

'I've only got two more clients, so I shouldn't be too long.'

'All right. But two people, both related to you, have been targeted. I'm worried, Mike. I think we should tell James and warn him, just in case.'

Mike sighed heavily. 'I suppose we should. But I didn't even know Michelle. Are we really sure she was my aunt? We only have Chapman's word for it at the moment, right?'

'The team will be looking into that – birth certificates and such,' Karen said. 'But I think warning James is the right move.'

'Could you call him?' Mike asked, sounding exhausted. 'I'm really tied up with this training. I should've cancelled it, my head's not really in it, but . . .'

'Mike, what's really going on with you and James? He wouldn't have just gone off to stay at a hotel for no reason.'

A long pause. 'I messed up and said something I shouldn't have.'

'What happened?'

'He told me he was feeling pushed out with all this talk about my biological father. And I just snapped. Told him he was being ridiculous, and I didn't have the energy to deal with him being needy and insecure.'

'Oh, Mike.' Karen imagined how deeply those words must have hurt James.

'I know,' Mike said quietly. 'The moment it came out of my mouth I regretted it. But I don't know why he's making such a fuss. None of this is about finding a new father – it's just about understanding where I came from. He knows he's the only father I'll ever need or want.'

'But that's just it,' Karen said. 'He doesn't actually know that, does he? Why don't you tell him?'

Mike sighed. 'I'm not really up for a deep heart-to-heart right now. Could you . . . Would you talk to him? He's fond of you. If I try, I'll just make it worse. Probably tell him he's being silly and to man up or something.'

Karen shook her head. Telling James he was being silly would *really* not help matters. 'I'll speak to him,' she said. 'But eventually, James needs to hear this from you. You'll both feel better when the air's cleared. And Mike, are you okay? I mean, relatively speaking. This news about Michelle is a lot to process.'

'I just want things to be normal,' Mike said, his voice weary. 'I want to have a few hours free from thinking about all this.'

'I know. Me too. Look, when you come home we can—'

The doorbell rang, a sudden, piercing sound that made Karen jump.

'Is there someone there? Who is it?' Mike's voice was sharp with alarm. 'Don't answer the door if you don't recognise them.'

She peered through the window and relaxed. 'It's okay, it's just Sophie and another colleague from work.'

'You're sure you're all right?'

'I'm fine, really,' Karen assured him, not entirely truthfully. 'Just a bit on edge from earlier, that's all.'

'Okay. I'll keep an eye out for the officers Morgan's sent to keep tabs on me.'

'It's for your own safety.'

'I know, and I'm grateful for it. I'll see you later.'

After Mike hung up, Karen let Sophie and Bridget Cunnings in.

'Well, you're both looking very serious,' Karen said as she shut the door behind them. Sophie and Cunnings shuffled into the hallway, avoiding her gaze. Cunnings kept her eyes downcast, while Sophie wrung her hands.

Karen's stomach tightened. This couldn't be good. 'What is it?'

Sophie spoke first. 'I wanted to check you were okay after finding Michelle Matthews's body. And Bridget mentioned your run-in with DI Falkner.'

'It wasn't the best morning I've ever had,' Karen admitted, leading them to the kitchen. 'Tea or coffee? I was just about to make some.'

They both opted for tea.

As Karen filled the kettle, she asked, 'Any leads from Michelle's murder yet? I hope you have more witnesses than we did for Lorraine's.'

'Nothing promising so far,' Cunnings said. 'But Falkner will get answers. He's like a dog with a bone when he's on a case.'

'He's not exactly my favourite person right now. Though I doubt I'm on his Christmas card list either.'

'He'll come around,' Cunnings said as she and Sophie sat at the kitchen table.

Karen retrieved mugs from the cupboard. 'I wasn't trying to interfere. But I'll admit, I wanted to ask Michelle questions about Lorraine's past and Mike's father. He still doesn't know who he is.'

Karen turned back from the cupboard with the mugs to see Cunnings and Sophie exchanging a loaded glance. It set Karen's nerves on edge.

She eyed them both. 'You're holding something back.'

Their silence only made her more uneasy.

'I'm not made of glass,' Karen said. 'However bad it is, I want to know.'

Sophie took a deep breath. 'It's actually why we're here. I discussed it with Cunnings, and we agreed you should know.'

'Know what?' Karen's gaze darted between them.

Sophie leaned forward, her expression serious. 'It's about Mike's father,' she said. 'We think we know who he is.'

Chapter Twenty-Three

Karen stared at Sophie. 'Who?'

'We believe Mike's father is a man called Kenneth Prescott.'

Karen's lips thinned as she pulled out a chair and sat down. 'That's the man Ava Claywood worked for when she died.'

'Yes,' Sophie said. 'We've spoken to DCI Whitmore, who handled the original Claywood investigation. He thinks Lorraine was involved with Prescott, but it ended badly. Apparently, Lorraine fell for Prescott while working for Chapman. Prescott was likely using her to get information about Chapman's operations.'

Cunnings added, 'They were both small-time back then, but fierce rivals.'

Karen leaned back, trying to process everything. 'So Chapman was angry at Lorraine for leaking information to Prescott?'

Cunnings reached for her tea. 'We don't think so. He might've been initially upset, but he ended up helping her. Prescott leaving the country was probably Chapman's doing. It's possible Chapman made him leave, or even that Chapman's reputation alone could have scared him into leaving.'

Karen exhaled slowly. She was relieved Chapman wasn't Mike's father, but now it seemed his real father might still be involved in crime. 'Is Prescott still alive?'

Sophie nodded. 'Living in Brazil.'

'It fits. It explains Chapman's involvement.' Karen paused. 'Though I'd have thought Chapman would be furious about Lorraine spilling secrets.'

'We're not sure she did,' Sophie said. 'It could be Lorraine wanted out of the relationship. That's when Chapman stepped in. Maybe he helped her out of a tough spot and continued supporting her as Mike grew up.'

Karen sat silent, knowing these weren't the answers Mike had hoped for. 'What's Prescott up to now?'

'Buying and selling yachts,' Cunnings replied. 'Probably dodgy. Brazilian police don't have much they can share with us, but we've no reason to believe he's gone straight.'

'Right,' Karen said, rubbing her temples. 'Does he know about Mike?'

'We're not sure,' Sophie admitted.

'Could he be angry enough at Lorraine to come back and hurt her after all this time?' Karen asked.

Sophie's expression was guarded. 'We're exploring all possibilities.'

Karen felt a flicker of annoyance at the stock phrase. 'Sophie, what do you really think?'

Sophie hesitated, glancing at Cunnings. 'Honestly, Prescott sounds nasty. It's possible that he could be involved.'

'Okay,' Karen said. 'But why now? And why Michelle?'

Both women shook their heads. 'That's where we're stumped,' Sophie said. 'But we think Lorraine reached out to Prescott recently. Harinder found—'

'Sophie,' Cunnings said sharply. 'Don't overstep. This wasn't what we agreed.'

'I know but—'

'No!' Cunnings turned in her seat to look at Sophie. 'You could lose your job over this.'

Sophie bit her lip and sent an apologetic glance to Karen.

'It's okay, Sophie. I know you just want to help,' Karen said. 'But Bridget is right. Don't risk your career over this.' She turned to Cunnings. 'What about Ava Claywood's murder? Is that connected?'

'It's possible. Maybe Prescott's responsible for the deaths of all three women,' Cunnings said.

Karen nodded slowly. 'Has Harinder had any luck tracing the person who's been sending me those emails?'

'Unfortunately, not yet,' Cunnings said. 'Our request has been logged by Swiss law enforcement, so now we have to wait for them to contact Proton Mail. They should cooperate, but it's going to take time.'

Sophie sipped her tea. 'I know it's tough being kept in the dark like this. If it was up to me, I'd tell you everything.' She shrugged. 'But it isn't up to me, and Morgan, Churchill and Falkner are keen on keeping you out of the loop.'

Karen understood. 'So, you don't want me telling them that you told me about Prescott?'

Sophie smiled. 'It might avoid some tension if you kept it quiet for now.'

'I understand,' Karen said, returning the smile. 'Thanks for telling me. I'll have to figure out how to tell Mike.' She paused, thinking. 'It should be easy enough to check if Kenneth Prescott's been in the country recently.'

'That's our next step,' Cunnings assured her. 'Don't worry, Karen. We'll get to the bottom of this.'

Karen scrolled through her messages. James still hadn't replied to her text. She thought she really needed to head over there, to try to sort out the bad blood between him and Mike.

But then her phone lit up with a message from her mum: *thinking of you* with a heart emoji, and something inside Karen cracked a little.

After everything that had happened – Lorraine's murder, those nasty emails, and now Michelle's murder too – she found herself driving towards her parents' house instead of James's hotel. She hadn't planned it, and hadn't even realised she was heading there until she was halfway down their street.

The familiar sight of the front garden brought a lump to her throat. Trust her dad to have the lawn looking like a bowling green even in December. The asters were still doing well, adding splashes of purple and deep blue to the borders.

Before she could even reach for the doorbell, her mum had the door open. One look at Karen's face and her arms were wide open.

'Oh, darling.'

The familiar scent of her mum's Estée Lauder perfume, the same one she'd worn since Karen was little, wrapped around her as she was pulled into a tight hug.

'I'm fine, Mum. Really.' But her voice wobbled as she pulled away.

'Hi, love.' Her dad appeared in the hallway, hands stuffed into the pockets of his ancient blue cardigan. Her mum had been threatening to 'accidentally' lose it for about five years now. 'Come here and give your old dad a hug.'

She managed a wobbly smile.

'Cup of tea?' Her mum was already heading for the kitchen, not waiting for an answer. 'I've got those dark chocolate digestives you like.'

For a moment, Karen felt like their little girl again. The kitchen was exactly as it had always been. The radio quietly playing Radio 2, and the slight squeak of the kitchen door hinge that her dad was always drowning in WD-40.

Her dad's strong hand rested on her shoulder as she sat at the familiar kitchen table. 'You don't have to be Superwoman all the time, you know. We're always here, love.'

'I know.' She wrapped her hands around the steaming mug her mum had set in front of her.

'How's Mike doing?' Her mum settled into her usual chair, opening the biscuits.

Karen chose her words carefully. No need to mention Michelle's murder or those creepy emails. They worried enough about her as it was. 'He's . . . struggling. I'm actually supposed to be heading over to talk to James. He and Mike seem to be having trouble communicating lately.'

'Want me to have a word?' her dad offered. 'Always liked James. He's a sensible bloke.'

His words took her back to being a child. She missed those simpler times, when it had seemed like her dad could fix any problem. It was tempting to accept his offer, but those days were over. She had to try to handle this herself. 'Thanks, Dad. I might take you up on that if my chat doesn't work.'

Four chocolate digestives later, Karen felt steadier. She watched her parents as her dad topped up her mum's tea without being asked, and the way he waited until she was distracted before helping himself to another two biscuits. She smiled at her mother pretending not to notice.

The thought of losing them one day made her throat tight. No wonder Mike was struggling. He now had a raw, empty space where his mother should be. James was all the real family Mike had left now, and Karen wasn't going to stand by while they pulled away from each other.

After leaving her parents, Karen drove up to Washingborough Hall, parking on the gravel to the right of the Georgian building. As hotels went, it was very nice. James had excellent taste. The Grade II listed building was surrounded by mature gardens and woodland, the eighteenth-century architecture quite a contrast to the modern cars parked beside it.

As she stepped out of her car, the crunch of gravel under her feet seemed unnaturally loud in the quiet afternoon. She glanced at her watch. Just gone three. The sound of muffled applause drifted over from a function room, where some sort of awards ceremony appeared to be in full swing.

The warmth from the roaring fire in the reception area hit her as she entered, chasing away the December chill. Karen remembered the lovely afternoon tea she'd enjoyed here for her mum's birthday just a few months ago. The scones had been delicious.

A woman behind the desk looked up with a bright smile. 'Good afternoon. Can I help you?'

'I'm looking for James Harrington,' Karen said. 'I think he's a guest here?'

The receptionist glanced towards the small bar to Karen's left. 'Is he expecting you?'

Karen spotted James sitting in a low comfortable armchair in the bar. 'It's okay. I can see him. Thanks for your help.'

The bar was all dark wood and plush furnishings, with cartoon-style sketches lining the walls. James sat alone at a small table, a glass of orange juice in front of him, staring at one of the sketches.

He looked up as she approached, surprise flashing across his face. 'Karen? What are you doing here?'

She slid into the seat opposite him. 'I think we need to talk, James. About what's going on between you and Mike.'

James looked away. 'I don't know what you mean.'

'Come off it, James. You shouldn't be staying in this hotel when you could be at home with us.'

He shrugged, still not meeting her eyes. 'Mike doesn't need or want me hanging around at the moment.'

Karen leaned forward. 'That's not true and you know it. Mike's just having a hard time. You're his dad and he loves you. You two need each other, now more than ever.'

James's shoulders sagged. He finally looked at her, his eyes bloodshot. 'I feel surplus to requirements, Karen. Mike's looking for his real father, and I'm just in the way.'

'You are his real father,' Karen said firmly. 'Biology doesn't change that.'

'Doesn't it?' James's voice was bitter. 'Lorraine never confided in me about any of this. I thought I was doing the right thing, not pushing her when she didn't want to talk about it. But now . . .'

'You were a good husband to Lorraine,' Karen said softly. 'You did the right thing.'

James blinked hard, his eyes shining. 'I keep thinking if I hadn't gone to golf maybe I could've been there, could've stopped whoever—'

'Don't.' Karen cut him off. 'If you had been there, James, we might be dealing with two losses instead of one.'

James nodded, but Karen could see he wasn't convinced.

'So,' she said, trying to inject some lightness into her voice, 'are you going to come back home with me?'

James hesitated. 'I just don't want to be a burden. And Mike might be better off without me there. Even as a child, he needed his own space to process things. His mother could always get through to him, but I wasn't very good at it. It was difficult to gain his trust. It had just been him and his mother for so long . . . then I moved in. If I'd been his real dad, maybe I'd have been able to connect with him better.'

'That's nonsense,' Karen insisted. 'You've been there for Mike in every way that matters. You are his real dad, no matter what we find out from here on in. Mike needs you right now, so are you going to pack your bags, or am I going to have to do it for you?' She grinned, letting him know she was joking.

He managed a weak smile and reached for his orange juice. 'All right, you win. I'll go pack.'

'James, before you go and get your things, there's something else you need to know, and I'm afraid it's not good news.'

James tensed. 'What is it?'

Karen took a deep breath, her voice softening. 'It's about Michelle, Lorraine's sister. I'm so sorry, James, but she's been murdered too.'

James's face drained of colour. He set his glass down with a shaky hand, nearly knocking it over. 'Like Lorraine? The eyes the same way?'

Karen nodded.

He shook his head, struggling to process the information. 'I never even met her. Lorraine never spoke about her.' He ran a hand through his hair. 'Why would someone target both Lorraine and her sister? It doesn't make any sense. They weren't even close anymore. What's happening? First Lorraine, and now Michelle? This can't be a coincidence, can it?'

Karen reached across the table, gently taking James's trembling hands in hers. 'We don't know all the details yet, James. The team are investigating, but they're keeping things close to their chest at the moment.'

James nodded absently. Suddenly, his eyes snapped back to Karen's, filled with panic. 'What about Mike? If someone's targeting Lorraine's family, could he be in danger too?'

'James, listen to me. The police are taking every precaution to keep Mike safe. There are officers watching the house round the clock. It's one of the reasons why we all need to be together right now.'

James nodded slowly, the tension in his shoulders easing a bit. 'You're right, of course. I know you're right.' He gave Karen's hand a gentle squeeze. 'I'm very glad you're here to look after us. I've been a silly old fool, running off to a hotel because my feelings were hurt.' He shook his head, looking embarrassed. 'Of course Mike has questions about his biological father. I need a thicker skin. Thank you again for putting up with me.' He sat up a bit straighter, sounding more determined. 'I need to pull myself together and be there for my son.' His smile was a bit sad, but genuine. 'Lorraine would be giving me a dressing-down if she knew how I was behaving.' He glanced up at the ceiling, his voice going soft. 'Sorry, love. I'll do better.'

James's gaze shifted to Karen's hand. He frowned, as if noticing something for the first time. 'Karen, that ring on your finger . . . is that an engagement ring?'

Karen smiled. 'It is. We were planning to tell you and Lorraine over dinner, but after everything that happened, it never seemed like the right time to bring it up.'

James beamed. 'That's lovely news. Sorry I've been so unobservant. My mind's been all over the place. But I'm genuinely happy for you and Mike. Lorraine would be so pleased for you both.'

James got to his feet and pulled Karen into a hug, holding on for a moment. 'I really appreciate everything you've done,' he said softly. 'I'll go grab my things now.'

She'd been so focused on Mike's grief that she'd missed that, as well as losing Lorraine, James had lost his sense of where he fitted in Mike's life. Karen had always respected James as Mike's stepdad, but now she saw him in a new light. He was grieving and hurting, but still trying to do right by his son. That was what being a real father meant.

As he got to the door, he paused. 'Thank you, Karen. The day Mike met you was a very lucky one.'

Karen watched him go off to pack and check out, wondering whether she should have asked him about Kenneth Prescott. But she decided it was only right that Mike hear about Prescott first. Besides, from what she knew, Lorraine hadn't told James much about her past, trying instead to move on in a new life with him.

As she waited for James, Karen glanced around the bar, taking in the elegant surroundings. The hotel was lovely, but it wasn't a home. And right now, home with Mike was where James needed to be.

Her phone buzzed. She pulled it from her pocket and her stomach dropped. Another email.

Subject: *Last Chance.*

> *You're getting too close. Lorraine and Michelle both learned the hard way what happens to people who don't mind their own business. Don't make their mistake.*

Karen looked up sharply, scanning the hotel bar. Was the sender here now, watching her reaction? The place was quiet. Nothing but an elderly couple having coffee.

The sender was clearly trying to spook her, and it was working.

She pulled up Morgan's number. Enough was enough. Whoever was behind these emails knew about Michelle Matthews. That information hadn't even been officially released yet.

It was time to find out who was playing games, before anyone else got hurt.

◆　◆　◆

Arnie stepped out of the car and massaged the small of his back, doing hip circles to relieve his sciatica. He grimaced as his joints popped and cracked.

Rick, who'd just got out of the driver's side, looked at him in horror. 'What on earth are you doing?'

'I'm loosening up my joints,' Arnie grumbled, continuing his awkward gyrations.

Rick pulled a face. 'It looks like you're doing pelvic thrusts. There's a time and a place, mate.'

'Sylvie showed me.' Arnie gestured vaguely. 'She said it helps—'

Rick held up his hands. 'Please, I'm begging you, stop.'

They both turned to look at the imposing residence in front of them that belonged to Quentin Chapman. The sprawling house stood in meticulously landscaped grounds, its grey-framed windows glinting in the late afternoon sun.

'Imagine living in a place like this,' Rick said, as they slowly walked towards the entrance.

Arnie sniffed. 'It's really not to my taste. I find it very nouveau riche.'

Rick smirked. 'I see, you'd prefer a two-up, two-down in Lincoln, would you?'

'At least it's got more character. This is a new-build; it can't be more than twenty years old. They all look the same. Bifold doors. Big open-plan kitchens. I prefer a separate kitchen anyway. Who wants to smell cooking in the living room?'

Rick shrugged, unfazed. 'You say that every time we speak to someone living in a fancy house. I wouldn't say no to a place like this.'

As they approached the front door, a security camera followed their progress, its movement telling them that they were definitely being watched.

'What's the betting he gives us the runaround?' Rick muttered under his breath.

'I'd be surprised if he didn't,' Arnie said, his mouth set in a grim line.

'You'd think DI Falkner might want to come himself and show us how it's done.' The bitterness in Rick's tone showed. He was still smarting from Falkner's condescending comments.

Arnie and Rick both knew they'd never get anything out of Chapman that he didn't want them to. He'd cooperated with them once before, but that was purely because it had benefited him.

When the door opened, two of Chapman's large employees blocked the entrance, their bulky frames filling the doorway. One had a shaved head with a tattoo on the side of his neck, the other had a ponytail.

Arnie and Rick went through the motions, showing their ID and introducing themselves. To Arnie's surprise, they weren't turned away. Instead, the one with the ponytail roughly pushed past them, muttering that he had somewhere else to be, but they were welcomed inside by the skinhead.

Well, *welcomed* was probably too strong a word. More like he waved a hand and grunted. But it was one up from having a door slammed in their faces.

He grunted something else and left them standing in the marble-floored hallway.

Rick was gawping like a goldfish as he turned in a slow circle, looking at the fancy chandelier and ornate furnishings. 'Yep, wouldn't mind a place like this myself,' he said wistfully.

A moment later, the skinhead grunted at them from down the hall and they followed him into an office. It was a cosy room lined with bookshelves and warm wood panelling. Arnie's boots sank into the plush burgundy carpet. The room smelled of furniture polish and aged leather.

Chapman stood behind an imposing oak desk, hands clasped behind his back. His silver hair was neatly styled. Every inch the sophisticated gentleman, except for the glint in his eyes that hinted at something far more dangerous lurking beneath.

Chapman spoke first. 'Gentlemen, what a pleasure. How can I help?'

'We've got some questions,' Arnie said. 'We think you can help with our double murder investigation.'

Chapman's forehead creased slightly. 'Double murder? So this isn't about the Lorraine Harrington case?'

'It's about the Lorraine Harrington case . . . *and* a second murder that took place this morning.' Arnie helped himself to a seat, not waiting for an invitation.

Rick hovered uncertainly for a moment before Chapman nodded. 'Please, sit down.'

Chapman lowered himself into a high-backed leather desk chair. He looked every inch the Bond villain as he steepled his fingers. 'Who is this other murder victim, and why do you think I can help you?'

'Michelle Matthews.'

Arnie was surprised to see Chapman react. He was a man who normally maintained impeccable control over his emotions. For a fleeting instant, shock flickered across his features before the mask slipped back into place.

'How unfortunate,' he said evenly.

'Yes, very unfortunate, especially since we got her name from you.'

A faint smile played on Chapman's lips. 'I believe that was a private conversation I had with Detective Sergeant Hart. I don't remember telling *you* anything.'

Arnie rolled his eyes, already exasperated. 'Regardless of how we found out, we know you knew about Michelle Matthews, so tell me about her.'

'I barely knew her,' Chapman said with a casual shrug.

'Then tell me what you do know.'

'Not much. I know she was Lorraine's sister, and they were very close forty years ago.'

'They weren't close recently, then?' Arnie probed.

'No.'

'Why not?'

Chapman's gaze was steady and unflinching. 'I'd say you should ask them, Detective, but sadly you can't. So, I suppose you'll never know.'

Arnie gritted his teeth, fighting back the urge to snap at the smug git. People like Chapman enjoyed making a police officer's job difficult. It was as though they *wanted* murderers to be left to roam the streets freely. All so they could maintain their reputations for never helping the police.

'Can you think why anyone would want to target both Lorraine and her sister?'

'I cannot.'

Arnie pressed on, undeterred. 'And are you aware of Mike Harrington's paternity?'

Chapman's expression didn't waver. 'No comment.'

Frustration crept into Arnie's voice. 'Look, if you know something, please stop messing about. We've got two murders.

Some nutcase is out there killing women. It would really help us if you could just play it straight for once.'

Chapman's eyes narrowed to slits. 'I'm prepared to talk to Mike Harrington about his paternity. I'm not prepared to discuss it with anyone else. Lorraine wouldn't have wanted me to do that.'

'It doesn't matter what she would want anymore. Someone killed her,' Arnie shot back.

'I disagree. I think it matters even more now,' Chapman said smoothly.

Arnie tried a different tack, going round the houses and asking a few more questions, but Chapman remained tightly buttoned up, refusing to spill anything.

He'd expected as much, but a small part of him had dared to hope for a positive result when they'd actually been allowed inside the house for a change.

'Don't you want to help Karen?' Rick said, his tone earnest. 'She helped you in the past.'

Chapman stared at him for a long moment before slowly saying, 'She did. And I'm not being deliberately difficult. I don't know who killed Lorraine and Michelle. But I am very sorry that they've both been murdered.'

'Does the name Kenneth Prescott mean anything to you?' Arnie asked, watching Chapman's reaction closely.

Chapman would have been a perfect poker player. The man didn't so much as flinch, even though Arnie knew from his research and from DCI Whitmore that he was well aware of Prescott. The two had been bitter rivals at one point, before Prescott left for Brazil.

'The name doesn't ring a bell,' Chapman said easily, checking the time on his Rolex. 'Actually, if we could wrap this up, I do have some meetings this afternoon.'

'And we have two murders to solve,' Arnie snapped, losing his temper. 'Why can't you help us? Is it because, by helping us, you'll incriminate yourself?'

Chapman remained silent, his expression unreadable.

'Was there a falling-out between you and Prescott?' Arnie persisted.

Nothing.

'Have you been in contact with Prescott since he left the UK?'

Still, Chapman said nothing, his lips pressed into a thin line.

Arnie got to his feet, recognising the futility of continuing the questioning. 'Come on, Rick, we're not going to get anywhere here.'

As they were leaving the study, Arnie turned back and levelled one final look at Chapman. 'If you know something about this, or if you're involved in any way—'

'I'm not,' Chapman said simply.

Arnie didn't believe him.

Chapter Twenty-Four

Sandy sat obediently beside Mike in the exercise area as they watched his client's excitable Labrador scamper around. The pale sun warmed Mike's face, despite the cold breeze ruffling his hair. For a moment, he could almost forget the nightmare of the past few days.

Almost.

When their happy way of life had been tipped upside down, they'd bolted to their respective safe zones – Karen to her investigations, and Mike to his dog training. At least they were consistent in their avoidance tactics.

He knew she wanted him to talk about what had happened and to stop bottling everything up. But that was rich coming from Karen 'I'm fine, just busy' Hart. Both of them were experts at dodging feelings by being good old-fashioned workaholics. While Karen buried herself in case files and witness statements, he found peace in the simple routine of training. Commands, rewards, routine. Simple. Safe.

'That's it, Bella. Good girl!' The client – a middle-aged woman named Janice – praised the dog as it successfully navigated the small agility course Mike had set up.

'She's doing well,' he said, forcing a smile. 'You've been practising.'

Janice beamed. 'Oh yes, every day. Though I think she still responds better to you than me.'

Mike chuckled. 'It's all down to practice.'

'And knowing who's boss,' Janice said, fussing over the dog. 'I'm afraid I'm a bit soft with her. She respects you.'

As if on cue, Bella bounded over to Mike, tail wagging furiously. He bent down to scratch behind her ears, wincing slightly as his bad leg protested.

'Are you all right?' Janice asked, concerned.

'Fine,' Mike said quickly. 'Just an old injury playing up.'

He straightened, pushing away the twinge of pain. Physical discomfort was nothing compared to the emotional turmoil. His mother, murdered. An aunt he'd never known existed, also dead. And now . . .

Mike shook his head, trying to dispel the thoughts. Focus on the present. On the dogs. On normality.

'Right,' he said, clapping his hands. 'Let's try that recall exercise again, shall we?'

As Janice led Bella across the field, Mike's mind drifted. How was he supposed to feel about Michelle's death? Grief seemed inappropriate, somehow. You couldn't grieve for someone you'd never met, could you? And yet the knowledge that another family member had been taken from him, before he'd even had the chance to know them . . .

It was too much. Easier to feel numb.

A flash of movement caught his eye. Mike turned, frowning as he saw a black Range Rover pull into the small parking area.

'Janice,' he called, keeping his voice level. 'Can you keep working on that recall? I just need to step away for a moment.'

She nodded happily, seemingly oblivious to the tension suddenly radiating from him. Mike whistled for Sandy, who immediately fell into step beside him as he strode towards the car.

His jaw clenched. What did Chapman want now? Hadn't the man done enough damage? Mike hated the idea that Chapman had somehow got his claws into Lorraine. His mother had been a good, honest woman. She wouldn't have had any dealings with someone like Chapman unless she'd had no choice.

As Mike approached, the rear door remained firmly shut. Instead, the driver's side opened, and a mountain of a man unfolded himself from the seat. Long hair pulled back in a ponytail, biceps straining against a tight suit jacket. One of Chapman's men.

'Mr Harrington,' the man said, his voice a low rumble.

'Chapman too busy to do his own dirty work?'

Ponytail shrugged, seemingly amused by Mike's hostility. 'Keep your hair on. I'm just the messenger.'

'Well, you can tell your boss I'm not interested in anything he has to say.'

'Sure. Anyway.' Ponytail rolled his eyes and reached into his jacket. 'I need to give you this.'

He pulled a plain white envelope from his inside pocket and held it out. Mike stared at it, making no move to take it.

'What is it?'

Another shrug. 'Above my pay grade. I just deliver things.'

Mike's eyes narrowed. 'And if I don't want it?'

'Then don't take it,' Ponytail said, his tone bored. 'Makes no difference to me either way.'

Mike's fists clenched at his sides. He wanted to punch that smug look off the man's face. But what good would that do? He'd probably end up with a broken hand and more of Chapman's heavies on his doorstep.

Curiosity warred with his anger. What was in that envelope? Information about his mother? About Michelle?

About his father?

Before he could stop himself, Mike snatched the envelope from Ponytail's outstretched hand.

'There,' Ponytail said. 'Was that so hard?'

'Shut up,' Mike growled.

The big man held up his hands in mock surrender. 'Hey, no need for that. I'm just doing my job.'

'You shouldn't.' Mike didn't know the ins and outs of Chapman's business, but he knew it was nothing good. 'Chapman threatens people, leaves them terrified, or worse. It's evil.'

A flicker of something passed across Ponytail's face. Amusement? Annoyance? It was gone before Mike could be sure.

'You're not wrong there,' Ponytail muttered. Then, louder, he added, 'Are we done here?'

Mike nodded curtly. 'Get off my property.'

Ponytail smirked and gave a mocking salute before climbing back into the Range Rover. The engine roared to life, and within moments, the car had gone.

Mike looked down at the envelope in his hand. No writing or text on the outside. It felt light, probably just a single sheet of paper inside. He should throw it away. Burn it. Whatever the contents, it couldn't be good news.

And yet . . .

A soft whine brought him back to the present. Sandy was looking up at him, head tilted in concern.

'It's all right, girl,' Mike said softly, reaching down to scratch her ears. 'I'm okay.'

Liar, a voice in his head whispered.

With a sigh, Mike tucked the envelope into his back pocket. Later. He'd deal with it later. Right now, he had a job to do.

Plastering on what he hoped was a convincing smile, Mike turned back to where Janice was still working with Bella.

'Sorry about that,' he called as he approached. 'Now, where were we?'

He slipped back into instructor mode and tried to ignore the envelope burning a hole in his pocket. Whatever Chapman had to say, it could wait.

◆ ◆ ◆

Back at Karen's, Mike slumped into a chair and placed the envelope on the kitchen table. He could hear water running from upstairs and realised Karen must be home and in the shower.

His stepdad was in the living room watching some quiz show on TV. Mike didn't want to tell him about this latest development. Digging for answers about his biological father was hurting James, and that was the last thing Mike wanted to do.

The memory of their falling-out pricked at him, sharp and unwelcome. He'd said something stupid: *Stop smothering me. I can't deal with your ridiculous insecurities on top of everything else.*

It had slipped out, bitter and thoughtless. His dad hadn't argued, or even looked angry. He'd just gone quiet. The silence was worse somehow.

He'd meant to apologise, but it was easier to try to pretend it never happened. But it lingered, heavy and unresolved.

James had been good to him and his mum, and Mike shouldn't be pushing him away, even if he did feel smothered and overwhelmed.

He suddenly felt bone-weary, as if the weight of the past few days had finally caught up with him. Sandy pressed against his leg, offering silent comfort.

'What am I going to do, girl?' he murmured, absently stroking her fur.

The envelope seemed to grow more ominous with each passing moment, like a ticking bomb on the table. He had planned to wait and talk to Karen before opening it. But the temptation was overwhelming.

'In for a penny, in for a pound,' he muttered, tearing it open with more force than necessary.

A single sheet of paper was inside. Mike unfolded it and began to read.

Mr Harrington,

I was very sorry to hear about your mother's passing. I understand your reluctance to engage with me, given recent events. However, I believe I have information that may be of great interest to you regarding your mother and your father's identity.

If you wish to discuss this matter further, please meet me at my residence tomorrow at 9 a.m. Come alone.

Regards,

Quentin Chapman

Chapman's address was printed at the top of the letter, and the body of the letter was written in an elegant, old-fashioned handwriting that seemed at odds with the man's thuggish reputation.

Mike read the note a second time. Then he crumpled the paper in his fist and shoved it into his pocket. Chapman was dangling this information like bait, and Mike was the fish circling the hook.

A surge of hot anger was quickly followed by a cold wave of dread at what he might learn.

Sandy whined softly, pressing her nose against his hand. Mike looked down at her, forcing himself to take a deep breath.

'What do you think?' he asked. 'Should I go?'

The dog lifted her head, then placed a paw on his leg.

Mike managed a weak smile. 'I know. You'd follow me anywhere, wouldn't you? Even into the lion's den.'

He straightened up, decision made. He'd go to the meeting. Karen might not like it, but this was something he needed to do.

He'd tell her about the letter, of course. Just as soon as she came downstairs. And if she wanted to come with him, then great. It would be good to have her there, thinking logically and making sensible decisions. Mike couldn't trust himself not to fly off the handle at the first sight of Chapman's smug face.

Chapman had specified Mike come alone, but it was time the old gangster learned he wasn't calling all the shots.

Mike sat back, his mind full of questions. Did Chapman know his father? How were they connected? And most importantly, could he trust anything Chapman had to say?

Tomorrow at nine a.m., Mike would finally get some answers. Whether they were answers he wanted to hear remained to be seen.

Karen headed downstairs. She'd taken a shower hoping to wash away some of the day's tension. It hadn't worked.

Mike sat at the kitchen table, his broad shoulders hunched, Sandy curled faithfully at his feet. He looked up as Karen entered.

'Hi,' she said softly. 'Tea?'

Mike nodded, then seemed to catch himself. 'Actually, Karen, I—'

The water filling the kettle drowned out his words.

She turned, eyebrows raised. 'Sorry, what was that?'

He shook his head. 'It's fine. Tea would be great.'

Karen busied herself with mugs and teabags, sneaking glances at Mike and noticing the set of his jaw, the tension in his shoulders. Perhaps this wasn't a good time to tell him about Kenneth Prescott.

But when would be a good time?

She placed a steaming mug in front of him, then settled into the chair opposite. 'So,' she began, then faltered. How should she broach the subject of his father? *Sorry, Mike, turns out your dad might be a criminal who's been living it up in Brazil all these years?* There had to be a more compassionate way of breaking the news.

Mike cleared his throat. 'Karen, there's something I need to—'

Sandy's bark, closely followed by the doorbell, cut through the air. They both jumped and tea sloshed over the rim of Karen's mug.

'Brilliant,' she muttered, grabbing some kitchen roll to soak up the spill. 'Who could that be?'

Mike's expression darkened as he got to his feet. 'If it's Chapman again, I swear—'

Karen laid a hand on his arm. 'Let's not jump to conclusions. I'll go and see who it is.'

She made her way to the front door, running a hand through her damp hair. Opening the door, she found herself face to face with Sophie and Rick, both wearing expressions of forced cheerfulness.

'Hello!' Sophie said, brandishing a casserole dish. 'We thought you two could use a home-cooked meal.'

Rick held up a shop-bought chocolate cake. 'And pudding,' he added with a grin. 'Because everyone knows cake makes everything better.'

'Rick!' Sophie glared at him. She turned back to Karen. 'Sorry about him. Obviously, we know it won't make things better, but we just wanted to do something to show we're thinking of you.'

'Karen knows what I meant,' Rick grumbled.

Karen smiled. 'Thanks. That's really kind of you both.'

'See?' Rick nudged Sophie. 'I told you the cake was a good idea.'

Sophie rolled her eyes. 'Yes, because a sugar coma is exactly what they need right now.'

'Better than your rabbit food,' Rick said, gesturing to the casserole. 'What even *is* that? The grains look like something my cousin would feed her budgie.'

'It's a quinoa and kale casserole,' Sophie said. 'It's healthy and nutritious.'

'It's green mush,' Rick said, before stage-whispering to Karen, 'Don't worry, I've got you covered with the cake.'

Despite herself, Karen felt a grin tugging at her lips. Their bickering was so familiar, so normal, it was comforting.

She led them into the kitchen, where Mike was throwing the tea-sodden kitchen roll into the bin. Sandy greeted the visitors, tail wagging happily.

'Look who's here,' Karen announced, a touch too brightly. 'Sophie and Rick brought us dinner.'

Mike managed a polite nod. 'Thanks. That's good of you.'

Sophie and Rick put the casserole and cake on the table. An awkward silence followed, broken only by Sandy's tail thumping against the floor as she eyed the newcomers eagerly, hoping for a tasty treat of her own.

'So,' Rick said, rocking back on his heels. 'How are you all holding up?'

Karen and Mike exchanged a glance. How could they even begin to answer that?

'We're managing,' she said. 'It's been difficult.'

Sophie nodded sympathetically. 'Of course. That's why we wanted to check in. Make sure you're all eating properly and everything.'

'Because nothing says "we care" like force-feeding your friends rabbit food,' Rick muttered, winking at Mike.

Sophie gave him a death glare. 'Ignore him. The casserole is delicious, I promise. It's packed with antioxidants and—'

'Tastes like disappointment?' Rick offered.

'Rick, one more word and you're walking home.'

'Well, we appreciate it,' Karen said. 'Both the casserole and the cake.'

Mike cleared his throat. 'Yes, thanks. It's kind of you to think of us.'

Another awkward pause. Karen saw the moment Sophie clicked, her gaze flicking between Karen and Mike, noting the tension, the unfinished mugs of tea, the way they both seemed poised on the edge of something.

'Oh!' Sophie said suddenly, far too loudly. 'I just remembered. We can't stay. Can we, Rick?'

Rick blinked at her. 'We can't?'

'No,' Sophie said firmly. 'We have that . . . thing. Remember?'

'Thing?' Rick repeated blankly.

Sophie's eyes widened meaningfully. 'Yes, that very important thing we absolutely cannot miss.'

Understanding dawned on Rick's face. 'Oh, right! That thing. How could I forget? Absolutely can't miss it.'

Karen bit back another smile. Subtle as a brick through a window.

'Thanks again,' she said, walking them to the door.

Sophie paused in the doorway. 'We're here if you need anything, okay? Anything at all.'

Karen nodded, throat suddenly tight. 'I know. Thank you.'

As the door closed behind them, Karen could hear their bickering start up again.

'Could you be any slower on the uptake, Rick?'

'You could have been clearer. You weren't making any sense.'

'I was improvising. It was obvious we'd interrupted something.'

Their voices faded as they walked away.

She made her way back to the kitchen, where Mike was examining the casserole with a dubious expression.

'I think it moved,' he said, poking at the dish.

Karen laughed. 'Be nice. Sophie means well. She's got a good heart.'

'I know,' Mike sighed, abandoning his investigation of the green concoction. 'They both do. They're good friends.'

The light-hearted moment faded, leaving them once again in weighted silence. Karen took a deep breath. No more stalling.

'Mike, there's something I need to tell you.'

At the same moment, Mike said, 'Karen, we need to talk.'

They both paused.

'You first,' she said quickly.

Mike shook his head. 'No, you go ahead.'

'Really, I insist.'

'Karen.'

She sighed, recognising the stubborn set of his jaw. 'Fine. But maybe we should sit down for this.'

Mike frowned, but he lowered himself back into his chair. Karen took her seat across from him, hands wrapped around her cooling mug of tea.

'Okay,' she said, then faltered. How should she even start? She took a deep breath. 'It's about your father. Your biological father.'

Mike went very still. Karen wondered if he already knew – or at least suspected – what was coming.

'What about him?' Mike asked.

Karen licked her lips, searching for the right words. 'Sophie told me some things earlier. Things the investigation has turned up.'

Mike gripped his mug. 'And?'

'They think . . .' She paused, steeling herself. 'They think your father might be a man named Kenneth Prescott.'

Mike's expression remained carefully blank, but Karen could see the storm brewing behind his eyes. 'For a moment, I thought you were going to tell me that Chapman's my biological father.'

'That possibility had crossed my mind,' she admitted.

'Kenneth Prescott,' Mike repeated slowly. 'I've never heard of him.'

Karen took a sip of the lukewarm tea, buying herself a moment. 'He was a rival of Chapman's, back in the day. Prescott left the country when you were a few years old and has been in Brazil ever since. Apparently, your mum might have been involved with him while she was working for Chapman.'

Mike's jaw clenched. 'Involved how?'

'Romantically,' Karen said gently. 'They think . . . Well, they think that's how you came to be.'

Mike pushed back from the table abruptly, his chair scraping against the floor. He paced to the window, hands clenched at his sides. Sandy whined softly, following him. 'So my father's a criminal? Fantastic.'

Karen wanted to hug him, but she sensed he needed space. 'Mike, we don't know anything for certain. It's just a theory based on what they've uncovered so far.'

He turned to face her, his expression showing his anger and pain. 'But it fits, doesn't it? It explains why Mum never wanted to tell me.'

Karen nodded reluctantly. 'It does seem to make sense of a few things.'

He ran a hand through his hair. 'All these years, I've wondered.'

'I'm so sorry, Mike. I know this isn't what you wanted to hear.'

He let out a bitter laugh. 'What? That my father is some criminal who's been living it up in Brazil while I grew up never knowing him? You're right. It feels more like a bad joke than a happy ending.'

Karen stood and made her way over to him. 'I know it's a lot to take in. But remember, this doesn't change who you are.'

Mike's expression softened. He reached out, pulling her into a hug. Karen held him close, feeling the tension in his body, and wished she could somehow take all this hurt away.

'Thank you. For telling me. For being here,' he said, then took a deep breath, seeming to steady himself. 'Okay. My turn now.'

Karen frowned. 'Your turn?'

'To share some news,' Mike said, moving back to the table. He pulled a crumpled piece of paper from his pocket, setting it on the wooden surface and smoothing it out. 'This was delivered to me at work today.'

'Delivered by whom?'

'One of Chapman's men. The one with the ponytail.'

'What? Mike, why didn't you tell me straightaway?'

He sighed, sinking back into his chair. 'I was going to. But then you came downstairs, and I could tell you had something on your mind, and then Rick and Sophie showed up.'

'So what does it say?'

Mike gestured for her to read it herself and Karen quickly scanned the note. She felt her frown deepen with each line.

'He wants to meet with you?' she said, looking up at Mike. 'Alone?'

Mike's expression was grim. 'He has information about Mum. And about my father.'

'You can't seriously be considering this.'

'Why not?' Mike said. 'He might have answers, Karen. Real answers, not just theories and maybes.'

'Because it's Chapman,' Karen said, exasperated. 'He's dangerous, Mike. You can't trust him.'

'I know that,' he snapped. Then, more softly, he added, 'I know. But, Karen, I need to know the truth. About Mum, about my father. All of it.'

Karen sank into her chair, the letter still clutched in her hand. Chapman was a manipulator who knew exactly which buttons to push. The letter was the perfect bait for Mike.

He'd draw Mike in with scraps of information about his family, then hold the favour over her head whenever he wanted something. *Your fiancé needs more information? Maybe we can help each other out* . . . She could already hear Chapman's smooth voice making the suggestion.

Karen being in a relationship with someone who owed him a favour would put her in exactly the spot Chapman wanted. She couldn't let that happen.

She understood Mike's need for answers. But the thought of him walking into Chapman's lair alone . . .

'I'll come with you,' she said.

'The letter says to come alone.'

'I don't care what the letter says. He manipulates people. Five minutes with him and he'll have you believing the sky is green,' Karen said. 'I'm not letting you face Chapman by yourself.'

A faint smile flickered across Mike's face. '*Letting* me?'

Karen rolled her eyes. 'You know what I mean.'

Mike reached across the table, taking her hand in his. 'I do. And if you want to come too, that's fine by me. Unless you think Chapman will clam up with a police officer present?'

'I'll get him to talk,' Karen said confidently.

Mike nodded. 'Then we'll talk to him tomorrow.'

They sat in silence for a moment, then Karen's gaze drifted to the casserole and cake.

'It's dinner time,' she said, attempting to lighten the mood. 'Quinoa and kale casserole or chocolate cake?'

Mike's nose wrinkled. 'Is takeaway not an option?'

She laughed. 'I like the way you think. But I'm going to try the casserole.'

Karen got a fork and loaded it up with green quinoa. Mike watched her expectantly as she tasted the first mouthful.

'Well? What's the verdict?' he asked.

'It tastes very . . . healthy.'

Mike grimaced and reached for his phone to order a pizza.

Chapter Twenty-Five

The following morning, Karen stopped the car in front of Quentin Chapman's house. 'Ready?' she asked, glancing at Mike in the passenger seat.

He nodded. 'Let's get it over with.'

They stepped out of the car, and Karen tugged at her coat, feeling underprepared. Mike wore his usual casual clothes: faded jeans, old boots, and the jacket he typically wore to work.

He shoved his hands deep in his pockets as he looked around at Chapman's fancy property with narrowed eyes.

A wave of protectiveness washed over Karen. She hated bringing him here. Mike was too decent for Chapman's games. He might share Kenneth Prescott's DNA, but that was where the similarity ended. From what John Claywood had told her, Prescott sounded like a ruthless crook only out for himself – but Mike? He volunteered at the local food bank, and she'd seen him rescue spiders from the bath before putting them safely outside.

She opened her mouth to say something reassuring, then closed it again. No words seemed right.

The front door opened. A burly man with a ponytail, one Karen recognised as Chapman's regular muscle, stood at the entrance.

'So, you decided to come then?' Ponytail smirked at Mike, his eyes gleaming with amusement.

Karen bristled at his smug tone but kept her expression neutral. 'We're here to see Chapman.'

Ponytail nodded, gesturing for them to follow.

He led them through the house. Expensive artwork hung on the walls, each piece probably worth more than Karen's yearly salary.

Ponytail stopped by Chapman's study, rapping his knuckles against the heavy oak door. 'They're here, boss.'

'Send them in,' came Chapman's muffled reply.

Karen squeezed Mike's hand briefly before they entered.

The office was dimly lit, the curtains drawn against the morning light. Dark wood panelling lined the walls.

It looked exactly as Karen recalled. Her gaze fixed on the spot where she'd once faced a gunman, the memory as vivid as if it had happened yesterday. She could almost hear the gunshot as she remembered the weight of Chapman slamming her out of the way. The bullet had hit Chapman instead of her. He'd survived, of course. Karen wondered if the man had nine lives, like a cat.

That moment still kept her awake some nights. Not just the shooting, but trying to understand why he'd done it. Every time she thought she had Chapman figured out as just another self-serving, vindictive criminal, he did something that didn't fit the pattern. After all this time, she still found him impossible to read.

Quentin Chapman rose as they entered the office. He had a smile on his face that didn't quite reach his eyes. His hair was neatly styled, and his suit was impeccably tailored. He looked every inch a successful businessman, not the notorious gangster Karen knew him to be.

'Detective Sergeant Hart,' Chapman greeted her warmly. 'And Mr Harrington. Please, have a seat.'

He gestured to the leather chairs in front of his desk. Karen sat, her back straight. Mike remained standing, his posture tense.

'Can I offer you anything? Tea? Coffee?' Chapman asked, his tone genial.

'We're fine,' Mike replied curtly. 'We're here for answers, not refreshments.'

Chapman's smile widened. He settled back into his chair. 'Very well. What would you like to know?'

Karen glanced at Mike, who gave a slight nod. She turned back to Chapman. 'You told Mike you had information about his mother and his biological father.'

'I do.' Chapman reached into a drawer, producing a small, leather-bound book. He placed it on the desk between them. 'This belonged to your mother, Mr Harrington. Her diary from a significant period in her life.'

Mike stared at the diary with apprehension. 'Why do you have my mother's diary?'

'Lorraine left it with me for safekeeping,' Chapman explained. 'She wanted you to have it, if anything ever happened to her. She said it would help you understand why she did the things she did.'

Karen's eyes narrowed. 'And you're just giving it to us now? Why?'

Chapman spread his hands, a gesture of innocence that Karen didn't buy for a second. 'I'm giving it to Mike. Just like Lorraine asked me to.'

'Why would she ask you to keep it?' Mike asked, his voice tight.

'We were friends. Your mother worked for me, many years ago. That's how she met Kenneth Prescott, much to my regret.'

Karen watched Mike's reaction closely and saw him flinch at the mention of his potential father.

'Kenneth Prescott,' Karen repeated. 'Tell us about him.'

'He ran betting shops in the late seventies and early eighties, and some other, less legal, betting enterprises. Prescott wasn't a nice man. But Lorraine, she seemed to like him at first. They became involved. It didn't work out between them, and I helped your mum out of a difficult situation.'

Mike's hands clenched into fists at his sides. 'And this Prescott bloke is my father?'

'Yes, he is.'

Mike crossed his arms over his chest. 'And why should I believe you?'

'Why would I lie?'

Mike shrugged.

'It can't be easy to learn your father was a crook,' Chapman said. 'Especially as you were such an upstanding officer of the law for many years.'

Karen saw Mike tense. He seemed ready to explode. She quickly said, 'Was this how Lorraine came into contact with Ava Claywood? Through Prescott?'

Chapman's eyebrows rose slightly at the change of subject. 'I believe so. Ava worked in one of Prescott's betting shops.'

'Did you ever meet Ava?' Karen pressed.

Chapman shook his head. 'I'm afraid not, Detective.'

Karen wondered if he'd tell her even if he had. With Chapman, every word was carefully chosen, every revelation calculated for maximum effect.

'Do you know who was behind Ava's murder?' Karen asked.

Chapman's expression hardened. 'No. And if I did, I wouldn't tell you. That's ancient history, Detective, and I'm not one of your informants. Remember who you're talking to.'

'I'm well aware, thank you. It may be ancient history to you, but it doesn't feel like that for the husband and daughter Ava left behind.'

Mike looked up from the diary. 'Why did you help my mum? Why did you protect her from Prescott?'

Something flickered in Chapman's eyes. Regret? Guilt?

'Lorraine was a good person,' Chapman said quietly. 'And Prescott had her terrified. She had a toddler – *you* – and nowhere else to turn. I did what anyone would do.'

'Right,' Karen said. 'Because you're such a humanitarian.'

'Believe what you want, Detective. But I cared about Lorraine. I supported her financially for years.'

'Out of the goodness of your heart?' Karen's tone dripped sarcasm.

'Watch yourself, Detective,' Chapman warned. 'I'm doing you a favour here.'

Mike's head snapped up. 'Don't talk to her like that.'

Chapman held up a hand. 'I understand you're upset, Mr Harrington. But I made a promise to your mother.'

'Why didn't she tell me any of this?'

'She wanted to, when the time was right.'

'And now she can't,' Mike said bitterly.

'Have you read the diary?' Karen asked Chapman, studying his face for any hint of deception.

Chapman's expression softened, an act Karen didn't trust for a second. 'Of course not. I respected Lorraine's privacy. Lorraine was a good person, caught up in a bad situation. I did what I could to help her.'

Chapman making out he was a protective friend and generous benefactor made Karen's blood boil. Her jaw ached from clenching it so hard. The thing that drove her mad was not knowing if it *was* an act. After all, he had helped Lorraine, whatever his reasons. That sadness in his eyes when he spoke about Lorraine seemed genuine. But trusting Chapman was asking for trouble. He had a reputation for a reason.

'How kind of you.' Karen's tone was cynical.

Chapman placed a hand over his heart, feigning hurt. 'You wound me, Detective. Is it so hard to believe I might do something simply because it's the right thing to do?'

'Yes,' Karen said bluntly.

A chuckle escaped his lips. 'Fair enough. But in this case, I assure you, my motives were pure. I provided Lorraine with financial support, helped her get back on her feet, and warned Prescott off.'

'Did you know Michelle?' Mike asked. 'My mother's sister?'

'Not well, but she and Lorraine were close once. I suggested to Detective Hart that she might want to speak with her. Then I heard from your colleagues that Michelle was also murdered.'

'Yes, and in the same way as Lorraine.' Karen leaned forward, her eyes locked on Chapman. 'Is there anything else you can tell us? Any idea who might be behind these murders?'

A shadow passed over his face. 'I'm afraid not, Detective.'

'Maybe an official interview might jog your memory?'

'The second you bring me in formally, I'll have my lawyer shut you down faster than you can say "no comment".'

'You really don't know who's behind this?'

'I don't. If I did . . .' He stopped, his thought unfinished. 'Lorraine didn't deserve what happened to her. Neither did Michelle.'

Mike abruptly made his way to the door. 'I need some air.'

Karen watched him go, torn between following and making sure he was okay and finishing the conversation with Chapman. She turned back to the gangster.

'What else can you tell us?' she asked. 'And don't give me any rubbish about ancient history. Two women have been killed this week. If you know anything that could help us find who did this, now's the time to share.'

Chapman was quiet for a long moment. When he spoke, his voice was low. 'I don't know who's responsible for killing Lorraine or Michelle. But I'll tell you this, Kenneth Prescott is a nasty vindictive man. It wouldn't surprise me if he is involved in some way.'

Karen nodded, filing the information away. 'And if we need to talk to you again?'

'You know where to find me,' Chapman said. 'But keep it off the record, Detective. If you make it official, you'll get nothing.'

'Understood,' Karen said grudgingly. She hated playing by Chapman's rules, but if it got them answers, she'd do it. For now.

She turned to go, then paused. 'Why did you really support Lorraine for all those years? And spare me the misunderstood-good-guy act.'

Chapman's lips twisted in a humourless smile. 'Maybe I'm not as cold-hearted as you think, Detective. Or maybe I just don't like loose ends. Take your pick.'

Typical Chapman, never giving a straight answer. It was infuriating, the way he could flip between cold-blooded criminal and playing the role of guardian angel without missing a beat. Rumour had it, he ordered his thugs to kneecap people over debts, but he'd also transferred money to Lorraine for years to help her bring up Mike without Prescott. Which version of Chapman was real?

Karen left the office and found Mike waiting in the hallway. His face was pale, eyes distant.

'You okay?' she asked softly.

He shook his head. 'Not really. But I will be. Let's just get out of here.'

They made their way back to the entrance hall. Ponytail was waiting by the front door, his expression bored.

'Leaving so soon?' he drawled.

Karen shot him a withering look. 'Just open the door.'

Ponytail smirked but complied. As they stepped outside, Karen heard Chapman's voice behind them.

'Mr Harrington?'

They turned. Chapman stood in the doorway.

'Your mother had her reasons for keeping certain secrets,' he said. 'Don't judge her too harshly.'

Mike nodded stiffly. Then, without another word, he turned and walked to the car. Karen hurried to catch up.

Inside the car, he said, 'What did you think?'

'I think Chapman's playing games as usual. But I also think there might be some truth in what he told us. I need to get that diary to the team,' she said, glancing at Mike. 'It could be crucial evidence. Do you want me to drop you at home first?'

His jaw clenched. 'I want to read it first. Before anyone else gets their hands on it.'

'But it could contain key evidence about a double murder investigation.'

'It's my mum's diary,' Mike said, his voice low and stubborn. 'Her private thoughts. I'm not just handing it over before I've even had a chance to look at it.'

'The team will make a copy of the text, and you'll get the original back when the investigation's finished.'

His eyes narrowed. 'And what if they don't let us take a copy? Have you forgotten how DI Falkner's been shutting you out?'

Karen winced. He had a point. Falkner had been less than cooperative.

'Look,' Mike continued, 'I'm not trying to obstruct the investigation. But this is personal. It's my mum. My family history. I need to read it first.'

Karen leaned back in her seat, weighing her options. She understood Mike's position, but she also knew the importance of following procedure. If they mishandled evidence, it could jeopardise the entire case.

'All right,' she said finally. 'You read it now. But then we take it to the station.'

Mike hesitated, then nodded. 'Okay. That's fair.'

Karen started the car. She hoped they weren't making a mistake. But then she glanced at Mike as he started turning the pages, and knew she'd made the right call.

Chapter Twenty-Six

Karen sat at the kitchen table with Mike. Between them lay Lorraine's diary.

James stood nearby, his expression tense. They'd explained Chapman had given them the diary, and now asked if he wanted to read it.

He shook his head. 'Lorraine's past isn't important to me. What's in there won't change anything. If it's all the same, I'd rather not read it.'

Karen exchanged a glance with Mike, wondering if James already knew what they were about to uncover. 'Are you sure?'

'Positive,' he replied firmly. 'I knew who Lorraine really was. Her past doesn't matter to me.'

As James retreated to the living room, Karen turned to Mike. 'Would you like some space to read this alone?'

He shook his head, his eyes never leaving the diary. 'No, I'd like you to be here. You can read it too, if you want.'

Karen moved her chair to sit beside Mike. Sandy curled up at their feet.

Mike flipped open the diary. The pages looked as though they could have been written yesterday. The handwriting was neat, almost painfully so, as if Lorraine had been trying to impose order on her chaotic situation.

The first few pages were filled with mundane details of Lorraine's life. She complained about a diet she was struggling to stick to, lamenting the loss of her favourite biscuits. There was an excited entry about a raise at work, praising Quentin Chapman for recognising her efforts.

3rd March 1981

Got a raise today! Mr Chapman called me into his office, and I was terrified. But he just smiled and said he was impressed with my work. The extra money will help this month as Mike needs new shoes. I never thought I'd say this, but Chapman really isn't that bad when you get to know him. Nothing like what people say.

A few pages later, Lorraine wrote about a dinner at the Chapmans' house:

17th April 1981

Went to dinner at the Chapmans' tonight. Their house is enormous! I felt so out of place, but Mrs Chapman was lovely. She kept asking about Mike, cooing over his photos. It's nice to know the boss's wife is so supportive of working mothers. Ken wasn't pleased I went, though. Said I should be home with Mike like a 'proper mother'. We argued again. I wish he could understand how much this job means to me.

And then another entry:

15th June 1981

Kenneth's been in a foul mood lately. I swear the air crackles when he walks into a room. I'm tiptoeing around, trying not to set him off. It's like living with a ticking bomb.

I've been keeping Mike out of his way, making excuses to take him to the park or to Michelle's. Anything to avoid those outbursts. Little Mike's the only light in this mess. Today, he tried to 'help' me fold the clean washing. Ended up wrapping himself in a sheet like a tiny ghost, giggling his head off. For a moment, I forgot about all the bad stuff.

Mike made a sound halfway between a laugh and a sob. 'I'd forgotten that. Used to drive her mad, messing up her neat piles of clean washing.'

Karen smiled. 'Bet you were a right little terror.'

'The worst,' Mike agreed, a hint of a grin flickering across his face.

They continued reading and found an addition at the bottom of the page:

Reality always comes crashing back. Kenneth came home reeking of whisky. I managed to get Mike to bed before the shouting started. God, how did we end up here?

Mike's jaw clenched, a muscle twitching beneath the skin. Karen watched him and noted the way his hands curled into fists on the table. She reached out and placed a hand on his arm.

'We can take a break if you need one.'

'No, let's keep going.'

They continued reading. Sandy, sensing the tension, moved closer to Mike, resting her head on his knee.

3rd July 1981

Ava showed up today, pale and shaking like a leaf, wanting to talk to me and Michelle. She knows about Kenneth's illegal betting ring and wants to go to the police. I wish I could support her, but I can't risk it. Not with Mike to think about. Kenneth would come after us, I know he would.

We talked for hours. She's terrified, and with good reason. The things she's uncovered . . . it's not just the betting. There's more, so much more. Money laundering, even whispers of a protection racket. How did I not see it? How did I let myself get tangled up in this?

Ava was determined to do the right thing. Michelle and I begged her to be careful, to think of her own safety. Ava was disappointed in us and called us cowards. I saw the look in her eyes as she left. She's going to do it, going to blow this whole thing wide open. And heaven help us all when she does.

The diary was more than a record of domestic violence; it was evidence of organised crime.

Mike turned the page, his hands shaking.

4th July 1981

Kenneth came home late last night. His clothes were muddy, and he had a wild look in his eyes. He had scratches on his cheek, too. He didn't say a word to me, just headed straight for the shower. I was too scared to ask how he'd got the scratches.

5th July 1981

Ava's missing. I'm scared out of my mind. What if Kenneth found out she was going to the police? What if he . . . No, I can't even think it.

I snapped at Mike earlier. He'd emptied his dinner all over the floor, and I was terrified Ken would be home any minute and kick off. Now I feel so guilty. I love Mike so much. I'd do anything to keep him safe. Anything.

The next entry made Karen's blood run cold.

6th July 1981

Ava's dead.

They found her body in Willingham Woods yesterday. I can't breathe. Can't think.

Michelle and I argued. She said we should have helped Ava and implied it was my fault we didn't. I hate her for saying it, but it's true. This is my fault. I should've done something. I should've helped her.

I'm thinking of running, taking Mike and disappearing. But where would we go? How would we survive? I'm trapped. If I go to the police, what happens to Mike? But if I stay silent, am I any better than Kenneth?

Karen looked at Mike and saw the pain etched into his face.

She wished she could say something to make it better, but what could she possibly say in a situation like this?

As a police officer, Karen knew she had a duty to investigate these revelations, or at least pass them on to the team so they could act. But right now, her priority was the man sitting beside her.

'Mike,' she said softly, 'I know this is a lot to take in, but your mum was protecting you.'

'Yes, it seems so.' Mike nodded at the diary. 'The Ava mentioned here must be Ava Claywood.'

Karen nodded grimly. 'I think so. Seems she stumbled on to something big and came to your mum for help.'

'Fat lot of good that did her,' Mike muttered.

'Your mum was scared,' Karen said. 'Listen to this bit. Your mum wrote: "I wish I could support her, but I can't risk it. Not with Mike to think about. Kenneth would come after us, I know he would."'

'She should have gone to the police.'

Karen raised an eyebrow. 'Easy to say in hindsight. But put yourself in her shoes. Trapped with a violent man, a young child to protect, no resources of her own. It's not as simple as just paying a visit to the local police station.'

Mike deflated, the fight going out of him. 'I know,' he said quietly. 'I just wish I could have done something.'

'You were a child, Mike,' Karen said. 'It wasn't your responsibility.'

They lapsed into silence, both lost in their own thoughts. Karen was piecing together the puzzle. Ava Claywood, dead in Willingham Woods. Kenneth Prescott, a violent man with criminal connections, with scratches on his cheek. And poor Lorraine and her sister, Michelle, caught in the middle of it all.

Karen nodded grimly. 'It's looking more and more likely that your father was involved in Ava's murder.'

'Don't call him that. He's not my father in any real sense of the word.'

'You're right,' Karen said quickly.

Mike put his head in his hands. 'What a mess.'

Karen agreed. She'd seen some twisted cases in her time, but this was a whole new level. 'Ready to read some more? There's only a few pages left.'

Mike nodded. As they neared the end of the diary, the entries became more erratic, filled with fear and paranoia. Then it was the last entry.

15th July 1981

I can't take it anymore. The fear, the uncertainty, it's eating me alive.

I broke down at work today. I was a gibbering wreck. Chapman made me tell him everything. He's promised to help. To get Ken to back off. Told me to take a few days' holiday and he'd sort everything out. He looked so confident I almost believed him. I know Chapman has a reputation, but is it enough to get Ken out of my life for good?

Last week, Ken said he'd kill us both if I ever left him. I can't risk Mike's life. But I can't keep living like this either. I just don't know what to do.

Karen and Mike sat in silence, letting the raw emotion of the final entry sink in.

After a moment, Mike spoke. 'It probably explains why she fell out with her sister, too. Perhaps they couldn't live with the fact they hadn't helped Ava when she'd needed them?'

Karen nodded. 'Maybe they blamed each other.'

'Then, thanks to Chapman's influence, it looks like Kenneth Prescott scarpered to Brazil. Mum met my stepdad a couple of years later I think.' Mike stood abruptly, his chair scraping loudly against the floor. He paced the kitchen, his movements agitated. 'I should have known,' he muttered. 'Should have pushed her harder when she wouldn't talk about my father.'

'Your mother made her choices to protect you. Don't blame yourself.'

'If she'd told me, maybe I could have done something. I should have realised there was a good reason for her holding back the truth about him.'

Karen sighed, running a hand through her hair. 'So should I. She told me once your father was a bad man. I should have dug deeper. But we can't change what's happened. Lorraine did the best she could under very difficult circumstances. She wouldn't want us to blame ourselves.'

'You're right,' he said, sinking back into his chair. 'Doesn't make it easier to come to terms with, though. Do you think he came back from Brazil to kill Mum and Michelle? Why, after all this time?'

Karen chose her words carefully. 'The way Lorraine and Michelle's eyes were sewn shut could indicate the killer wanted to emphasise keeping their eyes closed to a crime. Maybe that crime was the murder of Ava Claywood. Perhaps Prescott thought Lorraine and Michelle were going to tell the police what they knew after all this time.'

Mike leaned forward, his face intense. 'So you think he could have killed them?'

Karen shook her head. 'We don't know yet if Prescott was even in the country when they were murdered.'

'But what if he paid someone? He could have hired a killer from Brazil, couldn't he?'

'It's possible. But it seems unlikely. This feels personal.' Karen paused, considering. The crime did seem too personal for a hired hit, too vengeful. But Mike's words sparked a new train of thought. 'The team will need to look into whether Prescott has any other family. Maybe a brother or another child?'

'Another child?' Mike shuddered. 'I've hit my quota for family surprises. I don't want any more new family members popping up.'

Karen pushed the diary towards him. 'What do you want to do with this?'

Mike looked at the diary as if it might bite him. Then, he took a deep breath, picked it up and held it out to Karen. 'Take it,' he said. 'The team needs to see this. They need to nail the person who did this to Mum and Michelle, and Ava deserves justice after all this time.'

She stood and took the diary, feeling the weight of it in her hands. It wasn't just paper and ink she was holding, but fear, pain and secrets.

She wished she'd pushed harder to get Lorraine to open up before she died. She'd suspected there was more to the story, but this? She'd never guessed it would be as bad as this.

Chapter Twenty-Seven

Arnie sat at his desk, surrounded by stacks of paperwork and half-empty coffee cups, phone clamped to his ear. Most of the office were focused on Falkner reading the riot act. Again. Something about time running out. Officers forbidden from talking to the press. Blah blah. Arnie ignored him and focused instead on his task: pinning down Kenneth Prescott's whereabouts.

He pressed '2' as directed, drumming his fingers on the desktop as he waited to hear an actual human voice. 'Hello, Border Force? This is Detective Sergeant Arnie Hodgson. I need information on—'

'I'm sorry, sir. You'll need to speak with our records department.'

Arnie suppressed a groan. 'I just did. They told me to contact you.'

'That's not right. I'll transfer you now.'

'No, wait—' The line clicked, and Arnie found himself listening to hold music that sounded like it had been recorded in 1975. He glanced at his watch. He'd been chasing this for twenty minutes already.

Several more minutes crawled by before a new voice answered.

'Records department.'

'Finally,' Arnie muttered. 'I'm looking for information on Kenneth Prescott's travel history. I was told—'

'One moment, please.' More hold music.

Arnie leaned back, rubbing his temples. The chair creaked ominously beneath him. He really ought to put in an order for a new one, but the thought of dealing with more bureaucracy made his head ache.

The voice returned. 'I'm afraid I can't access that information. You'll need to submit a formal request to—'

'Listen,' Arnie cut in, his patience wearing thin. 'This is part of an active murder investigation. I've submitted the form. I sent it this morning. I don't have time for red tape. Can you please just tell me when Prescott last entered the country?'

'I'm sorry, sir, but procedures exist for a reason. I've checked and it seems the form you filled in is out of date. I can email you the new version of the request form if you'd like.'

Arnie bit back a sarcastic reply. 'Fine. Send it over.'

He hung up, resisting the urge to throw his phone across the room. Instead, he turned to his computer, pulling up Prescott's file. There had to be an easier way to track the man's movements.

As he scrolled through the information, DI Morgan appeared at his desk. 'Any luck with Prescott?'

Arnie looked up. 'About as much luck as a three-legged dog at Crufts. Every department's giving me the runaround.'

'Did you fill in the right form? It got updated six months ago.'

Arnie groaned, slumping further into his creaky chair. 'Of course you'd know about the form update. Let me guess – you've got it memorised?'

Morgan's lips twitched. 'Not quite. But I can pull it up for you if you'd like.'

'Please,' Arnie said, gesturing at his computer screen. 'Before I lose what's left of my sanity. They said they'd send the new form over, but they're taking their time.'

Morgan leaned over, accessing the correct file with irritating efficiency. 'There. It's not so bad once you know where to look. Now, let's delete the old form so this doesn't happen again.' He frowned at the screen. 'Just how many old forms have you got? Are you collecting them?'

Arnie shrugged, a defensive look crossing his face. 'I don't like to get rid of the old forms. You never know when you might need them.'

Morgan raised an eyebrow. 'They're outdated. That's the point. You'll never need them again. How can you work in such a mess?'

'We all have our own methods,' Arnie muttered, crossing his arms.

Morgan shook his head. 'I'm going to have nightmares about your file management.'

'You would say that. You probably colour-code your sock drawer,' Arnie said, squinting at the form. 'Look at all these boxes! Next thing you know, they'll be wanting blood type and shoe size.'

'Actually . . .' Morgan began, a hint of amusement in his voice.

Arnie held up a hand. 'Don't. Just don't.' He sighed, starting to fill in the endless fields. 'Seen Karen today?'

Morgan shook his head. 'Not yet. You?'

'No, but maybe it's for the best, eh? After what happened.' Arnie went quiet, remembering the grim scene at Lorraine's house. 'She could do with a few days off. If she does show up, Falkner will only have her counting paperclips or something equally thrilling.'

'True,' Morgan agreed. 'She needs time to come to terms with what's happened. This has been awful for her and Mike.'

Before Arnie could respond, Morgan's office phone began to ring.

He straightened up. 'Duty calls. Good luck with the form.'

'Yeah, thanks,' Arnie waved him off, turning back to his computer. He muttered curses under his breath as he navigated the dropdown menus and required fields. Finally, after what felt like hours but was probably only fifteen minutes, he hit submit.

His phone rang a few minutes later. Arnie snatched it up. 'DS Hodgson.'

'This is Amelia from Border Force. Thank you for sending across the correct form. I've got that information you requested on Kenneth Prescott.'

Finally. Arnie sat up straighter. 'What have you got?'

'Well, according to our records, Mr Prescott hasn't been back to the UK since 1982 . . . until this week.'

He'd come back this week? Arnie grinned. Old Kenny boy was looking more and more like a viable suspect.

'When exactly did he return to the UK?' Arnie asked, tapping his pen impatiently.

If Prescott had been in the country when Lorraine was murdered, he'd shoot straight to the top of the suspect list. This could be their first real break. Arnie was itching to get the old crook in for questioning, because—

'Mr Prescott flew into Heathrow on Tuesday,' Amelia replied, her voice crisp and professional.

Wait. Tuesday?

The realisation hit Arnie like a ton of bricks. Tuesday was the day *after* Lorraine's murder. His earlier excitement deflated faster than a punctured balloon. 'Tuesday? Are you absolutely certain about that?'

'Yes, sir. Our records are quite clear.'

'Is he still in the country?'

'Yes, he has a flight booked back to Brazil two weeks tomorrow.'

'Right. Thanks, Amelia. You've been very helpful,' Arnie said.

He hung up the phone and leaned back in his chair. So much for that lead. Kenneth Prescott couldn't have killed Lorraine if he wasn't even in the country. Back to square one, then.

Arnie rubbed his eyes, feeling the beginnings of a headache just behind them. He'd been so sure they were on to something with Prescott. His past involvement with Lorraine seemed too convenient to be a coincidence. Was the old man involved somehow, even if he wasn't the killer?

Kenneth Prescott had more crimes under his belt than Arnie'd had sausage sandwiches. He couldn't stop thinking that the old gangster had to be mixed up in this mess somehow. Maybe he'd arranged it from abroad? But why come back now? It didn't add up.

Arnie's musings were interrupted by an irritating voice.

'Hodgson!' DI Falkner called from across the room. 'Briefing room, now. And bring whatever you've found on Prescott.'

Arnie suppressed a groan. Falkner's briefings were about as enjoyable as a root canal without anaesthetic. He wasn't looking forward to telling him that Prescott had an airtight alibi.

He hauled himself to his feet, grabbing his notepad. Time to face the music and admit they were no closer to solving this case than when they'd started.

Arnie's backside had gone numb.

He shifted in his chair, trying to find a comfortable position. No chance. The plastic seat seemed designed specifically to torture coppers' rears during never-ending briefings. It would set off his sciatica again, and no amount of hip circles or stretches would help. He'd be limping about like a wounded penguin for the rest of the day.

Falkner droned on at the front of the room, his voice a monotonous buzz that made Arnie's eyelids heavy.

'DS Hodgson, update us on your progress with Kenneth Prescott.'

Arnie snapped to attention, blinking rapidly. Falkner's beady eyes were fixed on him.

'If memorising every form update in the database counts as progress, then I'm gaining ground.'

Falkner's frown deepened. 'This investigation isn't a joking matter, DS Hodgson.'

'Er, no sir,' Arnie said, scratching his stubbled chin. 'It turns out Kenneth Prescott has an airtight alibi for Lorraine Harrington's murder. He wasn't even in the country when Lorraine was killed. Flew into Heathrow the day after.'

Falkner's face turned an interesting shade of purple, somewhere between an aubergine and a bruise. 'And you're just mentioning this now?'

'Only just found out myself, sir,' Arnie replied, trying not to sound too defensive. 'Border Force finally got back to me.'

Falkner pinched the bridge of his nose. 'So we've made no progress? Fantastic.'

Arnie glanced around the room. Sophie and Rick looked as deflated as he felt. DS Cunnings was scribbling furiously in her notebook, probably jotting down ideas for new angles to pursue. At least someone was being productive.

'Prescott's still in the country,' Arnie continued. 'So far, I haven't been able to trace his movements. He's dodged us and slithered into a hole somewhere. No sign of him in Lincoln yet. But I'm working on it. I'll root him out.'

Falkner's lips thinned to almost nothing. 'I see. And what exactly have you been doing to find him?'

Arnie bristled. He'd only just managed to pinpoint the day Prescott had returned to the UK. But he'd been busting a gut to track him down even before the Border Force conversation. He'd been trawling through CCTV, even talking to DCI Whitmore to see if the retired detective had any ideas where Prescott might be lurking if he'd come back to the UK.

'Everything I can think of,' Arnie grumbled. 'Short of hiring a flipping psychic.'

A few chuckles rippled through the room. Falkner did not look amused.

'Perhaps you should consider that option, DS Hodgson. It might prove more fruitful than your current efforts.'

Arnie bit back a retort. No use antagonising the miserable git further. He slumped back in his chair as Falkner's attention moved on.

'DC Cooper, DC Jones? What have you uncovered about Prescott's family connections in Brazil?'

Rick spoke up. 'We've made some headway. Local records show Kenneth Prescott married a woman named Maria Soares in São Paulo back in 1992. They had at least one son, Liam Prescott, born in 1998. Mike should probably know about this. Liam is likely his half-brother . . .'

'He deserves to know,' Sophie agreed. 'It's his family history.'

Falkner held up a hand. 'Nobody tells Mike about this until I say so. When I completed my master's in Applied Criminology and Police Management at Cambridge—'

Arnie suppressed a groan. *Here we go. The famous master's degree again.* He'd bet a month's salary that Falkner had the certificate displayed pride of place in his home, strategically lit like a museum piece.

'Seems to me like we are keeping it from him for no reason,' Arnie said, interrupting before Falkner got too carried away.

Falkner turned on him. 'For all we know, Mike's already been in contact with Liam. We can't risk compromising the investigation if Liam finds out we're looking for him.'

'He's not in contact with Liam. Karen would have told us if he was,' Rick said.

'My decision is final. We keep this quiet until we have more information.' Falkner's expression was granite.

'Seems unfair,' Sophie muttered. 'Keeping him in the dark about his own brother.'

'Then I suggest you work quickly, DC Jones.' Falkner's smile didn't reach his eyes. 'The sooner we have answers, the sooner Mike can know.'

Arnie watched the exchange, thinking Falkner was about as compassionate as a brick wall. Probably learned that at Cambridge too. But Falkner was already moving on, clearly considering the matter closed.

'What else do we know?'

Sophie added, 'No criminal records or run-ins with local authorities that we can find. We're still digging, but so far it looks like Prescott has kept his nose clean during his time in Brazil.'

'Or he's been paying the right people to look the other way.' Cunnings shrugged. 'It happens.'

'More often than we'd like to admit,' Arnie agreed. 'That's probably more likely than Prescott becoming a saint overnight. Old dogs, new tricks, and all that.'

Rick frowned. 'Hard to know for sure, but the authorities in Brazil have been really helpful so far. If they had any info, I think they would have shared it. They seem genuinely interested in cooperating.'

'Next steps?' Falkner asked, flipping through a printed copy of his policy log.

'We need to check if Liam Prescott has travelled to the UK recently,' Sophie said. 'Could be important if he's been in contact with his father. He could be the one doing his father's dirty work.'

Falkner nodded, looking marginally less constipated than usual. 'Good work.' He sent a pointed look to Arnie. 'Good to see some of the team have been putting the effort in. See to it immediately.'

'Make sure you submit the right form for the international travel information request,' Arnie said. 'I had a nightmare with them, thanks to an out-of-date form.'

Rick grinned. 'No worries there. If anyone knows which form to use, it's Sophie. She lives and breathes paperwork.'

Sophie rolled her eyes, but Arnie caught the hint of a smile.

A phone buzzed, drawing Arnie's attention to Morgan.

'Sir,' Morgan said, interrupting Falkner mid-sentence. 'I've just heard from DS Hart. She's arrived at the station with new evidence. Lorraine Harrington's diary from forty years ago.'

The room went silent. Arnie felt a jolt of excitement fizz through him. Now this should be interesting.

Falkner's face darkened. 'How did she find that? The Harrington house was thoroughly searched after Lorraine's murder.'

Morgan shook his head. 'I don't know, sir. The message didn't say.'

Arnie watched Falkner's face turn that alarming shade of purple again. He looked ready to pop a blood vessel. Arnie couldn't blame him, really. If Karen had gone off investigating on her own, bypassing procedure, the brass would have Falkner's – and Karen's – guts for garters if anything went wrong.

Arnie was worried about Karen. She had a habit of taking risks. It was what made her a brilliant police officer, but it scared him sometimes. If she'd gone poking around on her own, who knew what kind of danger she might have stumbled into? Especially with that old crook Chapman involved.

Falkner's sharp voice cut through Arnie's thoughts. 'DS Cunnings! This is hardly the time for personal communications.'

Arnie glanced over to see Bridget Cunnings hastily shoving her phone into her pocket, looking sheepish.

'Sorry, sir,' she said. 'I was just checking messages, hoping to get some answers from the door-to-door enquiries around Michelle Matthews's residence.'

Arnie narrowed his eyes. He'd caught a glimpse of Cunnings's phone screen, and unless he was seeing things, whatever she'd been doing definitely hadn't been work-related. He smothered a grin. At least Cunnings was human, unlike the human cardboard cut-out leading their briefing.

There was a sharp knock at the door. Arnie's head snapped around, along with everyone else's. Then the door opened and Karen walked in. She looked flushed and slightly out of breath, as if she'd sprinted up the three flights of stairs. In her hand, she clutched a battered leather-bound book.

'Sorry to interrupt,' she said, her gaze sweeping the room before landing on Falkner. 'But I think you're all going to want to see this.'

Arnie leaned forward, his numb backside forgotten. From the look on Karen's face, that diary contained the breakthrough they'd been hoping for.

Chapter Twenty-Eight

Karen's fingers gripped the diary as she met Falkner's stern gaze.

She'd just told the team how she'd got Lorraine's old diary from Chapman and that it contained Lorraine's suspicions that Prescott had murdered Ava, after Ava had been talking about turning him in to the police for his crimes.

The room had fallen into a stunned silence, broken only by the steady tapping of Morgan's pen against his notepad. Falkner leaned back, his expression souring by the second.

'Let me get this straight,' he said, his voice dangerously low. 'You and Mike went to see Chapman? Alone?'

'I didn't have a choice. Chapman approached Mike. He had information that—'

'Of course you had a choice. Your recklessness could've got you and Mike both killed!' Falkner snapped, cutting her off. 'What on earth were you thinking? Have you not had basic operational safety training? You obviously need lessons in strategic policing to understand the importance of following proper protocols. I expect my team to operate at a higher level.'

His team? He wished. His assignment here was temporary, thank goodness.

'Let me explain this in simple terms,' he continued.

Karen braced herself for a lecture. Arnie hadn't been wrong about Falkner's superiority complex.

'Those of us who've studied advanced police methodology understand that lone-wolf heroics have no place in modern policing. My master's in Applied Criminology and Police Management from Cambridge taught me the complexities of strategic risk assessment.'

Karen should have known a lecture from Falkner couldn't be a proper lecture until he'd mentioned his master's degree.

Falkner shook his head as though he was deeply disappointed. 'But even basic training covers not walking into a known criminal's house without backup. My officers need to operate at a higher level.'

Karen bit her tongue. She didn't like being referred to as one of his officers, especially since she wasn't even officially working under him. Another few weeks or so and they'd be shot of him. She couldn't wait.

Yes, she'd gone to see the old gangster without backup. Yes, it was probably stupid. But it had got them a result.

'He gave it to Mike,' she explained, passing the diary to the DI. 'He said Lorraine asked him to pass it on if anything happened to her.'

Falkner's face flushed a deep red. 'And you didn't think to inform me?'

'I'm informing you now,' Karen said. 'There's important information in the diary. There are details on Ava Claywood's disappearance. And Lorraine suspected Prescott's involvement because he had scratches on his cheek around the time of Ava's murder.'

'The positive outcome doesn't negate the fact you were foolish.'

Cunnings tried to calm things down. 'What's done is done. The important thing is the diary's contents. Let's focus on—'

'Be quiet!' Falkner snapped.

Cunnings's mouth clamped shut, her eyebrows shooting up in surprise at his harsh tone. Karen felt a pang of sympathy.

Falkner rounded on Karen again. 'DS Hart, your continued interference in this case is becoming a serious problem.'

'With all due respect, sir, my personal connection gives me valuable insight.'

'Insight?' he scoffed. 'Or biased perspective? You're too close to this, Karen. Your emotions are compromising your ability to think clearly.'

Karen's cheeks burned. She wanted to argue and defend herself, but a small voice in the back of her mind whispered that Falkner had a point.

She shoved that thought aside. 'Sir, I understand your concerns, but—'

'Do you?' Falkner interrupted. 'Because I'm not convinced you do. Let's look at the facts, shall we? Ava Claywood was strangled more than forty years ago. Michelle and Lorraine were killed by blows to the head this week, then their eyelids were stitched together. The MOs don't match.'

Karen flinched as an image of Lorraine's mutilated eyes flashed through her mind.

She took a steadying breath. 'I'm not saying it's exactly the same. But there's a link here. We can't just ignore it.'

Falkner's eyes narrowed. '*We?* Karen, this is exactly why you can't work this case. You're too emotional. If you were thinking logically, you'd realise it can't possibly be the same killer. Prescott likely killed Ava Claywood in 1981, but Prescott wasn't even in the country when Lorraine was murdered.'

His words hit home with devastating accuracy. She'd been sure Prescott had to be behind Lorraine's death, somehow, but she struggled to find a flaw in Falkner's logic.

Still, she wouldn't let him see how much he'd affected her.

'I can remain objective,' she said, keeping her voice steady. 'We just need to—'

'*We* again?' Falkner's voice turned to ice. 'There is no *we*, Karen. You're not on this case.'

The words stung more than she'd expected. She'd tried her best to keep her distance, but it wasn't easy to step back when this case affected her life so directly. She'd already been sidelined. To be pushed out further felt like a betrayal.

'You're right,' she said, maintaining her composure, 'I shouldn't have gone with Mike to see Chapman without clearing it with you first. I apologise.'

Falkner stared at her for a long moment, his expression unreadable. Finally, he sighed. 'Fine,' he said grudgingly. 'You can stay in the loop. But I'm warning you, one more stunt like this Chapman business, and you're out, home on gardening leave indefinitely. Understood?'

Karen nodded. 'Understood, sir.'

As she left the briefing room, irritation simmered beneath the surface. At least she wasn't being frozen out completely. She was hanging in there, even if it was by the skin of her teeth.

Arnie and Morgan caught up with her in the hallway.

'Karen,' Arnie called, his voice gruff. 'Hold up a sec.'

She turned, forcing a smile. 'That went well, don't you think?'

'Could've been worse,' he said. 'He didn't actually ban you from the station.'

Morgan's piercing gaze saw right through her 'everything is okay' act. 'We're worried about you.'

'Yeah,' Arnie said. 'Falkner was over the top. You all right?'

These two were not just her colleagues, they were friends. But right now, their concern felt suffocating.

'I'm fine,' Karen replied quickly. She could see the doubt in their eyes. 'Really. I can handle it. I won't let my emotions get in the way.'

Arnie and Morgan exchanged a look. They weren't exactly subtle.

They reached her desk. Karen sank into her chair with a sigh. She hadn't been back in the station ten minutes, and already the weight of everything was pressing down on her.

Falkner's lecture was still ringing in her ears. The really annoying thing was that he might have had a point. She'd been so sure about Prescott, she'd practically started building the case against him in her head. Now that felt more like wishful thinking.

How was she supposed to step back when this case was so tangled up with her personal life?

Emotional investment was a tricky thing. Sometimes it drove you to dig deeper and find things others might miss. The trouble was, she couldn't tell if she was seeing real connections, or just seeing what she wanted to see.

Everyone was telling her to step back and let others handle it. But she was scared she'd miss something crucial if she wasn't involved.

The question wasn't whether she was close to the case – of course she was. The real question was whether that closeness would help uncover the truth, or send her on a wild goose chase.

'Anyway,' Arnie said, attempting to change the subject, 'I need you to review that photofit we're having made from Jason Wilkes's description of the man he saw going inside Lorraine's house the afternoon she died. Should be ready this afternoon. I had an early peak, and it looks like a young man. Much too young to be Prescott.'

Karen frowned. 'Someone working for him, then? A hired gun?'

'Could be.' Arnie shrugged. 'I'll let you know when it's ready.'

As Arnie and Morgan headed back to their desks, Karen leaned back in her chair, letting out a long breath. She closed her eyes, trying to calm her racing thoughts.

Delivering Lorraine's diary to the team hadn't gone as she'd planned. She'd thought they'd be happy to have new evidence. She hadn't anticipated the lecture.

Maybe she should have. Falkner was breathing down her neck, ready to boot her out at the slightest provocation. And if she were being honest with herself, she could see where he was coming from. She was emotionally involved. How could she not be? This was Mike's family.

But being emotionally involved didn't mean she couldn't do her job. If anything, it made her more focused on bringing whoever was responsible to justice. She just had to prove to Falkner, and to herself, that she could keep a level head.

Sophie stifled a yawn as she waited for the ancient coffee machine to splutter into life. She needed caffeine to face more hours of searching for Prescott's son, Liam. So far, she'd hit nothing but dead ends.

'Hello,' Callum said, appearing beside her with his own mug. 'Mind if I grab a coffee too?'

'Help yourself,' Sophie replied, stepping aside. 'Though I warn you, Arnie says it tastes like something scraped off the A15.'

Callum grimaced. 'I tried it yesterday. Definitely an acquired taste. You should have seen the fancy machine we had at my last job. All bells and whistles – although half the time it didn't even work. At least this one's reliable.'

Sophie's grip on her mug shook. Her hand weakened when she was tired, a lingering reminder of the attack. The doctors were happy with her progress though. One even described her as miraculous, which had pleased Sophie no end. She'd joked with the doctor that she'd always been an overachiever.

Callum focused on her trembling hand. Feeling self-conscious, she swapped the coffee mug over to her left hand and said, 'So, how's life in the land of spin and soundbites?'

He chuckled, reaching past her for the sugar. 'Oh, you know, never a dull moment. Though I suspect it's not half as exciting as your world of dramatic arrests.'

Sophie snorted. Hardly. Police work mostly involved mind-numbing paperwork and endless waiting.

Callum's phone rang. He glanced at the screen, and his smile disappeared. 'Sorry, need to take this.' He hurried off down the corridor without his drink, speaking rapid Portuguese into his phone.

Sophie froze, coffee mug halfway to her lips. Portuguese?

The penny dropped.

Hadn't Callum mentioned growing up in Brazil during that chat in the canteen earlier this week?

Sophie returned to her desk. She pulled up Callum's profile page on the internal system. Press Office, joined a month ago. Degree in Media Studies from Leeds. Master's in Journalism from City University. His previous job was press liaison and communications officer at some big tech firm in London. That must have paid a hefty salary.

Why would someone take a pay cut to work in police communications?

Sophie drummed her fingers on her desk. She couldn't access his HR file without raising flags, but something felt off. That phone call, his Brazilian background, the timing of his arrival . . .

Prescott's son would be in his mid-twenties now, about Callum's age. They only had the name Liam to go on, but who said that was his name now?

Sophie leaned back in her chair. If Callum was Prescott's son, they had a serious problem.

Was it possible? Could their new press officer really be Kenneth Prescott's son and inside man?

◆ ◆ ◆

Sophie spotted Arnie at his desk and headed over. 'Got a minute?'

'If it's about more paperwork, then no.' Arnie didn't look up from his computer screen.

'It's about Kenneth Prescott's son.'

That got his attention. 'Go on then.'

'I think . . .' Sophie hesitated. 'I think it might be Callum Turner.'

'Callum?' Arnie's forehead wrinkled. 'The new press officer? What makes you suspect him?'

Arnie's face was still flushed from his earlier conversation with Falkner. Maybe this wasn't the best time. But she'd already started, so . . .

'Well . . . I heard him speaking Portuguese on the phone.'

'And?' Arnie's eye twitched slightly. Not a good sign.

'And he was born in Brazil, like Kenneth Prescott's son.'

Arnie let out a sigh and threw his pen on the desk. 'Do you know how many people are born in Brazil?'

'No . . .' Sophie shifted uncomfortably. She was starting to think Arnie didn't think much of her theory. 'Do you?' she added, when he kept glaring at her.

'Well . . . no,' he admitted, some of the thunder leaving his expression. 'But it's a lot.'

Sophie wished she'd gone to someone else with this. Arnie was in a foul mood for at least an hour after dealing with Falkner. 'Callum's the right age, too. Plus, he only started working here a month ago.'

Arnie drummed his fingers on his desk, that dangerous glint appearing in his eyes which usually meant he was about to do something impulsive. 'You know what?' He pushed back from his desk. 'Let's just go and ask him.'

'What? Now?' Sophie stared at him. 'Just like that?'

'Why not?'

'Well, because we're not prepared. I don't have any evidence. We need an action plan—'

'No, we don't. We need to ask him. You can learn a lot not just from what people say, but how they say it.'

'But he might just lie and deny it!'

'Only one way to find out.' Arnie was already heading out of the office.

Sophie hurried after him. If Callum really was Prescott's son, they needed to be careful. His shy personality could be an act. They needed to prepare for all eventualities, make sure everything was done properly. Not confront Callum like a bull in a china shop.

Arnie knocked on Callum's door. 'Got a minute?'

'Of course.' Callum looked up from his laptop. 'What can I help you with?'

'Quick question,' Arnie said, settling into a chair. 'You know we're investigating Kenneth Prescott?'

Callum shook his head as Sophie sat down too.

'Ah. Well, he's a suspect in our murder investigation. Career criminal, now based in Brazil.' Arnie paused. 'Sophie here has an interesting theory about you being his son.'

Callum's eyes widened. 'Me? No, my father isn't called Kenneth Prescott.'

Sophie's eyes narrowed. Well, Callum would say that, wouldn't he? He was hardly going to come right out and admit to being the son of a wanted criminal.

'You were born in Brazil?' Arnie asked.

'Yes, my mum's Brazilian, but my dad's Bruce Turner. Runs The Swan just outside Milton Keynes.' He fumbled for his phone. 'Look, I can prove it. I've got pictures. I can show you his pub's Facebook page. Or I can call him right now. Or I can bring in my birth certificate tomorrow. Whatever you need.'

Sophie shifted in her chair, doubt creeping in. He did sound quite convincing. Had she just got way ahead of herself here?

'Calm down, mate.' Arnie held up a hand. 'You're not in trouble. We've just got suspicious natures, what with being detectives.' He glanced at Sophie. 'Sometimes our imaginations get the best of us. No harm done.'

Callum's hands shook slightly as he pulled up Facebook. 'Here, look. That's my dad. Behind the bar, that's him.' He scrolled through several photos, including one of himself and his dad at a football match, both wearing Arsenal shirts and grinning at the camera.

Sophie's stomach sank. She'd really messed up big-time. Callum looked absolutely distraught, his usual cheerful manner completely gone. The poor bloke was shaking.

'I can video-call him,' he offered, his voice trembling. 'Right now if you want. Or I can go home and get my passport and birth certificate.'

'That won't be necessary,' Arnie said. 'Sorry to have bothered you.'

'I'm so sorry,' Sophie said, feeling mortified.

Callum's phone buzzed. He glanced at it, then quickly turned it face down on his desk.

'We'll leave you in peace,' Arnie said, standing up.

Sophie couldn't get out of there fast enough. As they walked along the corridor, she turned to Arnie and said, 'I'm such an idiot.'

'Actually . . .' Arnie stopped walking. 'I knew he wasn't Prescott's son. I checked his background the minute Brazil came up.'

Sophie's mouth fell open. For a moment, all she could do was gape at him. 'What?'

'Yeah. Callum's dad's pub does a cracking Sunday roast according to Tripadvisor. Four and a half stars. Might pay a visit if I ever get the chance.'

'But why would you let me go in there like that if you already knew Callum had nothing to do with it?'

'I was trying to show you that you need to build your theories based on proper evidence.' He scratched his head. 'Except maybe I went about it wrong. Falkner's been winding me up, and I've got less patience than usual.'

Sophie's face was hot enough to fry an egg on. What a mess. They'd gone charging in without any proof and got Callum all upset for nothing. The poor bloke had looked ready to have a heart attack.

And now it turned out Arnie had known her theory was wrong . . . What a horrible way to teach her a lesson.

Arnie must have seen her embarrassment, because suddenly his expression softened.

'I'm really sorry, Sophie,' he said, his voice quieter than usual. 'Falkner's been annoying me, then you came to me with this half-cocked theory and I just—'

'Thought you'd embarrass me in front of Callum?'

He deflated. 'It was a mean thing to do.'

'Yes,' Sophie agreed. 'It was.' She stared at her shoes, her earlier confidence draining away. After her recovery from the attack, she'd finally started feeling like herself again. Now she just felt stupid.

'I really am sorry. You're a good officer, Sophie. Sharp instincts. You just need to back up those instincts with facts first.'

'I would have done,' Sophie shot back. 'But I came to you because I thought you'd want to know straightaway. I mistakenly thought you might help me check it out properly.'

Arnie winced. 'You're right.'

Sophie felt her anger fade. It was hard to stay cross with Arnie.

'Am I forgiven?' He gave her his best hangdog expression.

'I suppose so.' She sighed. 'You're just on edge because you're worried about Karen. And Falkner lording it over everyone doesn't help.'

'Still no excuse. It would have been nice if you *had* been right about Callum being Prescott's mysterious son though,' Arnie said with a remorseful smile. 'It would've saved us hours of searching. Oh well, back to the grind.'

Sophie watched him head off to his desk. That business with Callum turning his phone face down was odd, wasn't it?

But no, she was being ridiculous. She needed to focus on finding Liam Prescott, not get swept up in random goose chases accusing a colleague of being the son of a wanted criminal.

Heat crept up her neck as the humiliation hit her again. At least it was only Arnie she'd gone to with her wild theory. She'd never have lived it down if she'd gone to Morgan, Falkner, or worse still, DCI Churchill with this nonsense.

Still, something about Callum's reaction . . .

Sophie gave herself a mental shake. *Stop it.* She turned back to her computer. Time to find the real Prescott Junior.

Chapter Twenty-Nine

After dinner – when Mike had disappeared into the study and James had settled in to watch mind-numbing TV – Karen tidied the kitchen.

Earlier, Arnie and Sylvie had stopped by. Arnie had hesitated by the doorway, but Sylvie had bustled in with a bright smile and a book in her hand.

'I thought this might be useful,' she'd said, pressing the book with a faded green cover into Karen's hands. 'It helped me a lot when I lost my mum.'

The title was *Grief and Loss*.

'People just don't know what to do after there's been a death,' Sylvie continued. 'They want to help, but there are no words really suitable.'

Karen had nodded, understanding all too well. They couldn't exactly say, *Sorry to hear a maniac killed your future mother-in-law and sewed her eyes shut.* They didn't sell those types of condolence cards at Clintons.

Arnie and Sylvie's visit had been a brief respite from the gloom. It was nice to see them so close, and Karen had never seen him so content. Sylvie was good for him.

As Karen wiped down the counter, her gaze fell on a small pile of post on the sideboard. She might as well sort through it.

Anything to keep her busy. Bill, junk mail, more junk. Karen paused, frowning at an envelope addressed to Christine, their next-door neighbour.

It must've been delivered by mistake. Karen glanced at the clock. It wasn't too late to pop round.

Karen grabbed her keys and the misdelivered letter, calling out to Mike and James that she'd be back in a minute.

She pulled on a jacket before stepping outside into the crisp evening.

Karen paused by the unmarked car parked on the road. The officers inside were there to keep watch, in case the killer decided to target Mike or James.

'Everything quiet?' she asked, leaning down to the open window.

One of the officers, a red-haired young woman with freckles, smiled. 'All calm here. How are you all holding up?'

Her partner, a burly man with curly hair, looked over.

'We're getting there,' Karen said.

The woman nodded. 'We're here if you need anything.'

'Appreciate it,' Karen said. 'Can I get you two a drink? A cup of tea? It's chilly out here.'

The female officer smiled and shook her head. 'Thanks, but we're all set.' She lifted an insulated mug.

Her partner did the same. 'Got our own supplies. We came prepared.'

'I'm just nipping next door to drop off a letter. Won't be long.' Karen nodded towards Christine's house.

'All right. We'll keep an eye out.'

Karen felt a pang of guilt at the resources being used to keep them safe, but she was grateful they were there.

She headed to Christine's house. She liked Christine. It had been a while since they'd gone to the pub quiz. It was always a good night when Christine was on the team. She had an almost inexhaustible knowledge of trivia.

A tingle prickled the back of Karen's neck. Someone was watching her. She turned slowly, searching the shadows. Nothing seemed out of place. Just the unmarked car with the two officers inside. Karen shook her head. Of course they were watching her. That was their job, after all.

She looked around once more, just to be sure. The road was empty. No one else was about. She was just jumpy.

She rang the doorbell. Christine answered quickly, her round face creasing into a concerned smile as she opened the door.

'Come in, come in,' she said warmly. 'How have you been?'

Karen managed a smile. 'Oh, you know. Taking it day by day. This came to ours by mistake.' She handed over the letter.

Christine took the envelope, and Karen glanced over her shoulder, eyes scanning the shadows behind her. Still nothing. Just her imagination.

'Thanks for bringing it round. Fancy a cuppa?'

Karen hesitated, then shook her head. 'Better not. I don't want to leave Mike too long.'

'Such a dreadful business. I've been worried about you and Mike. If you need anything . . .'

'We appreciate that. It's been difficult,' Karen said, glancing out the window.

Christine followed her gaze. 'How's Mike doing?'

'He's managing. Grief is a strange thing.'

Christine changed the subject. 'I meant to ask what happened with that dodgy salesman? The one who turned up at your place acting suspicious?'

Karen blinked, having completely forgotten about him. 'I haven't seen him since. Did he come round to yours?'

'No, he didn't call here. I kept an eye out after you sent the text, but never saw him. Perhaps he was a ne'er-do-well and you scared him off?'

Karen frowned, remembering the man's odd behaviour – the way he'd tried to look over her shoulder and into the house. Like he was looking for something, or someone. 'Maybe.'

If the man was a door-to-door salesman, why would he skip Christine's house? Had he been casing the premises? Or looking for Mike or James?

Christine shrugged. 'I put a post up on the neighbourhood page after you mentioned it, but I never saw him.'

'Well, let me know if you see anything unusual,' Karen said as she headed to the door.

'Will do, and take care.'

'Thanks, Christine. Have a good night.'

She turned to leave and shivered. She had that feeling again . . . like eyes were boring into her. She walked up the driveway to the main road, looking for anything out of the ordinary.

The chill was sharper now. She zipped up her jacket, feeling uneasy. The night loomed dark around her, and the stars seemed to flicker like warning lights.

Karen nodded to the officers, then walked back towards her house. Christine's mention of the salesman nagged at her. Could he be connected to the case somehow?

With two members of Mike's family now dead she couldn't be too careful about someone potentially targeting him or James.

Then again, the salesman might have been genuine, or maybe even part of that burglary gang Cindy Connor had reported on recently. She made a mental note to take a screenshot from the security camera footage and pass his photo to the team working those cases, just to be safe.

As she reached the end of the driveway, that creeping sensation of being watched crawled over her skin again. Slowly, she looked across the road.

There. A shadow shifted. Someone was standing there.

She *was* being watched.

A figure lingered beside the trunk of a huge beech tree, half hidden in the darkness.

He moved slightly to the right, closer to the lamp post, and his face was lit up.

It was him. The man who'd been trying to sell things door-to-door.

He turned and bolted.

'Stop!' Karen shouted, breaking into a run. 'Police!'

She heard car doors slamming behind her as the protection detail scrambled to follow.

'What's going on?' one called.

'Someone was watching the house!' Karen yelled back, pointing ahead. 'He went that way!'

The man darted down the side street opposite Karen's house. He was fast.

She rounded the corner, only to find . . . nothing.

The street was empty. Karen spun around, chest heaving, gaze darting to every shadow and crevice. But the man had vanished.

The officers caught up, breathless and wide-eyed. 'Did you see where they went?'

Karen shook her head. 'He's gone.'

She swore, and leaned over, hands on her knees, as she tried to get her breath back.

The breathlessness wasn't only from the exertion, but the sheer flood of adrenaline and panic that was still flowing through her veins.

The officers exchanged a glance. As though they weren't sure whether to take her seriously.

'What is it?' Karen demanded.

'Are you sure you saw someone?' the curly-haired officer asked.

'Of course I'm sure,' Karen snapped. She sighed, then softened her tone. 'Sorry. I'm just on edge. There was a man standing behind the beech tree, watching me as I walked back from Christine's.'

'Right,' the woman officer said gently. 'We didn't see anyone. We saw you running, so we followed.'

That was odd. 'Well, I can assure you there was someone there. I didn't just imagine it.'

'Of course not.'

Karen shook her head, frustration and fear battling for dominance. Then a horrifying thought hit her like a bucket of ice water.

They'd all run after the man, leaving Mike and James unprotected. What if this had been a distraction to lure them away from the house?

'We need to get back, now!' she shouted, taking off at a sprint.

Without waiting for a response, she ran back towards home, her chest tight.

Please, let them be okay, let them be okay.

She burst through the front door, the officers close behind. 'Mike! James!'

Sandy barked twice, picking up on Karen's panic.

The TV was still on in the living room, the same mind-numbing game show playing. James levered himself out of the sofa. 'Karen? What's wrong?'

Mike appeared in the hallway, laptop in hand. 'What's going on?'

She sagged against the wall, relief washing over her. 'I thought . . . Never mind. False alarm, guys,' she added to the officers.

'We'll call it in and do a sweep of the area,' the male officer said. 'See if we can find anything.'

'Thank you,' Karen said. 'I appreciate it.'

They nodded, heading off towards their car.

Karen watched them go, then turned to Mike. 'I saw someone outside. We chased after them, but . . .'

'They got away?'

Karen nodded. 'I'm going to ring Morgan and get some more people looking.' She hesitated. 'The man looked like the same one who came to our door trying to sell things the other day.'

Mike frowned. 'It could just be the same bloke trying his luck again.'

Karen didn't think so. 'He was lurking. Watching the house.'

'Maybe he's part of that burglary gang, and was waiting for an opportunity to break in, but made a run for it when you spotted him.'

Karen wanted to believe that. It would be a logical explanation. But logic seemed to have taken a holiday lately, replaced by a constant worry that everything was connected. Was she seeing threats where there weren't any? Or was she right to trust her instinct that something wasn't adding up? The man who'd killed Lorraine and Michelle was still out there somewhere. What if he was watching, waiting for his chance to get to Mike or James?

Great. Now she even sounded paranoid to herself.

But with Mike and James's lives potentially at stake, wasn't being overcautious better than them ending up dead?

'First Lorraine, then Michelle . . .' James removed his reading glasses and rubbed his eyes. 'And now this man skulking about in the dark?' He fixed Karen with a shrewd look. 'You think he might be connected to Lorraine's murder, don't you?'

The directness of his question caught Karen off guard. But James deserved honesty. 'I don't know,' she admitted.

'Are we in danger?'

Karen wished she could give him a more reassuring answer. 'I'm not sure, James. But until we catch Lorraine and Michelle's killer, I'm not taking any chances with either of you. We've got the police officers parked outside, and I'm going to call Morgan now. He'll organise more officers to come and help.'

After she'd called Morgan, Karen found herself alone in the kitchen. Mike had retreated back to the study, saying something about making a start on his accounts. She knew keeping busy was his way of coping, but she wished he'd just talk to her. James had gone back in the living room to watch TV.

Karen locked up, double-checking every window and door. She could still feel that crawling sensation on her skin, as if eyes were watching from the darkness.

Less than twenty minutes later, the quiet hum of an engine outside caught her attention. Karen peered out, relief flooding through her as she recognised Morgan's car.

Morgan climbed out first. Arnie followed in his rumpled coat. She opened the front door before they could knock.

'You all right?' Arnie called out as they approached, concern evident in his gruff voice.

Karen nodded, stepping back to let them in. 'Yeah, I'm fine. Thanks for coming so quickly.'

Morgan gave her a reassuring smile. 'Of course.'

Mike appeared in the hallway, James trailing behind him. 'What's going on?' Mike asked. 'Has something else happened?'

'No, no new developments,' Morgan said. 'We're here to assess the situation.'

'You've not identified the person hanging around outside?'

'Not yet.'

They all crammed into the kitchen. Karen put the kettle on, more for something to do with her hands than any real desire for tea. As she grabbed the mugs, she filled Morgan and Arnie in on what had happened and what she'd seen.

'So it was definitely the same bloke as the door-to-door salesman?' Arnie asked, confirming what Karen had told them earlier.

Karen nodded. 'No doubt about it. It was him.'

Mike's jaw tightened at the reminder of how close the man had been to their home. He paced the kitchen, running a hand through his hair. 'Right outside our house. I take it you think he had more in mind than burglary.' Karen saw the fear beneath his anger. 'What was he planning to do?'

There was a pause before Arnie said, 'We can't say for sure, but I doubt his intentions were good.'

'I hate the thought of him prowling around our home . . . I'd prefer to get out there now and look for him.'

'That's the worst thing you could do,' Karen said.

'We've got officers nearby,' Morgan said quietly. 'He won't get close again.'

Arnie nodded. 'We'll catch him. Half the force are looking for him now.'

Mike stopped pacing and let out a breath. 'Thanks for being straight with us about what's going on. Knowing you're not keeping things from me makes it less scary somehow.'

'Of course, you have a right to know,' Morgan said.

Guilt churned in Karen's stomach. Now she felt really bad about the emails she hadn't mentioned. She should just tell Mike now. Rip off the plaster.

'There's something I need to tell you,' she said quietly. 'I've been getting threatening emails. Three of them now.'

'What?' Mike stared at her. 'And you didn't tell me?'

'I didn't want to worry you. You've got enough to deal with—'

'Stop.' Mike held up his hand. 'Just don't.'

Arnie cleared his throat awkwardly and became very interested in inspecting his nails.

'Mike, I'm sorry,' Karen said. She'd been doing exactly what Lorraine had done, keeping secrets from him 'for his own good'.

He had every right to be angry. She should have told him.

'Maybe I'm just stupid,' Mike said, his voice bitter. 'Or maybe I just walk around with my eyes closed. I don't see what's right in front of me. My own mother was living in fear, and I didn't notice. And you've been getting threats, and again, I'm the last to know.'

'Now, Mike,' James cut in. 'Karen's heart is in the right place. She's only trying to protect you.'

'Like Mum was?' Mike shook his head. 'I thought I could trust you to be honest with me, Karen.'

His words hit Karen hard. She'd been trying so hard to protect him, but somehow she'd only made things worse.

'What exactly did the emails say?' Mike asked.

Morgan turned his back and scrolled through his phone; Arnie began studying the kitchen ceiling as if he'd never seen one before.

'They were short. Threatening.' Karen's voice was quiet. 'Telling me to back off, stop asking questions. The latest one mentioned your mum and Michelle.'

'And you've had three of these?'

'Yes.'

'Have you traced who sent them?'

'Harinder's trying, but they're using an encrypted email service. Based in Switzerland. The sender's been careful. Very careful.'

Mike nodded slowly, processing the information. The betrayal in his eyes made Karen's chest ache.

'So someone's been threatening you. And everyone knew except me.'

'Not everyone,' Karen said softly. 'Just the team working on it.'

'Right,' he said. 'Just the team. Just the people you actually trust.'

Everyone was silent.

'Right,' James said after a moment. 'Well, I'm off to bed. Had enough excitement for one night.' He shuffled out of the kitchen without another word.

Karen felt terrible. James was a decent man who just wanted everyone to get along, and now she'd made him uncomfortable with this tension between her and Mike. She couldn't seem to do anything right at the moment.

Mike looked at Karen. 'Do you need me for anything?'

Karen shook her head. 'No, I can fill you in on everything in the morning.'

Mike nodded, then turned and headed back to his study. Karen watched him go. Navigating this situation felt like walking through a minefield.

Once Mike and James had left, Arnie's gruff voice filled the kitchen. 'So, this bloke just vanished into thin air, did he?'

Karen nodded, recounting the events for what felt like the hundredth time. She was tired of this. Tired of being scared Mike could be next; tired of feeling like a sitting target.

Arnie reached over and patted her hand. 'I know this is tough, but you'll get through it.'

He moved over to finish making the tea, which Karen had completely forgotten about.

Morgan was all business. 'We'll increase patrols in the area. Maybe set up a few extra cameras if we can get approval.' He paused, looking at Karen. 'Would you consider moving to a safe house? It might be necessary given the circumstances.'

The thought of leaving her home made Karen's stomach churn. This was where she usually felt safe. She didn't want to be driven out, but she had Mike and James to worry about, too. Were they safe here?

'I don't think we're at that stage yet,' she said.

Morgan didn't push the issue, but his frown deepened. 'All right. But we can move quickly if you change your mind.'

'You sure you're okay?' Arnie asked, his tone softer than usual. He handed Karen and Morgan each a mug of tea.

Morgan nodded his thanks and blew on his steaming mug.

Karen managed a weak smile. 'I'm fine. Just a bit rattled.'

And frustrated, and scared, and angry, she added silently.

'I'd better make a start,' Morgan said. 'Call me if . . . Well, if you need anything, call me.'

He left his tea on the kitchen table.

'Would you look at that? He only took one sip,' Arnie said in faux outrage. 'Last time I'm making him tea.' He took a slurp from his own mug, then said, 'Have you had a chance to look at that photofit yet?'

Karen blinked. The photofit. With everything going on, it had completely slipped her mind. Some detective she was.

'Sorry, Arnie. I completely forgot about it.'

'No worries. I emailed it over earlier. Give it a once-over when you get a chance.' Arnie stood and drained his tea.

Karen winced, wondering how he could gulp it down like that when it was still piping hot.

'We're going to organise a search just in case our little peeping Tom left something behind.' Arnie headed out to find Morgan.

After Arnie left, Karen went to talk to Mike. She wanted him to open up, but he was stubbornly insisting he was fine and just needed to finish off his accounts. Finally admitting defeat, she wandered back to the kitchen and reached for her phone.

She opened Arnie's email. His message read: *Jason Wilkes saw this bloke inside Lorraine's property the day she died. Ring any bells?*

The attachment loaded slowly. When it finally appeared on her screen, Karen's breath caught in her throat.

The face staring back at her was unmistakable. The same angular jaw, the same intense, deep-set eyes.

It was him. The same man she'd seen earlier, pretending to be a door-to-door salesman. The same man she'd chased earlier tonight.

And now she knew he'd been at Lorraine's house the day she died.

The face that stared back at her was youngish, probably mid-twenties. Sharp cheekbones and close-cropped dark hair. He had a brooding, handsome appearance. Definitely way too young to be Prescott, but there was something about him that sparked a flicker of recognition.

She zoomed in, studying the features more closely. Those eyes . . .

Karen had seen eyes like that before, in photos of serial killers and psychopaths. The kind of dead-eyed empty gaze that made you want to look away, but you couldn't.

Evil eyes.

She shivered.

Chapter Thirty

Morgan crouched beside a cluster of overgrown brambles. His eyes scanned the ground for any sign of their suspect. He guessed the man they were looking for had disappeared into the hedgerows bordering the side road near the location where Karen had given chase.

Beside him, Arnie grumbled as he poked through the undergrowth. 'Probably long gone by now,' he muttered. 'Scarpered across the fields. Ruddy coward.'

Morgan didn't respond. He kept his focus on the task at hand, knowing the importance of patience and diligence in police work. They had to be thorough and methodical in their search.

A small team of officers fanned out around them, combing through the surrounding area. Morgan heard their voices and the rustle of leaves as they moved carefully through the foliage.

Arnie straightened up and let out a low whistle. 'Morgan! Over here,' he called, waving him over.

Morgan made his way over to Arnie's position. The detective sergeant was standing next to a black rucksack, which was partially hidden beneath a pile of leaves.

'Reckon this is what we're looking for?' Arnie said.

'Possibly,' Morgan replied. 'Let's have a look inside.'

Arnie snapped on a pair of gloves and carefully opened the bag.

Morgan's stomach lurched as Arnie withdrew a coil of rope and a menacing knife.

A wave of revulsion washed over him. He met Arnie's gaze, both of them understanding the implications.

Arnie swore. 'You know what this means? What he was planning to do?'

'Yes. We need to get this to Forensics,' Morgan said. 'A DNA rush job if possible. We need to ID this guy.'

Arnie nodded grimly. 'I'm tempted to park myself outside Karen's all night – keep an eye out for him,' he said. 'This is the kind of evil that keeps me up at night.'

Morgan understood the sentiment. He felt it too.

'A sleepless night won't help anyone,' he said. 'You need sleep to do your job well.'

'Show some emotion for once,' Arnie snapped. 'This is Karen we're talking about, and she nearly . . . This guy was going to . . .'

'I know,' Morgan said quietly. He understood the danger Karen had been in and the evil their suspect could be capable of. But he had to keep his emotions in check if he was going to do his job effectively.

Morgan examined the ground, noting a set of tracks leading away from the bag. 'Probably fled that way. Through the hedgerow and across the adjacent field.'

Arnie swore again. 'I'd like to get my hands on him.'

Morgan ignored the threat, knowing Arnie's temper was getting the better of him.

Arnie's phone rang, and he answered it. His expression grew animated as he listened to the caller.

'Great work. Get Churchill to organise an arrest warrant . . . I don't know. Tell him what he needs to hear. Just make sure we get that arrest warrant. We need to trace his movements.' Arnie finished the call and looked at Morgan, a satisfied grin on his face. 'Finally, a breakthrough.'

◆　◆　◆

Sophie's monitor had turned into a blur of text. Her head throbbed, and the familiar pins and needles crept down her bad arm. Time for a break.

It was late, and the night air was a shock as she stepped into the car park. It was freezing, but there was no one around.

Perfect.

She swung her arms in wide circles, then did the stretches her physio had shown her. The exercises helped, even if they made her feel a bit silly.

She shouldn't feel embarrassed. Everyone had been incredibly supportive during her recovery. But she just wanted to be treated normally again, not watched for signs of weakness or asked if she was okay every five minutes.

Voices drifted across the car park. Sophie stepped back into the shadows beside the building, not wanting to be caught doing her exercises like an overzealous aerobics instructor.

One of the voices she recognised as belonging to Callum. Sophie peered around the corner. He was talking to someone – a woman with a rigid bright blonde bob that practically glowed in the dark.

Cindy Connor.

Sophie frowned. Cindy had written about the connection between Ava Claywood and Lorraine Harrington. How had she known about that? Perhaps Callum had been feeding her information about the case?

No. Hadn't she learned her lesson? What was wrong with her? She was leaping to conclusions without any evidence.

Callum was the press liaison. Talking to journalists was literally his job.

Even if meeting in a dark car park did seem a bit odd.

Cindy strode off towards her car, her heels clicking against the tarmac. As Callum turned back towards the building, he spotted Sophie.

'Oh, hi.' He gave her a small smile.

'Hello,' Sophie said. 'I really am sorry about earlier. You know, the Prescott-being-your-dad thing?'

'Don't worry about it. I've forgotten already.'

'Been talking to the press?' Sophie nodded in the direction of the journalist's car, where Cindy now sat, watching them like a hawk.

'Just trying to head her off. She's relentless when she gets hold of a story.'

'Must be challenging, dealing with the press.'

'Yes, but they do an invaluable job. They keep us honest.' He shoved his hands in his pockets. 'I only came out to my car to get something, and she cornered me. I thought if I gave her a few minutes, she might back off a bit.'

'Did it work?'

'No.' He laughed. 'She's tenacious. You okay? You look cold.'

'Just getting some fresh air. Been staring at a screen too long.'

'I know that feeling. Well, better head back.'

Sophie watched him disappear into the building. She was being ridiculous again. Of course Callum had to talk to journalists. It was his job.

She flexed her hand one last time. The pins and needles had gone. At least for now.

Chapter Thirty-One

The following morning, Karen leaned against the kitchen counter, cradling a mug of tea. Her gaze drifted to Mike, who was frying bacon. He hadn't said much, and Karen suspected he was focusing on mundane tasks to distract himself.

Karen had not slept well, haunted by how differently things could have turned out if she hadn't spotted that man watching the house. Arnie had told her they'd found a bag containing a knife and rope nearby. She shuddered, forcing away thoughts of what might have happened if the man had managed to get inside. The items in that bag painted a horrifyingly clear picture of his intentions.

Arnie had also informed them there'd been a breakthrough, although irritatingly had insisted that he couldn't tell Karen what it was yet. He'd been apologetic but firm. 'Falkner's already threatening creative forms of dismemberment if anyone leaks details. But we're getting close, Karen. Very close.'

She really hoped he was right.

Being shut out of the investigation reminded her uncomfortably of how Mike must have felt when she'd hidden things from him. She'd learned her lesson, though. No more keeping things from Mike. But rebuilding his trust would take time.

Karen sipped her tea. It was hard to reconcile the Mike she knew with the idea that his biological father was a man like Kenneth

Prescott. If she was finding it difficult, then it must be a hundred times worse for Mike.

Mike glanced up, catching her looking at him. He forced a smile. Karen hated seeing him like this. He was holding it together, but she knew he was struggling.

'I've been thinking. Maybe it would be best if you and James stayed home today.'

Mike's hands stilled. 'You want us to hide?'

'It's not hiding,' Karen said gently. 'It's being sensible. There are surveillance officers parked outside. Home is the safest place for you both right now.'

'What about you?'

'I'll be fine. I've got things I need to do today. I'm going to visit Brian Whitmore, the detective who investigated the murder of Ava Claywood back in the eighties. I'm hoping he can shed some light on Kenneth Prescott's past.'

Mike frowned, but didn't argue.

'Promise me you'll stay home today,' she said. 'Both of you.'

He muttered his agreement, and Karen felt a weight lift off her shoulders. At least he was out of harm's way, for now.

She set her mug down and walked over to him, wrapping her arms around his waist. He rested his chin on top of her head, his body warm and solid against hers.

'I really am sorry about keeping things from you,' Karen said. 'I should have told you everything from the start.'

Mike was quiet for a moment. 'I know you thought you were doing the right thing,' he said finally. 'But being kept in the dark makes everything worse. I keep thinking about Mum doing the same thing – she thought she was helping by handling everything alone.'

'I get it now. I really do.' Karen tightened her arms around him. 'No more secrets. I promise.'

'Even if you think the truth might upset me?'

'Even then.'

Mike pressed a kiss to the top of her head.

'You won't have to stay home for long,' Karen murmured. 'Arnie said they've had a breakthrough in the case. They'll catch him soon.'

Mike nodded, and Karen felt him relax, just a little, against her. She hoped she was right.

Karen pulled on to the drive of a small, tidy bungalow on Harmston High Street. Brian Whitmore's home. She had met him just once before – years ago, when he'd popped by to see her old boss, Anthony. Whitmore had been a tall, strapping man with a booming voice and a ready smile.

When Whitmore answered the door, Karen's breath caught in her throat. The man in front of her looked nothing like the man she remembered. He was frail and sat stooped in a wheelchair. An oxygen tank was attached to the back of the chair, the tube looping around his ears and beneath his nose. His skin, once ruddy, now seemed dulled by the weight of illness. It was hard seeing how much he'd changed.

'Detective Hart.' He greeted her with a smile that still held all of its former warmth. 'Come in. My wife just popped out to the supermarket, so it's just us.'

'Thank you for seeing me, Brian,' Karen said, stepping inside. The bungalow was cosy, filled with photographs and knick-knacks. 'I'm sorry to intrude.'

'Nonsense.' Whitmore waved her apology away. 'I was pleased to get your call. And I'm glad of the company. Would you like a cup of tea? I'm not exactly a whizz in the kitchen thanks to this contraption, but I can manage some tea.'

'No, thank you. I'm fine.'

'Come on, let's sit in the living room.' He wheeled himself into the room, and Karen followed and sat on the sofa. Whitmore turned his wheelchair so he was facing her.

'I knew your old boss, Anthony,' he said, his voice tinged with nostalgia. 'We worked together back in the day. Good man.'

'I remember – and he was,' Karen agreed, feeling a wave of sadness. 'I miss him.'

'When your number's up, it's up, I suppose,' Whitmore said. 'Happens to all of us eventually.'

'I'm here because I need your help, Brian. We're investigating a double murder. I think my colleagues came to see you a couple of days ago?'

'Yes, they did. They thought it might be related to the Ava Claywood case from back in 1981. I told them everything I know. I'd love to see Kenneth Prescott behind bars before I meet my maker.'

Karen decided to be honest about her connection to the case. 'One of the victims was my fiancé's mother, Lorraine Harrington. The other was his aunt, Michelle Matthews. So this feels very personal to me. I understand if you don't want to talk to me, due to my connection with the investigation.'

'Why on earth wouldn't I want to talk to you?'

'I just mean it would probably be frowned upon. Protocol and all that.'

Whitmore waved a hand. 'Protocol,' he scoffed. 'I won't tell if you don't.' His eyes softened with sympathy. 'I am sorry.'

'Thank you. What can you tell me about Kenneth?' Karen asked. 'Anything that might help us find him or understand his motives?'

Whitmore leaned back in his wheelchair, his gaze distant as he recalled the past. 'Prescott was always a slippery one. He had police officers and council workers on his payroll. And he was nasty with it; it wasn't just cash for favours. He'd threaten families and all sorts. Downright vicious. A thoroughly unpleasant character.'

Karen listened intently, trying to piece together a picture of the man who had fathered Mike.

'Can you tell me anything about Prescott's connections to Quentin Chapman?'

Whitmore nodded. 'They didn't get on. Chapman was much higher up in the pecking order, and Prescott resented that, I think. They were both brutal men, but I always thought Chapman had morals. Not the same morals as you or I, mind, but he had a code he lived by. Prescott would kill his own granny if he got a few quid out of it.'

The more she learned about Kenneth Prescott, the more dangerous he seemed.

They chatted a little longer, then Karen stood up to leave. 'Thank you, Brian. You've been a great help.'

Whitmore smiled, wheeling himself towards the door. 'I wish I could do more. Just be careful, all right? Prescott's a nasty piece of work.'

'I will,' Karen promised, stepping outside. She turned back to Whitmore. 'If you think of anything else, please let me know.'

'I will,' Whitmore said. 'And Karen?'

'Yes?'

'Good luck. I really hope you get Prescott for this.'

Karen thanked him again. She had a feeling she was going to need all the luck she could get.

Karen got into her car and pulled out her phone to check her emails before driving off. Another message. Subject: *Final Warning.*

You should have listened. It would be a shame if Mike paid the price for your stubbornness. Consider your next move carefully.

The words swam on the screen. Karen's chest constricted, her breath coming in short, sharp bursts. That was a direct threat against Mike. She gripped the steering wheel, forcing herself to take slow, steady breaths.

Four emails now, and they still hadn't traced the sender. Harinder was trying his best, but whoever was behind this knew exactly what they were doing.

Karen looked up, scanning the quiet street. The house opposite seemed to loom over her. An orange leaf swirled across the road in the breeze. No one in sight, and yet . . .

She twisted in her seat, checking the rear-view mirror. Nothing but empty pavement and parked cars.

But that crawling sensation on the back of her neck – the one that told her she was being watched – wouldn't go away.

Chapter Thirty-Two

Brian Whitmore shut the door after Karen left and wheeled himself back into the living room. His wife still wasn't back; she often popped into Costa Coffee for a pastry after going to the supermarket. He couldn't blame her – she didn't get out much these days.

He felt like a burden, weighing her down with his constant needs. They couldn't get about like they used to, not with him carting around an oxygen cylinder wherever they went.

Brian gazed out at his garden through the living room window. The once-pristine flowerbeds were now dotted with weeds. Ankle-length grass was buffeted by the breeze where a manicured lawn used to be. That lawn had been his pride and joy.

His wife would laugh at his attempts to get stripes from the mower. The smell of fresh-cut grass used to fill him with happiness, but now it reminded him that his wife had to struggle with all the house and garden upkeep herself these days.

He looked around the room. A jigsaw puzzle and wordsearch books cluttered the coffee table. The TV guide lay open at the afternoon quiz shows. This was his life now.

Still, it could be worse. At least he was still breathing. Just.

Meeting his wife had been the luckiest day of his life, and he still had visits from his children and grandkids to look forward to.

Plus, there was always a good game of online bridge to be had with his old pals.

Brian wheeled himself to the kitchen. His chest felt tight. He really needed his motorised chair back, but it was in for repair, which meant he had to struggle with the heavy, cumbersome one for at least another week.

The oxygen cannula rubbed against his nose. It was a constant irritation. His hand shook as he reached for a glass of water. Even simple tasks drained him. As he paused to catch his breath, the oxygen hissed quietly.

It was a lifeline and a cage. He couldn't go anywhere without it. The tank followed him like a faithful dog, but unlike a dog, it offered no comfort. Only reminded him of his frailty.

Brian closed his eyes. He pictured Ruth Claywood as she was back then. A skinny girl with long, tangled hair. Her eyes had been big and scared. She'd flinched at loud noises. Her father had tried his best to hold things together. But whenever he visited the house, Brian had noticed the smell of alcohol clung to John Claywood.

Ruth's clothes were sometimes dirty. Brian had been sure she hadn't been eating enough. He used to buy her fish and chips every time he called to update them on the case.

Brian had wanted to help more. But there were limits to what he could do. He wasn't about to report them to social services, and he knew the neighbours helped, dropping meals round and keeping an eye on Ruth.

It was nice to know Ruth had made a success of her life. Poor kid – she'd been so affected by her mother's murder.

He hoped Karen and the team would nail Prescott for Ava Claywood's murder – Brian was convinced Prescott had been the one to kill her. He had seen evil when he'd looked in Prescott's eyes. It was the biggest regret of his career that he hadn't locked the man up. After all these years, perhaps justice would finally catch up with him.

The chime of the doorbell snapped him from his thoughts. Who could that be? He wasn't expecting anyone else. He chuckled; he'd never been so popular.

He manoeuvred his way to the front door, bashing into the wall with the side of his wheelchair. No matter how long he'd been in the blasted thing, he'd never quite got the hang of it. And this non-motorised chair felt even more awkward and clumsy.

He opened the door to find a woman standing there – someone he didn't recognise.

'Can I help you?' he asked.

The woman's blonde hair was pulled back in a tight ponytail. Her smile seemed warm and friendly. 'I apologise for the intrusion. You must be tired of us dropping by. I'm DS Cunnings.'

'Oh, you're here about the Prescott case as well, are you?'

She nodded. 'I hope I'm not interrupting. I should have called first.'

'No problem at all,' Brian replied. 'Honestly, I'm happy to help. Please, come in.'

He wheeled into the living room, and Cunnings followed, shutting the door behind her.

'Can I get you a drink?' Brian asked.

'No, I'm fine. Just had a coffee, actually,' she said.

Brian's chair clobbered the wall, and he swore. 'Sorry. I'm getting sick of this thing. I did retire with plans of working in my garden and joining a walking club, but' – he jabbed a thumb at the oxygen cylinder – 'this thing has really slowed me down.'

Cunnings looked behind him, out of the window to the back garden. 'You've got a gorgeous plot,' she said. 'It's huge.'

'Don't get out there as much as I'd like. Even the motorised chair doesn't cope well with the crooked slabs on the path, and I've got no chance in this heavy thing.'

'Why don't we go out and talk out there, then?' Cunnings suggested. 'I'll push you down to the bottom. It'll save me a trip to the gym.'

Brian hesitated but then smiled. He could use some fresh air. 'Why not? Although, I'd better put a jacket on. It's a bit nippy out.'

'It is,' Cunnings agreed, looking around. 'I can get it for you.'

'There's one on the hook in the hallway,' he said. He wheeled his chair behind Cunnings as she went out and plucked the jacket off the peg for him. After he'd put it on, she pushed him through the kitchen, out the back door, and down the ramp they'd installed three years ago.

The air was bracing – cold but invigorating. He'd missed this. He hated being cooped up inside all the time. But he didn't like to keep interrupting his wife to ask for her help when she was working from home.

'Shall we go down to the bottom?' Cunnings suggested.

'Yes,' Brian said, giving her a thumbs up.

The garden stretched out before them. The path wound down the hill. Overgrown shrubs crowded the edges, and weeds poked through cracks in the paving stones.

It was a long, steep garden. Harmston was hilly for a village in Lincolnshire, but it afforded beautiful views. They set off down the path, and Brian relaxed, enjoying the sight of a little robin flitting from bush to bush, following them down to the bottom of the garden.

Beyond the garden wall, fields stretched to the horizon. The view was breathtaking. But Brian suddenly felt exposed. Vulnerable. The house seemed far away.

When they reached the bottom of the garden, they looked down over the wall. Cunnings sighed appreciatively. 'It's gorgeous here. What an amazing view.'

'It is,' Brian agreed. 'I've not been all the way down here for ages. I can't manage to push myself back up the garden. It's too steep. Even the motorised chair struggles.'

'Oh, that's a shame,' Cunnings said. 'Have you ever thought of moving somewhere a bit flatter?'

Brian smiled and shook his head. 'No, I think I'll be here till the end now. My wife loves it. We've got family nearby and—'

He didn't say it, but the doctors had been brutally honest; he didn't have much longer anyway, and selling the house would be a stress they didn't need.

'So, what was it you wanted to talk to me about?' Brian turned to Cunnings.

'Well, it's about Kenneth Prescott,' she said. 'You just had a visit from DS Hart, I believe?'

'Yes, that's right. Karen,' Brian said. 'Lovely to see her again. I knew her when she was a young DC. It's wonderful to see her thriving now, especially after all the tragedy in her past. She hasn't had it easy.'

'No,' Cunnings replied, 'not easy at all.'

There was a little wrought-iron table and chairs beside the wall. Cunnings pulled out one of the chairs. 'Do you mind if I sit down?'

'Course not,' Brian said. 'Help yourself, although that metal can be quite cold.'

Cunnings sat down. 'So, were you able to give Karen any information?'

Brian opened his mouth to reply, but hesitated. Cunnings hadn't actually asked any questions of her own about Prescott yet. He had been retired a while now, but some things never left you. Brian still had his copper's instinct. And something about Cunnings was ringing alarm bells.

'Oh, I managed to answer her questions, yes,' he said evasively.

Cunnings's smile lessened. 'I see. And what exactly did you tell her?'

'Oh, just background. Things about the old case.'

'Would you mind elaborating?'

'Well, I'm sure Karen will tell you back at the station, but I'm happy to answer any of your questions,' Brian said.

'I see,' she said. Her fingers tapped against her thigh. She seemed restless. Her voice was soft and pleasant, but there was an edge to it. He noticed her back was straight and her shoulders tense. Something wasn't right.

Brian stared at her for a moment. 'They got to you, didn't they?'

'What do you mean?' Cunnings asked, her expression carefully blank.

'This is how he's always operated. They look for weakness and exploit it to their advantage.'

Cunnings just looked at him, but Brian wasn't fooled. 'You're not the first, you know? Prescott's always gone after coppers and anyone else he can use. Kenneth's blackmailing you, isn't he? What is it? What has he got on you?'

'I don't know what you're talking about,' she replied stiffly.

But Brian knew he was right. Whatever he had over Cunnings was bad enough that she'd agreed to work for him. Whatever he'd told her now would get straight back to Kenneth. Well, DS Cunnings could think again. He wouldn't be telling her anything, and as soon as he got back inside, he'd call Karen.

'You've put me in a very difficult position,' Cunnings said quietly, looking at the rust spots dotting the surface of the table.

'What do you mean?' Brian asked, but she didn't reply. 'Look, he's a bad man. He's threatened you – maybe your family. People will understand. Come clean. It would be better if you do it now, because Prescott is going to get caught, and he'll take you down with him. You're kidding yourself if you think he'll be loyal.'

Cunnings laughed. 'I don't think he'll be loyal. I'm not that naive. But I also don't think he's going to get caught. The Prescotts of the world always seem to squirm their way out of trouble.' She checked her phone screen. 'Do you have your mobile?'

Brian patted his pockets. 'No, it's back in the living room.'

'I see.' She slid her phone into her pocket and stood up. 'I really am sorry about this, Brian. It was nice to meet you. I wish it could have been under better circumstances.'

'Right,' he said awkwardly. 'Well, could you wheel me back up to the house? I don't have the strength in my arms or the puff to do it myself.'

Cunnings looked sad. 'That's not going to happen, Brian.' She suddenly reached behind him and yanked out the tube trailing from the oxygen canister to the looped tubing around his nose and put it in her pocket.

'No, wait,' he said, immediately panicking as he felt the flow stop. 'You can't leave me here without my oxygen. I'll die.'

'I'm so sorry, Brian,' she said. 'But I can't let you live now.'

'You can't do this,' he wheezed as Cunnings began to walk back toward the house. 'My wife will be home . . . soon . . . I'll tell her what you did . . . I'll tell them all.'

Cunnings turned back. 'I think we both know you won't last that long, Brian.' Something flickered in her eyes – maybe regret, or fear. 'It's too late for both of us now.'

Then she turned her back on him and walked away.

Brian's chest constricted as he struggled for air.

He needed to stop panicking. That was making things worse. He needed to think. The neighbours . . . someone might be home.

'Help me . . .' His voice sounded so weak. He couldn't get enough air in.

His vision blurred as he tried again to shout for help. No sound came out. He gripped the arms of his wheelchair so hard his fingers turned white. He looked around wildly. The neighbour's house was so close. If only he could make more noise.

He opened his mouth again. A weak wheeze escaped. Spots danced before his eyes. He tried to push his wheelchair, but his arms felt like lead. It didn't budge.

Panic set in. He was going to die here. Alone. At the bottom of his own garden.

Desperation clawed at him as the world began to fade. The vibrant green and rich browns of the garden blurred into a dull haze. The faint rustle of leaves and chirping of birds sounded distant, as though he were submerged underwater. Each breath felt like a battle, a fight for survival, and he was losing.

In a final, frantic effort, he pushed against the wheels of his wheelchair, summoning every ounce of strength he had left. The chair lurched forward an inch, but it was not enough.

His heart thudded as cold sweat trickled down his back. He forced his head up so he could see the house, willing his wife to appear at the back door.

But the door remained shut.

Chapter Thirty-Three

Karen had intended to go home and check on Mike and James, but instead she found herself driving towards Willingham Woods. She felt the need to be outside, somewhere in the fresh air where she could think.

She parked up in the public car park and made her way through the wood, heading towards the area where Ava Claywood's body had been discovered. It was a crisp, chilly afternoon.

Twigs and leaves littered the muddy path through the trees. The air smelled green and clean, with hints of damp earth and ferns. As Karen walked deeper into the woods, the noise from the road faded away. She could only hear the soft crunch of leaves under her feet and a few birds singing nearby.

When she reached the spot where Ava's body had been found, Karen shoved her hands in her pockets and looked out over the calm water. Her boots sank into the mud. She wondered if Ava's feet had sunk in too when she'd stood here, fearing for her life.

Karen tried to put herself in Ava's place. Had she come here intending to meet Prescott, perhaps to talk to him, try to make him see sense? Or had Prescott followed her here, knowing it was somewhere she usually came to walk her dog, somewhere she was usually alone? Karen suspected the latter.

Had Ava known her life was in danger?

Did she try to run? Or had she been too shocked to move? Karen tried to imagine how terrified Ava must have been in her final moments, as Prescott's hands clamped around her neck.

It was a beautiful spot, so quiet and peaceful. It was hard to imagine such a horrific crime happening in the vicinity. A crime that had now gone unpunished for over forty years. She hoped they would finally get justice for Ava. If they could just get their hands on Kenneth Prescott, hopefully DNA would do the rest.

The evidence collected from Ava's crime scene was still in storage. If the DNA matched Prescott's, hopefully that would be enough to secure a conviction.

Ava's family had been left in the dark all these years. No answers, no justice. It wasn't right.

Karen knew something about the pain that could cause. Losing her husband and daughter had been horrendous. But not knowing who had done it, or why? That was a whole other level of pain. It had eaten away at her. The thought that someone out there had torn her world apart, destroyed the people she loved and had just got away with it. That had been the part she'd struggled with the most.

Karen was about to go when she noticed someone else by the lake. A woman in a dark coat, just standing there, staring out at the water.

As Karen approached her, she realised it was Ruth Claywood.

She stopped, not sure if she should intrude. This spot meant something to Ruth. Maybe it helped her feel close to her mother.

Ruth saw her and nodded. 'Detective.'

'Hello, Ruth,' Karen said.

'Were you looking for me?' Ruth asked.

'I wasn't. I just came here to . . .' How could she explain she'd come here to think – to try to get things straight in her head? 'I just . . .' Her words trailed away, but Ruth nodded as though she understood.

'I'm the same. I used to come here a lot after Mum died. Over the last few years I haven't come as often. But with it all coming back to the surface again, I felt like I needed to be here. I used to think if I came here, she might communicate with me somehow.' Ruth smiled sadly. 'Silly, isn't it?'

'No, it's not silly. There's something about this spot. It's beautiful and peaceful, despite what happened here.'

Ruth nodded. 'So . . . are you any further along with the case? Any progress?'

Karen hesitated, wondering quite how much to tell her about Prescott. It seemed everyone was sure Prescott was guilty, but until they had him in custody and had a sample of his DNA, it was going to be hard to prove it.

'We're looking at a suspect who was considered at the time of your mother's death. We're hoping that with DNA and other new technologies we might be able to get further along with a conviction.'

Ruth smiled. 'That's good news. Dad will be pleased.'

The sun was now low in the sky, and Ruth was shivering.

'I should probably get back,' Karen said. 'Mike will be wondering where I am.'

Ruth zipped her jacket right up to her chin. 'Yes, I should get home too.'

'How are your kids getting on at university?' Karen asked.

'Great. Well, at least I think so. I haven't heard from them for over a week. I can still check on their location app, though, which is reassuring,' Ruth said. 'I expect they're far too busy having fun to call.'

They continued to chat as they walked back to the small car park.

'You'll keep in touch?' Ruth asked as they stepped into the clearing. 'Let me know if there are any developments?'

Karen nodded. 'Of course. I'm not officially working on the case, but you will be updated.'

After she said goodbye to Ruth, Karen got in her car and headed home. It was getting dark, and she was hungry. She'd missed lunch again. After nagging Mike and James to make sure they ate properly, she wasn't following her own advice.

When she pulled into her drive, the first thing she noticed was that there was no police car outside and no officers watching the house.

That was odd.

Karen frowned. Had Morgan pulled the officers off duty without telling her? That wasn't like him at all.

She tightened her grip on the steering wheel. Perhaps DCI Churchill had run out of funding for the surveillance? Karen knew how expensive it was to keep officers on watch around the clock. But surely someone would have informed her if they were stopping the protection?

A sudden worry gripped her. What if something had happened to Mike and James?

She forced herself to take a deep breath. This was just like last time – she'd panicked then too, convinced something terrible had happened when Mike didn't answer his phone. And he'd been absolutely fine, just left his mobile at home. She was overreacting. Again.

Karen scanned the road, feeling increasingly uneasy. There'd been no new developments in the case to suggest Mike was any less at risk. The threat was still very real.

Mike's car was parked on the driveway, and so was James's. At least that was something. She quickly got out of the car and hurried towards the house.

The front of the house was completely dark. Not a single light shone from the windows. Karen paused and listened. Maybe they were both in the kitchen at the back of the house, she reasoned, trying to calm her growing anxiety.

Her hand trembled as she reached for her phone. Those threatening emails flashed through her mind . . . especially the last one, about Mike paying the price.

She called Mike's number, but her screen went black. Dead. She swore under her breath, angry with herself for not charging her phone on the drive back from Harmston. Her head was all over the place at the moment.

She couldn't even check the security cameras without the app on her phone.

She glanced at Christine's house next door. Should she go over? Get help? But she was being ridiculous. The house looked completely normal. The door was firmly shut, not hanging open like it had been at Lorraine's house or Michelle's. There was no sign of forced entry, no broken glass, nothing to suggest anything sinister.

With a deep breath, Karen slid her key into the lock and stepped inside. Silence. There was no Sandy barking or wagging her tail in greeting, which was very odd. The dog always came to the door whenever someone approached.

Maybe Mike and James had taken Sandy for a walk? She felt a surge of annoyance at the idea. Why would Mike leave the house when she'd made it crystal clear that staying home with the officers was much safer?

She reached for the light switch, but nothing happened when she flicked it on. She turned back to look out through the small window by the front door. Lights glowed warmly from the house across the road. Not a power cut then.

She thought through the possibilities. Maybe a fuse had blown? That was the most likely scenario, but she couldn't afford to be careless. This could be a trap.

She waited, listening.

Nothing.

Keeping her back to the wall, she edged inside.

'Hello?' she called out, but the house was silent.

As her eyes got used to the dark, she looked at the familiar surroundings of her home and saw so many potential hiding spots.

She stopped by the telephone. They hardly ever used the landline anymore. She quickly dialled Morgan's number, but it went straight to his voicemail. 'Morgan, it's Karen. The officers aren't outside my house. Call me back immediately on my home number please.'

She moved carefully along the wall towards the kitchen. The usual hum of appliances was missing. It felt wrong.

'Mike?'

Peering into the dark kitchen, she noticed the digital clock on the oven, which usually glowed bright blue, was off.

Karen spotted a sheet of paper on the kitchen table. Squinting in the dim light, she fumbled over to grab a torch from the drawer beside the oven. She turned it on and used the beam of light to read the scrawled note. Mike's familiar handwriting jumped out at her:

Gone to Home Curries for takeaway. Back soon. Ordered you a chicken biryani. Mike x

Karen let out a long breath, feeling both hugely relieved and a bit miffed. At least they were safe. But Mike hadn't mentioned anything about the missing officers. Had he even noticed they were gone? Had they told him why they'd left their post?

She set the note back on the table, shaking her head. While the knot of worry in her stomach loosened slightly, she wouldn't feel completely at ease until Mike and James were back home where she could see them with her own eyes.

Still, a takeaway sounded pretty good. Karen's stomach rumbled, reminding her how hungry she was. She could murder a biryani right about now, so she couldn't be too cross with Mike.

First though, she needed to sort out this power situation, and figure out what was going on with the surveillance officers.

Karen opened the door to the cupboard under the stairs where the fuse box was kept. She leaned in and saw that one of the switches had tripped.

The tension drained from her shoulders as relief set in. She had started to think perhaps someone had deliberately turned the electricity off. Talk about paranoid. A simple blown fuse and she'd practically convinced herself someone had broken in to cut the power. This whole situation had her jumping at shadows. Mike and James were fine and probably halfway to the curry house with Sandy by now.

Karen reached in to reset the switch on the fuse box as her home telephone rang. It had to be Morgan calling her back.

There was a soft creak behind her. But before she could turn, something heavy slammed into the back of her head.

Pain exploded through her skull. Her vision blurred. She stumbled forward and crashed into the cupboard. Her legs gave out, and she fell to the floor.

Then everything went black.

Chapter Thirty-Four

Karen's eyes fluttered open as she regained consciousness. Her kitchen came into blurry focus. A dull throb pulsed behind her temples, and her mouth felt like sandpaper.

She tried to move but found herself bound to a chair with plastic cable ties digging into her wrists. Dizziness washed over her as she tried to straighten up.

A scuffing sound behind her told her she wasn't alone. The chair scraped against the floor as she tried to turn around.

A familiar shape moved beside her. 'Mike, what's going on?' The height was right, the build . . . but something was wrong. The way he moved, the silence. Then he turned and Karen's heart stopped.

It wasn't Mike. Cold dread settled in her stomach as she recognised the man standing beside her.

The same bloke who'd pretended to be a door-to-door salesman. The same one who'd been watching the house.

'What do you want?'

The man's eyes darted around the room, never settling on Karen for more than a second. Sweat shone on his forehead as his fingers twitched at his sides.

'Shut up,' he growled.

He stepped towards her, then jerked back as if burned.

Karen watched his twitchy movements, the darting glances. The man was erratic and volatile.

Something nagged at her brain as she looked at him – something about his face . . . And then it hit her. The realisation made her stomach drop to her shoes.

She'd been blind not to see it before. His features were an echo of Mike's. Not exact, but still close enough to make her blood run cold.

Karen stared at him. The shape of the nose, the strong jawline.

It was like looking at a distorted version of Mike's features. The photofit hadn't had quite enough detail for her to see it, and when she'd chased him, she'd been a bit too far away, but now, up close, it was obvious. This man had to be related to Mike. That was why he'd seemed so familiar when he'd called at the house.

'This has all gone wrong,' he said, starting to pace the kitchen, wringing his hands. 'All of it. This wasn't meant to happen like this. Where is he?'

Mike, Karen thought. He was after Mike.

'Who are you?'

'Can't you see the family resemblance?' He sneered. 'I'm Liam, Mike's brother. While Mike lived a charmed life, I had to stay with our old man.'

Karen felt sick. It was like someone had taken Mike's face and warped it into something twisted and cruel to form Liam's.

Mike's eyes held warmth, but the man beside her had eyes like a shark's – empty and soulless. Evil.

The pieces started falling into place. While Mike had grown up safe and loved, Liam had been raised by Kenneth Prescott. Had that turned him into this? Was this his twisted way of making Mike pay? Had he murdered Michelle and Lorraine just to make his brother suffer?

Liam grew more frantic. 'Where are they? They should be back by now. This is ruining everything!'

'Look, Liam, let's just talk about this.' Karen was trying to stay calm.

Mike would be back soon with their dinner, walking straight into danger. And James would be with him. She had to find a way to warn them.

He jabbed a finger at her. 'Shut up,' he screamed. 'Just shut up.' He turned. 'I told you to put a gag on her.'

Was he talking to someone else?

Karen tried to twist around to see who that person was. But she couldn't quite see right behind her. She wasn't sure what was worse: the thought of having to overpower two people, or the idea that he was talking to thin air – an accomplice that didn't exist.

But someone else *was* there. She could sense them. Better to face two real people than deal with someone like Liam hallucinating, she supposed. His agitated behaviour made her wonder if he was high.

She took a deep breath, but it did nothing to slow her hammering heart. 'Liam, what are you planning to do?'

'I told you to shut up,' he screamed, spittle gathering at the corner of his mouth as his face flushed red.

'No, I won't,' Karen said. 'You have no right to do this. This is my home. You can't break in here and tie me up. Let me go right now.'

Liam's jaw dropped. His eyes widened. Then a laugh burst from him, high-pitched and unnatural.

The cable ties hadn't actually been pulled that tightly around Karen's wrists. If she could get Liam and his accomplice out of the room, she might be able to work them loose.

'What's that?' Karen said, deliberately staring at the kitchen window. Outside, nothing but darkness pressed against the glass.

'What?' Liam turned to look.

'There's someone outside,' Karen said urgently. 'They were just looking in the window.'

'Who?' he said, peering out. 'I can't see anyone.'

'They were definitely there,' Karen said. 'You'd better check.'

He turned back, eyes narrowed with suspicion. But curiosity won out.

'All right, don't let her move,' he said, again talking to the spot behind Karen.

A soft female voice replied, 'I won't. Just check outside.'

Karen recognised the voice.

'Cunnings?' She twisted further in her chair. 'Bridget?'

Cunnings finally stepped into view, her expression a blank mask. But her guilt showed in her eyes.

'Sorry about this, Karen. Nothing personal.'

The words hit like a physical blow. Karen had trusted Cunnings, even been grateful for her help. Now, seeing Cunnings standing there, complicit in this nightmare, her anger and betrayal surged past the fear.

'Nothing personal?' Karen spat. 'What exactly do you call kidnapping and tying up a police colleague, then? A fun team-building exercise?'

Cunnings shrugged.

'Where are the officers who were supposed to be outside? And where is Mike? What's Liam planning?'

But the answers were already falling into place.

Cunnings wasn't on her side. She was with Liam. The Prescotts had got to her somehow.

Karen shouldn't be surprised. It wasn't her first brush with police corruption. But she'd *liked* Cunnings. If anyone had been bent, she'd have put money on the annoyingly brash and condescending Falkner.

Cunnings pulled over a chair, sitting in front of Karen. 'Look, this isn't what I wanted to happen at all. But Liam is not the most stable person in the world. You'd better just humour him. I'll try to get us out of this.' She shifted, glancing away. 'I'm sorry about all of this. I really do like you, Karen. I had hoped we'd get to know each other better.'

Karen raised an eyebrow. 'Really? Well, in my experience, that usually happens over coffee or a nice chat. Tying someone up isn't generally part of the process. Maybe bring cake, not cable ties, next time.'

She knew there wouldn't be a next time, though. Not now she knew Cunnings was corrupt. They couldn't let Karen go, not with everything she knew. They'd have to silence her.

'What about Mike? Where is he?' Karen asked.

'We don't know,' Cunnings said. 'That's why Liam's here. He wants to confront his brother. Apparently, he thinks their father is about to change the will and leave everything to Mike.'

'Why would he do that?'

'Honestly, I don't know. I think it's probably something Liam's just got in his head and got confused. You saw him. He's not exactly the full ticket, is he?'

'But why are you helping them?' Karen said. 'You know what these people are capable of. We're sure that Kenneth Prescott killed Ava Claywood. The Prescotts are not good people.'

Cunnings laughed. 'Believe me, I know that better than anyone. But they're forcing me to help them.'

'Forcing you? How? What have they got over you? Are they threatening your family?'

Cunnings gave a small shake of her head. 'I almost wish they were. At least that would be more understandable. Maybe people would feel sorry for me then. But no.'

'Then what?' Karen asked.

'They . . . It's complicated.'

'And what are you going to do with me? Are you going to let him . . .' Karen couldn't finish the sentence.

'I . . . don't know. But I'm not the one in charge, Karen. I don't want anything bad to happen to you. I wouldn't be here if it was down to me.'

'What about the officers outside? They'll help us. Where are they?'

'I sent them back to the station. I told them they were relieved from duty and I was taking over the shift.'

'And they *believed* you?'

'Why wouldn't they? I'm a detective sergeant.'

'So what happens now?' Karen said.

Cunnings took a deep breath as Liam's footsteps echoed off the tiled floor and he stomped back inside. Then she looked at Karen. 'Now we wait.'

'There's no one out there, you lying cow,' Liam snarled at Karen as he returned. His face contorted with rage as he paced the kitchen. 'You don't understand,' he spat, turning to face Karen. 'Mike's been living the life of Riley while I've been putting in the work. Years! Years I've been there, dealing with our father's moods, his demands and his business. And now?' He laughed, harsh and bitter, making Karen flinch. 'Now the old man wants to change his will. For Mike! A son he hasn't seen in decades!'

Karen watched him. Mike wouldn't want a penny of Kenneth Prescott's money. The very thought would disgust him. But contradicting Liam now would only enrage him further.

Liam's eyes fixed on Karen with frightening intensity. 'You think he's so much better than me, don't you? Perfect Mike and his detective girlfriend.' He leaned in close, his breath hot on her face. 'I'm going to ruin your life. You'll know what it's like to suffer soon enough.'

Despite her fear, anger flared in Karen's chest. 'I don't *think* Mike is better than you,' she snapped. 'I *know* he is!'

Cunnings stepped forward, her face tight with worry. 'Karen, don't wind him up if you know what's good for you.'

But Karen was beyond caution now. 'Mike is worth a million of you.'

Liam sneered. 'Don't make me laugh.'

'At least he hasn't killed anyone,' Karen shot back. 'What sort of person kills a woman in her sixties and sews her eyes shut? You're evil.'

Surprise flickered across Liam's face. 'What are you on about? I never killed her.' He whirled to face Cunnings. 'They think *I* killed her? You were supposed to tell me everything!'

Cunnings raised her hands defensively. 'I did what I could to distract attention—'

'Useless!' Liam exploded. 'You're absolutely useless! I should have known better than to trust a cop!'

As Liam ranted at Cunnings, Karen's stomach lurched. If Liam hadn't killed Lorraine, who had? And what did Cunnings know about it?

She twisted her wrist, trying to activate the emergency SOS on her smartwatch while Liam was distracted. She pressed the little side button.

The watch gave a soft beep. Liam's head snapped around. His eyes locked on to the device.

'What do you think you're doing?' he snarled, lunging forward.

His fingers closed around her wrist. With a violent yank, he tore the watch off.

Karen watched helplessly as Liam hurled the watch across the room. It skidded across the tiles, coming to rest by the fridge.

A robotic voice emanated from the device: *I'm sorry, I cannot connect at this time.*

Liam strode over, raised his foot, and brought it down hard. The crunch of plastic and electronics echoed through the kitchen.

'That was expensive,' Karen said, trying to sound unfazed.

Liam turned back, his eyes blazing. 'Oh, poor little detective can't afford a new watch? Maybe Mike will buy you another one. That's if you live long enough to enjoy it.'

Cunnings wrung her hands. 'Liam, Karen hasn't done anything to you. She—'

'Shut up!' He leaned in close. 'I know all about you, you know? You and Mike, planning your perfect little wedding. White dress, flowers, the works, is that it?' His lips curled into a sneer. 'Maybe I'll mess up that face of yours. I wonder if he'll still want to marry you then?'

Liam's hand shot out, grasping Karen's chin roughly. She tried to pull away, but his grip was too strong.

'Get your hands off me,' Karen said through gritted teeth, glaring at him. 'You're pathetic, Liam. Jealous of a brother you barely know.'

Cunnings stepped forward, her expression tense. 'Liam, calm down. This isn't helping anyone.'

Liam whirled around, lashing out with a vicious backhand that caught Cunnings across the face. She stumbled back, her hand flying to her reddening cheek.

'Don't tell me what to do!' Liam roared. 'You're supposed to be on my side!'

Karen watched the scene unfold with horror. She'd hoped Cunnings might help her, but now they were both at Liam's mercy.

She needed a plan, and fast.

Chapter Thirty-Five

When Liam spoke again, his voice had turned cold. 'Gag her, now. I'm not having her screaming out when he gets back.'

'No, wait,' Karen said. Her pulse thudded in her ears as she searched for a way to reason with him. 'What are you planning to do to Mike? He's never done anything to you. He's a good man.'

'Is he?' Liam said. 'How touching.'

Karen tried one last time. 'Listen, he's your brother. Why not talk to him? You might actually like each other. You probably have more in common than you think.'

'Don't make me laugh,' Liam said. He grabbed a tea towel from the counter and started cutting it in half with her kitchen scissors, helping himself to her things as if he owned the place.

The sight of him casually rifling through her kitchen made Karen's blood boil. Here she sat, bound and helpless, while this thug treated her home like his own.

He tossed the cut cloth to Cunnings. 'Do the honours.'

'Sorry,' Cunnings whispered as she shoved the makeshift gag into Karen's mouth, crushing her lips against her teeth as she pulled it tight around her head.

Karen twisted away but couldn't escape. The fabric pressed against her tongue and tasted of washing powder. She struggled to breathe through her nose as panic rose in her chest.

A key scraped in the front door lock.

Liam's head jerked towards the sound. He grabbed the biggest knife from the block and pressed himself against the wall behind the door, blade raised. His eyes glinted as he waited. Cunnings went into the utility room to hide.

Karen waited until the door opened, praying Mike would hear her through the gag. 'Mike,' she tried to shout, but it came out as a muffled *mhmmm*.

Karen's chest felt tight with panic. She had to warn them somehow. She stamped her feet on the floor, trying to make as much noise as possible.

Liam glared at her, then pressed a finger to his lips.

Still, Sandy heard the noise. The dog started barking straightaway.

'Karen?' Mike called. 'Why are all the lights off?'

She tried again to force sound through the gag. *Please let it be enough to warn him before—*

Mike appeared in the doorway. He peered into the gloom. Karen stared at him, willing him to realise Liam was lurking behind the door with a knife.

'What's going on? I think we've got a power cut,' James said, walking straight into Mike's back where he'd frozen, staring at Karen.

She met Mike's eyes and flicked her gaze towards the door, giving a tiny nod. *Come on*, she thought. *Notice what I'm trying to tell you.*

He did. Mike grabbed the door handle and shoved the door backwards hard.

But Liam was ready, dodging it with a cat-like grace. He slashed out with the kitchen knife, barely missing Mike's arm.

Liam smiled at the look of shock on Mike's face. He lifted the knife. 'I'm going to enjoy this.'

Sandy erupted into fierce barking, leaping forward to protect Mike. The dog's hackles were raised, teeth bared, as she growled at

Liam. His confident smile flickered for just a moment as he took half a step back.

'Who are you? What do you want?' Mike raised his hands defensively as he edged sideways, trying to put more space between them.

'What – don't you recognise me? Don't you think I look familiar?' Liam grinned. 'I'm your little brother. The one you're trying to steal from.'

'I don't know what you're talking about.' Mike's back came up against the wall. His eyes darted between the knife and Liam's face.

'Course you don't.' Liam's laugh was hollow. 'You're the golden boy, aren't you? You grew up in a nice house with your perfect family. While I got beaten if I so much as looked at the old man the wrong way.'

Sandy launched herself at Liam, snapping and snarling. He stumbled back, the knife flashing as he swung it defensively.

'Cunnings!' Liam shouted. 'Get that dog out of here or I'll slit its throat!'

Karen's stomach lurched at the threat, but Sandy just kept barking, positioning herself between Mike and Liam.

'Sandy, settle,' Mike ordered.

To Karen's amazement, Sandy stopped barking instantly, though the dog's body remained coiled with tension, a low growl rumbling in her throat as she stared at Liam.

'Get rid of the dog,' Liam hissed at Cunnings. 'Put it out in the garden. If it makes another sound . . .' He left the words hanging.

Karen watched as Cunnings edged towards Sandy, clearly nervous. 'Come on, boy.'

The dog's growl deepened.

'Sandy, follow,' Mike ordered, pointing at Cunnings. Despite the fear in Mike's voice, his command was clear.

Sandy reluctantly followed Cunnings to the utility room, her tail low and muscles tense, every step showing how desperately she wanted to stay with Mike. Through the open doorway, Karen heard the click of Sandy's claws on the utility room floor, then the squeak of the back door opening and closing.

As soon as the back door closed, Liam lunged again with the knife. Mike tried to dodge but his bad leg twisted. He stumbled, catching himself on the counter. Karen's heart hammered against her ribs. She pulled desperately against the restraints, trying to make eye contact with James to communicate he needed to go for help. But James was inching closer to them.

'Bet dear old Dad never mentioned me in your cosy little chats, did he?' Liam sneered, circling Mike like a predator.

'I never even knew you existed,' Mike said. 'And I haven't spoken to or seen your father since I was three. Whatever issues you have, they are nothing to do with me.'

'They're *everything* to do with you,' Liam screamed.

James crept closer, but Liam's head snapped around. 'Well, if it isn't Grandad to the rescue.' Liam sneered at James. 'Going to try to protect your precious boy? Better watch your blood pressure. Wouldn't want you having a funny turn.' He laughed. 'Look at you all, playing happy families,' he spat. 'Mike gets a nice new dad while I got left with a monster. My own mother wouldn't even stick around when he started knocking her about – she ran off and left me there. Seven years old, alone with *him*. But you wouldn't have a clue what that's like, would you, Mike? At least your mum took you with her.'

'Just leave us all alone,' James said, his voice shaking. 'Leave now before the police arrive.'

Liam's fist shot out, driving deep into James's gut. James doubled over with a harsh gasp, crumpling to his knees. His face went slack with shock as he collapsed, wheezing and clutching his stomach.

The sight of James going down made something snap in Mike. He surged forward, smashing his fist into Liam's face with enough force to snap his head back.

Karen watched as Liam stumbled, wobbling and swaying like a drunk. For a second, she thought his legs would give out and he'd collapse. But then he steadied himself, lifting the knife as he found his balance again. His bloody grin looked more animal than human.

Mike tried to sidestep the blade but his bad leg buckled again.

'Nasty limp you've got there,' Liam said, wiping the blood from his split lip on his sleeve. 'What happened? Skiing accident at some posh resort? Can't work anymore? Is that why you're coming after the money Dad promised me. The money I earned?'

'I want nothing to do with your father or his money.'

'Liar!' Liam's eyes blazed with fury. His boot connected with Mike's bad leg with a sickening thud.

Mike went down hard, crying out in pain. His face was grey, contorted in agony as he tried to push himself up. But his leg wouldn't hold him.

Liam raised the knife. 'Any last words?'

James staggered to his feet.

Karen screamed against her gag, thrashing wildly in the chair. Not like this. She couldn't watch Mike die.

'No!' James charged forward with a roar that seemed to shake the walls. He slammed into Liam, the unexpected attack sending them both crashing into the line of kitchen cabinets. The knife spun away into the corner of the room.

But Liam was younger and stronger and fuelled by years of hate. He threw James off easily and scrambled towards the knife.

Mike's face tightened in determination as he dragged himself across the floor and grabbed Liam's ankle. His brother kicked out viciously, catching Mike's jaw with a blow that made Karen wince.

Mike lost his grip, but didn't give up. He launched himself at Liam, ignoring the clear pain in his bad leg. They crashed to the floor and Mike used his weight to pin Liam down. Blood dripped from Mike's face on to his brother's shirt as they struggled.

They crashed around the kitchen floor, knocking over a chair as they grappled. Mike's fist smashed into Liam's jaw again and blood sprayed across the white kitchen tiles.

Liam fought dirty, ramming his knee between Mike's legs, but Mike shifted just in time and landed a punch that made his brother grunt in pain. Liam retaliated by driving his fist into Mike's gut.

The sound of Mike struggling for air made Karen's insides twist. She yanked harder at the cable ties, not caring that they were cutting into her wrists. She had to do something.

Liam scrambled on top, drawing back his fist with hatred in his eyes. This wasn't just about hurting Mike – this was about finishing him.

But they'd all forgotten about James. He grabbed the toppled chair and swung it full force against Liam's back.

Liam slumped on to Mike like a ragdoll. James wobbled forward on shaky legs to help heave him off Mike.

Mike rolled Liam on to his stomach, twisting his arms behind his back. His hands were shaking but his grip was firm. 'Stay down,' he muttered, though Liam was clearly out for the count. Still, it was better to be safe than sorry when dealing with knife-wielding psychotic half-brothers.

'Get Karen free,' Mike called out to James, his voice rough. Blood dripped steadily from his nose on to Liam's jacket.

Mike kept one knee planted firmly in Liam's back while he checked for a pulse. 'You all right, Dad?'

'I will be. Just a bit winded.' James pressed a hand against his ribs as he made his way to Karen. 'And I'm far too old for all this excitement.'

James started yanking at the cable ties. Karen winced as they dug deeper into her wrists. James grabbed the scissors Liam had used to cut the tea towels, and began hacking through the plastic.

The moment her hands were free, Karen ripped off the gag, gasping in air.

'James, can I use your phone please?' She looked at Mike. 'Are you okay? You look terrible.'

'You should see the other guy.' Mike nodded down towards Liam and tried to laugh, but it turned into a wince.

James handed Karen his phone, then nodded to a plastic bag on the counter. 'Let's use the cable ties he brought with him. Might as well put them to good use.'

He threw a couple to Mike.

'He definitely came prepared, though I bet he didn't expect to be wearing them himself.' Mike yanked the cable ties tight around Liam's wrists.

Karen's fingers shook as she dialled for backup on James's mobile.

'What happened? Where are the officers that were meant to be outside?' Mike asked when Karen had finished the call.

'Cunnings told them to go.'

'Why would she do that?'

'She's been working for the Prescotts all along.'

'Is she still here?'

There was no sign of her in the utility room. 'She must have slipped out during the fight. Keep an eye on Liam. I'll see if I can find her.'

One of the panes of glass on the back door had been smashed, which was obviously how Liam and Cunnings had gained entry. Karen dashed into the garden, blinking in the darkness.

Wet grass squelched under her feet. Her heart hammered as she searched the shadows. How long ago had Cunnings made a run for it? She *had* to catch her.

Sandy charged over to greet her, tail wagging madly.

'Where did she go?' Karen muttered.

There – trying to climb the back fence. Cunnings was clawing her way up the wooden slats, her shoes struggling for purchase.

Karen bolted forward, heart pounding, with Sandy barking furiously beside her. When they reached the fence, Sandy leaped up at Cunnings, teeth snapping at her feet. Cunnings screamed, slipping just enough for Karen to grab her legs and yank.

They crashed on to the grass, the impact knocking Karen's breath away. Blood filled her mouth, but she held on, locking her fingers around Cunnings's ankles. Sandy circled them, barking frantically.

Cunnings thrashed, her heel smashing into Karen's ribs.

Pain shot through her side, but she gritted her teeth and kept her grip.

They both scrambled to their feet, and Cunnings drove an elbow into Karen's face. Light exploded behind her eyes.

'Get off me!' Cunnings sobbed.

'Not likely,' Karen muttered, clinging on. After what Cunnings had done, she wasn't getting away.

Mike appeared, skidding to a stop as Karen wrenched Cunnings to her feet. Sandy bounded over to Mike, jumping up excitedly to greet him before returning to bark at Cunnings.

With both of them holding an arm each, Cunnings couldn't escape. She finally stopped struggling. The fight going out of her all at once. Karen and Mike held her tightly as they made their way back to the house.

Inside, James hovered nervously beside a semiconscious Liam, who was now groaning as he came around.

His face was a mess of bruises. One puffy eye was already closing. Despite looking like he'd gone ten rounds, his eyes still held that evil glint.

The atmosphere was tense as the brothers faced each other.

'Dad never mentioned you were so handy with your fists, bruv,' Liam said, spitting blood on to the kitchen floor. 'Doesn't matter. You're still not getting his money.'

'I never wanted his money,' Mike said. 'And I never wanted a brother like you.'

◆ ◆ ◆

Morgan and Sophie were among the first to arrive on the scene.

Sophie hovered over Karen, eyes wide with worry. 'You should go to the hospital.'

'I told her that already,' Mike said, putting his hand on Karen's shoulder. 'But she's stubborn.'

'I'm fine,' Karen said, though her head was banging, and nausea rolled through her stomach. 'I want to know what Liam has to say for himself.'

Morgan shifted uncomfortably, glancing between Karen and Mike. 'There's something you both should know. We found out yesterday that Liam Prescott was in the country when both murders happened.'

Karen's head shot up. She immediately regretted the movement as pain stabbed at the base of her skull. Mike's hand tightened on her shoulder.

'What?' Karen stared at Morgan. 'You found out *yesterday*? Arnie mentioned there'd been a breakthrough but said he couldn't tell me . . .'

Mike's voice was quiet. 'You knew about Liam, and you didn't warn us?'

'That was Falkner's call.' Morgan swallowed hard, his jaw tight. He didn't look like he had it all under control, which wasn't like him. He turned to Mike. 'He was insistent you couldn't know. On the off chance you might have been communicating with Liam . . .'

'How could I?' Mike's voice cracked. 'I didn't even know he existed until he tried to kill me in my own kitchen.'

Karen squeezed Mike's hand. 'I didn't recognise him when he came to the house . . . I should have seen it.'

'I don't know,' Sophie said gently, looking at Mike. 'There's only a slight resemblance really. Same build and colouring, but Liam's got a nasty face. He looks cruel.'

Mike lifted his face to the sky, hands jammed deep in his pockets, as though he wanted to escape the conversation entirely.

'We have a witness, a delivery driver, who saw a man in Lorraine's house the day she was murdered,' Sophie started to say.

'Sophie.' Morgan's voice held a warning tone.

She lifted her chin defiantly. 'I think it's about time we started being more open with them both. If we had, we might have avoided all this.' She gestured behind her at Karen's house, which was now a crime scene.

Morgan sighed. 'Fair enough.'

Sophie continued, her voice gentler as she addressed Mike directly, 'The delivery driver identified the man he saw at your parents' house as Liam Prescott.'

Mike went rigid. Even his breathing seemed to stop. 'So my *half-brother* killed my mother?'

She'd seen the photofit, but this was all coming as a surprise to Mike. Karen wrapped her arm around his waist, wishing she could take him away somewhere safe until this nightmare was over.

'I'm really sorry,' Morgan said. 'Keeping the information about Liam from you was the wrong thing to do. I should have gone to Churchill and had Falkner overruled.' He looked at Karen. 'I really thought with the officers stationed outside, you'd be safe.'

'You were following orders, and you couldn't have known Cunnings would get the officers outside to leave,' Karen said.

'I'm glad it's over now,' Sophie said. 'Liam's in custody, and if we're lucky, maybe he knows the truth about his father's involvement with Ava Claywood's murder.'

'Even if Liam does know whether his father killed Ava, he's unlikely to tell us,' Morgan said.

'I suppose you're right,' Sophie said. 'Family loyalty.'

'I have a spare room for you and Mike,' Morgan said to Karen. 'And James is welcome to take my room. I'll kip on the sofa.' The offer was typical Morgan – practical, and thoughtful without making a fuss about it.

'Thanks, that's really kind,' Karen said. 'But Christine next door has already offered to put us up for the night. She's got plenty of room. James is there already.'

James had gone next door for tea with Christine. Karen envied him a bit. A cuppa sounded pretty good right now.

Morgan checked his watch. 'Okay. First priority is getting Liam and Cunnings interviewed tonight. We need their statements while everything's fresh.' He pulled out his phone. 'I'll get the custody sergeant to set up two interview rooms.'

'It will be good to get them interviewed while they're still rattled,' Sophie said. 'One of them has to know where Kenneth Prescott is hiding out. Now he's in the country, we have a shot at linking him to Ava Claywood's murder with a DNA sample.'

'Agreed. Brian Whitmore is convinced Kenneth killed her,' Morgan said. 'Now we have the tech to actually prove it.'

'But only if we find him before he goes back to Brazil,' Karen said. The Claywoods had waited so long for answers. They couldn't let Kenneth escape justice again.

'Once Prescott hears about these arrests, he'll probably try to flee the country,' Morgan said. 'We'd better update the Border Force alert, make sure every airport and port's watching for him.' He looked up as another police vehicle arrived at the entrance to

Karen's driveway, its flashing lights casting a blue glow over the garden. 'For now, we process this scene and get statements from everyone involved. Karen, you and Mike have given me what we need. We can go over things again tomorrow when you've had some rest.'

Karen envied his composure. Her own thoughts were scattered in every direction.

'So, did Liam say anything about murdering Lorraine and Michelle?' Sophie asked. Morgan shot her a look. She flushed and glanced at Mike. 'Sorry, that was insensitive of me.'

'He didn't confess anything to me,' Mike said. 'Karen, did he say anything before I got here?'

'He denied it. He seemed shocked I suspected him.'

They watched as officers led Liam out of the house in handcuffs, towards a waiting police car. It was hard to believe that the violent man they'd faced tonight was related to Mike.

'We'll question Liam thoroughly,' Morgan said. 'And investigate his connection to Lorraine and Michelle's deaths.'

'But I mean he *must* have done it,' Sophie said. 'Liam was in the country. His father wasn't. And we know Kenneth Prescott got that email from Lorraine telling him she had kept things secret long enough. So he probably sent his son to, you know . . .' Her voice faded, leaving the rest unsaid.

Karen's eyes narrowed. 'What email? This is the first I've heard about it.'

Morgan shot Sophie an irritated look. She stared at her feet.

'Come on then,' Karen said. 'Tell me.'

Morgan rubbed the back of his neck, clearly debating how much to share. Eventually he said, 'We found a deleted sent email on Lorraine's computer. It was to Kenneth Prescott via one of his companies, warning him that she was going to come clean. She said: "I've kept things secret long enough."'

Karen tried to process this new information, her tired brain struggling to make sense of it.

'What secret?' Mike asked. 'Me being Prescott's son?'

'Maybe,' Morgan said. 'Or about Ava Claywood, if she knew something about Kenneth's involvement?'

'Either way, the email could have triggered Kenneth and Liam to silence her,' Sophie said.

'Hence her eyes being sewn shut,' Karen said quietly. 'Lorraine was no longer willing to turn a blind eye to what Kenneth had done. They weren't just punishing Michelle and Lorraine for knowing or seeing too much. They were sending a message to anyone else who might be tempted to look too closely. *Keep your eyes closed to my crimes, or this is what happens.*'

But even as she spoke, something bothered Karen. If silencing Lorraine and Michelle was the goal, why sew their eyes shut? Wouldn't their mouths have made more sense?

She pushed the niggling doubt away. Trying to understand the logic of someone who could murder and then mutilate their victims was probably a waste of time. There might not be any logic to find.

She glanced at Mike. His face looked grey. He stared, unseeing, at the ground. Karen reached for his hand, feeling the tension radiating from him.

'Liam also thought his father was about to change his will to include Mike. Hence his hatred for him,' Karen said.

Mike frowned. 'Why would Kenneth Prescott include me in his will? It's not like he's ever been interested in me.'

'I'm not sure he really intended to,' Karen said. 'I suspect it could be something he used as leverage against Liam, something to keep him on his toes.'

'Well, as far as I'm concerned, I want nothing to do with either of them – Kenneth or Liam,' Mike said. 'I wanted to know where I came from, but I've had all the answers I can stomach. I'm grateful Mum got me away from Prescott when she did.'

Karen's road had turned into a crime scene circus. She watched the forensics team sweep her front garden in their white suits, torches bobbing across the grass. The whole thing felt surreal.

She winced at another throb of pain in her ribs. At least there had been no murder this time. But it had been close.

Morgan and Sophie went off to perform their assigned tasks. Morgan headed towards the crime scene manager for an update, while Sophie walked over to the nearest parked van, checking in with the officers cataloguing the evidence bags.

'Are you really okay?' Karen asked Mike now they were alone. There was a red mark just above his right cheekbone, which would be a nasty bruise by morning.

'I should be asking you that,' he said. 'They hit you over the head. Was it Liam or Cunnings who attacked you?'

Karen touched the tender lump and pain shot through her skull. She tried not to show it. 'I'm not sure. I didn't see. But I suspect it was Liam.'

'We should probably get you to the hospital and checked out for concussion.'

'I've had a paramedic shine a light in my eyes. She was satisfied. So I'm happy. I don't want to go and sit in A&E for ten hours. I know the warning signs to look out for: dizziness, being sick, a headache that gets worse.' She ticked them off on her fingers. 'But how are you feeling? That was all pretty . . . intense.'

'Yes, not exactly the ideal family reunion,' Mike said. 'Liam seemed extremely . . . troubled.'

The memory of the anger in Liam's eyes made her shiver. His smile – so like Mike's, but twisted with a coldness that Mike's never had – gave her the creeps.

'I still don't understand why he would kill my mum,' Mike said, his voice cracking.

'The only thing that makes sense is he took that email your mum sent to your dad's company as a threat.'

'Don't call him my dad,' Mike said automatically, then sighed. 'Sorry, Karen. It's just this is all so . . .'

'Sorry. James is your dad. I know that. I meant to say your biological father,' she said, mentally kicking herself. She noticed the dark circles under Mike's eyes and how rigidly he held himself. 'If Liam saw that email, maybe he thought he was protecting his father and their business by stopping your mum from telling whatever she knew.'

Mike raked his hands through his hair, leaving it sticking up. 'What d'you reckon she was planning to reveal? Was it about me? My real dad? Or was it about Ava?'

Karen chewed her lip. 'Honestly, Mike? I'm not sure. Could be any of those, or something we haven't even thought of yet.'

'Anyway, Liam and Cunnings have been arrested. So I suppose it's a pretty good outcome.' But Mike didn't sound convinced.

'Yes, now we've just got to find Kenneth Prescott,' Karen replied, but something nagged at her. The case felt unfinished – a jigsaw with missing pieces.

A familiar feeling was there at the back of her mind, the one that said things weren't adding up. Sure, they had Liam and Cunnings, but Liam's denial about killing Lorraine and Michelle kept playing in her head. The shock in his eyes had seemed real. But could she trust that? Cunnings had fed him information all along. How much had that muddied the waters?

Karen frowned. Yes, Liam being around when Lorraine had died was suspicious. But his reaction? Something didn't fit. What were they missing?

DI Falkner's arrival changed the atmosphere instantly. Officers straightened up and conversations hushed. He marched towards Karen.

'DS Hart,' he barked, eyeing her head wound. 'You should be at the hospital, not lingering at a crime scene.'

She tensed. 'I'm fine. Paramedics cleared me.'

Falkner's jaw clenched. 'Right. Well, we need to talk about Cunnings. How did none of us spot what was going on? Didn't you suspect anything?'

Karen's temper flared, her headache making it worse. 'Hang on, you've known her longer than any of us. If anyone should've suspected something, it was you.'

Falkner deflated visibly. He suddenly looked very tired. 'You're right. I'm sorry, Karen. I should've seen it.' He cleared his throat awkwardly. 'Right, well, I need a word with DI Morgan.'

As he headed off to find Morgan, Sophie suddenly appeared beside Karen. 'So sympathetic, isn't he? Thought he was going to bite your head off for a second there.'

'I suppose he did apologise,' Karen said with a shrug.

'We think we know why Cunnings was working for the Prescotts.'

'Why?'

'Arnie saw Cunnings using a betting app a while back. Turns out she's up to her eyeballs in debt. We think that's how the Prescotts got their claws into her.' Sophie stopped talking as Falkner and Morgan walked past. 'Well, I'd better go and see if I'm needed,' she said, darting after the two senior officers.

Karen watched her hurry away. So that was it. Cunnings had sold her colleagues out for gambling debts. But if that piece of the puzzle was solved, why did everything else still feel wrong?

Three dead women. Two pairs of eyes sewn shut. And a missing millionaire gangster. Somewhere in the middle of all that was the truth.

Chapter Thirty-Six

Morgan sat across from DS Cunnings in the interview room, studying her. She'd insisted on starting without her police rep, though her solicitor didn't look happy about it.

The stuffiness of the room wasn't helped by the solicitor's overpowering aftershave. Cunnings gnawed at her thumbnail while her solicitor tapped an expensive pen on the table, looking bored.

'Would you like to explain what you were doing at DI Hart's house this evening?' Morgan asked, keeping his voice steady despite the anger churning inside him. He'd only known Cunnings for a matter of days, but this still felt like a betrayal.

Cunnings stared at the table, her lower lip wobbling. Her usual bright smile was nowhere to be seen. Morgan thought about how competent she'd seemed when she'd first joined the investigation. What had gone wrong?

Cunnings adjusted her ponytail, hands trembling. 'I'm sorry,' she said quietly. 'I really didn't want any of this to happen.'

Her solicitor frowned. 'My advice is to wait for your rep,' he warned.

Cunnings shook her head. 'I need to start now.'

Falkner was more than happy with that. He pushed some A4 sheets across the table. 'Your bank records, DS Cunnings,' he said. 'A number of payments to betting apps, and several cash withdrawals.

You're considerably overdrawn and have multiple credit cards, all at their maximum limits. You've also taken out four loans, and your credit rating is through the floor. Is that how you were targeted by the Prescotts?'

Cunnings gripped the edge of the table. 'It's an addiction – like any other. People with different addictions get sympathy and support. But gambling? It's like you're instantly judged, like you're some horrible person. Everyone thinks you should just snap your fingers and stop. And when you can't . . . you're just written off as a failure,' she said, her words spilling out in a rush.

'I needed to place bets, and I'd been cut off from every betting app and three bookies in Sleaford. I was out of options. Then I heard about this betting ring. The odds were unbelievable – it felt like a lifeline.' She looked down at her bank statements, seeing her debts in black and white, and sighed. 'I couldn't resist. Looking back, I know they'd set it up to pull me in, but at the time, when I was winning, it was such a rush.'

Her shoulders sagged. 'Then I started losing. Big-time. The debts piled up, but I kept thinking – just one more bet, one big win, and I'd fix everything. But that win never came, and if you don't pay your bills to Prescott's guys, you don't just lose access to a betting app and get declared bankrupt with a county court judgement. They break your legs.'

She laughed bitterly. 'I got a phone call from a man who said he could help me out. Later, I realised it was Kenneth Prescott. He promised they'd forget my debt if I did a little work for him. At first, it was small things, just bits of information on different cases. Nothing serious. Not until this investigation. I volunteered to transfer over with DI Falkner. This case made everything ramp up.' She paused, her lower lip wobbling. 'It wasn't just about cutting off my access to betting or handing me over to the heavies running the ring. They said they were going to kill me if I didn't cooperate. And I believed them.'

Morgan's emotions warred between sympathy and disgust. He'd seen officers go bad before, but this was different. How had they all missed the signs? Had Cunnings just played her part too well? Her betrayal left a bitter taste.

'Well, at least you're talking and telling the truth now,' DI Falkner said, his tone kinder than before. 'That's a start. Tell us everything you know about the Prescotts, and we can get them locked up. You can make amends—'

'Oh, I can't,' Cunnings interrupted, tears welling up. 'I've done something really terrible.'

The solicitor snapped to attention, his boredom vanishing. 'I need private time to discuss this matter with my client,' he said sharply. He reached for Cunnings's arm, but she shrugged him off.

'No,' Cunnings said, voice shaking. 'I have to tell them.'

The solicitor's jaw clenched. 'DS Cunnings, I strongly advise—'

'I never meant things to get this far.'

Morgan caught Falkner's eye, both of them thinking the same thing. Whatever Cunnings was about to say, it was big.

'What do you mean?' Falkner asked, frowning.

'You've committed another crime?' Morgan wondered if this was about today's events or something else.

Cunnings broke down sobbing. 'You need to go and check on him.'

'Who? Who do we need to check on?' Morgan asked.

'DCI Whitmore.'

Morgan leaned forward, staring at Cunnings's tear-stained face. Hearing Whitmore's name made his stomach drop. He'd only met the retired DCI once. He'd been frail when he and Arnie had spoken to him about the Ava Claywood case.

'Why do we need to check on DCI Whitmore?' Morgan asked, keeping his voice low despite his rising panic. 'What have you done, Cunnings?'

Cunnings's sobs grew harder, her shoulders heaving. 'I panicked. He realised I was working for Prescott, so I . . . I . . .' Her words dissolved into unintelligible mumbling.

Morgan stood, his chair scraping the floor. He nodded to Falkner, a silent understanding passing between them. He pulled out his mobile as he strode to the door, dialling Whitmore's number.

With each unanswered ring, Morgan's apprehension grew.

Tracy Whitmore climbed out of the car and heaved her shopping bags from the boot. She'd taken longer than planned and felt guilty about leaving Brian alone.

She'd bumped into Jess from her old book club at Tesco. They'd gone for coffee, and the time had flown by. It was so good to have a catch-up. But she should've texted Brian to let him know she'd be late. Then again, he was always telling her to get out more and take time for herself. *You're not just my carer*, he'd say. *You need a life too.*

Inside the house, she blinked in the dim light. She was looking forward to their usual evening routine – a quick dinner followed by an old *Poirot* episode. They both loved crime dramas. Brian always liked to guess the killer before the reveal. He took it very seriously.

Life had changed since Brian's diagnosis. At first, they'd managed day trips and pub lunches. But slowly, everything had got harder. Even with his oxygen, getting in and out of the car exhausted him. Bit by bit, they'd stopped going places, put off by the effort involved. The electric wheelchair had helped for a while. But it kept breaking down and they'd had to switch back to the manual one.

The handles of the bags dug into her fingers as she carried the shopping down the hall. Something felt off straightaway. The telly wasn't on, and Brian wasn't in his usual spot doing his puzzles. She checked behind the living room door. No Brian. The kitchen was empty too.

Tracy assumed he was in the loo. She started unpacking the shopping. As she reached for the eggs, her eyes drifted to the window.

It was dark, but she could just see a shape at the bottom of the garden.

Right at the end of the path. It looked like . . . but it couldn't be.

He wouldn't have gone out there alone.

Her stomach lurched.

The egg carton slipped from her hands.

Tracy bolted outside. Her feet slapped against the paving stones, her breath coming in gasps. The smoke from a neighbour's bonfire scratched at her throat.

Brian was slumped forward in his wheelchair at the end of the path, arms dangling limply.

'Brian! Brian!' Her voice cracked, but he didn't move.

Why had he come out alone? Oh, the silly old fool, why couldn't he have waited until she got back?

She rushed towards him, tripping over her own feet and almost skidding into him. As she reached him, everything seemed to slow down. She could hear herself panting, feel the rough wool of Brian's cardigan as she pushed back his jacket and grabbed his shoulders.

'Brian!' She shook him gently.

His oxygen tube was still hooked round his ears and under his nose, but when she checked the tank, she saw it had been disconnected. The linking tube was nowhere in sight.

She lifted his head. It fell forward again.

She tried to feel for a pulse and at the same time grab her mobile phone from the back pocket of her jeans. Her instinct was to call for help, for an ambulance, but Brian had a 'do not resuscitate' order, so they wouldn't do anything anyway – would they?

She pressed her fingers against his neck, desperate to feel a pulse.

Tracy's thoughts were all over the place, jumping between memories. They'd been through so much – bringing up their three children, his forced early retirement from the police after finding out he was ill. Then all the hospital visits. The good days and the bad. And she couldn't bear for it to end, not like this.

Life wasn't like before, but it was still good. They still chatted and laughed and watched old films.

Her hands shook as she tried to find Brian's pulse, silently begging for a sign he was still with her. After so many years by his side, the idea of being on her own was terrifying. She waited, hoping to feel even the tiniest flutter under her fingers.

'Please, don't go, Brian,' she said. 'I'm not ready to be on my own yet.'

Chapter Thirty-Seven

DS Arnie Hodgson grimaced as he swallowed a mouthful of cold coffee.

Cunnings had been a surprise. Knocked him for six. He'd thought she was *nice*. One of the good ones. Now, if it had been Falkner, Arnie wouldn't have been surprised. But *Cunnings*? That had been a bolt out of the blue.

But he supposed that was how people like the Prescotts worked. They took advantage of weaknesses, and betting had been a huge weakness for Cunnings.

He drummed his fingers on the desk, itching to be in the interview room with Liam Prescott. But Churchill and Sophie had taken the lead on this one. He'd watched a bit in the viewing room. Liam was disturbed. Probably messed up from having Kenneth Prescott as a father – but he was clearly a nasty piece of work either way.

Liam had confessed to going to Lorraine's house, so Jason Wilkes really had seen him there. Liam had planned to scare Lorraine, to shut her up before she could spill whatever dirt she had on his father to the police.

But when Liam had got there, so he claimed, Lorraine was already dead, her body sprawled on the dining room floor.

Liam had insisted he wasn't the one who'd killed Lorraine or Michelle. Arnie really wasn't sure what to believe.

Could Liam be sick and twisted enough to kill someone in such a cruel manner? Yes. Evil enough to sew the women's eyes shut? Again, probably, yes.

But Arnie couldn't shake the possibility that maybe he was telling the truth. Maybe Lorraine really was already dead when Liam arrived at the scene. Maybe he'd never gone to Michelle's house.

But then, who had killed them? Kenneth Prescott had an alibi for Lorraine's murder. He hadn't even been in the country.

The fact they still hadn't tracked Kenneth down was really getting under Arnie's skin. It felt like they were chasing shadows, always one step behind the elusive criminal.

The sharp ring of his desk phone yanked him back to the present. 'DS Hodgson.'

'Hello,' a woman's voice said. 'I'm calling because I have some news for you regarding an all-ports alert on Kenneth Prescott. There's a private jet booked from Humberside Airport for tonight.'

'Tonight? Where's it flying to?' Arnie asked.

'Brazil.'

Arnie's grip tightened on the phone. 'Passenger names?'

'Only one. Kenneth Prescott.'

'When is the flight scheduled to depart?'

'In an hour and a half,' the woman said.

'And can they go all the way to Brazil from there, or are they stopping to refuel en route?'

'Um,' the woman said, clearly overwhelmed by all his questions. 'No, they don't need to stop en route. The plane is a Gulfstream G650ER. It can fly all the way to São Paulo without stopping for refuelling. We don't get many of those here. It's an advanced long-range private jet.'

334

Arnie did a quick mental calculation. Humberside Airport was roughly thirty miles north of Lincoln. He could get there and arrest Prescott himself, which would be very satisfying.

After thanking the woman and hanging up, Arnie gathered his things. 'Farzana, Prescott's trying to fly out of Humberside Airport. I'm going after him.'

She grabbed her coat. 'I'll come with you.'

They sprinted to the car park. Arnie gunned the engine, and they sped towards the airport.

Farzana's phone buzzed constantly as Harinder fed them updates. 'We need to make sure the airport's ready to stall if Prescott tries to leave early,' she said as Arnie took a roundabout a bit too fast.

Local units had headed to the airport too, so if Arnie didn't get there in time they could stop the flight.

Arnie's phone rang, and he put it on speaker. 'DS Hodgson,' he barked.

'Sir, the pilot's requesting an early take-off,' an airport official reported.

'Absolutely not!' Arnie shouted. 'Tell them there's a severe weather warning. Unexpected fog or something!'

'But sir, it's a clear night—'

'I don't care! Make something up!' Arnie slammed his hand on the steering wheel. 'We're almost there. Just keep that plane on the ground!'

Farzana winced as Arnie swerved around a slow-moving lorry. 'Maybe ease up on the accelerator a bit?'

'No time,' he said. The speedometer crept higher.

When they finally arrived, Arnie screeched to a halt in front of the terminal. They flashed their badges at security, but still had to wait as the guards scrutinised their IDs.

'Come on, come on,' Arnie muttered, tapping his foot impatiently.

'Procedure, sir,' one of the guards said, unmoved by Arnie's glare.

After what felt like a lifetime of bureaucratic dawdling, they were waved through. A harried-looking airport official appeared. 'DS Hodgson? Follow me.' He led them through a maze of corridors and out on to the tarmac.

The sleek private jet loomed ahead, an auxiliary power unit humming quietly to run the air conditioning. Arnie's eyes widened at the sight of the Gulfstream G650ER. It was a far cry from the plane used on the budget-airline flight he'd taken to Málaga last summer. He'd been wedged between a snoring old man and a toddler with sticky fingers.

Arnie spotted flashing lights in the distance. Police backup. Comforting, but he wanted to do this himself.

'Come on,' he said to Farzana, and took the boarding steps two at a time, his heart thumping.

He burst into the cabin, where he came face to face with Kenneth Prescott.

'What is all this?' Prescott demanded, slapping down the newspaper he'd been reading. Despite being seventy-nine years old, Prescott looked far younger. There was no justice in the world, Arnie thought.

An airline worker stood just behind Prescott. 'What's going on?' she asked.

'Step back please, madam,' Arnie said, his gaze focused on Prescott.

Prescott's silver hair was immaculately styled, and his tailored suit probably cost more than Arnie's monthly salary. Despite the polished exterior, there was a certain tightness to his skin, especially around the eyes, and a hint of puffiness in his cheeks.

He looked like he'd had a lot of work done.

His expression was unreadable, locked behind a mask of fillers and Botox.

'This is the end of the line, Prescott,' Arnie said. He pulled out his handcuffs. 'Your flight's been cancelled.'

Prescott's eyes widened. One eyebrow awkwardly tried to frown while the other stayed firmly in place, immobilised by the cosmetic procedures he'd undergone. The uneven reaction was enough to show his shock, and his frozen features couldn't mask the flicker of fear in his eyes.

Arnie grinned. When things came together like this, the job satisfaction was hard to beat.

'I don't think so, Detective,' Kenneth Prescott said. And he yanked the flight attendant from the middle of the aisle and held something sharp to her throat.

Arnie couldn't quite see what it was, but the flight attendant looked terrified.

Arnie shook his head. Why couldn't they ever come quietly? And what kind of security let someone carry anything sharp on to a plane?

On his last holiday, he'd had to take his shoes off and shuffle through the scanner hoping no one noticed the big hole in his sock. He supposed private terminals had different standards. More champagne and less shoe removal, but someone had seriously dropped the ball here.

'How exactly do you see this playing out?' Arnie asked, settling into one of the leather seats, facing Prescott. From here, he had a clear view of Prescott and his hostage. 'We're on a grounded plane, soon to be surrounded by armed officers. Not exactly a foolproof escape plan, is it, Kenny?' He let out a sigh of pleasure at the plush cushioning. 'These seats are comfy. It's like sitting on a cloud. Makes those budget-airline seats feel like sitting on a park bench.'

Prescott looked perturbed. Arnie wasn't reacting in the way he'd expected.

'I'm gonna stab her,' he said.

'Really?' Arnie replied, sounding bored.

He'd noticed that what Prescott was holding wasn't a knife at all, but a fancy-looking pen. Still, it wasn't nice to see it pressed against that poor woman's throat.

'I will,' Prescott yelled.

'Fine,' Arnie said. 'If you do, we'll have you for another murder, won't we? Whatever the outcome here, I'm still going to arrest you, and you're not flying anywhere.'

The stewardess looked horrified that Arnie was being so blasé.

'I think there's probably protocol for this, Arnie,' Farzana said awkwardly.

'I've got a hostage,' Prescott yelled at Farzana. 'Both of you get off the plane and don't try to stop me.'

'Not going to happen,' Arnie replied. 'You've reached the end of the road, sunshine.'

'Tell the pilot to take off immediately!'

Prescott still thought he was in control. He wasn't.

Arnie chuckled, reaching over and picking up Prescott's discarded newspaper. 'Absolutely not,' he said, casually flicking through the pages.

Farzana stepped forward, hands raised placatingly. 'Mr Prescott, please. Let's talk about this. There's no need for anyone to get hurt.'

Prescott sneered at her. 'Shut up, you stupid girl. You have no idea who you're dealing with.'

'That's enough,' Arnie snapped, his tone sharp. He stood up, fixing Prescott with a steely glare. 'You're not as important as you think, Prescott. You're just another criminal. We've dealt with plenty like you before. So why don't you drop the act and face the music like a man.'

Arnie turned to Farzana. 'You go out on to the tarmac. We've got backup, but they'll be wondering what's going on. Let them know that he's now decided he's taking a hostage.'

'Get off my plane!' Prescott screamed.

'No,' Arnie said. 'You can throw all the tantrums you like, but you are not flying to Brazil, Kenneth.'

Prescott looked like he might be about to explode. He let go of the hostage and lunged towards Arnie with the pen.

Arnie lamped him squarely on the jaw and watched, satisfied, as Prescott fell in a crumpled heap in the aisle.

'Not bad for an old bloke, eh?' he said, rubbing his knuckles. He turned to look for Farzana, but she was already outside.

'You all right?' he said to the flight attendant, who was rubbing her neck.

'Not really, no,' she said stiffly. 'You didn't sound very concerned about my safety.'

'Oh, I was very concerned,' he said. 'I've just had a lot of practice hiding it.'

Prescott groaned on the floor. Arnie kneeled so he could turn him over and look him square in the face. Prescott glared up at Arnie with pure hatred. The mighty Kenneth Prescott, finally brought to account.

'Kenneth Prescott, you are under arrest on suspicion of the murder of Ava Claywood.'

As Arnie read him his rights, he watched the last traces of arrogance drain from Prescott's eyes. Money might buy private jets, but it hopefully wouldn't buy Prescott's way out of a murder conviction.

From private jet to a prison cell. Prescott wouldn't be too thrilled with the downgrade. The fall was going to be a long, hard one. And in Arnie's opinion, it couldn't happen to a more deserving man.

Chapter Thirty-Eight

Sophie found Harinder in the tech lab, already pulling on his coat.

'Heading off?' she asked, leaning against the doorframe.

'Just about. You?'

'Working late.' She stifled a yawn. 'I'm questioning Liam Prescott alongside DCI Churchill. We're taking a quick break.'

'That's a big deal.' Harinder smiled. 'Good for you. Nice that Churchill picked you out for that. He must think a lot of your interview skills.'

'Hmm. Maybe.' The truth was, most of the team were tied up elsewhere. Arnie had been chasing down Kenneth Prescott and had just arrested him in a dramatic scene at Humberside Airport; Karen had just been attacked by Liam in her own home; Cunnings had turned out to be working for the Prescotts, and Morgan was questioning her with DI Falkner. Still, she'd take what she could get. And Churchill *had* asked her to do the interview instead of Rick, so there was always that.

'Actually, I'm glad you're here,' Harinder said. 'I finally heard back from the Swiss authorities about those anonymous emails Karen's been getting. I was just on my way to see Churchill with the good news.'

'Oh?' Sophie straightened.

'They were sent from Lincolnshire. Not really a surprise.' Harinder grinned, sliding back into his chair and switching his computer on. 'But we've narrowed it down further.'

He pulled up some data on his screen, clearly enjoying his moment. Sophie had to smile. His enthusiasm for tech was sweet, even if she rarely understood half of what he was talking about.

'Go on then, impress me with your skills.'

'See these IP addresses? Once we got through the encryption . . .' He paused for dramatic effect.

'What?'

'It was DS Cunnings. She sent the threatening emails to Karen.'

Sophie's stomach dropped. 'What? All this time, those creepy threats?'

'Yes. I'm just about to tell Churchill before I go home.'

'I can do it, if you're on your way out.'

Harinder shook his head. 'Better coming from me in case he has questions. I'll do it before I leave.' He paused. 'How's Karen doing?'

'Recovering. That bump on the head was nasty, but you know Karen. She's already wanting to get back to work.'

'Tell her to take it easy.'

Sophie headed for the vending machine, still reeling from the second revelation about Cunnings that evening. She'd really managed to pull the wool over everyone's eyes.

The canteen had closed ages ago, but Sophie needed something to keep her going. She scanned the options through the scratched plastic front. Chocolate bars, crisps, more chocolate. She dismissed three different varieties of cheesy corn snacks and something claiming to be a protein bar that was probably just chocolate in disguise.

Finally, she spotted a packet of vegetable crisps lurking in the corner. She fed in her money. At least vegetables had been

341

involved at some point in their production, even if they were now drowning in oil.

She'd just pulled the packet through the flap at the bottom of the machine and was grimacing at the salt content when footsteps echoed down the corridor. Callum appeared, a file tucked under his arm, phone pressed to his ear.

'I told you I can't just give you that information. People will start to—' He stopped dead when he saw Sophie. The colour drained from his face. 'Got to go,' he muttered into the phone and hung up.

'Evening,' Sophie said carefully.

'Oh, hi.' Callum shifted the file to his other arm. 'Working late too?'

'Yes.' She held up her vegetable crisps. 'Dinner of champions.'

'Right.' He glanced towards the exit. 'I just need to grab something from my car.'

Sophie watched him hurry away. That phone call . . . Something wasn't right.

She waited a few seconds, then followed.

The car park was dark except for the glow of the security lights. Sophie hung back as Callum approached a familiar silver Audi. Cindy Connor's car.

The journalist was waiting in the driver's seat. Callum slipped into the passenger side and handed her the file.

Sophie's blood boiled. So that was how Cindy had known about the connection between Lorraine and Ava Claywood almost immediately after they'd found those newspaper clippings at Lorraine's house.

Callum wasn't just doing his job as press liaison. He was feeding Cindy information about the case.

She'd known something dodgy was going on. And to think she'd even apologised to him! Technically, she'd got it wrong – he wasn't Kenneth Prescott's son. But he was still up to no good.

Sophie strode towards the car and rapped sharply on the window.

'This isn't what it looks like!' Callum scrambled out of the car. 'I was just explaining some public statements to Cindy, that's all. Standard stuff. Nothing classified or—'

'Oh, for goodness' sake,' Cindy cut in, lowering the window. 'Grow a pair, Callum. You don't owe her an explanation. She has no proof.' She turned to Sophie. 'And this is none of your business. What goes on between the press office and journalists isn't your concern.'

'It is when Callum's leaking details of an investigation, potentially compromising it.'

Cindy rolled her eyes. 'Oh, don't be so dramatic. This is how it's always worked. A little give and take between the press and police. No one gets hurt.'

'No one gets hurt?' Sophie's hands clenched. 'What about the families of victims having to read about that stuff before the police have had a chance to break the news to them? What about compromising an active investigation?'

'Leave it to the grown-ups, sweetheart. We know what we're doing.'

Sophie turned to Callum. 'What have you got to say for yourself?'

At first, he looked ashamed, shoulders hunched like he was a schoolboy caught cheating in an exam. But then something shifted in his expression.

'You know what? No. I'm not going to apologise,' Callum said, straightening up. His voice took on a fevered edge she'd never heard before. 'The public has a right to know what's really going on. Do you have any idea how much gets covered up, buried in bureaucracy?'

'Well, I agree a bit of modernisation would help, but—'

'The police service needs dragging into the modern age. Proper accountability, real transparency.'

'Oh, come on. This isn't about transparency, you—' Sophie started.

'It is!' Callum's face turned scarlet. 'People deserve to know the truth. The public deserve answers, not only what the police deem suitable for release.'

Sophie blinked at this sudden transformation from meek press officer to passionate radical.

'I left my banking job and took a massive pay cut. Because someone needs to shine a light on what really goes on behind those walls.' Callum jerked a thumb towards the station.

'By leaking confidential information to the press?' Sophie asked incredulously.

'By making sure the truth can't be buried or forgotten!' He was almost shouting now. 'You're part of the problem if you can't see that.'

'No, Callum, *you're* the problem. You can explain yourself to the super.'

He seemed to shrink back into himself. 'Wait, Sophie, please. The public needed to know. The Claywoods had been forgotten. Abandoned by the system. I thought a few articles would attract righteous indignation from the public, which would force the service to reopen the case.' His voice trembled. 'I was only trying to do the right thing. You've thought about it too, haven't you? How much we keep from people?'

'You sold us out.'

'It was just one time—'

Sophie almost laughed. 'One time? The Ava Claywood connection to Lorraine's murder was published before we'd even finished processing the scene. How many other leaks have there been?'

Callum's silence was answer enough.

'I'm reporting this,' Sophie said.

Cindy's patronising smile didn't waver. 'Are you sure that's wise? After all, sometimes it's better to play nice with the press. You never know when you might need me.'

Sophie met her gaze. 'I'll take my chances.'

◆　◆　◆

Morgan spotted Tracy Whitmore as soon as he entered the hospital waiting area. She sat hunched in one of the plastic chairs, her face pale and drawn, hands clutching an oversized handbag in her lap.

'Mrs Whitmore.' He hurried over. 'How is he?'

She looked up. 'He's hanging in there. Tough old thing.' She managed a weak smile. 'They're transferring him to a ward now and said I can see him once he's settled.'

Morgan let out a long breath. When he'd learned Brian had been found unconscious in his garden, he'd feared the worst. After getting answers from Cunnings, he'd come straight to Lincolnshire County Hospital.

'I don't understand how it happened,' Tracy said. 'He was in his manual chair. There's no way he could have wheeled himself to the bottom of the garden. His oxygen tube has never come disconnected before. Ever. He's so careful with it.'

Morgan hated to see her confusion. She was trying to make sense of something that had no sense to it.

Now came the hard part. He sat down beside her.

'Tracy, there's something you need to know. About what happened to Brian.' He hesitated. 'It wasn't an accident. It was DS Cunnings. She visited him at home on the pretext of asking questions about an old case. She removed his oxygen tube and left him to die.'

'What?' Tracy's bag slipped from her fingers and on to the floor. 'A police officer did this? But why would they . . . ?'

Morgan picked up her bag and patted her hand awkwardly, wishing he was better at this. Before he could explain further, a doctor appeared.

'Mrs Whitmore? You can see your husband now.'

Tracy grabbed Morgan's arm. 'Come with me? If Brian's strong enough, he'll want to talk to you and make a statement.'

The hospital ward was quiet. The lights were dimmed except for the one over Brian's cubicle. He looked small and frail, but his eyes were alert. A nurse adjusted something on the monitor beside him.

'He's doing well,' she said cheerfully. 'Aren't you, Brian? Gave everyone quite a scare.' She checked the equipment one more time. 'He's on four litres of oxygen, but we might be able to reduce that soon if he keeps improving. You didn't like the mask, so we're trying the nasal cannula, aren't we, Brian?'

'Feel like I'm suffocating with that thing,' he said, giving a tired nod to the clear plastic mask.

'Thank you,' Tracy said.

As soon as the nurse left, Brian reached for Tracy's hand. Their fingers intertwined, and they shared a look that made Morgan feel like an intruder.

After a moment, Brian's gaze shifted to Morgan.

'Cunnings,' he said, his voice sounding rough. 'She's working for the Prescotts.'

'We know,' Morgan said gently. 'She's been arrested.'

'But why target Brian?' Tracy asked. 'It doesn't make sense. He's been retired for years.'

'I think it might have to do with Brian's still razor-sharp detective skills,' Morgan said with a smile at Brian. 'Once a DCI . . . You sussed out she was crooked, didn't you, Brian?'

Brian smiled and breathed in deeply through his nose.

'I figured it out when she came to the house. The way she was asking questions. I guessed they had something on her.' He paused to inhale deeply again. 'When I confronted her about it, she disconnected my oxygen and left me at the bottom of the garden to die.' Another deep breath. 'She knew I couldn't make it back to the house and wouldn't live long without my oxygen.'

'I hope you throw the book at her,' Tracy said, gripping Brian's hand.

'We intend to. Cunnings was also with Liam Prescott when he attacked Karen and Mike in their home,' Morgan said.

Brian's eyes widened in alarm.

'Karen's okay,' Morgan added quickly. 'Everyone's safe. We arrested Cunnings at the scene. If you feel up to making a statement, we'll add attempted murder to her charges.'

Brian nodded. 'Why did she do it?'

'Gambling debts. She owed some very dangerous people a lot of money. Kenneth Prescott offered to clear her debts if she helped them.'

'All this for money?' Tracy's voice shook with anger.

'Cunnings bet on the wrong side,' Morgan said. 'And now she's lost everything.'

Chapter Thirty-Nine

Karen was feeling surprisingly good considering yesterday's events. She'd left Mike and James at Christine's while she made her way to the station. She was trying to avoid Falkner. If he saw her there, he wouldn't be happy.

Christine had fed them a huge full English breakfast and then lunch, making them feel at home. But Karen's mind had been elsewhere the whole day.

She kept circling back to why Lorraine and Michelle's eyes had been sewn shut. It was a message, though its meaning still didn't quite make sense to her.

It sort of fitted with the Prescotts sending a warning. Lorraine and Michelle knew what Kenneth had done to Ava, and when he thought they wouldn't keep their eyes closed to his crimes any longer, he made sure their eyes were shut – permanently.

But that felt like a stretch. Like a jigsaw piece being forced into a hole it didn't really fit.

In the AV room, Karen accessed yesterday's video stream from Liam's interview. Her mouth went dry as his face appeared on the screen. She shuddered as she recalled regaining consciousness in her kitchen with him looming nearby.

Liam had clearly struggled to control his temper in the interview, ranting and raving at Sophie and Churchill. But when they asked him about Cunnings's involvement, he readily gave her up.

Karen scoffed. Honour amongst criminals? The Prescotts wouldn't know a moral code if it slapped them in the face.

The interview went on for hours. For most of it, Liam stayed stubbornly silent, and Karen fast-forwarded those sections. But his occasional outbursts were interesting.

Liam showed no remorse. He described his plan to rough Lorraine up and warn her about the consequences of going to the police. But he insisted, 'I didn't kill her or sew her eyes shut. That's pretty twisted. Whoever did that must have had a childhood more messed up than mine.'

Karen wasn't sure what to think. It had to be Liam; they didn't have any other suspects. It made sense. Lorraine had sent the email. Kenneth had felt threatened, so he'd sent his son to warn her off.

It wasn't too hard to imagine Liam getting carried away, hitting Lorraine over the head, and then deciding to leave a macabre message by sewing her eyes shut – a warning to others to keep their eyes closed to Kenneth Prescott's crimes.

But then Karen felt her stomach drop as a realisation hit her. She paused the playback.

Of course it wasn't Liam.

How could she have missed it?

The *eyes*.

She knew who the real killer was. Or, at least, she thought she did.

The more she considered it, the more it made sense. It was the only thing that did.

Karen grabbed her coat. She paused, halfway to the door. Should she tell Morgan and Falkner?

She knew Morgan would be all for making a plan and, knowing him, a risk assessment – he always did.

Falkner wouldn't be happy if she interrupted him, especially if her hunch turned out to be wrong, and technically she wasn't even supposed to be at work today.

Come to think of it, Morgan wasn't exactly known for supporting hunches. No, she'd deal with it herself and tell them afterwards.

She headed back to the open-plan office area and looked around, expecting to find Arnie, but he was gone. There was no sign of Sophie, Rick or Farzana either.

She debated whether or not to go on her own. It was reckless, and she'd already come quite close to losing her life yesterday.

She shrugged on her coat, and just as she picked up her bag, Rick walked into the office, shaking rain off his umbrella.

'It's really coming down out there,' he said, wiping his face.

'Just the man I wanted to see,' Karen said. 'Fancy going on a road trip?'

Rick raised an eyebrow. 'In this weather? Where are we off to then?'

'I thought we might pay a visit to the Claywoods,' Karen said. 'I think it's about time we found out the truth.'

'About what happened to Ava, you mean?'

'Amongst other things,' Karen replied.

The rain pelted the car, and the windscreen wipers squeaked in protest as they fought a losing battle against the downpour. After a slow journey thanks to the terrible weather, they pulled up to the Claywoods' house in Market Rasen.

Rick peered through the sheets of rain. 'Nice place. Looks cosy.'

'Yes,' Karen said, parking up. 'Let's hope they're in.'

They knocked on the door. Ruth answered, wiping her hands on a tea towel.

'Oh, hello,' she said with a warm smile. 'Have you got some news for us?'

'Yes,' Karen said. 'We've made an arrest. We want to tell you and your father about it.'

As they stepped inside, Rick glanced around. 'Smells good in here,' he said.

'Lasagne,' Ruth replied. 'I was just making dinner. It'll keep. I think Dad's tinkering in the shed again. Freezing out there, but he's happy.'

Pictures of Ava lined the hallway. She'd been a beautiful woman, and younger than Ruth when she'd been murdered.

'I'll just go and ask Dad to come in.'

'Actually, Ruth, let's go out there to talk to him,' Karen said.

She looked surprised. 'Oh, okay.'

John Claywood looked up as they entered the shed. 'What's all this then?' he asked gruffly.

'They've brought some news, Dad,' Ruth said. 'They've made an arrest.'

The shed was cramped but meticulously organised, with tools hanging neatly on pegboards along the walls.

John watched them warily from his workbench. Karen's gaze swept across the tools until it fell on a hammer. A standard claw hammer with a wooden handle worn smooth with age. Raj had been specific about the murder weapon: blunt force trauma, likely from a hammer or similar tool, struck at a downward angle. The head would be about two inches wide.

She glanced at John's hammer again.

Rick followed her gaze, his eyes widening slightly as he made the same connection. He shifted his weight and gave a subtle nod.

John turned to see what they were looking at.

'Well?' he said. 'Are you going to tell me about it, or stand there gawping at my tools?'

'We've arrested Liam Prescott,' Karen said.

John narrowed his eyes. 'Liam?'

'Kenneth Prescott's son,' Karen said.

John thought for a moment, then frowned. 'What have you arrested him for? He wouldn't have murdered Ava. He'd have been too young.'

'You mean you've arrested Liam for murdering Lorraine and her sister?' Ruth asked.

'He's been arrested, and he's being questioned,' Karen said.

John snorted. '*That's* the update? You could have done that with a phone call.'

'Dad,' Ruth said, shooting him a look before turning back to Karen. 'Sorry about that. We do appreciate you coming all the way out here, especially in this weather.'

'When Liam was being questioned, it got me thinking,' Karen said.

'Really,' John said drily. 'Do tell. Can you get to the point, duck? It's cold out here and it's nearly dinner time.'

But Karen didn't rush. 'There was something you said to me when we talked about Ava. You told me that the police were trying to look at Kenneth Prescott, but everyone around him refused to talk. They all *closed their eyes* to what happened.'

Ruth's fingers twisted the tea towel she was still holding. 'Well, yes,' she said. 'It's true. They all clammed up. People pretended not to see anything.'

'Everyone acted blind when it came to Prescott,' John said. 'None of them would tell the police what they knew.'

'And you decided Lorraine was one of those people who shut their eyes to the crime,' Karen said softly. 'Michelle too?'

John frowned. 'What are you talking about? I don't think I like the way this conversation is going.'

Karen turned to Ruth. 'Did you decide they needed to pay for their silence?'

352

Ruth's face paled. Her hands turned white as she gripped the tea towel.

'Hold on a minute,' John said sharply, leaning forward on his workbench. 'What are you implying?'

Ruth gave a brittle nod. 'If they knew something, they should have spoken up.'

'Why did you do it?' Karen asked.

'Do what?' John demanded. 'What are you talking about? I hope you're not accusing my Ruth of committing a crime.'

'Dad, it's okay,' Ruth said, taking a shaky breath. 'I've been expecting this. I knew there was a high chance I'd get caught. I'm not stupid. I'm a PCSO, I knew the risk. I decided it was worth it.'

'What are you talking about?' John stared at her, confusion and then fear crossing his face. He held up a hand. 'No, don't say anything. Don't talk to the police. We'll get a solicitor.'

'No, Dad.' Ruth shook her head. 'I want to confess.'

'No,' John insisted. 'Think of your boys.'

'They're fine. They're at university now. They don't need me anymore.'

'Of course they need you. You're their mother. What are you talking about? You needed your mother, didn't you?'

'Yes, I did,' Ruth said, her voice breaking. 'When I was twelve years old. But she was taken from me.'

'Neither Lorraine nor Michelle took her from you,' Karen said gently.

'They may as well have done,' Ruth snapped, then she sighed. 'What gave me away?'

'The eyes,' Karen said simply. 'When we first discussed your mother's case, you described everyone 'turning a blind eye' to Prescott's crimes.'

Something about Liam's words in his interview – *That's pretty twisted. Whoever did that must have had a childhood more messed up than mine* – had sparked the memory for Karen.

Then she'd remembered DCI Whitmore describing Ruth having to deal with her mother's death and her father's alcoholism at only twelve years old.

A difficult childhood, followed by over forty years of pain from a lifetime of knowing her mother's killer went unpunished because people kept their eyes shut to his evil.

Ruth had been just a child, trying to cope while her father drowned his sorrows and her mother's killer walked free.

Ruth's shoulders sagged. 'I've rehearsed this moment in my head a thousand times since I killed them. Every night since, I've lain awake, wondering when I'd get a knock at the door.'

'I don't understand, Ruth. Why now? After all this time, why?' John asked, his voice wavering.

Ruth wiped tears from her cheeks. 'Because – well, a couple of reasons really.' Ruth turned to Karen and Rick. 'Dad just got his terminal diagnosis. Liver cirrhosis.'

John's face fell. 'Ruthie, I'm old. Something was always going to get me at some point. Don't say you did this because of me.'

'No, Dad, I didn't. I did it now because Lorraine came to me. Two weeks ago. She turned up at the house. Told me she'd been diagnosed with lymphoma and didn't have long to live. She said that before she died, she wanted to apologise.' Ruth took a deep breath. 'And she told me everything. How Mum had gone to her and her sister, Michelle, for help, and how they'd turned her away. And then, even knowing it was Kenneth Prescott who'd killed Mum, they did nothing. They let him get away with it for years . . . I was *twelve*, struggling to keep our lives from unravelling as my dad drank himself to sleep every night. I was . . . *alone*,' she said, her voice trembling.

John covered his face with his hands and smothered a sob. 'I'm sorry I let you down. I'm so sorry, Ruth.'

'It wasn't your fault, Dad. Not after what you'd been through. It was Lorraine's fault. Her and her sister.' Ruth's voice grew cold, her eyes distant. 'Lorraine came here expecting to get absolution. She'd refused to help Mum and then wouldn't lift a finger to bring her killer to justice. She closed her eyes to it all.' Ruth's hands clenched into fists. 'So I decided to close her eyes . . . for good.'

The room fell silent.

The confession hit Karen hard. There was little comfort in having her suspicions confirmed. She had hoped she'd got it wrong.

Mike's face flashed in her mind. How on earth was she going to tell him?

They had all seen Ruth as a victim, not a killer.

Karen exchanged a glance with Rick. He looked sombre. Neither of them found satisfaction in closing the case like this.

'We're going to have to take you into custody now, Ruth. You understand we have to do that, don't you?' Rick said gently.

'Oh no, please,' John said, looking between them with desperation. 'Please don't.'

'We have to, Mr Claywood,' Rick replied firmly.

'You don't understand. This has ruined my family once. Can't you just show some compassion. For forty years nobody got justice for Ava. Crimes go unpunished all the time. Locking Ruth up won't bring Lorraine or Michelle back. Please don't arrest my daughter.'

'She committed murder, Mr Claywood,' Karen said. 'We can't just ignore that.'

'Sometimes justice takes a long time,' Rick added. 'But it doesn't make it right to take it into your own hands.'

'No!' John shouted. 'Don't take her. It was me. I did it. I killed Lorraine and her sister. Please, Ruth, say it was me.'

'No, Dad. I did it,' Ruth said firmly.

A storm of emotions crossed John's face – from disbelief to despair. He sank back against the wall, knocking tools to the ground.

'Ruth,' Karen said softly. 'You need to come with us now.'

Ruth looked at her, eyes filled with relief and sadness. 'Okay.'

Rick stepped forward. 'Shall we go, then?'

Ruth put the tea towel on the workbench. 'Yes,' she said. 'Let's go. I'm ready.'

Her father followed as they led her out of the shed, through the house, and out the front door.

By the time they reached the car, the rain had eased to a drizzle. Karen glanced back.

John Claywood stood by the doorway, his hunched, sobbing figure a dark silhouette against the warm light inside.

Chapter Forty

The following week, the team was huddled around a cramped table in the Plough Inn, celebrating a breakthrough in the Ava Claywood case. The lab had worked its magic on the decades-old evidence and found a DNA match between Kenneth Prescott and samples taken from the scene. After all these years, the past had finally caught up with him.

'Fantastic result,' Arnie said, lifting his pint. His grin was infectious, spreading around the group.

'Absolutely brilliant!' Sophie said, then her gaze flickered to Karen. 'Sorry. Not brilliant. Bad word choice. But I'm glad we nailed Prescott and arrested Ruth for Lorraine and Michelle's murders.'

Karen felt a pang of sadness at the mention of Lorraine. She ignored it, pasting on a smile. 'No, you're right,' she said, surprised at how steady her voice sounded. 'It was a brilliant result. We caught Lorraine's killer, and we solved two further cases.'

Churchill tapped his finger on the table. 'You know, we could really use some positive press on this one. What do you say to a quick photo op for the local paper? Just a shot of the team, maybe a quote or two about our successful outcome?'

Karen shot him a look that could've frozen hell over. 'Not a chance, sir.'

'Karen's right,' Arnie said. 'Bunch of parasites. I'd rather wrestle a dozen angry badgers than have anything to do with Cindy Connor's rag.'

As if summoned by the mention of her name, Karen's phone buzzed. Cindy's name flashed on the screen. Karen declined the call with a vicious jab of her thumb.

'Fair enough. I suppose I should buy a round,' Churchill said, to cheers from the rest of the group. 'All right, all right,' he said, holding up his hands. 'Don't make me change my mind.' He weaved through the Friday night crowd to the bar.

Sophie was scrolling through her phone, her face illuminated by the faint glow. 'Have you seen all the stories already online?' she asked Karen. 'I'd avoid social media for a few days if I were you. It's a proper circus.'

'I intend to,' Karen said, picturing herself hurling her mobile into the River Witham. 'Might treat myself to a new book and stay offline completely this weekend.'

'Oh wow, Cindy's got a story out already,' Sophie said, her eyes widening. 'Listen to this—'

'You're not helping, Soph,' Rick said, giving her a gentle nudge. 'You just told her to avoid social media, so she doesn't see this stuff, and now you're about to read it out.'

'Sorry,' Sophie said, with an expression that wouldn't have looked out of place on a naughty puppy.

'It's fine,' Karen said, waving a hand. 'Cindy's already been calling, trying to get the inside scoop. I swear, that woman would trade her soul for a front-page headline.'

'I still can't believe it was Callum feeding her information all along,' Rick said, shaking his head. 'He seemed so meek. Wouldn't say boo to a goose.'

Karen nodded, taking a sip of her drink. 'That's what made him perfect for it, I suppose. No one suspected the quiet lad from press relations.' She remembered the search of Callum's computer – page after page of radical forums campaigning to limit police powers. 'Not so meek online though, was he?' It had turned out the mild-mannered press officer was quite the keyboard warrior.

After a few months of interacting with those groups, he'd given up a six-figure salary in London to 'make a difference'. Some difference. Karen thought back to his interview – how passionate he'd become when defending his actions. Gone was the timid press officer, replaced by someone convinced he was fighting the good fight.

'That's what happens when people spend too much time in echo chambers online,' Rick said. 'He started off as a believer in greater transparency – which is a good thing – but when he joined those anti-police groups, they radicalised him. Convinced him that all the problems of the justice system came down to the police hiding things from the public.'

Karen agreed. Callum had seen himself as some kind of crusader for justice. Instead of what he really was – just another leak putting cases and convictions at risk.

'Well, he had me fooled,' Rick said with a shrug.

'Me too,' Karen said. 'But Sophie knew there was something dodgy going on with him, didn't you?'

Sophie let out a self-deprecating laugh. 'Yes, but I got it completely wrong at first. I was convinced he had to be Prescott's son because he'd been born in Brazil. That was properly embarrassing.'

'Don't be too hard on yourself,' Karen said. 'You admitted your mistake and didn't let it put you off. You kept your eyes open. If it weren't for you, we might still have Callum sneaking information to Cindy.'

Rick added, 'On the bright side, we caught him and put a stop to it. And Cunnings too. Sounds like she'd been in bed with the Prescotts for a while. It's been a right mess, hasn't it?'

Karen nodded grimly. 'Two leaks in one case.'

'Any word yet on whether Callum will be charged?' Sophie asked.

Karen shrugged. 'Not sure yet. He's definitely lost his job, but whether they'll press charges is still up in the air. I suppose it depends on how much damage they think he's done.'

Sylvie bustled into the pub like a friendly whirlwind. She leaned over and planted a kiss on the top of Arnie's head. 'Hello, darling.'

'What can I get you?' he said, standing up.

'G and T, please. Make it a double. It's been that kind of week.'

'Churchill's getting the round, but I'll get yours. We're celebrating.'

'I know. Great job on the case.'

'It's a triple celebration.' Arnie beamed. 'Five members of that burglary gang were apprehended yesterday. And – drum roll please – the canteen overlords have caved. Real sausages back on the menu from Monday.' He frowned. 'Suppose that means I owe Cunnings a fiver.'

'She really did like a bet, didn't she?' Rick said.

Arnie sighed. 'She did. I should've picked up on that.' He turned back to Sylvie. 'Here, have my seat.'

'How are you?' Sylvie asked, shuffling closer to Karen. Her eyes were full of concern.

'I'm okay,' Karen said. 'But it's been tough.'

'And Mike?'

This wasn't something he could bottle up and move on from. But so far, he was still her Mike, brooding and introspective. That was the thing with Mike. He'd talk in his own time. He wouldn't be rushed. 'He's dealing with it surprisingly well, all things considered.'

'Why did Liam have such a hatred for you and Mike? That's the part that just doesn't make sense to me.'

Karen felt a wave of exhaustion. How did you ever really know what went on in someone else's head? And did she even want to try to understand Liam's twisted reasoning? 'Kenneth thought that by treating Liam badly, it'd keep him on his toes. He used him more like an attack dog than a son. He lied to Liam that he was going to cut him out of the will and put Mike in. Of course, Liam wasn't happy about that.'

The will business had been just another of Kenneth's mind games. He'd laughed when they'd asked him about it. Typical controlling behaviour. The threats about the will had just been another way to keep Liam dancing to Kenneth's tune.

Karen's thoughts drifted to Cunnings. The CPS was building a strong case against her, not just for her part in the attack on Karen, but for what she'd done to Brian Whitmore too. She was acting all repentant now, probably hoping for a lighter sentence when it came to court.

Sylvie thanked Arnie as he brought over her G&T. And Churchill arrived with a tray of drinks and began handing them around.

'To a successful case. Well done,' he said, lifting his glass.

After everyone joined in the toast, Morgan leaned over and asked Karen, 'You doing all right?'

Karen saw the genuine concern in his eyes. Morgan might not be the most expressive member of the team, but he'd been there for her through thick and thin. 'I've been better, to be honest, but I'm getting there.'

She thought about the evening ahead with Mike and James. She'd suggested picking up fish and chips, comfort food for an impossibly uncomfortable situation.

She and Mike were going to accompany James back to his house – the house he'd shared with Lorraine until her murder – now that the investigation was over.

James would be sleeping there alone tonight, in the bed he used to share with Lorraine.

Would he lie awake, staring at the ceiling, imagining his wife's final moments?

Going back to the house would mean Mike would have to walk past the spot where he'd found his mother's body. Karen was sure he had replayed that moment in his mind a hundred times since it happened, just as she had.

Karen had spent the day helping Mike and James with the funeral preparations. Choosing Lorraine's favourite flowers – white roses and irises – and picking out readings. It felt surreal.

Not long ago, they'd been planning to announce their engagement over dinner with Lorraine and James. Now, instead of wedding preparations, they were organising a funeral.

Falkner was still keeping Karen at arm's length from the case, like she was some kind of contamination risk. It grated, but she understood. He was worried it might damage their chances of conviction. Cunnings had already thrown a spanner in the works and they didn't need things complicated further.

Ruth's arrest was still a sore point for Falkner. Karen winced, remembering his meltdown afterwards. Red-faced and spluttering, he'd waved his arms about like an unbalanced windmill as he read Karen and Rick the riot act.

'Shame about Chapman,' Rick said, and took a sip of his pint. 'Slippery snake.'

The group murmured in agreement. Chapman was still out there, carrying on his dodgy business dealings as if nothing had happened. The evidence just wasn't there, at least not yet. Maybe one day they'd nail him, but for now he was too careful, too well connected. Sometimes you had to accept that you couldn't get everyone, not all at once. They'd got Kenneth and Liam Prescott, caught Ruth, and Cunnings would face justice. That would have to be enough for now.

Karen glanced around the table. Surrounded by the team, she felt herself relax, something she hadn't done since the day she and Mike discovered Lorraine's body.

A hush fell over the pub. Karen looked up to see DI Falkner entering, his face as serious as ever. He made a beeline for their table.

'Detective Hart, a word?' he said, his tone clipped.

Karen excused herself and followed him to a quiet corner of the pub. She braced herself for another lecture about the need to distance herself from the work involved in wrapping up the case.

To her surprise, Falkner's expression softened. 'I wanted to apologise,' he said, catching Karen off guard. 'I may have been too hard on you during this case. You've done good work, despite your personal connection to events.'

Karen blinked, momentarily speechless. 'Thank you,' she managed. 'I appreciate that.'

'I have to admit,' he continued, 'Ruth was never on my radar as a suspect.'

Karen nodded, remembering Ruth's confession. The murder itself was shocking enough, but sewing her victims' eyelids closed? That was the stuff of nightmares.

It wasn't a quick, angry act. It had required planning. Karen felt bile rise in her throat as she imagined Ruth calmly threading a needle, leaning over Lorraine's body, ready to stitch through her skin with a steady hand.

Ruth had seemed so normal. Unremarkable, even. All those interactions with her, and Karen hadn't spotted the sinister undercurrent beneath that mild exterior.

Even after Ruth's confession, part of Karen's brain had kept trying to reject the truth and find some other explanation. Because if Ruth could hide such a twisted side from her, what did that say about Karen's ability to read people?

'Well,' Falkner said. 'I'll let you get back to the team.'

Karen made her way back to the table. The case was closed, Ruth had confessed to killing Lorraine and Michelle. Prescott would be behind bars for the rest of his life for killing Ava Claywood four decades ago, and even Falkner had acknowledged Karen's efforts.

She glanced at her phone, realising it was time to head off. The taxi she'd booked would be arriving soon. She said her goodbyes to the team.

As she stepped out into the chilly evening air, Karen's emotions were still all over the place. The case had been brutal, revealing dark secrets, and it had torn the Claywood family apart. But there was also a sense of justice finally being served after so many years.

Karen hoped that Mike and James could work through their grief in a healthier way than Ruth had. They had advantages. They were adults, while Ruth had been a child when she'd lost her mother. Unlike Ruth, they weren't left knowing a killer had walked free.

All those years of not knowing who was responsible, of suspicion and resentment. No wonder it had twisted Ruth. How different might things have been if Ava's killer had been caught back in 1981?

Karen tried to imagine Lorraine's state of mind all those years ago. Young, frightened, weighed down by knowing what had happened to Ava and fearing she could be next. She'd had Quentin Chapman's help to escape Prescott. But had she ever really escaped?

Lorraine had been a victim too. And her attempt to make things right had backfired so tragically.

She'd stayed silent about Ava for years because she'd been scared. Scared of Kenneth, her abuser. Scared for Mike, and how the truth about his biological father might damage him.

That fear had built walls around Lorraine, making her seem distant and prickly. But now Karen saw her behaviour for what it was – a desperate attempt to protect herself and Mike.

The cruel irony was that when Lorraine had finally found the courage to open up and tell the truth, it had got her killed.

Chapter Forty-One

Ruth perched on the edge of her bunk. Her cellmate's snores filled the cramped space, and Ruth longed for the quiet of her bedroom at home. It wasn't easy to sleep in prison. The constant racket, doors clanging, someone always shouting, was worlds away from her peaceful street back home. Ruth knew she'd get used to it eventually, but right now, it was doing her head in.

She squeezed her eyes shut as memories of those first awful days without her mum came flooding back. She'd been so young, yet suddenly responsible for everything.

She remembered one evening when she'd forgotten something in the oven. The smoke alarm had gone off, its piercing screech echoing through the house. She'd had to drag a chair over, climbing up to wave a towel frantically at the alarm, trying to clear the smoke. All the while, her father had been out cold in the living room.

The constant fear of mucking things up, of disappointing her grief-stricken father. The loneliness of it all. No one had been there to help her, to guide her. She'd had to figure it all out on her own.

Maybe Lorraine and Michelle hadn't killed Ruth's mother, but they'd left her defenceless to face Prescott on her own. They'd refused to go to the police and had hidden the identity of her mother's killer for decades. Then, after Lorraine got an attack of conscience after being diagnosed with terminal lymphoma, she'd wanted to come clean and ask for forgiveness from Ruth.

She'd been so patronising, so infuriatingly matter-of-fact, as though she expected Ruth to just shrug and forgive her.

The rage she'd felt when Lorraine had confessed . . . Ruth's mind flashed back to that conversation.

'Ruth, dear,' Lorraine had said. 'I need to tell you something. It's about your mother. She came to me for help, all those years ago. And I'm ashamed to say I turned her away. I couldn't get involved. I had a child, you see.'

Ruth had stared at her, disbelief and anger rising like bile in her throat. 'What?'

'I'm so sorry. I know it doesn't make it right, but I was scared. I had Mike to think about. He was just a child.'

Ruth's voice had been ice-cold when she replied. 'And what about me? I was a child too. Did I not matter?'

Her hands clenched into fists at the memory. She'd lost her mother, then had to try to keep the house together while her father drank himself into oblivion every night. She'd had to learn how to cook, to wash her own clothes, to be the adult when she was still just a kid herself.

After Lorraine had left, she'd planned everything carefully. She'd taken her dad's hammer from the shed, and the sewing kit from her quilt-making set.

She'd cleaned the hammer with bleach, knowing that would help destroy evidence soap and water would leave behind. But deep down, she'd known getting caught was inevitable.

It had been surprisingly easy. When Ruth had turned up at her house unannounced, Lorraine was delighted to see her. She had taken Ruth into the dining room.

'Come and look at this,' she'd said, leading Ruth to where her son's police graduation photo sat on the sideboard. She'd gone on about how both Ruth and Mike had grown into people who helped others. And despite Ruth's setback, Lorraine was glad she'd made a success of her life.

Setback?

Ruth's fingers had closed around the handle of the hammer in her bag while Lorraine droned on about making amends, about her plan to report Kenneth to the police the following day. Like Ruth should be grateful she was finally growing a conscience after forty years.

When Lorraine turned back to the photo, reaching out to adjust its position, Ruth had known it was time. One clean hit was all it took.

Michelle had been harder. Now Ruth knew what it felt like to really kill someone, and she'd nearly bottled it. Her hands had been shaking, sweat trickling down her back as she stood in Michelle's kitchen. She'd blamed it on the change.

'These hot flushes are awful,' she'd said, fanning her face. 'Mind if I use your bathroom?'

Michelle had been sympathetic. 'Of course, love. First door on the right.'

When Michelle turned away, Ruth had known it was her moment. She couldn't lose her nerve. The second time hadn't been as clean as the first, but she had done the job.

Ruth squeezed her eyes shut, trying to block out the memories. She hadn't enjoyed it. But that was what everyone would think, wouldn't they? That she'd relished their deaths. But she hadn't. It had just needed doing. Like putting down a sick animal. It was necessary.

The sewing had taken longer. But it was important. They'd chosen to pretend to be blind to her mother's fear and to Ruth's childhood struggles. So, she'd made their blindness permanent.

Like her father said, for bad things to happen, all people had to do was close their eyes to evil.

In the end, the police had done their job. They'd caught Kenneth Prescott. But could they have arrested him if Ruth hadn't killed Lorraine and Michelle? Would they have even bothered to reopen her mother's murder case? Ruth had her doubts.

Ruth's mind drifted back to when her dad had come to visit yesterday. He'd looked so old and broken. His eyes had been bloodshot, his hands shaky, and his skin yellow – clear signs that the cirrhosis was winning. Ruth felt sick with guilt. The stress of her arrest had pushed him back to the bottle. After years of staying mostly dry, he was drinking heavily again.

She missed her sons desperately. Neither of them had come to see her yet, and that hurt. But she understood. They'd grown up knowing their grandmother had been murdered, but Ruth had carefully hidden her obsession. To them, their grandmother's death was a sad family story, not the reason behind a burning need for vengeance it had become for Ruth.

Now she was locked up, Ruth probably wouldn't get to know her grandchildren, if her sons had any. Or if she did see them, they'd have to be brought to the prison visiting room.

The bitter irony wasn't lost on her. In avenging her mother's death, she'd robbed her own children of their mother too, just in a different way. Yes, they were grown men now, not twelve-year-old girls, but she'd still chosen revenge over being there for them.

Ruth glared at the ceiling. She still felt justified. Lorraine and Michelle had let her mother die and protected her killer for decades. They had deserved it. But a small part of her wondered if she'd just continued the cycle of pain.

Her sons would never look at her the same way again. Her father was drinking himself to death. And for what? The hollow satisfaction of knowing she'd made Lorraine and Michelle pay?

She'd spent years dreaming of this moment, of her mother's killer being locked up. But Prescott was in jail, Lorraine and Michelle were dead, and she felt empty.

The result she'd wanted for so long hadn't brought her mother back. It hadn't healed that scared twelve-year-old girl that still lurked inside her. It had just created more victims, more pain, and more broken families.

Was this what justice was supposed to feel like? Because it was nothing like she'd imagined.

Ruth wiped away her tears with trembling fingers. It hadn't turned out the way she'd planned, but that was life, wasn't it?

The only thing that really mattered was that, after all this time, the people responsible had finally paid for what they'd done to her mum.

And now all Ruth could do was cling to the memories of her mother, which were all she had left.

It wasn't fair. It wasn't nearly enough.

'You could sell up, you know,' Mike said, turning to James as they looked around the house.

The second they walked in, Karen had noticed the air seemed still and heavy. It was as if the house knew what had happened and was holding its breath. She watched Mike and James closely, noting their tense shoulders and tight expressions.

Karen worried about how this was affecting them both. Mike had never been one for deep conversations at the best of times, and now there was all this business about Prescott being his biological father. She'd seen how James had withdrawn, feeling pushed out by the revelation.

They needed to talk about it properly, but Karen knew Mike. He'd rather eat his own shoes than have an emotional heart-to-heart.

'Yes,' James said, hands shoved deep in his pockets. 'Might have to, eventually.'

'You could stay with us until the place sells and you find somewhere else?' Karen suggested. She and Mike had discussed it earlier. James coming back to live in a house where such an awful thing had happened to Lorraine wouldn't be easy.

James managed a slight nod. 'Appreciate that. But we had good memories here. More good than bad. I'll cope, for now anyway.'

'Right, well, shall we eat the fish and chips?' Karen said, lifting the bag. 'Before they get cold.'

They made their way to the kitchen and got out plates and cutlery, then carried them through to the dining room. Karen's stomach clenched as they entered. She couldn't imagine how hard this was for James and Mike.

As they ate, Karen tried to keep a light conversation going. 'These chips are great.'

Mike nodded, poking at his fish. 'Mum liked the ones from Washy best.'

'Yes. "Proper chips, and not too greasy," she used to say. We never found better ones anywhere else.' James reached for the salt. His hand shook slightly as he sprinkled it over his food. 'She always told me off for using too much salt.'

Karen caught the look, loaded with years of shared memories, that passed between father and son.

After dinner, they settled in the living room. No one wanted James to face his first night back alone with his thoughts.

Mike broke the silence. 'Remember that Christmas pudding Mum made?'

The corner of James's mouth twitched. 'What a disaster that was.'

Karen looked between them, curious.

'She'd put about half a bottle of brandy in it,' Mike explained to Karen.

'Set it alight and whoosh! The flames nearly reached the ceiling,' James said. 'I was panicking, but your mum just picked up the cream and poured the whole lot over it.'

Mike grinned. 'We always got one from M&S from then on.'

After a moment, James cleared his throat. 'Look, about Prescott—'

'Don't,' Mike cut in. 'He might've contributed some DNA, but that's all. Nothing worth discussing.'

James nodded, something easing in his shoulders. He stood up and walked to the cabinet, pulling out a photo album. Karen watched as he settled back down, opening it carefully.

The photos were a collection of moments from their family life. Lorraine at the coast, windswept and laughing. Mike paddling in the sea. Christmases with paper hats from crackers and terrible jumpers. Mike pulling faces at the camera. Ordinary moments that seemed so precious now.

Karen studied a photo of Lorraine in the garden, trowel in hand, a huge smile on her face.

Mike's hand brushed over a picture taken at a family barbecue. 'Oh, look at Mum's face. She was fuming. Do you remember? The sausages were like charcoal.'

'I'd had a few too many drinks before I lit the barbecue. Your mum never let me live it down,' James said with a chuckle.

They fell into silence again, but it was different now. Less heavy. The house didn't feel quite so oppressive anymore.

James closed the photo album. 'What about you two? The engagement . . . is that still . . . ?' He was clearly unsure whether he should ask.

Mike reached for Karen's hand. 'Course it is.'

'We're just going to wait until after the funeral to think about dates and plans and things,' Karen added.

James smiled. 'Good. That's something to look forward to.'

He accompanied them outside as they left. They paused by Lorraine's roses. Lit up by the porch light, they were nothing but thorny stems at this time of year.

'They'll burst into bud again come late spring,' James said, shoving his hands in his pockets. 'Life doesn't stop, does it? Carries on even after the harshest winters.'

Mike nodded. His breath clouded in the frosty air. 'Mum would've liked that thought.'

They said their goodbyes and headed for the car.

Karen thought about Ruth, locked in her cell, and wondered if revenge had given her the peace she'd hoped for. She doubted it.

You couldn't fix the past by creating new victims. All you could do was try to build something better from what was left.

As she'd watched Mike and James tonight, Karen realised they'd be okay. DNA didn't define family. It was who chose to be there when it mattered.

They would get through this. Not because of any grand gestures or emotional heart-to-hearts, but because of evenings like this one – having a chippy tea, looking at old photos and sharing memories.

That was all they needed. That, and time.

ACKNOWLEDGEMENTS

The fabulous editors past and present who have worked on the Karen Hart series deserve a massive thank you. It's been a pleasure to work with such a talented group of people at Amazon Publishing. Huge thanks to my new editor Maisie, who has embraced the series with such enthusiasm.

Thank you also to the talented Russel McLean for his help and invaluable attention to detail over the series, and to the meticulous Gemma Wain for her careful copyediting.

To my family, I'm so lucky to have your support – and as always, special thanks to Chris for his support.

And finally, most importantly, thank you to the readers who have read and recommended my books. Your kind words and encouragement mean the world to me.

If *See No Evil* had you absolutely gripped, and you can't wait for Karen's next case, have you read *Bring Them Home*? Two little girls disappear without a trace. Can Karen bring them home safe and sound? Turn the page for an exclusive extract!

Prologue

'I'm not sure about this,' Sian Gibson muttered to her friend as they crept along the school corridor. There was no one else around as the other children had gone back to the classroom.

Emily turned around and pressed a finger against her lips. 'Shhh. Do you want someone to hear? Mrs Morrison will go mental if she catches us.'

Sian wished someone would hear them. She wanted to get caught before they left the school grounds. Her mother would be furious if she found out she'd skived off.

It was different for Emily. She was always in trouble and didn't seem to care. In fact, the entire Dean family were trouble, according to Sian's mother.

Emily looped her arm through Sian's and pulled her along. As they made their way past the line of colourful coats hanging from hooks on the wall, Emily grinned. She passed Sian her yellow coat before putting on her red anorak. Sian's coat was only a month old, but Emily had the same anorak as last year. The cuffs were ragged, and there was a small hole by her right elbow.

She usually turned the sleeves up carefully so the other children wouldn't notice the frayed hems, but today she was too excited to care. The girls were mounting a daring escape and leaving school a full five minutes before the bell signalling the end of the school day.

Ahead of them, the door to the playground was open. Nothing stood in their way. Sian felt her stomach tighten. She couldn't back out now. Emily would think she was a baby.

As they left the school corridor and stepped out into the cold October afternoon, Sian shivered. She looked back over her shoulder towards the classroom windows. Their classmates would be sitting cross-legged on the floor listening to the teacher reading another chapter of *The Magician's Nephew*. Sian wished she was back there in the warm with them.

Emily tugged her arm. 'What's the matter with you? Don't you want to see the ponies?'

'I didn't say that. I just don't see why we have to leave school early. We'll be in so much trouble if Mrs Morrison finds out. What if she calls my mum?'

'She won't find out if you get a move on. Hurry up.'

Sian's mother said Emily was a bossy little madam and she didn't like her spending time with the 'Dean girl'. Sian had begged to be allowed to go to Emily's for tea and had been surprised when her mother had finally relented. She'd be having kittens if she knew they were creeping out of school early.

It was only five minutes, though. Surely that couldn't get them into much trouble. Emily had insisted they leave school before the bell rang because she said she didn't want any of the other children finding out about the ponies.

Emily was horse-mad at the moment. All she'd talked about for the past six months was ponies and horses. Her parents had told her they weren't wasting money on horse-riding lessons, but Emily walked to the stables every Friday afternoon and watched Sian's weekly lesson with her Welsh cob Florence.

Emily watched those lessons with such longing it made Sian feel guilty. Now, Emily was about to have her own riding lesson.

She was glad for her friend but didn't understand why they had to keep it secret.

Sian loved horses. There was something comforting about the smell of the stables, and stroking the soft muzzles of the gentle ponies was the best feeling in the world, so she didn't know why she was feeling so nervous.

It was probably because she was afraid of being caught. Emily was right. She was a baby. She hated getting into trouble.

It was silly really. If anyone should be panicking about getting caught, it was Emily. After all, Sian would probably be given a stern telling off and not allowed to watch TV for a week, but if Emily's mother found out, she'd tell Emily's dad. Sian was terrified of Emily's dad. He was a huge man with a temper. But his shouting and threats didn't stop Emily getting into trouble. She didn't seem to care.

Sian followed her friend, crossing the path and heading towards the fence that ran along the side of the playground.

The girls climbed over the wooden fence but Sian stumbled, landing on her hands and knees on top of a pile of soggy brown leaves.

Emily rolled her eyes but held out a hand to help her up.

Sian took a last longing look at the warm lights of the classroom glinting between the trees. Finally, she brushed her clothes free of leaves and bracken and followed her friend into the woods.

She'd been excited about going to Emily's for tea. Sian's mother always picked her up from the front gates, but Emily was allowed to go home on her own even though she was only ten. She used a shortcut along the side of the playground and the wood which led out on to Longwater Lane. But today they weren't going straight to Emily's house. Today they were meeting Emily's new friend, who was going to take them to see some ponies and let Emily ride one.

At the thought of the ponies, Sian perked up a bit and walked a little faster. She shoved her hands deep in her pockets as the cold, damp October air made her shiver. It wasn't raining, but drips of moisture fell from the branches above them, landing on their hair and coats.

'Where's your friend meeting us?' Sian asked, no longer whispering now there was no one around to hear them.

'Just through here,' Emily said, pointing deeper into the woods. She grinned at Sian. Her eyes were sparkling and she bounced with each step like a puppy.

Suddenly she turned to Sian, the excitement on her face replaced by fear. 'What if I can't do it? What if I fall off? Or the pony doesn't like me?'

Sian shook her head. 'Of course the pony will like you, and you won't fall off. Somebody will hold the reins for you if it's your first lesson.'

Emily nodded but didn't look convinced.

Sian reached out to squeeze her friend's hand, then both girls jumped when they heard leaves rustle in front of them.

The afternoon was dark and gloomy, making it hard to see. A prickling sensation ran along Sian's spine as a tall, thin figure loomed in front of them.

At first, nobody spoke and then Sian stammered, 'Is this your friend?'

Emily finally found her voice. 'Yes, the one with the ponies.' Emily's voice was louder than usual.

Sian wished Emily's friend would step away from the trees so she could see them properly, but in the next moment, she wished they'd just go away. For some reason, she felt an overwhelming need to run back to the classroom.

'I told you not to tell anyone.' The voice was gruff and angry.

Sian's hands tightened into fists in her pockets to stop them from shaking. She shuffled back a few steps. Sian wanted to return to school, but she was scared for her friend. She shot a glance at Emily and saw she was frowning.

'I'm sorry,' Emily said. 'It's just that Sian really likes horses too, and she always lets me come to her lessons.'

Sian waited for the figure to reply, but for the longest time all she could hear was ragged breathing.

'Fine. This way,' the figure said finally, before turning around and heading deeper into the woods away from the school and Longwater Lane. Sian had never gone in this direction before.

'Is this the way to the stables?' Emily asked. Her voice wasn't as loud now.

The figure walking in front of them said nothing.

Chapter One

DS Karen Hart collected the evidence files from her desk with a sigh. The case was going nowhere and, much as it pained her, she was going to have to clear it from her active cases. Mary Clarke, a domestic abuse victim, was now refusing to give evidence against her husband. For the past few days, Karen had been trying to persuade her to move to a women's refuge in Lincoln. It had all been for nothing. An hour earlier, Mary – purple bruises still on her arms and neck – had slammed the door in Karen's face after threatening to have her charged with harassment.

'What's up, boss?' DC Rick Cooper asked, nodding at the files in Karen's arms.

'I'm taking the Mary Clarke paperwork to be filed. The case is finished.'

'Not enough evidence for the CPS to press charges?'

'Not if Mary keeps insisting she fell down the stairs.' Karen clutched the blue cardboard folder. 'There's not much we can do unless she decides to accept our help.'

Rick frowned and leaned against the desk. 'Let's just hope we get a chance to help her before her husband finishes her off.'

Karen shuddered.

'Sorry, boss. That was an insensitive thing to say.'

Karen shook her head. She knew Rick was right: Mary's life was in danger, and it was frustrating and infuriating to watch the situation unfold.

DC Sophie Jones looked up sharply from where she was sitting at her desk in the open-plan office. 'Surely there's something else we can do, Sarge. We can't just give up.'

Sophie was a new member of the team and had only recently achieved the rank of detective constable. She was a hard worker, but idealistic. Karen thought she'd eventually make a good officer, though she'd only worked with Sophie for two months. The young woman was a stickler for rules and punctuality, and Karen imagined she must have been the class swot when she was at school.

With her curly brown hair, pink cheeks and angelic expression, Sophie was a stark contrast to Rick. If she looked like an angel, he resembled a mischievous imp.

Rick was a good-looking man and he knew it. He had tanned skin, evidence of his Italian ancestry on his father's side, and wore his dark hair slicked back. His cocky smile was quick to surface, and he always wore a little too much aftershave. That aside, Karen was glad he was a member of the team. He worked hard and she trusted him.

'No one's giving up,' Rick said to Sophie. 'But we can't prosecute if Mary doesn't want us to.'

'But that's ridiculous,' Sophie said, getting to her feet and walking around the desk. 'There has to be a way we can make Mary Clarke see sense.'

Rick glanced at Karen and rolled his eyes as if to say, 'See what I have to deal with?'

'In an ideal situation, we'd push ahead with the charges, Sophie,' Karen explained. 'But from experience, I know it's not going to stick.'

Sophie was about to open her mouth to protest again when DI Scott Morgan entered the office area with Superintendent Michelle Murray and the three officers looked up expectantly.

Superintendent Murray didn't often visit the CID offices. She had a large office on the top floor of Nettleham police headquarters, and only occasionally came down to the lower floors to attend key briefings. Today she looked concerned, her dark eyes even more intense than usual.

Beside her stood DI Scott Morgan, as immaculate as always. He'd been the leader of Team Three for just over a month, and Karen hadn't yet worked out what made him tick. Her last DI had been an open book. But Scott Morgan didn't give much away.

Superintendent Murray spoke first. 'We've had a report of two missing girls, both ten years old, from Moore Lane Primary School in Heighington.'

Karen dumped the files on her desk and checked her watch. It was only just after four p.m. 'How long have they been gone?'

'They were seen just before three o'clock when the class finished rehearsing for the school play. Their teacher noticed they were missing at three fifteen.'

That was unusual. Children tended to disappear on their way to and from school rather than during the school day.

Karen shifted her attention to DI Morgan. Unlike the superintendent, who looked tense, his face was impassive.

'Is there any reason to suspect foul play?' Rick Cooper asked.

DI Morgan replied, 'Not yet. A uniformed unit is already on the scene, conducting a preliminary search of the woods beside the school and the surrounding streets, but it's possible the girls decided to leave early of their own accord and will turn up at home wondering what all the fuss was about.'

'Let's hope so,' Superintendent Murray said in her soft Scottish accent. Karen had never heard her raise her voice. She didn't need to. Everyone at Nettleham HQ knew Superintendent Murray's gentle tone was deceptive, and woe betide anyone who assumed she was a soft touch.

'It's Heighington again, boss,' Rick muttered, looking at Karen.

She gave a curt nod, understanding what Rick was getting at. She turned her attention back to the superintendent, who was issuing instructions to DI Morgan.

'You and DS Hart should get to the school straightaway. I'm sure DC Cooper and DC Jones can set up the incident room in your absence. Keep me updated.'

Superintendent Murray turned and walked away, and Karen reached for her coat.

When they were in the fleet car with DI Morgan at the wheel, Karen asked, 'What do we know about the girls so far?'

'Two girls. Both ten years old. Sian Gibson and Emily Dean. The head teacher of the primary school is Jackie Lyons. She's the one who reported the girls missing. The girls' teacher is Roz Morrison, and she says that although Emily Dean is a difficult child, it's unlike her to sneak off during the school day, and it's very out of character for Sian.'

Karen nodded. 'And we haven't spoken to the parents yet?'

'Not yet,' DI Morgan said. He put his foot down as they pulled away from a junction. 'But they've been informed.'

Karen was about to suggest that she talk to the parents of the two girls while DI Morgan spoke to the teachers, but before she could, DI Morgan asked her about Rick's comment.

The car came to a stop in front of traffic lights, and Karen turned to look at DI Morgan. She hadn't realised he'd picked up on it as he'd been talking to the superintendent at the time.

Less than eighteen months ago, Karen had been seconded to DI Freeman's team after a young woman had disappeared from Heighington. Heighington was only a small village and normally very safe and Karen couldn't help thinking it was a pretty big coincidence to have a similar case in such a short period. Hopefully this one was a false alarm and the girls would turn up safe and well. It still ate away at Karen that they hadn't been able to track down Amy Fisher, the nineteen-year-old who'd disappeared without a trace. Even though Karen had only been on the periphery of the case, it still stung that they hadn't been able to get a result.

'Did you hear about the Amy Fisher case?'

DI Morgan nodded. 'The nineteen-year-old who went missing from a village in Lincolnshire over a year ago? Yes, if I recall correctly, there were plenty of suspects but she wasn't found.'

Karen was impressed. DI Morgan had been based in the Thames Valley when Amy Fisher went missing. Then again, she should have guessed he would recall some details of the case. In the short time she'd known him, she'd noticed he liked to accumulate knowledge.

'Amy lived in Heighington,' Karen said quietly.

DI Morgan considered that information for a moment before replying, 'It's unlikely to be related to our missing girls. Emily and Sian are ten. Amy Fisher was nineteen. If the incidents were related and we were dealing with a predator targeting young girls, we'd expect them to be in a similar age range.'

Karen knew he was right but his reply irritated her. It sounded like something straight out of a textbook.

Nettleham was north-east of Lincoln, and they needed to cross the River Witham to get to Heighington. Travelling on the congested A15 was not ideal but, fortunately, the route wasn't as busy as usual, and they reached Canwick Hill within ten minutes.

Karen's mobile beeped. It was a message from her sister on the family group chat they'd set up with their parents. She'd check in with them later. After muting the app, she slid the phone back in her pocket.

As DI Morgan turned left on to Heighington Road, he asked, 'Do you have any local knowledge of the area or know anything about the girls' families?'

Karen lived just two miles away from Moore Lane Primary School in the neighbouring village of Branston. She'd moved there with her family ten years ago. Branston was full of happy memories. After her husband and daughter had died in a car accident, Karen hadn't wanted to leave the area. If she did, she felt she'd be leaving a part of them behind.

'I know the head teacher, Jackie Lyons, is well respected and active in the community. I'm not familiar with Sian Gibson's family, but I think Emily Dean could be the daughter of one of the Dean boys.'

DI Morgan frowned but didn't take his eyes off the road as they sped past the open fields. 'The Dean boys?'

'The Dean family are known to the local force. They're forever getting into trouble, petty crime mostly.'

'Go on.'

'It goes back to Matthew Dean, their father. I guess he's about sixty now and does a few jobs here and there. If you ask him, he'll tell you he labours on local farms, but I suspect most of his income comes from criminal activities. He's been prosecuted multiple times, and he's been inside twice for long stretches. Once for actual bodily harm, and once for stealing farm machinery. He's got two sons and the youngest, Dennis, is as bad as his father. I can't say for certain, but I'm pretty sure Dennis has a daughter called Emily.'

DI Morgan nodded slowly. 'We'll have to find out if they're involved in any active feuds. In my experience, criminal families like that don't tend to get on well together, and if someone holds a grudge against the Deans . . .'

Karen looked at him. 'The Deans are a pain in the neck, but even so, it's hard to imagine anyone targeting two children to get back at them.'

Karen leaned forward in her seat, willing DI Morgan to travel faster along the straight road. She knew uniform were already on the scene and had started the search, but in a case like this every second counted.

'I have heard rumours that Dennis's wife kicked him out a few months ago,' Karen said.

'If that's true, and Dennis Dean feels he's being denied contact with his daughter, it's possible he made a grab for Emily.'

Karen exhaled heavily. If Emily was, in fact, a member of the notorious Dean family, things could escalate quickly. The fact that another child was involved made her feel uneasy.

As they turned off Heighington Road and entered Moore Lane, Karen swore under her breath. The lane was packed with parked cars, but DI Morgan took it all in his stride and parked a distance away from the school.

Irritated by the precision of his parallel parking, Karen yanked the door open as soon as the car was stationary.

They walked quickly towards the small school. Groups of parents stood close to the entrance, many of them holding their children's hands, reluctant to let go after they'd heard about the two missing girls. They were hanging around, anxious for any news, but Karen wished they'd go home. Unless they had information to pass on, they were just getting in the way.

In a crowd like this it would be easy to miss something important. Karen scanned the gathering, looking for anything suspicious, but all she saw were the concerned faces of parents and the wide-eyed, confused expressions of the youngsters, who didn't really understand what was going on.

A young mum, wearing a navy-blue jacket and tight jeans, pushed her way towards them. 'Are you the police? What's going on? Have you found the little girls yet?' She tossed her long brown hair.

'We don't have any news at present,' Karen said and walked around the woman, heading quickly to the double doors at the entrance to the school.

Before they managed to get inside, Karen felt a tug on her sleeve. She swallowed a sharp retort, and DI Morgan slowly and deliberately leaned over and removed the man's hand from Karen's forearm.

'I understand that you're extremely concerned, sir, but we need to get inside and do our job.'

The man swallowed and ran a hand through his light brown hair. 'Of course, sorry. It's just I think I've got some information for you.'

Karen had already turned away and had one hand on the door ready to enter the school, but his words stopped her dead.

'What information?' DI Morgan asked.

'Well, actually it's not me. It's Danny, my son.'

DI Morgan and Karen looked down at the young lad standing beside his father. He had brown hair and big, expressive brown eyes, and he looked absolutely terrified.

'Do you have something to tell us, Danny?' Karen asked.

The boy's lower lip trembled, then he looked up at Karen and replied, 'I saw them climb over the fence in the playground. I saw them leave.'

ABOUT THE AUTHOR

Born in Kent, D. S. Butler grew up as an avid reader with a love for crime fiction and mysteries. She has worked as a scientific officer in a hospital pathology laboratory and as a research scientist. After obtaining a PhD in biochemistry, she worked at the University of Oxford for four years before moving to the Middle East. While living in Bahrain, she wrote her first novel and hasn't stopped writing since. She now lives in Lincolnshire with her husband.

Follow the Author on Amazon

If you enjoyed this book, follow D. S. Butler on Amazon to be notified when the author releases a new book!
To do this, please follow these instructions:

Desktop:

1) Search for the author's name on Amazon or in the Amazon App.
2) Click on the author's name to arrive on their Amazon page.
3) Click the 'Follow' button.

Mobile and Tablet:

1) Search for the author's name on Amazon or in the Amazon App.
2) Click on one of the author's books.
3) Click on the author's name to arrive on their Amazon page.
4) Click the 'Follow' button.

Kindle eReader and Kindle App:

If you enjoyed this book on a Kindle eReader or in the Kindle App, you will find the author 'Follow' button after the last page.

Printed in Dunstable, United Kingdom